About the Author

Mark Hayden is the nom de guerre of Adrian Attwood. He lives in Westmorland with his wife, Anne.

He has had a varied career working for a brewery, teaching English and being the Town Clerk in Carnforth, Lancs. He is now a part-time writer and part-time assistant in Anne's craft projects.

He is also proud to be the Mad Unky to his Great Nieces & Great Nephews.

Also by Mark Hayden

The King's Watch – Conrad Clarke

The 13th Witch
The Twelve Dragons of Albion
The Eleventh Hour
Tenfold
Nine of Wands
Eight Kings
The Seventh Star
Six Furlongs
Five Leaf Clover
Tales From the Watch (Novella Anthology)

Operation Jigsaw
(Conrad Clarke & Tom Morton – prequels to the King's Watch)

A Piece of Blue Sky
Green for Danger
In the Red Corner

Tom Morton Crime
(following Operation Jigsaw)

A Serpent in Paradise
Another Place to Die

All available from Paw Press

Five Leaf Clover

The Ninth Book of the King's Watch

MARK HAYDEN

www.pawpress.co.uk

First Published Worldwide in 2021 by Paw Press
Paperback Edition Published
June 01 2021

Cover Design – Rachel Lawston

www.lawstondesign.com

Paw Press – Independent publishing in Westmorland, UK.
www.pawpress.co.uk

ISBN: 1-914145-02-X
ISBN-13: 978-1-914145-02-5

For Ethan Thomas

Proud Irishman.

(one day)

FIVE LEAF CLOVER

A Note from Conrad

As usual, there are new people to meet and new magick to discover in this book. The Ahearns of Galway get their own special introduction in Chapter Six, and there is, of course, a full list of everyone and a glossary of magickal terms on the Paw Press website:

www.pawpress.co.uk

And now on with the story.

Thanks,
Conrad.

Part One

A Grand Tour

1 — Like Son, Like Father

It seems like years since I slept in a bunk, and it definitely is years since I shared a room with my father. To do both at once was something of a shock to the system, even more so to do it on the overnight ferry from Valencia to Palma, Mallorca. Shall we just say that the top bunk was not designed for someone my height.

I – we – had been staying with my parents at their Spanish villa while I convalesced from a punctured kidney. Mina had gone back to London on her own, and I was arriving in Palma on the first leg of what was going to be something of a magickal road trip. I had a lot to sort out, a lot to discover and possibly a lot of danger ahead of me. Not today, though. I wouldn't take my dad anywhere that was genuinely dangerous. I couldn't comment on whether he would do the same to me.

Yesterday had been sunny and dry at San Vicente, and relatively warm. Despite being one of Britain's favourite holiday destinations, the island of Mallorca was anything but warm, sunny and dry. By the time we'd made it away from the docks and up into the old town, I felt like I'd been digging ditches in the fens all day. Everything seemed wet and gloomy without it actually raining very much, a sort of penetrating foggy drizzle that got inside your coat without knocking. 'Is it always like this here?' I asked.

'In December, yes it is. Makes it easier to find people,' said Dad. 'No one wants to go anywhere in weather like this, so when you knock on their door, you can be a little ray of sunshine in their lives.' He gave me his sideways grin. 'I had a couple of very good trips here when we first came to Spain.'

'Buying or selling?'

'Selling. By the time we'd settled at the Villa Verde, all the good stuff had been cleared out of Mallorca years before. This chap we're meeting – we were partners in a little venture selling authentic Royal Balearic dressers, handmade by Poles in the same factory that churns out stuff for IKEA. That's what Francisco said. He worked on the Mainlanders, I worked on the ex-pats.'

He stopped at the top of a flight of steps to catch his breath, and I shook out my leg. 'Was it worth it, Dad?'

He brushed some condensation off his coat. 'I'll say, son. We made double on every dresser, and it got me away from your mother. By the time I went back, she was ready to put the business with Sofía behind her. She'd joined three bridge groups and made friends with Isabella. This way.'

I've often wondered how my parents' marriage survived the shock discovery of Dad's daughter, my half-sister Sofía. It was probably a good thing that they didn't let on to Rachael and me that she existed, and that gave them a chance to figure it out on their own, and today they seem as close as ever. So long as we pretend that Sofía and Mercedes don't exist while Mother is in the room, and pretend that magick doesn't exist while Dad is in the room, everything is normal. Or as normal as it gets in my family.

Dad led us to one of the private houses that fronted on to the street and rang the buzzer. The speaker crackled, and a heavy male voice said, '*¡Hola Alfredo!* Mind your head.'

'Catch 'em, Conrad,' said Dad.

I stepped back from the wall and looked up. A window rattled open and a set of keys descended through the drizzle. I caught them, and Dad shouted up to the man who'd dropped them. '*Gracias, Francisco. Hasta luego.*'

Francisco (who could have been Father's long-lost Spanish twin) waved and retreated. I was already unlocking the van and stowing the luggage by then; anything to get out of the damp and get some warm, dry air blowing on my leg.

'You guessed which van, then,' said Dad.

'The *Antiguedades Escorial* on the side was a bit of a clue. Perfect cover. Do you know the way?'

'To Esporles? Sure. It was a happy hunting ground for us. Just turn right at the end of the road and follow the signs to the motorway. Nice new van he's got. Must be doing all right for himself. Or he's diversified.'

'So long as he hasn't diversified into drug smuggling and put this van on the watch-list, I'm pleased for him.'

'I'll tell him you said that. He'll be tickled.'

It only took twenty-five minutes, and we'd have done it in less if I hadn't been keeping to the speed limits and taking it carefully. I turned in to the football ground's car park and left the engine running. At eight o'clock on a December's morning, we pretty much had the valley to ourselves, but I didn't want to risk going any closer. Just in case. I got my rucksack and opened the bottom section. 'Let's get you kitted out, Dad.'

For the first time since I'd suggested this venture, Dad started to look uneasy. I took that as a good sign: I'd eliminated all the risks I could, but I'd rather have my father nervous than blasé. I fitted the button camera on to his coat and stashed the transmitter in his pocket. He didn't complain when I ran through the procedure again.

'Open the App from inside the van, and don't get out until you've had a message. Right?' He nodded. 'Here's the WiFi jammer. Keep it in your pocket and only turn it on if you can see a new video doorbell. Fallback meeting place is the Cafè Nou.'

'Right. Is it usual to wish someone luck before a mission?'

It was scarcely a mission. More of a message, and he was more at risk every time he cold-called a farmhouse looking for antiques, if his stories about farm dogs and runaway bulls were true. 'Good luck, Dad.'

I got out of the van stood watching until he'd adjusted the seat, the mirrors and the heating. I waved him off and went in search of shelter.

It took him ten minutes to find the villa and message me that he was starting the camera. As you know, I've fought against having a smartphone for years now, until Mina forced me to use one. It's amazing what you can do with them if you want to break the law, which sort of justifies my point. For now, I was grateful for it, and opened the remote App for the body camera. 'Well done, Dad,' I muttered to myself.

In glorious monochrome, I could see the dashboard of the van, proving that Dad was still inside it. 'Clarke Senior to Clarke Junior. Can you read me, son?'

I tapped a quick message and heard it ping a few seconds later.

'Right, here we go.' I'd told him not to give a running commentary, but through nerves or love of the dramatic, he couldn't help himself.

'I've definitely never been here before,' he said. 'Far too classy for the likes of me. And a bit gloomy, if I'm honest. No sign of a video doorbell. I'd better shut up now.'

From what I'd already seen of the villa on the Internet, and from what I could see now, the place might as well be called *DunSpelling*. It was rambling, heavy and overhung by the mountains that surround Esporles. It was exactly where you'd expect a Mage to go to ground for the winter – the out-of-season rental was dirt cheap.

Dad pressed the old-fashioned doorbell and used the iron knocker for good measure. Then he stepped well back from the door and tried not to look threatening. When I'd briefed him, I'd told him to aim to look like a man from the letting agency.

The large wooden door opened, and there he was, still in his dressing gown: Piers Wetherill, erstwhile Watch Captain of the Marches and a man with whom I had a bone to pick.

'Can I help you?' said Wetherill, loud and clear over the link.

'Sorry to disturb you,' said Dad. I could hear the charming smile in his voice. 'I'm Alfred Clarke, and my son, Conrad, would like to talk to you. Just a chat. I give my word.'

Piers is older than Dad, and has wisps of white hair that he hadn't bothered to tame this morning. His face gave nothing away when Dad made his speech, but as soon as he'd finished, Wetherill looked around, his deep-set eyes invisible. I've seen enough Mages now to know when they're using their Sight, even over video.

'Is he here?'

'He's waiting in the town. He said to offer you breakfast. Your choice of venue.'

Wetherill snorted. 'Is your word binding, too, Mr Clarke?'

'It is.'

'Then I'll see you in half an hour.' He named a slightly more up-market café than the one I'd chosen and closed the door firmly but not rudely.

'Mission accomplished, son,' murmured Dad. 'Now for part two.' I watched as he moved over the villa's forecourt and stop by Wetherill's car. I saw a cigar emerge from Dad's pocket, and then his lighter, which he dropped. While bending down to pick it up, he slipped the tracker under the car. I even heard the *clunk* as the magnets took hold.

I'd planned it like this to minimise the chance of Wetherill feeling immediately cornered, which is why I'd stayed well out of range of Wards and Alarms. He might still do a runner, though, hence the tracker.

'Disconnecting now, son. See you in a minute. You know what to get.'

I was already heading through the perpetual wet towards the café and switching to the tracker app. I beat Dad to it by a few minutes, and I was admiring the beauty of the honey-coloured old buildings that makes Esporles so popular with well-heeled tourists who can afford private villas with pools. But not in December.

Dad arrived at the same time as the waiter brought two carajillos outside.

'Cheers,' said Dad. 'I've earned this.'

I wouldn't normally dream of starting the day with espresso and brandy, but it suited the day and the mood. We enjoyed a smoke, and I told Dad that he'd done a superb job. Which he had. When the tracker said that Wetherill was in the town centre, we adjourned inside and got the breakfast menu.

When Wetherill realised that my father was joining us for breakfast, he got a little testy. Sign of a guilty conscience. Dad poured himself a coffee and said, 'Tell you what, I'll go outside and finish my cigar while we wait for the food. Give you chaps a moment.'

'How in the name of all the gods did you find me?' said Wetherill, while Dad was still in earshot.

'Electoral roll. You used your second identity. After that, I got Ruth Kaplan on it.'

'Does everyone do your bidding now?'

I took out the paper I'd brought and tore it in half before passing it over the table. He unfolded the remains and grunted. 'Clever. Mundane warrant issued by a court martial.'

'And already cancelled. Once I'd found you'd taken a six month lease, I knew you weren't going anywhere.'

He shook his head and pushed the warrant away. I took it and screwed it into a ball. 'Just so you know, Piers, my father is blind to the world of magick. Despite being present at the Newton's House bombing, it's a blank to him. He's going to leave us alone again after breakfast.

I let Dad make the running over the food. Wetherill's patch used to be the Marches – Shropshire, Herefordshire and chunks of Cheshire and Gloucestershire, and Dad had spent his working life scouring them for antiques. They soon found some common ground. When Dad left to check out the town, we got down to business.

Piers Wetherill owed me some answers. To become Deputy Constable of the Watch, I'd also had to take on the role of Lord Guardian of the North and Priest of Nimue's Altars, and that meant a close encounter with the Spirit who guards Caledfwlch, aka Excalibur. Nimue is patron of the King's Watch, and we use the symbol of Caledfwlch in her name. She is also slightly unhinged.

To bind us together, she'd drunk some of my blood. Instead of the syringeful she'd taken from Hannah Rothman, the Nymph had taken two armfuls and two legfuls as well as immersing me in freezing spring water. I'd nearly died of hypothermia brought on by exsanguination, and only survived because Piers Wetherill was present and ready to call an ambulance. He also had a compression bandage and my medical details in his pocket. He'd known it was coming. Or that it might be. And he hadn't said a word to me about it.

He didn't wait for me to start. 'I'm sorry, Clarke. I had no idea things had got so bad. I wouldn't have let you near her if I'd known.'

'But you were expecting something bad.'

He looked uncomfortable and rubbed his stomach as if he was getting indigestion. Good. 'The Constable shouldn't have left it so long before appointing a Deputy.'

'Don't blame the Boss. You should have told me the risks.'

'Then you wouldn't have done it, would you? Hannah more or less blackmailed you into taking the job, and if she'd known how hungry Nimue was, she wouldn't have let you. You're her favourite.'

There was a touch of camp malice in the last statement that I didn't like. 'Hannah looks after all her team, and I think you'll find that if she sent Christmas cards, I wouldn't be on the list.'

'She has not once broken bread at any other house but yours, but that's beside the point.'

'What is the point, Piers?'

'The point is that she doesn't understand Nimue, never has, and has never made the effort to understand her. And that's rubbed off on you. I thought a close encounter with her might be an education for you. It was wrong of me. I can't apologise enough. When I saw what I nearly did to your fiancée, I knew I was too old for this job. I've been too old for years.'

'For your sake, Piers, I hope you've got something better than what you've come up with so far.'

'That sounds like an *or what* statement, Clarke. Your father gave me his word that all you wanted was to talk.'

'And I do. I also have to go home to Mina, and if she's not satisfied, I'd move if I were you. Argentina or Brazil to start with.'

He didn't know what to make of that. If he had any sense, he'd take it literally: when I kissed Mina goodbye at the airport on Thursday, she told me that her vow to kneecap Wetherill in both knees was only on hold, not cancelled.

'I think I need a brandy.'

I ordered two brandies and gave him a moment.

'Where exactly have you met Nimue?' was his question after sniffing the brandy.

'Merlyn's Tower, Middlebarrow, under Draxholt and under Windermere.'

'Damn. That explains it.' His shoulders slumped even further. He stared at his glass for a second, then looked up. 'Nimue's realm is deep underground. Mostly. Wherever the groundwater is, she moves, and she comes to the surface where springs, wells and lakes are found. She also needs Lux, of course, but the old Ley lines have mostly been replaced. I've been telling the Earthmasters about this for forty years, but none of them have listened to me. The activities of our water companies haven't helped either. That's why she's so fractured: she finds it hard to translocate and manifest.'

'And the need for blood? It can't be the Lux – I felt more Lux in her realm than I'll ever have in *my* body.'

He shook his head. 'You're devoted to Mina. I can see that. You turned down the chance to lie with Nimue, didn't you?' My face must have given him the answer. 'Your choice, of course, but she needs the DNA. If you'd donated some sexually, she wouldn't have needed to take so much from your blood.'

I was stunned. 'DNA? Why would a Spirit need billions of partial DNA samples?'

'Because she's not a Spirit. Not really. Despite what they teach in Salomon's House, she's a creature of flesh and blood in ways that are hard to understand. Like the Fae, she needs human DNA.'

I sat back and tried to digest what he'd said. The brandy didn't help it go down.

He could see that I was unhappy and waved his hands in a gesture that said he couldn't put it into words I'd accept. 'You know about Changelings, right?'

I nodded and paused. To become a Prince or Princess in the Fae world means a process of exchange with a human child that results in the child's death and replacement. There are rules about how and when they can do it, but do it they must or they die out. I also know that a Fae Queen will take a

Fae Prince as her consort and mate with him. Wetherill was about to add something else.

'Fae Queens also mate with young men,' was his message. 'For variety.'

I thought about Cara, the Queen of my wolf pack. 'What about the Dual Natured?'

'I heard that you'd become a Protector. That offer is purely symbolic.'

'How come this is news to me?' I asked. 'And to all of the Mages I've talked about it with?'

'Blame the Victorians. Their attitudes to sexuality have cast a long shadow, especially over Salomon's House. I've spent a lifetime in the Marches unlearning that.'

If what he said was true, it was an explanation of sorts. I gained a lot from my encounter with Nimue, and I *had* survived. On the other hand, Wetherill had used me as a combination of guinea pig and sacrificial lamb.

'You should have told me, Piers. Not Hannah – me. You should have told me the risks.'

'Yes, you're right. And that's why I ran away. Once again, I'm sorry.'

'You can start to make up for it by telling me what's going on in Windermere. What's so special about Nimue up there?'

'I wish I knew. I did everything I could to avoid the Particular, but you've jumped straight in with both feet. If you met her on Windermere, I'm not even sure it's the same Nymph. I know it has something to do with the rock underneath, but that's it.'

The Gnomes of Clan Skelwith had told me to avoid contacting Nimue on England's largest lake for reasons connected to my encounters with her elsewhere. I would very much like to know why.

'What are you doing out here, Piers? You're not married, are you?'

'I'm what used to be called a *confirmed bachelor*.' He didn't go on to say whether that meant he was gay. Instead, he added, 'I've been writing a book. It covers a lot of the same ground we've been going over. I hope Chris Kelly and that Mowbray kid read the bloody thing. His father certainly didn't want to know.'

'Lord Mowbray?'

Wetherill snorted. He's the first Mage I've met who's had a bad word to say about the late master Geomancer. Professionally, at least.

My father was back in the doorway, giving me a raised eyebrow. 'What's your new number?' I asked. Wetherill gave me a card. I put it in my pocket and gave him one in return. 'If you value your kneecaps, Piers, a substantial donation to that charity would help.'

He stared at the writing. 'The Mission for the Education of Women in Gujarat?'

'That's the one. Message the receipt to the number on the other side. And if you see my number calling you, take the call.'

'I will. Take care, Lord Guardian.' I left him and joined my father outside.

Dad gave me a shopping bag and said, 'I've put the electrical stuff at the bottom, including the tracker from his car. On top are some sobrassada sausages. They're just about ready now. I know that Myfanwy likes them.'

'Thank you very much.'

He checked his watch. 'If I'm driving, you should make the early flight to Manchester.'

'You're definitely driving, Dad. I've had three brandies already.'

'The van's down here.'

He didn't ask how it had gone with Wetherill, and I didn't offer to tell him. He's good like that.

I received the message late in the afternoon, while I was painting Vicky's toenails. I told her to check my phone and carried on. She couldn't unlock it, of course, but she could see the message and her foot squirmed.

'Hold still! If I get red glitter on your carpet, it will be your fault.'

'Aye, I know, but why has an unknown number sent you a message saying they've given five grand to your cousin's charity?'

'That will be Piers Wetherill, trying to escape retribution, now hold still or I will stop work and you will have to finish them yourself.'

I was helping Vicky to get ready for a date, and she was helping me get ready for dinner with Hannah Rothman. And drinks with someone else, but we'll come to that later.

'Is Piers off the naughty step?' said Vicky.

'For now. If what he said to Conrad is true. Other foot.'

I have been back in England for a couple of days now after we spent some time with Mary and Alfred in Spain. Mary had arranged for us to go out for a sumptuous Diwali feast in Valencia, which was good, and right, but I felt like I'd missed out on the communal part of the festival, which is why I was very much looking forward to Christmas.

I love Christmas because it is a chance to be as tacky as you like without anyone raising an eyebrow. This afternoon I had managed to persuade Vicky to put far more tinsel on her tree than she thought was acceptable. I count this as a victory; whether Desirée will think the same when she gets back is another matter.

While we were away in Spain, Vicky had an eventful time at the debut of Sofía's Fire Games (and even more so afterwards), and I was glad I could be there to help her come down. I miss having her around, and so does Conrad. And if she starts dating this man, who knows what could happen.

I cast my eye over him when he turned up to collect her, and over the pictures of the Fire Games, and I wished them a good evening. He seemed nice, if a little wet. I went back to Vicky's room to re-adjust my saree and put some more jewellery on before I summoned a black cab to take me to the Savoy. I would need another one to take me to the kosher restaurant, but my first call had been suggested by someone I never expected to share a drink with, let alone cocktails at the American Bar. She was waiting for me and slid a glass of pink liquid along the counter.

'Cheers, Mina. That colour really suits you.'

'Cheers, Eseld. It suits you, too.'

We didn't kiss or embrace. I sipped the drink – it was as dry as the desert – and considered why she'd asked to meet me as we went to find a table.

Eseld Mowbray was wearing the same shade of blue as me, somewhere between royal and navy, but mine was in a saree and hers in a long sleeved velvet evening gown that made her look a lot more feminine than she usually does. Don't get me wrong, Eseld is a striking woman in anything she wears, so long as she covers her shoulders. They are rather broad: all that horse riding, I suppose. And she'd kept the hair extensions she'd put in for the Edwardian costume.

'I love the drape of the skirt,' I said. 'What's the occasion?'

'I'm going to the ballet as Rachael's guest. Part of her programme to introduce me to the world of mundane money. Dad took me to see *Nutcracker* when I was little. I always preferred riding boots to pointe shoes, but I'm looking forward to it.'

Eseld has become the new BFF of Conrad's sister Rachael for complicated reasons that have to do with Rachael's Entanglement in magick and Eseld's change of career after her father's murder. This would be merely *interesting* in normal circumstances, but there was an elephant in the room here: Conrad.

I am not a therapist, but no woman who worshipped her father like Eseld did and who hates her mother to the point of ostracism will find it easy to make relationships. I should know, because it's something we have in common. Less so in my case, but the pattern is similar.

Within twenty-four hours of meeting Conrad, she propositioned him. Since then, she has saved his life, helped him magickally, taken both his sisters under her wing and she shows no signs of going away. In return, Conrad has avenged Lord Mowbray's murder and saved Morwenna's life. In any other story, it would be her wearing his engagement ring, not me. Very few Mages can read thoughts, I am told, but Eseld seemed to do just that.

'You deserved better of me, Mina. Right from the beginning in Cornwall.'

I was supposed to graciously acknowledge the apology, and with someone else I might have. 'Why didn't I get it, Eseld?'

She nodded and messed with her hair. To suddenly go from spiky to a cascade takes a bit of getting used to. 'I saw you as a short, mundane accountant who'd got swept along in the Dragonslayer's wake. I know better, now.' She tipped back her drink. 'Want another?'

My glass was empty. How had that happened? 'Please, but remember, I am still short and mundane. I do not have your capacity for alcohol.'

'I deserved that.' She raised her glass and the waiter came over. When he'd gone, she put her hands on the table. 'I need Conrad, and I would never do anything to hurt him, and that means I would never do anything to hurt you. I also think you throw a great party. What else can I say?'

It was the sticking point: could I forgive her? Could I accept her in Conrad's life? Could I welcome her into our home for her own sake?

'You could say that I am stunningly attractive and clearly superior. Or you could get yourself a girlfriend. Or a boyfriend. Any of those would work.'

She blinked. She frowned. The waiter interrupted her meditation, and she came to some sort of decision. When he'd gone, she raised her glass. 'To Rani Mina Desai, a Princess in the world of magick.'

I bowed my head in acknowledgement. 'Better.' I couldn't keep it up after that, and burst out laughing. 'You should see your face. I wish I had a camera or one of those Parchment things.'

She gave me a murderous look, but said nothing.

I smiled at her and leaned in a little. As much as I could without risking my saree coming into contact with the table. 'Now that's on record, what did you really want?'

'How does Conrad keep up with you, Mina?'

'I try not to let him. By the way, if you were after an invitation to the wedding, don't worry. Rachael has been angling for you to be a bridesmaid for some time.'

'I … erm … What?'

It was a lie, of course, but she didn't need to know that. 'The hen party will be epic and span several countries. You can lend us the Smurf. And Leah Kershaw, if she's up to it.'

'Right. You are winding me up, aren't you?'

'Perhaps. I can multi-task, you know. I can wind people up and be serious at the same time. It's cultural.'

She had finished her second drink and looked longingly at the empty glass. She also checked the time on a very slim and elegant white gold watch. 'We need your help, Mina. The family does. I'd ask Conrad, but this is your department, not his.'

'Have you been hit with death duties?'

'In your capacity as Officer of the Cloister Court. When you see the Constable tonight, could you tell her that Cador is going to make an application next week to move the writ of election for the Staff King of Kernow.'

It was my turn to be put on the wrong foot. When Eseld's father, the late Lord Mowbray, started down the road of becoming a Staff King, he also started down the road that led to his death. We were all down there in Cornwall when he split the Kingdom of Wessex in two and became, for one night only, the first Staff King of Kernow.

'You told Conrad that Kenver would get it,' I said with a frown.

'I did. I had a long talk to Ethan and Lena last week, and I think that it's too much for Kenver. I persuaded Ethan to stand.'

I sat back, stunned. Kenver Mowbray is a nice boy with great potential, but he is still a boy. He may be nineteen, but he's led a sheltered life and never had any responsibility. Suddenly, he is the second richest man in Cornwall (after Prince Charles), and hundreds of lives depend on his decisions. He also feels incredibly protective towards his older sister, Morwenna, who has just burst into their lives after being presumed dead for many years.

Conrad needs to see Morwenna soon, so this could not have come at a better time. For me anyway. 'How soon?'

'Next weekend?' she suggested.

'Why not?' I replied.

'And talking of Morwenna, can you deliver this?'

Her bag was a bit larger than one I'd have chosen for the Royal Opera House. Probably because she's a smoker. It also gave her enough room for an envelope made from heavy cream paper with the Mowbray boar stamped on the back. It was addressed to Matthew Eldridge in the Lakeland Particular.

'I shall make sure Conrad hands it over on Tuesday.'

'Thanks, Mina. I'd better go.'

I slid out of the booth to give her a hug. 'Consider yourself enrolled,' I said.

'In what?'

'In the Desai Dating Bureau, of course. There is definitely scope for a Matchmaker in the world of magick.'

'Good luck with that. I can't see you enrolling anyone who'd match my tastes. Apart from Conrad, of course.'

Damn. She'd managed to get the last word. I didn't know she had it in her.

I waited a moment and walked out to get a cab. On the journey north, I reflected on whether I could truly like her, and decided that I couldn't. Yet. I was reassured, yes, and I can see that she has many qualities. Underneath, she may even be a good person. She is also a rich Mage who has no interest in anything but magick and parties. Until she grew up a bit more, she would remain Rachael's friend and Conrad's sidekick.

2 — *Home is where the Howl is*

Now this is what I call rain: proper rain, lashing down from the west with a strong breeze and sheets of water slamming against the window. None of your Mallorcan drizzle on Ullswater. It's good to know that you can rely on the Lake District to be *truly* wet. Perfect weather to go and stand at the edge of the lake and feel the full force of nature. Mina was less enthusiastic.

'I will catch pneumonia and die out there. Or I will be blown away like a leaf and drown in the lake.'

We'd stopped at one of the outdoor clothing shops in Ambleside yesterday, and Mina was now wearing so many layers that she wouldn't get wet and would probably float if she got blown on to the lake.

'You'll be easy to spot,' I observed. 'That coat is very colourful.' The temptation to push her buttons was just too strong. 'You don't have to come, you know. You could wait here.'

She jabbed a Goretex finger at me. 'You are meeting a VIP. I am not going to hide away like the little woman. And no heightist comments. Why don't you move the pack to somewhere warm, like Spain?'

I'd treated myself to a waxed cotton hat with a big brim that actually fitted. I put it on and headed for the door. 'Good idea. Mother could teach the pack to play bridge and Dad could train them to break into houses, like an Anglo-Spanish Fagin. Coming?'

'What is a Fagin? Wait for me!'

It has been a month since the encounter on the last six furlongs of the Fae Gallops, and a fair bit has happened since then. The wolves from the Ripley pack have been merged into my existing crew, and they were on their way from Northumberland to take possession of their new home and new name. In their absence, Clan Skelwith has been busy constructing a small landing stage for easy access from the Lake (the eastern shore of Ullswater is pretty much beyond the back of beyond), and Erin has been in negotiations with the Fae Queen of Derwent about moving into her territory. It is the Queen's representative who was about to arrive at the new dock. And Erin was late. Again.

Mina ran to catch up with me, then had to fall back because the path isn't wide enough for two. The pack ground only has two buildings at the moment, a shed where the Evil One forced them to live, and a large cottage where she cowered in fear that the pack would break their bonds and eat her alive. Sura Ripley should never have been left in charge of a pack of Dual Natured wolves, and the pain she inflicted would take a long time to heal. Longer to heal than the stab wound she gave me right before her nightmare came true and the wolves ripped out her throat.

The Queen of Derwent has her own pack of wolves over in Lunesdale, and their Protector is Prince Harprigg, the Royal Huntsman. He wasn't coming today, but their Madreb was. A pack needs a human Mage, ideally one in permanent residence, and Erin was going to do the job for me. Madreb means Auntie, and Erin being Erin, she'd insisted on Guardian. Fine by me. How long Erin would be able to keep it up was another matter. She does have a day job as well.

The Madreb of the Derwent pack wasn't alone on the boat, and I don't mean the young girl at the controls or the lumbering Fae Squire who helped her get on to the rather narrow pier. Another female figure jumped out of the boat and landed with sure feet on the planks. And then she winced with pain and rubbed her hip.

The Madreb came first, almost as well wrapped up as Mina. I'd been trying to find out how a Witch from Jamaica called Omnira had ended up as Madreb to wolves in Westmorland (and Prince Harprigg's Consort), but I'd drawn a blank. She came up to us and we bowed to each other.

'Welcome to Birk Fell, Madreb Omnira,' I said. 'This is my fiancée, Mina Desai.'

'Namaste. Welcome,' said Mina.

'Thank you.' Omnira turned and ushered the other woman forwards. 'This is Lowri, if you find her worthy of the name.'

The woman who'd jumped from the boat was limping a little now, and I got the chance to get a good look at her. She was the only one hatless out here, and the rain ran streaming off her long, black and silver hair. Her face was lined and sun-burnt and put her about sixty. She was actually twenty. She was a Mannwolf.

With much discomfort, she got to her knees and bowed her head.

'Lowri, you are worthy of your name and welcome here,' I told her.

Before she could move, Mina was at her side, offering a shoulder to lean on. Lowri looked like she was going to spurn it, then relented and gripped Mina while a grimace passed over her face as she stood up.

Omnira had suggested – almost insisted – that the new Birkfell Pack needed a local Elder, and Lowri was her candidate.

Someone, somewhere had bred, bought or kidnapped all of my adult wolves and sold them, some to the Ripleys in Westmorland and some to an Octet of Gnomes in Cheshire. One day I would track that person/creature down and have words with them. Until then, I had a pack of nearly feral wolves on my hands.

The relatively short lifespan of a Mannwolf means that they rarely bother to learn how to read, and the wisdom of the pack is normally preserved and passed on orally by Elders. The ex-Ripley wolves were all young adults or cubs. The ex-Cheshire pack had an Elder, a lovely woman who was also very old. It made total sense to import an Elder with knowledge of the area beyond Birk Fell and with the wisdom of a more established pack to share. Whether Lowri was the right Elder is another matter.

Omnira had been upfront about Lowri's position in the Derwent pack. 'Queen for a day,' she'd said. 'Literally.'

There had been a change of leadership, and Lowri had come out on top. Briefly. She had been too old to be a long-term queen, and had displaced the previous top wolf to keep the crown warm for her daughter. The rest of the pack weren't happy, and blood was shed. It doesn't happen often, especially under Omnira's stewardship, but there was a vicious fight, and Lowri's daughter had been killed. Lowri herself had fled.

Omnira had two choices: send Lowri to Borrowdale to live out her days as a servant to the Fae Queen or send her to another pack, and that's why she was standing here in front of me, water running off her nose and dripping from the hem of her skirt.

She had a gaunt face with a pointy jaw and fierce eyes that were trying to mask pain with fortitude. She wiped the water away from her mouth and said, 'I seek protection, my lord.'

I like to think things through. Did I think that Lowri would spy on my pack for Omnira? Yes. Almost certainly. Did that bother me? No, because I wasn't planning to attack the Fae Queen, and if she was planning to attack me, it wouldn't just be the pack she was after. I couldn't see that happening. I'm not saying it wouldn't happen, just that I couldn't see it.

What worries me more is that Lowri might want revenge on the Derwent pack. Mina had said that this was a given and suggested a way forward. It was a bit extreme, but it beat anything I had to offer.

'Lowri, what do you think of the Derwent pack?' I said.

Shock and confusion flashed across her face, and she looked to the side, at Omnira. Her Madreb said nothing and didn't make eye contact. When she finally answered, at least she was honest.

'I don't know what to say, my lord. What would you like me to think of them?'

'Nothing. You may have my protection if and only if Cara and Alex welcome you, and only if you give me your word never to speak of your former running mates. That is the condition.'

Omnira didn't look happy on many levels. She was worried that Lowri might say no, and she works for the Fae, so she's used to getting her own way in dealings with humans. She's an astute woman, and she also saw where I was coming from, so she said nothing.

'That is a heavy price to pay, my lord.'

It was Mina's turn to be Good Cop. 'You may speak of your daughter,' she said. 'Of course you may. I wouldn't ask any mother not to do that. Focus on her life, not her death. Focus on what you had, not what you lost. I want to know about her.'

Lowri nodded. 'It is as my lord wishes.'

'Good. Let's get out of the rain.'

Mina took Lowri away to show her the kitchen, while I led Omnira to the shed, now renamed as the Pack Hall. Clan Skelwith had patched the roof and lined the walls with insulation and plywood, but it was still a steel shed. Around the back were four deluxe portable toilets.

'I've seen worse,' said Omnira, lowering her hood and taking off her woolly hat. Black hair sprang out and formed a halo. 'What are your plans?'

'I'm going to leave that to the pack. I've done a deal with Skelwith Construction to hire tradesmen as tutors. It's not ideal, but they're fast learners. So long as they can master basic carpentry, there's plenty of wood around. It'll do for this generation.'

She nodded. 'I have two gifts from my Queen for you. The first is simple: we will leave by car. The boat is gifted to the pack.'

'That is very generous. Thank you.'

'The second gift is different. For one year and a day, her grace has generously offered to take all of your pack into hers. You heart is in the right place, Mr Clarke, I have seen that with my own eyes, but you are not a rich man. Keeping a pack is a very expensive business, especially if you can't hire them out for hunting parties.'

She wasn't wrong. The land around us had been handed over by the Ripleys as compensation for what they did, but that was it. I had already spent a lot of money to make the place barely habitable and functional, including a satellite dish and microwave Internet connection for the cottage.

'Thank you again, Madreb Omnira. And thank her grace, too. It's a very generous offer, and one I won't hesitate to take up if it's in the best interests of the pack. A year is very generous, and should be long enough to see if they can make it work.'

She looked amused. 'I take it you have a plan?'

'I always have a plan. I'll keep it quiet for now, in case it goes horribly wrong. Here's the tea.'

Mina and Lowri had a tray each which they deposited on one of the foldaway tables. From outside the Pack Hall, a voice shouted, 'Sorry I'm late, sorry I'm late.'

Erin ran out of the rain and stopped, breathless in front of Omnira. She swallowed and bowed. 'Bloody traffic on the lake road. Who drives a tractor in December? I swear they lie in wait.'

'Never mind, Erin. We have an alternative now.'

While Lowri served tea, I explained about the Queen's gifts. Erin was impressed and looked like she wanted to give Omnira a hug, but the Madreb's face suggested otherwise. Then Erin turned to Lowri. They'd met before, and Erin gave her a proper hug, so hard it almost squeezed water out of her. Omnira frowned: in her book, the Madreb should not be so tactile with the pack.

The Fae Squire who was acting as Omnira's minder appeared in the doorway. I invited him out of the rain, and he said that the car was waiting, so it was down to the real business of Omnira's visit.

'Have you got the maps?' I asked Erin.

'On it,' she replied. She opened a new cupboard and took out a stack of Ordnance Survey maps. After I'd taken off my coat to avoid drippage, we spread them on the table and gathered round. Lowri was included, because she would need to remember this and because she could read maps. Up to a point.

In the New Year, I'm going to be chairing a commission into the future of Dual Natured wolves in England. At the moment, they don't have any legal status at all, even though it is widely known that several Fae nobles keep a pack. The magickal establishment was forced to stop turning a blind eye when I not only encountered Princess Birkdale's pack but acquired one of my own.

Between themselves, the Fae have agreements that divide the land in different ways, and we were here to strike a deal. Or rather, I was here to receive the Queen's generosity and discover what she was going to allow us. When it comes to the Fae, you should always think twice before starting an argument.

Omnira ran her finger down the Lune Valley, all the way from Newbiggin-on-Lune to Glasson Dock. 'These are our forage lands.'

Wolves need to hunt. And eat. For one pack to trespass on the forage lands of another would be an act of aggression that would be met with fangs. Omnira moved her finger to Hartsop, a hamlet at the top end of Patterdale, south of Ullswater. 'The Birkfell Pack should find enough forage from here to Brougham Castle, where the Eamont joins the Eden.' She traced out the Ullswater catchment and drainage then reversed it to include the River Lowther. 'You can have that, too, but steer clear of the Lowther Estate. Understood?'

Erin, Lowri and I all nodded. Mina was frowning.

'Now we come to hunting.'

Omnira kept her face neutral, but did I detect a slight tremor in her finger? Obviously, our packs hunt for food, but that's none of our business. "Hunting" in this context means the Fae. 'The Eden Valley is Royal Hunting Ground, as are the northern fells and the Derwent lands.' She looked up. 'Should you wish to take your amusement in Windermere or the Cartmel peninsula, we would have no objection.'

'Understood.'

'And steer clear of Coniston, of course.'

'I will. Whose toes am I avoiding over there?'

It was Erin who answered. 'The Greenings. You've not met them yet. I'll tell you later.'

I'd read about the Greenings of Grizedale in a very old book, and I'd seen their name on the list of Officers for the various Unions that make up the Lakeland Particular. 'Good. Thanks,' I said to Erin.

'I should be going,' said Omnira. 'Thank you for the hospitality, and may the gods smile on you.'

The Squire had an umbrella ready for her, and she made her way into the rain. Lowri watched until she'd disappeared, then turned to me. She'd been leaning on the table to take the weight off her feet. Before she spoke, she stood up straight, rubbed her arms and shivered.

'May I see Great Fang, Lord Protector?'

I unsheathed my sword and laid the blade flat on the board, keeping hold of the hilt. She swallowed hard and became very still. Slowly, she moved her fingertips across the table, stopping just short of the cutting edge. 'Prince Harprigg has nothing like this,' she said, not taking her eyes off the gleaming steel.

I lifted the sword and sheathed it. Lowri zoned back in and said, 'I will work hard to prepare the ground for my new pack's return later. Do you want more of me now?'

'No thank you.'

She bowed and started clearing the tea things with Mina's help. When they were gone, I dragged a chair to the doorway and lit a cigarette. Erin came to join me. We had been in touch regularly since I left Preston hospital, so I was pretty much up to date. 'The Greenings?' I said.

'Another of the big Lakeland Families.' She shifted in her chair and frowned. 'They're big into magickal animals, hunting and racing. Rowan's joined them.'

'Oh.'

In my first visit to the Particular, I'd locked horns with the Sexton family. Two were now in jail and young Rowan Sexton had been cut out of the line of succession; Erin is now working as tutor to the girl who'd replaced Rowan, leaving Rowan to pursue her career as a jockey.

'How's it going with Pihla?'

She nodded. 'Good, thanks. She's a talented kid.'

'Thanks for everything you've done, Erin. It can't be easy minding the pack from a distance and getting to grips with a new job. Not to mention getting to grips with Barney.'

'Oy! Less of that, thank you. He's got a new job, too, you know. I'm sure he'll tell you all about it tomorrow. Where are you staying?'

'At Sharrow Bay.'

'Get you! I've been tempted, but it's just too expensive.'

The Sharrow Bay hotel, where sticky toffee pudding was invented, used to have the gastronomic crown of Lakeland. That's passed to Simon Rogan at l'Enclume now, but Sharrow Bay is still pretty special, and it's just up the lake from Birk Fell.

'Mina insisted, and it really is handy. What about you? Fancy bedding down with the pack?'

'Not funny. I've got clothes all over the place. The woman in Kendal's Boots thinks I'm ditzy because I keep buying new electric toothbrushes. I've even left one in Barrow.'

'Right. I'll see you after lunch for the arrival.'

We stood up and put the chairs back. I jammed my new hat on my head and went in search of Mina.

The rain hadn't abated much by the afternoon, and putting wet waterproofs back on has never been my favourite activity. Before you accuse me of leaving the dirty work to Erin and Lowri, I should point out that it had been a working lunch at Sharrow Bay.

The Ripleys had refused to transfer the land to me until the pack was actually here, and I had only been lying a little bit when I pretended that Lowri was the whole pack. I signed the final deed, signed the bill, waited while Mina witnessed things, then we headed back to Birk Fell.

We didn't want to drip all over the cottage, so we gathered in the Pack Hall. 'They'll be here soon,' said Erin. 'You're up to something, Conrad, aren't you?'

'He's always up to something,' said Mina. 'You need to be more specific.'

I raised my eyebrows at Erin and waited to see if she'd take the bait. Of course she did.

'Every time I've tried to talk about the next couple of weeks, you've changed the subject, that's why. You're planning something.'

'Seriously, Erin, I don't know. You could say that I was gathering intelligence. Where that will lead, only the gods know, and the Allfather has been quiet lately.'

'They're coming!' shouted Lowri from the other side of the yard.

'Brace yourselves,' said Erin. 'I haven't told you about Maria yet.'

'Who? Why?'

Erin walked into the rain. 'Didn't want to spoil the surprise.'

'Don't look at me!' said Mina. 'I am as worried as you are.'

Two small coaches drove up to the gate. The pack would have fitted on one, but one large coach would never have got down here, never mind got out again. The drivers opened the doors, and the pack flooded out, cubs and children first with adults shouting for them to wait.

There are Dual Natured creatures all over the world. The basic trick of occupying two bodies simultaneously, one on this plane and one on the next, has been around so long that no one knows which race came first. What I can tell you is that through large parts of Western Europe, the Fae offered sanctuary when Mannwolves were hunted and killed. I've checked, and I'm the only human who admits to being Protector of a pack.

We also use a translation of the Fae words for the pack leaders: king and queen. My king and queen are Alex and Cara, leaders of the old Brookford Pack, and I'll share the Fae wisdom of how that works: the king leads the pack, and the queen tells him what to do.

When the dust had settled after the encounter at the Six Furlong Gallops, I found myself with a new, smaller pack and a second queen, Mary. I told them (and her) they could join the re-named Elvenham Pack if they submitted to Alex, which meant that Mary would have to submit to Cara.

Violence does happen within packs. Lowri is a testament of that. According to Erin, despite also being a greater user of magick than Cara, Mary had submitted happily enough, so what was the problem?

Alex led the way, with Cara at his side. She was expecting again and looked very happy to be at their new home. Both of them wore fleeces to keep out the cold and kilts because they'd be Exchanging very soon; it's pretty much the uniform for wolves. But not for the one behind them.

'Please tell me that's the Witch,' said Mina.

'Oh no, love, Dawn is only just getting off now.'

The Witch who's been looking after my pack is Dawn, one of the Northumberland Shield Wall, a mixed coven of Witches from the North East. Dawn is also a Goth, in a fairly mild way, and as you'd expect she was pretty wrapped up. Not so the girl behind Cara.

I'd last seen Mary dressed as Elsa from Disney's *Frozen*. Since then, she's moved on from Disney Princess and has copied her Pack Witch's look. In spades. I must say that the sight of a seemingly teenage ultra-Goth leading a toddler through the rain to a metal shed is not one I'll forget in a hurry. I had to tear my eyes away and remember who was really in charge.

We did it outside, with Mother Nature our witness. Alex and Cara knelt down to renew my role as Protector, and I pronounced their new name. 'From today, I name you the Birkfell Pack. These are your lands, and this is your home.'

They stood up, and Cara stood aside, ushering Mary forwards. She must have spent hours on her makeup alone, and in a short while she'd have to take it off or risk getting it in her eyes when she Exchanged.

'Here is one who would have a new name,' said Cara. 'I have told her that there is only room for one *Mary* in our Lord Protector's life. We have agreed on *Maria*, if it pleases my lord. Maria would also like to be known as Pack Chantress. I have said that is your decision, sir.'

Mary knelt and got mud all over her fishnets. 'If it please my lord.'

She had saved my life twice over on the Gallops. I wasn't going to say no if Cara didn't object, was I?

'I name you Maria, Chantress to the Birkfell Pack. Welcome.'

The pack were all assembled in front of me now, and had been casting inquisitive looks at Lowri, who was trying to keep her face neutral. Erin had warned them about their new member, and Cara had been positive. In theory.

'I would like to introduce a new member. Alex, Cara, this is Lowri.'

Lowri came forwards and submitted. Cara noticed the grimace, and went to help her up. Once on her feet, Cara turned back to me. 'There's one more, sir.' She whistled and waved to the driver of the first coach, who leaned down behind the wall.

When he stood up, a familiar black and white missile shot down the slope, barked loudly and jumped at me.

'Hello you,' I said to Scout. 'Have you been a good boy?'

'Arff!'

He didn't know which way to turn. He ran a few paces to Mina, then dashed to the shed, then back, and finally stood between Maria and me, turning his head. 'Arff?'

'Here.'

He came to me, and I gave him a good scratch. We were getting soaked out here, and there was a fair bit of stuff to unload from the coaches. 'Lowri will show you the cottage. If the rest could help the drivers, Alex and Cara, I need a word.'

The humans and the pack royalty took seats around the table while the rest ran off. When I saw the pained look on Scout's face, I sent him to be with Maria and her little girl.

Dawn had very kindly agreed to stay with the pack for a couple of nights while they settled in and found their way around. After that, Erin would be in charge. I had a horrible feeling that it was going to be a while before I saw them again, and I hadn't realised that I missed Scout so much until I saw him today.

I spent a few minutes explaining to the king and queen what I expected of them, then a fresh-faced Maria and Lowri brought refreshments out. Of course: Maria had done most of it with a (very convincing) Glamour. The clothes were real, though, and when the tea was delivered, she dashed back to get changed, Scout still at her heels.

Alex broke off from admiring the workbench to speak. 'We'll give Maria a minute, sir, then if you permit, we need to Exchange. The coaches are gone now as well.'

'Of course. Listen carefully to Lowri. And Maria. This was her home and she knows the woods and the fells.' I smiled and dangled a set of keys. 'Who's going to be Pack Boatman? There's a motor launch down at the lake.'

Alex licked his lips. 'I think that will be me, sir.'

'For now,' added Cara. 'Let's go.'

The whole Pack crowded in to the shed, and their original Elder corralled the smallest children into a corner. They wouldn't be Exchanging today.

I stood by the doors and spoke up. 'Go, with my blessing, and explore your new home.'

Alex and Cara led, slipping out of their clothes and dumping them in the shed, then running naked into the rain. When all had followed them, they Exchanged into wolf form.

The process takes a few seconds as the two bodies are swapped over. If you've really good Sight, you can see them flicker in and out. One of the things that young Mannwolves learn is to portray it as a transformation, not a swap. It *looks* like they're growing tails and fur, but they're not.

As naked humans, it had been easy to spot the survivors of the Ripley Pack, because they were all covered in scars and old wounds, many inflicted by Sura Ripley herself. As wolves, some of them had white patches where there should be grey, but that was about it.

With an ear-shredding collective howl, the Pack poured out of the compound and down towards the lake. It was a good job it would be dark soon.

We returned to tea, cake, maps and documents.

'What's this?' said Erin.

'Your budget,' said Mina. 'From today.'

'You didn't say anything about a budget!' said Erin.

'There is always a budget,' replied Mina, as if imparting the wisdom of the gods.

Actually, she was. Ganesh loves a budget.

3 — Up North

He was wearing a new suit. Of course he was. When Barney was considering whether to become a detective, he'd look at the male DCs he came across and wonder whether he'd go for something that was cheap and replaceable or more expensive and durable. As it was December, he'd gone for something a bit warmer. He took a deep breath and walked up to the back door.

Police officers enter the imposing bulk of Cairndale Division Station via the secure car park. Most use their pass to buzz the security door within the building, but Barney had to ring the bell and wait for someone to come and see what he wanted. There was no sliding hatch or counter round here, just a glass window.

A civilian with a pleasant smile came over and said hello through the intercom. He took another deep breath and stated his business. 'Trainee Detective Constable Smith from Barrow. I have an appointment with Commander Ross.'

She smiled again and picked up a note that was on the desk that fronted her side of the armoured glass window. 'The Commander came down this morning and gave his apologies. He'll see you tomorrow and says that Detective Sergeant Swindlehurst will look after you.' To make sure he realised how favoured he was, she continued, 'He said that personally.'

Commander Ross, hewn from Aberdeen granite, inspired universal respect in his officers and complete fear of falling short of the mark. Barney was quite happy that his first taste of the detective life would not be in the Commander's office. 'Thanks.'

'I'll give her a call. One sec.'

The intercom died, and Barney stepped back to watch the woman make the call. There were a couple of nods and she finished with another smile. Friendly bunch here. The intercom came alive again. 'She says she's coming down and that you're going straight out to see the magistrate. Won't be long.'

All that Barney knew about DS Swindlehurst was that she was a she. He tried to remember her first name and came up empty. Never mind. The important thing was that he'd not heard anyone bad-mouthing her at Barrow nick, so he'd have a clean slate. He hoped.

The security door clicked open and DS Swindlehurst emerged. Like 99% of the Division's officers, she was white; apart from that, she was average height and in her thirties. Being a detective is stressful, and most detectives spend long hours on the phone or at the computer chain-snacking and have the figure to match. DS Swindlehurst was no exception.

'Hi,' she said as she shook hands. 'You're Barnabas, right?'

'Barney, please.'

There was no invitation to use her first name. Instead, she looked at the outside door and said, 'Is it still raining?'

'Yes.'

She rolled her eyes. 'Bloody typical. It's a swine to park at the courthouse. Let me get a brolly.'

It was also quite a short walk – no more than ten minutes. And good exercise. His new sergeant returned and breezed out of the station. She spent the walk through the leafier part of Cairndale asking about mutual acquaintances at Barrow station and in CID. It was a polite way of finding out who his friends were.

She cheated at the courthouse by using the prisoner entrance and bypassing security; the guard at the back clearly knew her very well. In a couple of minutes, they were sitting in the police seats of Colonel Will Shepherd's courtroom, watching him dispose of licencing requests. He barely looked up when the Clerk announced them and passed over the papers for him to sign.

Barney stated his name and details before repeating the oath. Shepherd looked up at that point and took his measure. 'About time we had a new detective up here. Are you sure you're ready for days of frustration and paperwork, DC Smith?'

'Absolutely, sir.'

'Then you'll fit right in. All we need now is a new senior detective. Shame you're too young, Elizabeth.'

'I don't feel it, sir,' replied his new boss. He filed away the name *Elizabeth* for future reference.

'Witness details?' said the Clerk, who was clearly in a big hurry.

Barney's new boss stated her full name for the record, and Barney was frozen to the spot.

'Elizabeth Caroline Skelwith Swindlehurst, Detective Sergeant at Cairndale Division.'

What the fuck? *Skelwith?* Shit. She was one of them. Barney dropped his newly acquired warrant card and spent a few moments picking it up in an effort to regain his equilibrium. DS Swindlehurst was trying to hand him stuff, and he nearly lost the plot completely. He accepted his security pass, a load of paperwork and somehow managed not to say anything.

'The bail applications are ready,' said the Clerk.

'Let's get out quick,' said Swindlehurst. 'We'll detour via the Market Square and get coffee. I'm about ready.'

Back in the rain, she gave him a look. 'Colonel Will doesn't normally have that effect on one of us. Big moment for you, eh?'

'I was thinking of my Granddad. He was a copper. Sorry, Sarge.'

'We're on first name terms at Division. Too much of a bear pit and too many empty desks for hierarchy, so I'm Liz.'

They crossed the old bridge over the River Cowan and trekked up the short hill to the Market Square and then to the coffee shop. On the way in, Liz said, 'Rumour has it this place might change hands soon. I hope the new owners don't spoil it.'

'I'll get them,' he said, before Liz could say anything else about the new owners. 'Can I buy you a Danish?'

'You don't need my permission to buy me pastries. I'll have a large latte.'

They completed the circle back to the station with Liz pointing out the curry house (excellent), the pizza shop (avoid at all costs) and a couple of favourite places for drug deals to take place. Barney listened as carefully as he could, but part of his mind was elsewhere. Should he say something? Liz made him try his new pass on the security door and then they were heading through to CID.

She stopped inside the open-plan room and pointed out all the desks. 'Vacancy, Vacancy, long-term sick, holiday, yours, mine.'

That covered six of the desks. Of the others, some were presumably out detecting, and that left three detectives. Two were on the phone and hadn't looked up, which left one: DS Les Gartside, a face Barney knew well. Les raised a hand in greeting, with an amused look on his face, and then went back to reading a thick wadge of papers. Barney had also noted that his own desk was nose-to-nose with Liz's. No surprise, really. He was going to be the new boy for some time.

'And this is the escape room,' said Liz, pointing to a large, glassed-in office at the end. 'It should have a senior detective, but as you know, we don't have one and have to make do with loan signings. The current one is from Lancaster and likes to sit in the team. When she's in, that is. Let's grab a bit of privacy while I take you through the coursework.'

As well as getting signed off by Liz, Barney would have to pass a stiff test in advanced rules of evidence and principles of detection, but that wasn't what was on his mind. He followed his sergeant into the empty DCI's office and closed the door behind him. She took the boss's chair and waved for him to sit down on the other side of the desk.

He did so and tried to summon up some courage. Before Liz could launch into an explanation of modules and assessment, he spoke up. 'I hope we're not going to be late tonight. I have to be in Ambleside.'

She wasn't expecting this, and frowned at being knocked off course.

He ploughed on. 'I've got a dinner engagement with Special Constable Clarke and Matthew Eldridge. Conrad is overseeing the ground for his new pack today.'

She blinked hard, then sat back in the comfy chair and stared at him. He kept quiet. 'Well, well, well,' she said. 'You're a dark horse, Barney Smith, aren't you?' She leaned forwards again. 'But are you a Trojan Horse for the King's Watch? That's what I want to know.'

He was already shaking his head. 'No, Sarge. Absolutely not.'

'When did it happen? It must have been recent.'

'I helped DCI Morton on the Eldridge case, and Matt Eldridge dragged me along to Sprint Stables.'

'Shit. Really? There's a huge blanket of silence over the supernatural side of that case, and the police files are locked tighter than the Bank of England. You were really there?'

He nodded.

'But why is Conrad Bloody Clarke inviting you to his party if you're not in his pocket, Barney?'

'I'm a plus one, Sarge.' He coughed. 'I'm dating a Witch, but it's early days yet. She's doing some work with the pack.'

'Wonders will never cease. How did you clock me, because you had no idea when you arrived here, did you?'

'No. It was when I heard your full name.'

'And you guessed I was a Daughter of the Earth. Well spotted.' She looked around the office as if seeing it for the first time. 'So how are we going to do this, Barney? How are we going to get along?'

'I just want to be a detective. I'm not here to rock the boat or fight someone else's battles. How many cases actually involve magick anyway?'

'Enough to wind up the Commander, but you're right. It could be six months before there's another one, and we have more than enough crime to go round.' She rubbed her nose and put her hands on the desk with a smile. 'Shall we start again? I'm Liz, my father is in the Third House of Clan Skelwith and I'm married to a haulage contractor, of all things. We have two children who drive me to drink. Who are you dating?'

'Erm, Erin Slater. She's an Enscriber who's just moved up here.'

'Clearly a fast worker.'

Erin was a fast worker, in more ways than one. Dating her had been a whirlwind, and she was already looking at property in the area. He smiled at Liz and didn't add anything.

She lifted herself half out of the chair and plonked back down on it. 'Talking of DCI Morton, do you know what Project Talpa is and what he's doing in the Counter-Terrorism room?'

That was an easy one. 'I have no idea. None whatsoever. He gets all sorts of odd cases, or so I hear.'

She thought that was funny. 'And do your sources have anything to say about whether he's going to make this office his own? I've heard that Ross has offered it to him.'

'Then you've heard more than I have.' He reflected for a moment. He did know *something*, and sharing it with Liz might be a sign of good faith. 'I've met his girlfriend, and she's the one who's buying the coffee shop. She's already got one in Garstang and one in Southport that I know of.' He slipped in an extra detail. 'You know her father is Gary White?'

'No!' She shook her head. 'You must have worked with Morton a bit. What's he like?'

'He wears very expensive, hand-made suits and has a thing for spreadsheets. And he's not afraid of Mr Clarke, which says something. Oh, and he makes excellent tea.'

She opened the top drawer absentmindedly and seemed surprised not to find Haribo in there (Barney had already clocked her waste basket and knew her snacks of choice). 'Good. Right. I have very little involvement in the Particular. Other than through my father, of course. I'd like to keep it that way. Apart from gossip, of course. Deal?'

'Yes, Sarge.'

'Good. I do want to hear about the pack, though. You can tell me tomorrow when you drive me round the patch. Right. Back to proper policing.'

Barney took this as a sign to remove his Police Issue waterproof. He'd had his hand in the pocket since they'd entered the bolthole, wrapped around the Merlyn's Tower Irregulars badge that Clarke had given him. He relaxed inside and sat up straight. Never had *Application for Search Warrants in Computer Crime* seemed so appealing.

'Ready, love?' I asked.

'I'm not sure I can ever be ready for something like this,' said Mina, lifting her eyes to look at the top storey of the building in front of us.

I've stood here before, outside, but this would be my first time inside the Oak Tree Hotel. The grey stone hotel and restaurant is located in Ambleside, one of the Lake District's honeypot Towns. A honeypot if you're a tourist; one of its centres of power if you live in the world of magick.

A Mage called Harry Eldridge had made the Oak Tree his mundane home, and inside was his widow and young daughter: it was their room that Mina had been trying to focus on. Harry had woven himself a very tangled web, and those of us left behind after his violent murder all had some responsibility to untangle it.

Harry had once loved a girl called Lara Dent, a champion jockey who'd ended up working for the Fae, then quitting, and then drowning in a terrible accident. After that, Harry had become a bookmaker at various occult sporting events. He had also fallen for a Ukrainian woman called Zinayida Zinchenko, who bore a striking resemblance to the late Lara. Harry had invested all his remaining capital in buying a hotel in partnership with Zinayida and her chef brother, Anatoly.

To compound the confusion, Harry had told Zinayida that Lara was his deceased sister, and they'd then called their daughter Lara in her memory. It was a testimony to Harry's devious nature that none of his magickal employers or even his half-brother had known anything about this.

Harry loved horses. A broken back had cut short his own career as a jockey, and an unwise bet had left him bankrupt and bought out by the Fae Prince Galleny, a big player in the sporting world and consort to the local Fae Queen. It was a stressful and difficult life for Harry, having to ride two horses at the same time, but he'd managed it well enough until something changed. Radically.

For reasons we don't know, Prince Galleny had sent Harry to raid an archaeological dig being carried out by the Ripleys on what is now the Pack ground. Galleny had used the stick of Harry's debts, but it was the carrot that was giving me headaches. Somehow, the Fae had kept a Memorial Artefact with most of Lara Dent's memories and skills in them, and they'd recruited (or bought) a human vessel to wear that Artefact.

I'd seen her in action, riding a High Unicorn, and she was the absolute spit of Lara Dent. And the similarity had gone beyond surface looks, because Harry had spent at least one night with her, and that human vessel was now pregnant with Harry's twins. When the Artefact was ripped off her, Lara Dent had returned to being Morwenna Mowbray, and that was another can of worms altogether, a can so big that it would have fed the Lord Mayor of Moles for a week.

I took Mina's hand and we walked into the hotel's reception area. Waiting to greet us was Matthew Eldridge, the late Harry's half-brother. The final strand in Harry's web of deception had been to say nothing whatsoever to Zinayida about having a male sibling. The Eldridge brothers hadn't got on well in later years, and Matthew worked for the Lakeland Particular as an Assessor – their version of the King's Watch.

I went to shake Matt's hand after Mina had made Namaste. 'How are things?' I asked, trying to be sympathetic without being saccharine. Matthew – Matt – is a solitary, undemonstrative and taciturn man at the best of times. He's also a good one, and has become little Lara's champion in the world.

He's also Harry's executor, and that was why Eseld Mowbray had given Mina the letter for him.

'Better,' said Matt. He gestured at the Christmas tree in the corner of reception, and a little shiver ran down my back: it was the perfect memorial to Harry Eldridge and his life, because the tree was covered in silver thread made to look like spiders' webs.

'Spiders?' I said. 'Really?'

'Ukrainian tradition,' said Matt, oblivious to the symbolism. 'Doing the tree was good for Zina, and she's been well enough to cope with the Christmas rush, so that's helped take her mind off things. She'll be down in a minute. How are you Conrad? You certainly look better than when I waved you off in the air ambulance.'

'Pretty much healed, thanks. I'm still on sick leave for now, though. What about you? Did you follow Tom's advice about the Chief Assessor?'

The politics of magick in the Lakeland Particular are even more twisted than Harry's web of deception or Zinayida's tree. As Deputy Constable of the Watch, I have no authority here unless the victim is mundane. Harry was a Mage, and the Chief Assessor had been criminally negligent in her supervision of the investigation, a point made to Harry by DCI Tom Morton. I would never dare say that.

'I told my Union Chair,' said Matt. His mouth twitched but never made it to a smile. 'He's told me to take another month's compassionate leave, that way he won't have to process my complaint. He did do one thing, though. He jumped up and down and insisted that Kian Pike was prosecuted for attempted murder, not assault. He's in court next week.'

The attempted murder in question was directed at me, and I do take things like that personally. 'Good. I hope he gets two years in the Esthwaite Rest.'

A blast of cold air announced more arrivals – Erin and Barney, and today was his first day as a trainee detective. When we shook hands and I asked him how it had gone, I got a swivel of the eyes and a curt, 'Fine, thanks sir.'

'Tom and Lucy are already here,' said Matt.

'Then can I grab you for a moment before we settle down, Matt?' I said. 'In private.'

'Of course. We'll go out the back and grab a beer on the way.'

'We'll find the Mortons,' said Mina. Tom and Lucy are not married or engaged, but it can't be far off.

The Oak Tree has a small smokers' area at the back of the hotel, complete with infra-red heater and enough light to read by. Matt handed me a beer, and we clinked bottles. I took out the letter and showed him the direction. 'It's from Morwenna, via Eseld and Mina. Do you want me to give you some privacy?'

'No. You're the only person who knows everything, Conrad. I'll read it here. No one will disturb us.'

We sat down, and Matt had to fumble for glasses. 'I've only just realised I need these,' he said. He opened the envelope and we lapsed into silence. I took out my cigarettes.

It didn't take him long to read it. He read it again and offered it to me. I told you he was a man of few words.

Dear Matthew,

I know how much you lost when Harry was taken. I am so sorry. I hope that one day we will meet in peace and remember him. If the Goddess wills it that my babies come safely into the world, I hope that you will stand in Harry's place at the naming.

Until then, I know that you have a hard job to do. I have spoken to my brother Cador the lawyer, and he says that I can renounce the babies' share of Harry's inheritance, so long as I put the same value into a trust fund for them. I promise you that I will do this, but Cador says I can't do anything until they're born.

I am not going to leave Kernow while I'm expecting, but you are welcome here whenever you want.

Hoping we can live in peace,
In Harry's memory,
Love, Morwenna Mowbray.

I passed the letter back, and Matt folded it carefully. 'Are you going to see her soon?' he asked.

'Within a few days.'

'Then thank her for me. I doubt I'll be down there beforehand, but I'll be proud to stand for Harry at the naming. I'll write to her next week. It's a weight off my mind, certainly.'

'One of the weights, Matt.' I echoed Mina by pointing to the family accommodation. 'What about little Lara? Are you going to tell Zinayida the truth about magick?'

It was an important issue, and one that got harder to deal with every day. Zinayida knew nothing of magick. Nothing at all. Nor of Harry's other life. She still thought that Lara Dent was Harry's half-sister, not his great lost love.

That was all fine in theory, but if little Lara developed magickal talents, she would inevitably find out the truth about her father.

'No,' said Matt. 'Harry chose not to. He knew the potential risks and decided they were worth it. I'm not going to go against that.'

The door opened and a shadowy figure in a long skirt was outlined by the internal lights. 'Matthew? Why are you here?' The accent was strong, the voice strained. Zinayida.

He sprang out of his chair and rushed up to her. 'Sorry, Zina. Business, I'm afraid. We're coming in now.'

She backed inside, and Matthew made the introductions in the hotel corridor. Zinayida Zinchenko was wearing the Ukrainian national dress that all front of house staff sported, including the Polish and English ones. She had blonde hair, tied back in a plait, but otherwise she could definitely be Lara Dent, older and sadder. I shook hands and met her blue-eyed gaze.

She gripped my hand and didn't let go. 'You are the one who killed her, yes? You took revenge for Harry?'

It was a Mannwolf who'd ripped out Sura Ripley's throat in reality. In the official version, it was me. 'Yes.'

'Thank you, Mr Clarke. Thank you.'

I could have handed over that letter anywhere. That wasn't why I was here. The reason was Zinayida herself, abetted by Matt. She wanted to gather everyone who'd been involved in the investigation of Harry's murder and thank us with dinner. In the mundane world, Zinayida would have been told (politely but firmly) that this was not an option; in the world of magick, it was considered a good idea.

We entered the bar area and I saw that Erin and Barney were talking to Tom Morton. Barney looked very uncomfortable, as you might expect with his girlfriend sounding off to a senior officer, and Tom was trying to get a word in edgeways, not always easy when Erin was in full flow. Today's topic for Erin was the ludicrous price of houses in the Lake District. Mina and Lucy were huddled in the corner, no doubt discussing their plans for tomorrow.

Our party weren't the only guests – the restaurant was open for business as usual and was doing a brisk trade from winter tourists wanting hearty food. I even heard the head waitress telling a couple of walk-ins that there was nothing until nine o'clock. Matt led us through to the restaurant and we took the table for eight that had been given quite a bit of room to breathe. Before we sat down, Zinayida made us all drink a toast to Harry with a shot of Horilka, the Ukrainian national spirit. She held off raising her glass until her brother had joined us.

Anatoly Zinchenko was younger than his sister, and very young to have his own kitchen. When we sat down, he outlined what he was serving for us and left us to get on with it.

While Matt was still asking who wanted which wine, Mina put her hand on Zinayida's arm. 'You must have your phone in one of your pockets,' she said.

'Yes?' said Zina with a frown.

'I have heard so much about your daughter, you must show me pictures, please.'

And with that, I breathed a sigh of relief. By the time Mina had squeezed dry the topic of little Lara, Zina had almost forgotten why we were here, especially when the food arrived. It was very good, by the way. Mina drew Matt into the conversation and asked about the hotel business, and I thought we'd gotten away with it.

We were struggling to find room for a very light babka cake when Zina pointed her fork at Matt. He was opposite her and looked suddenly very uncomfortable. He blinked rapidly a few times and drew his chair back. When he crossed his legs, he half turned to his right, where I was sitting.

Zina glanced my way, then lifted her chin and wagged the cake fork. 'Now the avengers are here, perhaps you can answer my question, Matthew.'

'I … I don't know what you mean, Zina.'

'You know very well. You were the only one who had met this woman before. Could she have done this to Harry on her own?' Before Matt could answer, Zina turned to Barney, who did a very good impersonation of a stranded fish. 'Barnabas, you saw Harry hanging from the tree. Could a woman on her own have done *that* to him? All those things? And Thomas, are you happy with this?'

Erin, Mina and Lucy glanced at each other while their men were put on the spot, and they decided to say nothing. I looked at Tom, because I have a permanent need to stay on his good side. He inclined his head very gradually towards Matt, and in seconds everyone was looking at him to take the lead.

When none of us leapt straight in, he shifted in his seat and uncrossed his legs. He leaned forwards and shocked Zinayida by taking the fork out of her hand, placing it on the table and taking her right hand in his. 'Yes, Zina. She was a cruel, evil woman. Tell her about the dogs, Conrad.'

What? Oh. Right. 'She kept a pack of guard dogs on her farm,' I said. Then I shook my head. 'It was terrible. We didn't want to add to your pain by telling you how badly she mistreated them.'

Zina flinched, but she didn't draw her hand away from Matt's. She turned to Tom. 'No one will tell me why he was at her farm. You must know, Thomas.'

'Another thing we wanted to spare you,' he replied. 'Harry was breaking and entering. The dogs caught him.'

She managed a weak smile. 'Thank you, Thomas, and you Conrad, and Barnabas. Thank you.' She slowly withdrew her hand from Matt's and made eye contact with him. She said something to him in Ukrainian, something that sounded grateful, then suddenly stood up. We all followed suit. 'And now I must go. The babysitter needs to leave. You will always be welcome here. Please stay and enjoy yourselves. Matthew will look after you. Good night.'

Mina and Erin stopped her from running by giving her a brief hug. They let go when they saw her crying. The head waitress came over and offered us coffee. 'I think I'll take mine outside,' I said.

'I'll join you for a moment,' said Tom.

'Erm, there's something I need to tell both of you,' added Barney. 'If I may, sir.'

Tom put his arm round Barney's shoulders (which meant reaching up a fair bit), and said, 'We went past *sir* after the second toast, Barney. It's a good job that no one's driving.'

The coffee arrived and we adjourned outside. I think that Matt had given Zina a moment and then followed her upstairs, which left Barney, Tom and me to spread out behind the hotel.

'I still can't get used to it,' said Tom. 'All this fraternising and familiarity isn't good.' He said it with a smile because fraternising with a witness is exactly how he'd ended up dating Lucy. He turned to Barney. 'This is all to come for you if you stick with Erin.'

'Erm, yes. About that. There's something I need to tell you.' His tone made Tom and I sit up a bit straighter. 'My mentor is DS Swindlehurst. Do you know her, sir?' He directed his question to Tom, who shook his head. 'Her second surname is *Skelwith*.'

Tom looked at me. We already knew that Inspector Gibson in Barrow was a Daughter of the Earth, and that there was probably a magickal presence in CID. He raised his eyebrows and said to Barney, 'Does she know you know?'

'Yes. It's out in the open, including Erin.'

'Thanks, Barney. Do you think it will cause you problems?'

He rubbed the back of his neck. 'Honestly? No. Her priority is County Lines drug dealing around Morecambe Bay.'

'Good to hear. Tread carefully.'

'I will, sir. Thanks. I'd better be going. Early start tomorrow. Goodnight, Mr Clarke. Great to see you looking better.'

Tom watched Barney's retreating back. 'That was brave of him. I hope it doesn't come back to bite him on the arse.'

'Me too.'

He turned his attention to me. 'We've finished Project Talpa. You can come and see for yourself tomorrow.'

I didn't know what to say at first. You may recall that many of my troubles in the world of magick go back to a book called the Codex Defanatus, a book that is in circulation partly thanks to two of my ancestors. Finding that book and who has been selling secrets from it has been a top priority for the Watch, except that everyone we caught who'd been involved had either been killed or had zipped their lips so tightly that we couldn't pry them open. We'd called it *Project Talpa*, and at my suggestion, the Boss had commissioned Tom to see if there was a mundane way of tracking back to the source. I wetted my lips and said, 'Did you get a result.'

Tom gave a very self-satisfied smile. 'We did.'

'And?'

'And you'll have to wait. Elaine did most of the work, and I'm not going to steal her thunder. She'd make my life a misery.' Lucy calls DC Elaine Fraser *Scarywoman*, a fairly apt nickname. Talking of his work partner made Tom think of mine. 'Is there a reason why Cordelia isn't here tonight?'

Cordelia Kennedy has one of the hardest jobs in the King's Watch: keeping me out of magickal trouble. There were a lot of reasons for her not being here, including the fact that this was a private evening. I chose to give Tom the diplomatic answer. 'Someone has to mind the fort in Cheshire, and I'm still not officially back yet. I've got an appointment with a private specialist on Thursday morning, and he might not sign me off. Shall we see what the girls have been plotting?'

On the way back to the dining room, we passed through reception, and Matthew was showing out tonight's babysitter. Ambleside is home to Charlotte Mason College of teacher training, and Zinayida has a roster of girls who babysit during evening service. They're a conscientious lot, apparently, and Zina sometimes has to kick them out because they're so deep into their lesson planning for their teaching practice. This girl, however, was no trainee teacher.

She was younger and shorter, for a start, with a wiry figure and her hair in a Goddess Braid. As soon as she saw me, she blanched and ducked out of the front door. I'd seen her once before, riding a High Unicorn, and I knew that she was one of Harry's students in magick at Waterhead Academy.

'Was that Persephone?' I asked Matt.

'Yes. Perci was devoted to Harry, and I let her represent the Academy at his funeral. She came back here and fell in love with little Lara. It doesn't hurt.'

'Was she also representing the Queen of the Derwent at the funeral?'

Matt shocked me with his answer. 'No. The Queen came herself. To the interment, of course.'

'Of course.' No Fae Queen would ever set foot in a church – or mosque or synagogue. It was a very high honour, and I'm not entirely sure what it meant. I don't think Matt knew either.

We went through to the dining room, and I muttered to myself, 'Perci doesn't half remind me of someone. I wish I knew who it was.' If Tom or Matt heard me, they didn't offer any enlightenment.

Matt did, however, offer more wine. When we finally called it a night and left for our various hotels, Tom and I agreed that we'd have a late start in the morning. On the walk back, I held Mina's hand and gave it a squeeze.

'Poor Matt,' she said. 'I shall have to sign him up for the Desai Dating service. And quickly.'

'You're right. He's got it bad for Zinayida, hasn't he?'

'He has. And I really hope that she finds love again one day. We both know that it won't be with Matt, don't we? I don't know which will be more of a challenge, him or Eseld … What? What's so funny?'

4 — The Road South

'Bad news, I'm afraid,' said Tom the next morning when I presented myself to the desk at Cairndale nick.

'How bad?'

'Commander Ross somehow knows you're back in circulation. We've been summoned to his office. Now.'

It's a moot point as to whether Police Commander Allister Ross knows about the world of magick. I suspect that he's like my father: he blocks it out. What he does know all about is that the Union Assessors are allowed to take some cases off him. He does not like that, and I don't blame him.

Ross supported my application to carry firearms on two conditions. The first was that I do my best to break the Particular Unions' stranglehold on certain cases – I said I'd do my best. The second was non-negotiable: I had to become an unpaid Special Constable in the Lancs & Westmorland Police, which meant that when I walked into the police station, he treated me like one of his own officers. Which is what I was.

Allister Ross is from Aberdeen and was a captain in the Army before joining the police. According to Barney, bets are taken on the order of priority for the great passions in his life: policing, Mrs Ross, his daughters and rugby. Stepping into his imposing office, I sincerely wished that I was in uniform. RAF uniform. Then I'd outrank him.

Tom and I stood in front of his desk and he looked me up and down. His frown was directed at my second-best Barbour coat, I think. 'Well, laddy, how're you doing? You were in a pretty bad way according to Morton.'

'Much better, thank you sir.'

Harry Eldridge's murder had started off as Ross's case. He'd recruited Tom to take over, and Tom had recruited me when he realised that magick was involved. Ross was not happy when the Cloister Court ruled that it was none of our business, not that he knew anything about the Cloister Court.

'Good. Now then, Clarke, I want you to look me in the eye and tell me the truth about poor Eldridge's killer.'

I did look him in the eye; I didn't tell him the truth. I finished by saying that she'd died at my hand.

'Well, Clarke, unless you used some sort of ray gun, where's the woman's body? Or was that you, Morton? Did you spirit away the corpse while Clarke was in the Air Ambulance?'

Tom was very quick to dodge that one. 'MI7 took custody of the body, sir.'

That would be us – our new cover ID is MI7, an organisation so secret that we don't officially exist. It did give me a way out, though. 'Sura Ripley's remains were an extreme bio-chemical hazard, sir. They had to be disposed of safely. I can get the Home Office to confirm that, if you want. Her family know all about it, too. The only secrecy is at the inquest, and even then we've named her as Harry's killer.'

He grunted. 'I suppose I'll have to make do with that. Did those Assessors get any comeback for what they did or didn't do?'

'It's in hand, sir. Their bosses are not at all happy.'

'Even better. Now, Clarke, tell me straight: does this mission of Tom Morton's have any implications for my Division?'

'I honestly don't know, sir, because Tom hasn't told me yet.'

This time, Tom was willing to commit himself. 'No, it doesn't, sir. Absolutely nothing to do with Cairndale Division whatsoever.' He risked a smile. 'But I don't want to spoil the surprise for Conrad.'

'Go away, both of ye. No, wait. Tom, have you given any more thought to my offer?'

'Yes sir, and we're still thinking. I'll let you know before the new year.'

'Fair enough. What are you still doing here?'

Naturally, we were both sweating profusely by then. The release of tension made us both laugh in the corridor. 'It's alright for you, Tom. Blue eyed boy and all that. He just hates me on principle.'

'That's how he shows his affection. The more he shouts at you, the more he loves you. He'll be calling you bro before you…' He stopped suddenly when we rounded a corner and came face to face with Barney Smith. And his mentor.

DS Swindlehurst was a large woman with paper-white parchment skin and fine fair hair. We were blocking the corridor, so I stepped to the side, well out of the way. Barney suddenly realised that it was his job to introduce us. He only stammered a bit while he did so, and while he did, Swindlehurst looked me up and down.

'How d'you do,' I said, shaking hands. 'And don't worry, I'm leaving soon.'

'Why would that worry me?' she said, which was fair enough. She glanced at Tom. 'You must be DCI Morton, sir. Barney forgot that I don't know you. Are you leaving soon as well, because that might have more of a bearing?'

'I honestly haven't decided,' said Tom. 'If I stay, I'm looking forward to working with you.'

'Ditto, sir. Come on, Barney, the Commander's waiting.' She paused and looked at me. 'You haven't been winding him up, have you?'

'No more than usual. Nice to meet you, sergeant.'

She gave me a baleful glare and moved on. I did not envy Barney Smith's next ten minutes.

'There's a kettle in the bunker,' said Tom. Elaine should have a brew on by now.'

He wasn't joking about the bunker. Counter-Terrorism North West don't have a permanent presence in Cairndale, but they do have first dibs on the hyper-secure incident room. Tom scanned his fingerprint on the door and led us into a windowless space that had been decorated by someone who thought Institutional Grey was a colour-palette and not a form of psychological warfare. He wasn't lying about the tea, though.

I've said that Cordelia's job is to keep me out of trouble. My previous partner, Karina Kent, did exactly the opposite: when faced with a direct order to take out a Mannwolf, she'd chosen to shoot DC Elaine Fraser with a hunting arrow. Right through the thigh. The first order of business was to compare notes on our convalescence; Elaine was doing better than me, and had started using the climbing walls again. She can lift her whole body weight with just her fingers.

'Karina's been released from the Undercroft,' I told her. 'No permanent damage, they don't think.'

'Here's your tea,' she replied. 'Can that place really drive people mad in three weeks?'

'Yes.'

'Right. Shall we get down to business, sir?' She'd addressed the question to Tom. Elaine does not call me sir, not with me being a Special Constable. Tom went to get some files, and she pointed to a seat. I sat.

She lowered the lights a little and turned on an overhead projector. On the big screen, a big map of Europe appeared. When Tom was ready, she stood next to the map with a laser pointer in her hand and began. 'We've been through Home Office and Foreign Office passport logs, flight and ferry manifests, credit card and bank statements and, where possible, mobile phone data. You were right about one thing, Conrad.'

I snagged a biscuit. 'Only the one?'

She ignored me. 'Your Mages do seem a bit clueless about Big Data. They made very little effort to hide their movements. Out of all the subjects, we detected one significant anomaly.'

Tom was holding a stack of folders. He slipped the top one into his right hand, cradling the others to his chest. 'Keira Faulkner,' he announced. 'No significant pattern.' He dropped the file on to the desk and brandished the second one. 'Adaryn ap Owain, no significant pattern.' Drop. For the next file, he waved it about with some relish. 'Surwen and Gwyddno from the Dragon conspiracy.'

Elaine snapped her pointer to the map, to the western edge of Ireland. 'Five years ago, they took a family holiday to Galway and rented a cottage in the summer. At the end of October, Surwen went back on her own.'

'The end of October?' I said.

'Yes. Tom's told me all about Samhain.'

'Ivan Rybakov, aka Isaac Fisher,' said Tom.

Elaine waited until the file had thumped down. 'He went to Ireland multiple times, but he was in Galway at the same time as Surwen.'

'Irina Ispabudhan.' Another thump.

'Was with him. They stayed at the best hotel. As did…'

'Eilidh Haigh.'

Tom moved through the next four folders quickly. 'Diana Sexton: nothing. Harry Eldridge and his associates: nothing. Stella Newborn/Ripley: nothing. The Octet of Gnomes: nothing, and they were the hardest to track down. And that leaves me with Deborah Sayer.'

Debs Sayer was the one who started it all for me. She had recruited Keira Faulkner and they had tried to summon Helen of Troy. Tom waved the file and placed it down.

'Deborah Sayer was there, too. In the summer and at Samhain. But she was there with an unknown male. We can't access the hotel's records, but we know she paid for a second driver to be on her hire-car insurance. It was a false name, and none of the people she flew over with – or back with – went anywhere near Galway. So there you go.'

Tom squared the edges of the folders. 'We've prepared a report with the dates and names of the hotel and cottage accommodation, but we can't give you the source data. When Hannah negotiated access to the records, we were told they were for our eyes only. Sorry. Any questions?'

I did have questions, and I'm afraid that they didn't add much to what they'd already told me. When I was winding down, instead of standing up, Tom made himself more comfortable. 'I had a chat to Erin last night.'

This was not going to be good news. Erin has many qualities, and I've discovered that when she is told that something is a secret, she will keep it even under the influence of copious quantities of alcohol. When she doesn't know something's a secret… 'Oh yes, Tom?'

'I asked her about her name, and whether she had Irish roots, and that segued neatly into your Irish counterparts. When she told me, I'm afraid that the Gaelic went in one ear and out of the other.' He took a biscuit and waited for me to respond.

'I'm afraid that I'm better at Germanic languages than Celtic ones.' I closed my eyes and dragged the pronunciation out. '*The Fiosrúchán Aontaithe na hÉireann*, also known as the United Irish Inquisition or the F-A-E. You don't want to be pronouncing it as one word for obvious reasons.'

'Quite. I got the impression that they don't play nicely with the King's Watch. Not that Erin would be an expert, I suppose.'

Tom Morton went to a much better school than me, and all that legal training makes him a fiendish, if very dapper, inquisitor. His casual comment was a gauntlet thrown down: what was I going to do with the information I'd just received? He and Elaine deserved something approaching a straight answer.

'It's not that we don't play nicely with each other. We do. Only last year we sent a pair of Mages back to answer for their crimes, and they routinely respond to background queries about their ex-pats in England. It's more that the world of magick doesn't have international organisations or institutions. Or not any more. No one has ever extradited a Fae noble, and I don't have any jurisdiction over there. This is for others to sort out. At least in the short term.'

He didn't look entirely happy, and I don't think I've ever seen Elaine look entirely happy (maybe she is at home). He'd done his bit, though, and he trusted Hannah completely. He didn't have anywhere to go with his questions that wouldn't be rude.

When he sat up, I reached for my rucksack. 'Thank you both. Very much. This is from me, personally.' I slid a pair of envelopes across the desk towards Tom. 'Two nights bed and breakfast at the Little Langdale Lodge. Valid six months.'

Elaine frowned. Tom smiled and took the nearest envelope. 'That's very kind, Conrad.' He slid it back to me. 'I don't mind accepting your hospitality socially. And Mina's. But this is professional. Elaine?'

'Of course, sir.'

I collected both envelopes, and the single page report. I couldn't help notice that a copy had gone to the Boss, too. Only to be expected, I suppose. It would mean a very awkward conversation at some point in the near future.

'Right. That's it,' said Tom. 'If you volunteer to clean up and hand the bunker back to Division, Elaine, you can go home.'

'Cheers, sir. Are you off to see Lucy?'

It was there again. Vicky had spotted it, and so had Mina: there was an edge to Elaine's relationship with Lucy that didn't seem to go away. Tom either didn't notice or (more likely) put up with it. 'Yes. Both of us are.'

There were no more encounters with DS Swindlehurst on the way out, and we were soon heading into the Market Square. Tom had checked his phone as soon as we left the bunker and received confirmation that it had all gone through: Lucia Berardi, or her company, were now the proud owners of the Cairndale Coffee House, soon to be re-branded as Caffè Milano in Cairndale. Mina is barred from practising as an accountant for life on account of her money laundering conviction. However, there's nothing to stop her acting as a consultant, and that's what she'd been doing for Lucy.

They were waiting for us outside the rather Gothic Victorian building with smiles on their faces. That didn't stop Mina from having a go at Lucy, though. 'And I'm telling you that the goodwill is worth nowhere near that much, never mind the furniture. As for the state of the flat…'

'You tell her, Mina,' said Tom. 'She needs to be more realistic. All sorted, Lucy?'

By way of an answer, she threw her arms round Tom and gave him a big kiss. He looked thrilled and mortified in equal measure.

I patted him on the back. 'Don't worry. No one took a picture. Your reputation at Division is safe. Does this mean you're more or less likely to take the job here?'

'No comment. Are you staying for a celebratory cappuccino?'

'I wish we could, Tom: Cairndale is only the first stop on our grand tour. We're off to the Fylde now.'

There was a round of hugs and goodbyes, and we headed for the car. Mina cast a sidelong glance at the dentist where she'd had her teeth rebuilt, but didn't say anything today, and instead asked me about Project Talpa.

'Bad news, I'm afraid. It's Galway.'

She grabbed my arm and linked us together. 'You are being too negative. I say that it is good news. You don't want to be risking almost certain death twice, do you?'

'That's one way of looking at it.'

What Tom Morton didn't know was that exploring Morwenna Mowbray's issues would almost certainly lead to Galway as well. I had someone to talk to about that tonight, but first we were off to Ribblegate Farm. I may have been rather drunk last night, but as soon as Tom had told me they'd got a hit on Project Talpa, I'd called a meeting for this afternoon. The people I'd summoned all had one thing in common: they could keep a secret.

When I pulled out of the car park, I had a feeling that I wasn't just heading to see the Kirkhams, I was starting on a journey that would take me towards a metaphorical river: the Rubicon, the one that Julius Caesar crossed without authority, taking his legions to Rome, to triumph and to death.

He did it because he was nothing if not ambitious. Climbing the greasy pole of Roman power-politics was his be-all and end-all, and which was about the only thing that Shakespeare got right. Okay, that's a bit harsh.

If I crossed my own personal Rubicon, the legions would be at most a few people, but the effects could be devastating for them, for me and for the friends and family left behind. I wouldn't be doing it for power, that's for certain. I could tell myself I was doing it for justice and for the greater good, and maybe I was. It was the other motives that I tried to bring into focus: vengeance and shame. Not exactly edifying.

The trouble was that I couldn't think of what else to do that wouldn't leave me feeling impotent and redundant. If anyone asks, it was definitely for justice. And talking of justice, I needed to speak to my lawyer. 'Can you drive, love?'

'If I must.'

While Mina was moving the driver's seat, I called someone who I never thought I'd be on speaking terms with: Augusta Faulkner.

'Mr Clarke? Is Keira okay? Has something happened to her?'

Augusta's daughter is in exile in France. She tried to kill me several times, and although I always take attempts on my life *very* personally, the motivation on her part was purely business. So, when the wheel turned and Keira needed my help, I was able to hold my nose and set her off on a mission for the King's Watch that nearly got her killed; you can read about it in the story of my French Leave.

'As far as I know, she's fine. I was hoping you could give me an update on her.'

Augusta breathed a sigh of relief. 'Yes. We only spoke the other night. She's doing well, keeping her nose clean and working hard. She even has a mundane boyfriend. A more suitable one.'

Keira has a thing for married men, so this one must be single. 'Glad to hear it.'

Augusta was a top barrister in the Cloister Court, and had retired until her daughter's shenanigans forced her back to work to pay the enormous costs and debts that Keira had racked up. Augusta's default mode is sandpaper dry. 'I'm sure you are glad to hear it, Mr Clarke. I'm also sure that my daughter's health isn't the reason for your call.'

'It isn't. I'd like to become your client.'

'Is Cador Mowbray not good enough?' The mundane Mowbray is very much an up-and-coming barrister, and yes, he's done work for me. Augusta chuckled. 'Unless you're suing the Mowbrays, of course. I'd enjoy that.'

'No. The Mowbrays are still on the guest list for the wedding, but I don't tell everyone all my business. The one thing I'm sure about with you, Ms Faulkner, is that if you take me on, I get total confidentiality.'

'You do, but forgive me if I'm sceptical. From what I've heard, you have a habit of recruiting people to help you brush things under the carpet. I need to know more.'

'I need an opinion. It's on international law. No court work, just an opinion. I haven't done anything. Yet. You don't even need to meet me to write it.'

There was a pause. 'Curiosity will be the death of me yet. I agree, if only for the pleasure of taking your money.'

'Good. Can you give me a secure email address? This will need to be encrypted.'

My connection to Ribblegate Farm goes back some way. Well before magick came into my life, I'd recruited the Kirkham family to Team Conrad, now re-named the Merlyn's Tower Irregulars. That's not to say that magick hasn't visited the farm: Joe's first question was, 'Where's Scout?'

My former Familiar was born here and became magickal here; the bond was later severed, and Scout is now just a rather odd border collie.

'On holiday in Lakeland,' I replied. 'I had to leave him with some friends when I was injured.'

'Aye. How are you?'

Mina had already gone inside. The sight of a shed full of beef cattle is upsetting, and she wouldn't have come if she hadn't made friends with Joe's wife, Kelly. Before Joe could offer to show me the bull they'd named in my honour, a diesel engine laboured up the track and a horse transporter appeared. The driver parked it out of the way and got out. She did not look happy to be here.

'Afternoon Mrs Bentley,' said Joe. 'Nice to see you.'

'It's nice to see *you*, Joe' replied Olivia. 'What's this all about, Conrad? Why have you summoned me here?'

I've known Olivia even longer than the Kirkhams. Years and years. I once proposed to her younger sister, Amelia, who turned me down, and I thank the gods every day for that. Olivia, her husband and her family got involved in some nasty business, and then she became involved on the fringes of magick. She actually likes me as a person. I think. What she doesn't like is the hold I have over her, something I was about to reinforce.

'I heard that the enquiry had finished,' I said lightly.

She gave me a dark look. 'Only just. No criminal charges, thank God, but the Inland Revenue want their pound of flesh.'

'Which is why you're here,' I added. 'We might have a job for you.'

She looked at Joe. 'Don't look at me,' he said. 'I know less than you do.'

'Let's get the back of the transporter down,' I said. 'Someone else should be here shortly.'

We were standing looking at the inside of the vehicle when a people carrier bounced over the potholes. The driver got out and stared at the yard. He decided it wouldn't ruin his shoes and went round to open the passenger door.

Lloyd Flint, Chief of Clan Salz, is a Gnome, and we are bonded in blood. He helped his wife, Anna, out of the car, and she waved at me with a smile before the smell hit her. She's pregnant, and *eau de cowshed* clearly did nothing for her. I pointed to the farmhouse and shouted, 'In there.'

Lloyd shut the door and came over, looking around as he did. 'Alright, Conrad? Is he here?'

'No, Scout's with Alex and Cara.'

'Thank the gods.'

I said that Scout was odd. He did spend quite a bit of time being someone else, and his doggy senses got warped as a result. Not only can he smell magick some of the time, he thinks that Gnomes are incredibly, aphrodisiacally tasty. It's not a pretty sight.

I made the formal introductions, and everyone stood looking at me. This wasn't the Rubicon moment – that might come later – but this was the moment I started planning for it. I unzipped my Barbour because it had suddenly got warm in the yard, and I fished in my pocket for my cigarettes.

'I want to adapt your horse transporter, Olivia. It might come to nothing, in which case I'll turn it back, or I might need you to transport something to Ireland in the near future.'

She flinched and folded her arms. 'You mean smuggle something. I thought you were working for the state now. I thought you'd left all this sort of thing behind you.'

'As you know, the Crown no longer has jurisdiction in Ireland.' I let that sink in for a second. 'Your job isn't dangerous, and you won't be stopped. Lloyd will see to that.'

'Why can't he drive, then?'

Lloyd answered for me. 'Because I don't have an HGV licence, Mrs B, and I'm not a registered horse trainer or dealer.' He added the winning smile at the end, the one that had captivated Anna when they met in a Birmingham nightclub. From her response, it was clear that Olivia had no problem spending hours in a cab with Lloyd.

I followed that win with the fee I'd pay her for converting the transporter and the fee for the trip, if it came off. 'Plus expenses, of course.'

'Of course,' said Olivia.

'Excellent,' I said. 'Why don't you leave us to measure up the transporter. There's tea on in the farmhouse.'

'And cake,' added Joe. 'Natasha's teaching Kelly to bake.'

Olivia looked confused. 'Isn't Kelly your wife, and Natasha her daughter?'

'Aye. I didn't marry Kelly for her cooking. I think the baking gene skipped a generation in her family.'

Olivia left us to it. I don't know whether to applaud in admiration or shake my head in sorrow at her capacity to turn away from awkward questions. I turned to Lloyd. 'What do you reckon?'

Joe Kirkham is a prize winning dairy farmer, but we all know that milk prices have been very volatile – and his father is still the actual farmer. To diversify, Joe did a course in basic engineering and welding. He's good, and he made the weapons box in the back of my car. This project, though, would need a magickal component too, hence Lloyd's presence. Lloyd and Joe stood in the back discussing weights and grades of steel sheeting for a few minutes, then swapped numbers and shook hands.

Joe left us to prepare for afternoon milking, and I stood in the lee of the farmhouse with Lloyd. 'How's the First Mine coming along?'

'I'm blowed if I know why the stupid gits decided to dig a mine through rocksalt. And they didn't do a brilliant job with the landscaping, so the top started to wash away in the last storm.'

With my help, Lloyd and his mates had hijacked a hole in the ground shortly before it was due to be consecrated into the First Mine of a new clan, the magickal, religious and ceremonial power base of Gnomes. I am honorary Swordbearer to Clan Salz, a post that I hope doesn't become actual, because that would only happen if they were under attack. He said that relations with the other clans were good. So far.

'While we're here, can you take a look at something? I'm afraid I've had some bad news from Hledjolf the Dwarf: there's a new Ancile schema in circulation that defends against my enhanced rounds.'

'Shame. It was bound to happen sooner or later, though. Is it hard to make?'

'Yes, but that won't stop the sort of people I'm likely to come into contact with, will it?'

He laughed. 'You'm right there, Conrad. What is it you want me to look at?'

I took out the Hammer, the Dwarvish copy of a SIG P226 handgun that contains my Ancile and my Badge of Office. I pointed to the Badge and said, 'Can you get that off and put it on my sword?'

I wonder what women do when asked a question like that? Every man I've ever come across, from mechanic to decorator to gardener to cricketer does the same thing: they rub their chin with their non-dominant hand and say, 'Mmm, well.' Even Lloyd used his left hand, and his is a prosthetic.

Having rubbed and muttered, Lloyd took the gun off me and examined it closely. When I became a Watch Captain, Hannah melted some Alchemical Gold and used the pommel of Caledfwlch to stamp it into a circular disk in a recess on my gun. That Badge identifies me and gives me powers of arrest everywhere that Nimue holds sway.

'Yeeeesss. But there's a problem. Well, two problems actually, but one of them I can sort out. Your sword needs to have a re-worked hilt. I can knock that up no problem if you let us have it.'

'Go on, what's the big problem?'

'Only Nimue herself can loosen the bond with the gun or refashion it on the sword, and I'd need to be there with a portable forge to finish the job.'

I was wearing my sword in anticipation of this, not that anyone but Lloyd could see it. I lifted the scabbard from around my shoulders and handed it to him. 'I'll see you at the Haven around eleven o'clock tonight.'

'You what?'

'I'm off to Cornwall on Friday, and I don't want to be without either Great Fang or my Badge.'

'Don't want much, do you?'

I clapped him on the shoulder. 'For a man of your capabilities, Lloyd, it should be a mere bagatelle.'

I shoved him gently towards the farmhouse and he didn't resist. He did, however, have a question. 'I've heard that before. What the blazes is a *bagatelle* anyway?'

'An easy piece of music. I think. After you, and don't forget to take your shoes off inside.'

Twenty minutes later, I told Natasha that she should enter the Junior Bake Off, and we left. By then, Anna Flint had done her work and softened up Olivia Bentley nicely. You could see her thinking *How could anyone as wholesome as Anna be married to anyone devious or underhand?* If only she knew.

I could have done with an early night, to be honest. Last night's rather stressful dinner was going to be followed by a very stressful day tomorrow, and the last thing I needed was a midnight rendezvous with a slightly deranged Nymph. Still, you do what you must. At least Lloyd had brought a trolley to wheel his portable forge from the gate to the small grove of trees where Nimue has an altar. I've spent more time here – at Middlebarrow Haven – than I have at home lately.

Middlebarrow Haven is the official residence of the Deputy Peculier Constable: me. The rather nice Arts & Crafts villa comes with a housekeeper, Evie, and a Custodian, her mother Saskia. We were keeping Saskia out of the loop on this one.

The forge itself was basically a big cylinder, about four feet long and one in diameter. I had to carry the propane gas cylinder. Mina brought the battery powered LED worklights, and Evie Mason brought the batteries.

We were also keeping my work partner, Cordelia, in the dark, for entirely different reasons. I'd sent her into Manchester to make sure things were ready for tomorrow to keep her out of the way. Privilege of rank and all that.

'I still say you're absolutely mad,' said Evie. 'Where do you want these?'

'Of course he's mad,' said Mina. 'You get used to it. Over there, thanks.'

'That's what Cordy says,' muttered Evie. 'No matter how bonkers things are, Conrad Bloody Clarke can always take them to the next level of bonkers. After the last time with Nimue, I'm sure you must have a death wish.'

She'd said the last bit louder, loud enough to warrant a response. 'I'm the one who nearly died, Evie. Are you staying?'

'Of course. You might die, and that would be great for my creative writing course. We have a unit on tragedy coming up soon.'

Lloyd had been working quickly and in silence, connecting his forge by touch, and he fired up the gas before we'd finished sorting out the lights. As soon as the casing started to heat up, it also started to glow with Runes.

He stood back and rubbed his hands on a rag. 'Here we go. Doesn't take long. Worst case scenario, I can't protect the gun and it melts. Well, there is an even worse case scenario, but we won't dwell on that.'

'I want to dwell on it,' said Evie.

'If Hledjolf has booby-trapped the gun, the Work might discharge and kill everyone except Conrad.'

'Don't worry, Evie,' I said. 'I've got your tutor's details. I'll write it up and ask them to give you the MA posthumously.'

'Men! You're all the bloody same.'

'No they're not,' said Mina reasonably. 'Only one of them is being serious, the trouble is that I don't know which.'

'Now's as good a time as any,' said Lloyd.

It was cold, very damp and thoroughly miserable out here. I gave thanks that it wasn't actually raining and slipped off my coat and turned to the spring from which Nimue would rise. At least there was plenty of water flowing today.

'By the Mother!' said Lloyd.

'Ooh, errr, umm,' said Evie.

'What in the name of Albion are you up to?' demanded Nimue. She'd already arisen and presumably been watching. I took that as a good sign and bowed low. Everyone else followed suit, especially Lloyd. In her water form, Nimue is a stunning sculpture of liquid life. Having met her in her own realm, the reality is more impressive but less striking.

This was my show, so I got on with it. 'My Lady, forgive me for performing magick at your altar. I crave a boon: would you help us relocate your Sign from this weapon to that one.'

Her form moves constantly, water running down and rearranging itself. The one thing you don't get is the eyes, and for a few seconds she danced in front of me and I got a feeling that she was amused. Don't ask me how.

'You are my Priest and the Lord Guardian. Do it yourself.'

Oh. I hadn't thought of that. Lloyd did not look happy at the thought of me performing advanced magick with dangerous Artefacts. He was too loyal to say anything out loud, but his eyebrows were sending distress signals in my direction.

Before I could speak, Nimue moved her liquid hand to her watery hair. 'I forget. You haven't yet held the sword. It is time, I think. Present me the firing weapon.'

Lloyd was now looking like he'd rather be taking tea with the Fae than standing here. He shoved the Hammer into my hand and stepped well back. Mina grabbed his arm and stopped him retreating any further. He swallowed hard and went glassy eyed.

I turned back to Nimue and bent the knee, offering her the weapon.

She lowered her hand and droplets of water supercharged with Lux dripped on to the stock like a rain of diamonds. With a *ping*, the disk of red gold popped off and I dropped the gun to catch it.

'Now your blade. Take it and plant it in the earth as deeply as you can.' She swayed for a second. 'If we had a stone, we could use that, but I prefer a bigger audience for that sort of thing.'

Was it just me, or did she seem a lot more together today? For one thing, she hadn't asked her go-to question: *How fares the Realm.*

Mina shoved Lloyd in the back and pointed to Great Fang. He snatched it up and threw it to me, not wanting to get any closer. At least it was still in the scabbard. I drew the blade, reversed my grip on the hilt and plunged it into a damp looking spot.

Down it slid, and waves of magick came through my arm until the hilt was nearly in the grass, and at that moment I felt a different vibration, a sense of something normally only heard in a First Mine: the Song of Mother Earth.

I looked up in sharp surprise. Nimue was smiling at me, and she whispered words that didn't carry beyond the two of us. 'How did you think a Water Nymph made a sword of iron, of bronze, of flint?' she asked. 'It can be our secret. Now, mortal, give me something to chew on.'

Yes, you heard it right: the guardian spirit of Albion was hitting me with a double entendre. I swallowed hard, offered her my left forearm and closed my eyes.

They flew open again the moment the cold hit me, and I saw her shimmering face greedily taking blood from my arm, her figure filling out with red as she did so. In the distance, I could hear shouting. Then the shouting was louder and the intimate circle I was sharing with Nimue dissolved.

'…it now! Stop it!' shouted Mina.

Nimue stood upright and glowed pinkly. I stayed down on one knee and wondered if I were going to to faint. No. Not today.

'Place the Badge on the pommel,' said Nimue. I did so and looked up. She reached down into the waters where her feet should be and pulled out Caledfwlch, the sword also known as Excalibur. It doesn't look like it does in the films: instead of a long, cutting blade, it's a short, Roman stabbing sword.

She took it by the blade, watery hands oblivious to the edge, and offered it to me. I took the hilt and grasped it firmly. Colour exploded around me, and I was blown backwards to land on a soft grassy mound that tickled where you shouldn't be tickled. Hang on, that meant…

Yes, I was naked under a starlit sky and a lot warmer than I'd been in Middlebarrow. I sat up and nearly cut my leg open with the sword that was still gripped in my hand. Caledfwlch had morphed into a long flint dagger with leather cord wrapped round the hilt. I stared at the crude blade – crude by modern standards – and felt no magick whatsoever. Oh.

'Ladagalhoo,' said a high pitched woman's voice from behind me. I twisted round, and even though I was sitting down, I was nearly eye level with a creature that was both human and not-human. She was about four foot tall, with dark skin and long black hair. Yes, she was naked, too, and looked irritated, as if I'd woken her up for no good reason.

While I was still processing this, she said something else, and when I clearly had no clue what she was saying, she impatiently gestured towards the blade with a *give it here* gesture. I got up on to my knees and gingerly offered it to her hilt first. With equal impatience, she gestured for me to turn it round.

With a swift slash of her left hand and a hiss of pain, she drew her palm down the blade and offered it to me to taste, cupping the blood to stop it dripping. I moved my head down, and she shoved her palm at my mouth. When I drank, I finally felt the power of Caledfwlch, and I was more scared than at any moment since the Allfather had Enhanced me. This was a depth of magick that I didn't know was possible, a power that ran deep into the earth.

And then the blood turned to ice water, and I was back in the grove, drinking from Nimue's hand and gripping the Roman version of Caledfwlch.

'Quickly. Strike while the iron is hot.'

Steam was pouring up from the ground, from where Great Fang was embedded. I brought down the pommel of Caledfwlch on to the pommel of Great Fang, and a blaze of Lux flashed around.

'Good strike,' said Nimue. 'Now can I have it back?' I returned Caledfwlch and she held it aloft. 'Draw your blade, Lord Guardian.'

I moved my hand towards the hilt of Great Fang and then stopped. The bloody thing was still glowing. With mundane heat as well as magick. Shit. I dipped my hand in the water running around Nimue and thought of the Arctic winds of Norway as I drew Lux. My hand went blue with light, and I gripped my sword. I pulled it out of the ground and held it up.

'Until we meet again, Lord Guardian,' said Nimue.

'My Lady.'

She dissolved down into the water, drawing Caledfwlch with her into the ground. The grove went back to being lit by LEDs and the glow from Lloyd's forge. Mina, Evie and Lloyd himself were clinging on to each other at the edge of the circle, and Lloyd recovered first.

'Isn't this normally when you collapse?' he said.

'Not tonight, Lloyd. Not yet, anyway, though I could use a change of clothes.'

I dropped the sword on the ground and held out my arms. Mina broke ranks and ran up to me, jumping up so that I had to swing her round or fall over. I stayed upright and took a kiss.

Mina joined in for a second, then flinched, then doubled down for a few seconds more before breaking off and letting me lower her to the ground.

'Eurgh, Conrad, you taste of rusty nails. I hope that isn't permanent.' She frowned. 'You haven't been…?'

'No. Just a little mutual blood donation with … I don't know who with.'

I was excused carrying anything but Great Fang and the Hammer back to the Haven, and while the others cleared up, I got in the shower. Evie brought mugs of hot chocolate and iron tablets to the study, and we sat round the fire.

'Nice dressing gown,' she said when she handed over my mug. 'Birthday present?'

'His mother wanted him to have something to open on the day itself,' said Mina cryptically. 'So she sent this. I allow him to wear it because the alternative is even worse.' She turned to me. 'Well? What happened this time?'

I looked around the group. 'Does it stay in this room?'

'Of course.'

'Yes.'

'If that's the price of finding out, then yes.'

I described what had happened, and Lloyd's eyes darkened even further. 'What were her, you know, her breasts like?'

'Lloyd!' said Mina. 'I hope there's a good reason for that question.'

Lloyd looked very embarrassed and also deadly serious. He emitted a strangled sound that might have been *yes*.

'She didn't really have any to speak of. She was definitely female, though, and I am *not* going to go there.'

Lloyd swore in proto-Germanic, the language of Gnomes. Like a good friend should, he's been teaching me the swear words. You'd be surprised how little changed they are in modern English.

He looked around and his accent wandered back to his roots. 'I think yow've met the First Daughter of Mother Earth, Conrad. But what was she doing *here* and *then*? I wish I hadn't promised to keep this private.'

'Did you learn anything?' said Mina.

'Sort of.' I cast around for a suitable metaphor. 'You know how you need permission to climb Mount Everest?'

Mina put her hand on my forehead and announced dramatically, 'He is not delirious, but I have no idea what he is on about.'

I took her hand off my forehead and held it close, loving the feel of her fingers. 'Well, I now know how to summon Caledfwlch. In that same way that I might have permission to climb Mount Everest. I'm *allowed* to do it, but I haven't got a hope in hell of *actually* doing it.'

I put my mug down. 'And we all have an early start in the morning. Are you coming, Lloyd?'

'If Anna's okay, then yeah, that would be great.'

'Thanks, everyone. I promise not to do that again in a hurry.'

Lloyd muttered what the other two felt: 'I should bloody well hope not, too.'

5 — The Will of the People

Cordelia

The marble floor echoed with the sound of military footwear as Cordelia Kennedy marched up and down impatiently. Where is he? How could he do this to her? For the umpteenth time, she stopped and tried to still herself inwardly. Just because she'd been forced to wear her dress uniform it didn't mean that she actually had to march. She could stand patiently and wait. Surely she could do that.

The only other person in the entrance hall of the Manchester Alchemical Society stopped arranging the flowers and gave her a sympathetic smile. Cordelia had been told the man's name, but she couldn't remember it. The other council members of the Society were in the Agora, the huge chamber inside the building that they were so proud of. This man had been left to welcome the official party, only the official party were running late, which was most unlike Conrad.

It had been weeks since she'd seen him. She'd only seen him once before he'd disappeared to Spain, and the few phone calls they'd shared had been all business. When she'd collected him from the hospital, he'd been gaunt, ill and haunted by something. He'd slept almost the whole way from Preston to Middlebarrow. In their calls, he'd been solicitous, of course: *How are you coping? Are the Fae behaving themselves?* But nothing about what the hell was going on and what he was going to do about the situation in the Lakeland Particular. And now he was back and he'd dumped *this* on her?

While he went up to Lakeland to do the Goddess only knew what, she was down in Manchester dealing with these jumped up wannabes who thought that they were better than Salomon's House, as if that were something to be proud of.

Finally the door opened and … Erin Slater breezed in, pulling a small wheelie suitcase behind her. Damn.

'Hi Cordy,' she shouted.

While Cordelia clicked over to the door (*damn these shoes*), the flower-arranger welcomed Erin to the Society and showed her the signing-in book.

When Erin had finished, she turned and went to give Cordy a hug. The straining jacket and tight skirt almost stopped Cordelia from responding, but Erin is not the sort of person to let starch get in the way of spontaneous emotion.

'You're looking very … military,' said Erin. 'How are you? It feels like ages.'

Cordelia couldn't bottle it up any longer. 'Stressed. Do you know where his lordship is? They're late.'

'Aah. Hang on a sec.' Erin took out her phone and checked it. 'I think Mina must have messaged me by accident. *Late start and bad traffic on the M56.* I got the message twice, the second time with emojis, so she must have meant you the first time. I should have let her know.'

Typical. He hadn't even sent the message himself. Cordy was about to get worked up again, when the doors opened for a second time and the official party were finally here.

The doors were held open by a Gnome who Cordy hadn't seen before, and first through were Saskia and Evie, followed by Conrad and Mina. She gave a small gasp when she saw him. He really didn't look well, despite the impeccable uniform. He was pale and his eyes were sunk deeply back. As soon as he saw her, he came over with a worse limp than normal. She only remembered to salute at the last moment.

'Good to see you again, Cordy. Everything okay?'

'Fine, yes sir. Are *you* okay?'

'Feeling a bit rough this morning.'

Mina had caught up with him and positioned herself very close to Conrad's side. She had left her rich palette of Indian colours behind and dressed like she was due in court, which in a way she was. 'You have to tell her,' she said to Conrad.

He smiled ruefully. 'I had another close encounter with Nimue last night. Less blood involved this time, but more magick. See?'

Cordy hadn't noticed that he was carrying a sword at first, and not just any sword. She recognised the abstract runes on the scabbard, but something was different about the grip…

'Your Badge! Is it new?'

'Relocated. Ah, can I introduce Lloyd Flint, Chief of Clan Salz. You've heard me talk about him often enough.'

'Pleased to meet you,' said Lloyd, offering a firm handshake. 'I've heard a lot about you, too. All of it good. I doubt he's had anything good to say about me.'

It was delivered with a confident smile that Cordelia couldn't help but return. Nor could she help glancing at the Gnome's left hand. His whole arm hung limp from the shoulder while he was shaking hands with her, but when he stepped back, it moved naturally. She could see that it was a prosthetic and sensed the magick. It seemed that Lloyd lost control of his left arm when focusing on the right.

Erin had been standing back, and came forward to say hello while the functionary from the Society signed them in. And then the doors opened for a third time and Cordelia added an involuntary jerk to her small gasp of surprise. *What are they doing here?* she wondered.

She had seen the new arrivals a few times when she was Page to Raven, and how she wished that Raven were here now to stand in front of her and disguise the fact that the cream of Salomon's House would see her dressed up like one of the corps de ballet from an aggressive production of the Nutcracker. At least she wasn't the only one in a state. The flower arranging man let out a long, low, 'Shiiiiit,' then bolted for a hidden door at the side of the grand staircase. As he left, he muttered, 'Hold them up for a minute, will you?'

'Me?' squeaked Cordelia.

Erin placed a hand on her arm. 'Don't worry, I've got this.' Without waiting, she slipped past Saskia and bumped into Conrad, earning herself a frown from Mina. 'I know Cora and Selena, but who's the ginger and the Grumpy Twins?'

'Tell me she didn't just say that,' whispered Cordelia to Lloyd, who seemed to be the only other sane person here today.

'I was thinking exactly the same thing, but I wor – sorry, I *wasn't* going call her a ginger.'

'That's Dean Cora Hardisty and Lady Selena Bannister! How did you get on first name terms with them?'

He shrugged. 'One of Mina's parties. They're great levellers. Sort of. It was funny to watch the Dean stand behind the old school teacher in the village pecking order.'

Erin had forced Conrad forwards and there was a great deal of hand-shaking and namaste-making going on, and to be fair to Conrad, he looked as surprised as she'd felt by the new arrivals. If he'd known, he would have briefed her about it: the mission always came first.

Today was the Northern Hustings for the election of the new Warden of Salomon's House. Cordelia's former sisters at Glastonbury would never admit it, but the Warden was the premier Mage in Britain. Just about. The proper election was still a while off, but the Manchester Alchemical Society had organised a hustings so that their members could decide which of their number would take on the internal candidates from London.

For a few weeks, everyone thought that Dean Cora Hardisty, head of the Invisible College, would be the natural successor, but then she'd dramatically pulled out "For personal reasons," and the field had become wide open.

One of the candidates was Cora's friend, Lady Selena Bannister, who had the distinction of being the tallest woman in the entrance hall. She was nowhere near as tall as Raven, though.

'Go on then,' said Lloyd. 'Who are they?'

Cordy discreetly pointed to the two women that Lloyd had designated *The Grumpy Twins*. She tried not to giggle when she said, 'The one on the right is Heidi Marston, Custodian of the Great Work and a shit-hot Artificer, as you might say.'

'I might say that. I wouldn't say it to her face, though.'

'No, don't do that. She doesn't suffer fools gladly. Not that you're a fool or anything.'

'Thank you for the vote of confidence. Who's her friend?'

'I didn't know they *were* friends. She's Gillian Priestley, Master of Synthesis. That's Healing and Herbalism. She's a Herbalist.'

The final member of the Salomon's House party was standing just behind Dean Cora, and Cordy was sure that she'd just exchanged a meaningful look with Conrad. What could that be all about? Surely he wouldn't…

'Which leaves…?'

'Sorry. That's Oighrig Ahearn, if I've pronounced her name right. She actually is Irish, unlike all the Witches with faux-Celtic names.'

'What does she do, and why is she wearing a Glamour? Is it because she looks way too young to be keeping company like that?'

'She really is that young. Younger than me at any rate. Then again, I'm only old by Watch Officer standards.'

There was a glint in Lloyd's eye, and Cordy knew exactly what he wasn't saying: *You're not that old.* What he actually said was, 'So if the Glamour's not to hide her age…?'

Cordy didn't get to answer the question because the central doors between the twin staircases flew open and the proper welcoming party emerged. Conrad looked round and gave her a smile. He also beckoned her forwards. Damn. She straightened her spine and went to stand at his left.

Cordelia went to whisper to Lloyd, but he was hiding in the background, so she couldn't tell him that the woman with the big chain of office was the President of Malchs, as the Alchemical Society likes to call itself. Nor could she tell him that Marjorie was lovely and nearly crippled with the Mage's Curse, so much so that she couldn't shake hands properly. Perhaps that was why she was brief and to the point.

'Welcome to the Society, or welcome back if you've been here before. I hadn't expected to see you all at once.' She paused and lifted an eyebrow. 'To have so many visitors makes the honour almost overwhelming.' Having made her point, she smiled. 'My daughter will get you all signed in and show the Salomon's House guests to the room we've made available. The doors will open properly in half an hour.'

'Thank you. I'm sorry we're so early,' replied Cora.

Half the party were led to the signing in book, which left all the remaining eyes on Cordelia. 'Where are we then?' said Erin.

'And did you get the kettle sorted?' added Conrad.

'Yes to the kettle, and follow me. We're upstairs.'

In her one and only case so far with Conrad, Cordelia had ended up on a joint team with two detectives from the mundane police. The three of them, had drunk more tea than Cordy believed was humanly possible, so getting the kettle had been a must. She'd been out to the corner shop bright and early this morning, and cartons of milk were sitting in a bowl of chilled water. Should she claim that on expenses?

She led them up the grand staircase and into the Upper Meeting Room, where Mina promptly stared at the carpet. The others had fanned out, and Mina turned to Cordelia. 'Have you ever been to Newton's House?' When Cordy shook her head, Mina put her left hand on her hip and pointed to the carpet with her right. 'Newton's House has custom made carpet. This is generic. Do you think it bothers them that they lag behind in soft furnishings?'

Cordelia tried to keep it in for a second, then shook with laughter. 'They're so up themselves, aren't they?'

Mina stood closer, and Cordy got a whiff of her perfume. She was wearing much more than ever before, and there was musk and vanilla with just a hint of patchouli. 'I hope you're less nervous than I am,' said Mina, 'because I hate being the centre of attention.'

Mina looked – and smelled – like a rich, sophisticated and cosmopolitan professional. Cordelia had got to know her in Cornwall, and watched her stand on scaffolding to take the roll in the Staff King election. She'd seen Mina order people around and get Conrad to do pretty much anything she wanted. Now that they were in each other's personal space, she could see the truth of it. Mina was only truly relaxed when she was with what she thought of as family.

A small lump came into Cordy's throat: Mina thought of her as family, too. With Mina's heels, they were the same height, and Cordy leaned to whisper into Mina's gleaming black hair. 'If anyone tries to take a picture of me in this outfit, I may need to borrow the Dragonslayer's gun and shoot them.'

Mina put her arm round Cordelia's waist. 'Article 4, section 12: No Photography. I have memorised the bloody thing because if I put a foot wrong…' She gave Cordy a squeeze and stepped back as Erin approached, speaking more loudly. 'Actually, the people here are really lovely. Very welcoming. Almost Indian. But as an institution…'

'Tell me about it,' said Erin. 'Shall we get set up?'

There was much moving of tables and chairs, and unfolding of giant cloths with the Malchs coat of arms. And making of tea. At one point Cordy asked Lloyd what he was doing here.

'Waiting for the meeting. Conrad's going to nominate me for membership, and Clan Blackrod are going to second it. It was either hang around outside or muck in here. I won't be staying for the hustings, 'cos I can't vote.'

'Why not? Too soon?'

'Nah. Only members who can vote in the actual Warden election can vote in the hustings.'

That seemed reasonable. A minute later something else struck her. 'So you came in from Middlebarrow Haven today?' He nodded. 'Which means you were there last night.'

'Yep. I don't want to meet her again in a hurry.'

She knew better than to ask what had really gone on, because no matter how friendly he'd been this morning, if she pushed him, Lloyd would grin and change the subject. Gnomes were like that.

When they'd finished arranging the room, Erin disappeared, returning with a great stack of Enchanted Parchment. She also took a die stamp and tools out of her bag, together with a whole bunch of little steel-nibbed pens and a shallow dish for the ink which went on a side table.

'How does this work?' she asked the others.

Mina began. 'The Mage presents themselves to me and states their name. I check it against the list. If they're good, I give them a ballot paper and write down the number.'

Erin took over. 'I take the paper and stamp it. Then I hand it over with a smile because I'm the nice one.' Mina shook her head at that point and said nothing. 'Then the voter takes it over there and votes.'

'When they're done, we take over,' said Conrad. 'The Mage folds their ballot with the stamp showing and when we've seen it, they drop it in the box. That's still downstairs.'

Cordelia was impressed. 'That's very well worked out. Who came up with the idea.' Conrad and Mina stared at her with blank faces. 'What? What have I said?'

Mina frowned. 'Have you never voted in a mundane election, Cordy?'

'Why would I?' Conrad thought that was funny for some reason.

'I have,' said Erin. 'And it's exactly the same system. Apart from the Declaration Charm, which is your job. Yours to create and yours to destroy when the result is announced and agreed.'

Formal gatherings of Mages often had these. Someone would craft a double circle on the ground and fill it with Charms, the net result of which was to strip away all Glamours and record what the Mage said. It was exactly how most elections were conducted in the world of magick: open and on the record. Here, the circle would only record the Mage saying their name, presumably to prevent impersonation.

'Fine, but that takes ages.' She checked the clock on the wall. 'Doesn't it start soon?'

'You don't really want to be sitting on the top table listening to the speeches, do you?' said Conrad.

'No, but I did want to sit at the back and listen.'

He seemed unmoved. 'Sorry. It doesn't work out that way. Someone has to be on guard up here anyway. Mina, have you got spare manifestos?'

Mina searched her bag. 'Here. Once the Charm is finished, you can have a read. I don't think the speeches will add anything important.'

Conrad was getting his coat. 'I hope Seth adds a few jokes to the proceedings. He might as well, because he's not going to win.'

There was general movement now. 'How do you know?' said Cordy.

'Read those,' said Mina. 'You'll see. Come on, Erin. Let's go in search of the bathroom before we have to make our grand entrance.'

'Speak for yourself, Rani, but yeah, this hair needs serious work.'

The two women left together, and Conrad turned to Lloyd, taking off his sword as he did so. 'Can you mind the shop for five minutes while Cordy has a break?'

'Yeah. Course.'

Conrad laid his sword on the pile of ballot papers and did something she couldn't see. 'Could you use some fresh air for a minute?' he asked her.

It looked like her only chance of getting him on his own, so she agreed. He took her to a little courtyard she didn't know existed and lit himself a cigarette.

'I handled Caledfwlch last night,' he said. 'I hope I never have to do that again, and I'd rather it wasn't broadcast.'

She fiddled with her uniform tie as his words sank in. This was enormous. If he was telling the truth, he'd handled the oldest Artefact in Britain – in Albion. 'What was it like?'

'Scarier than flying into a snowstorm.'

That didn't help much. She was about to ask him more when his face changed. Something closed down when he looked at her, and she didn't think she'd like what was coming.

'Sorry to load this on you, Cordelia, but you're going to have to do most of the duty today. I desperately need to sleep for a few hours. I'm flying the Smurf to Cornwall tomorrow, and it could be another late one tonight.'

A special Manchester wind sought her out and blew down her back. What was he doing? His tone had made it clear she wasn't going to be included, and she could guess why he was going there. She said it out loud. 'Morwenna. You're going to see Morwenna, aren't you?'

He nodded. 'Yes. You deserve to know that much. You were part of saving her life, and the Mowbrays won't forget that, Cordy.'

'I don't care about the Mowbrays. I care about what we're supposed to be doing up here.'

He hooked his thumb at the building behind them. 'This is up here. The hustings is our job today. I've got a note from a consultant here that says Light Duties Only.'

She *tsked.* 'Don't try that. Flying the Smurf is not "Light Duties". What are you going to do to the Queen of the Derwent when Morwenna has made her statement? That's our job, too.'

'No it isn't. We have no jurisdiction in the Particular. When I've taken her statement, it will be *case closed* as far as the King's Watch is concerned. We'd better get back. I'll relieve Lloyd and give you a chance to freshen up.

Mina and Erin were just finishing when she entered the expensively refurbished ladies room. Erin was looking in the mirror and caught sight of her face. 'Are you okay?'

Mina saw her, too, and gave a tiny shake of the head: *Erin isn't involved.*

'Yeah, fine,' said Cordy. 'I just haven't done a Declaration Charm for ages.'

'Dur!' said Erin. 'There's a copy in my case. Sorry. Should have said.'

Cordelia's stomach was still churning when she got back to the Upper Meeting Room. Conrad was up to something, and he was cutting her out. If he was planning on an assault against the Fae bitch, he would do it with Cordelia at his side or not at all. And as for getting up to mischief, two could play at that game. He'd see.

Ten minutes later, she found herself pacing up and down the room without realising that she'd even started. She took a deep breath and centred herself. She had her plan, now it was time to get on with the day job.

She searched Erin's bag and found the notes. She also found a padded envelope with Conrad's name on it and magick protecting it. She weighed the envelope and put it back. Too dangerous. With Erin's notes, the Charm was hard but doable. She finished and checked it out, then realised that the meeting was going to be going on for a while yet, so she made a cup of tea and picked up the manifestos.

The very idea of a written manifesto was alien to the Daughters of the Goddess. There were power struggles aplenty in Glastonbury, but they were all decided in the open – literally, under the sky, with voices on record. She knew almost nothing of mundane politics and didn't really care, either. Some of the Daughters had insisted on registering to vote in the Brexit referendum, but they were a small minority.

She started with Seth Holgate, and couldn't stifle a smile at the cover. Seth looked like a big man, and he certainly had a big beard. For some reason he had his arms round a man and a woman. She peered at the small print. The man was a Gnome and the woman a Fae Princess, no less. Her face seemed familiar from somewhere. Interesting. Inside, the ecumenical theme continued. Seth said that a truly inclusive Salomon's House would welcome *all* users of magick, not just humans. That was one of his themes, as was establishing a new Invisible College North, here in Manchester. It was all very reasonable and Cordelia liked his style. She put Seth aside and picked up the manifesto of Dr Lois Reynolds.

Her picture was much smaller, and she'd gone out of her way to show off her Goddess Braid. Very interesting. Lady Selena wore one and made no secret of the fact that she was happy to both take the Oath of Allegiance *and* worship in a Circle of Witches. When she read on, she realised why Lois's proposals were so radical.

Dr Reynolds wanted to completely split the Invisible College from Salomon's House's role as the professional body for Mages. She wanted education to continue as now and yes, to open a branch in the North, but all the post graduate registration, fees and monitoring would be completely separated into a new institution that covered *all* Mages and which would absorb the King's Watch into a new Occult Constabulary. No more Witchfinders.

When Conrad re-appeared with Mina and Erin, the first thing she did was wave Lois Reynold's manifesto at him and ask, 'What does the Boss think of this?'

'I'm afraid my Yiddish isn't good enough to tell you,' he replied. 'Nor would I want to swear that much in public.'

Mina bustled around to the back of the table. 'I told her to calm down and have another drink because it will never happen. I think Lois will become Warden and then a committee will be set up that rejects it out of hand. Places everyone, here they come.'

By six o'clock, half of Mina's prediction had come true, and Doctor Lois Reynolds had become the Society's Preferred Candidate. By a considerable margin. Cordelia got to watch Mina reveal the result in the Agora, and she had the chance to observe Seth and Lois properly.

Before Mina was announced, Seth had been standing in a little group with a slightly younger woman and an even younger one who had clearly got her looks from him. Poor kid. Seth looked very upbeat, in contrast to his daughter, who was giving Lois the evil eye. Seth even had a pint of beer in his hand from somewhere.

Across the stage, Lois was sitting rigidly in a hard chair, and her campaign manager was standing behind her with his arms folded. Cordelia only knew who he was because Erin had whispered his name during the voting. He had come into the Upper Meeting Room with Dr Reynolds and stood well clear at the side, coming nowhere near the business end of the room and then leaving with his boss, who turned out also to be his mother. He hadn't voted because he had no magick.

Cordy didn't get to hear the acceptance speech, because Mina and Conrad bolted as soon as Mina had handed back to the President. The only truly shocking moment had come before the result, when Madam President had personally thanked *Lieutenant Kennedy* for her hard work and pointed her out.

At least Conrad looked more human after sleeping all afternoon. *Where? – In the Lower Meeting Room – How? – Years of practice and a long settee.* Evie and Saskia hadn't stayed for the result, either, and a mouthwatering spread was waiting for them at Middlebarrow Haven when they got back. And so was a surprise: Dean Cora and Oighrig Ahearn. The two guests had been there a while and were ensconced in the Salon with Saskia.

'Why are they here?' Cordelia whispered to Mina when they cut and ran upstairs for a quick change without announcing themselves.

'Personal guests of the Deputy Constable. We'd have Selena, too, but that would be favouritism. We'd even have Heidi and Gillian if there was room.'

Feeling infinitely more comfortable, Cordelia paused outside the Salon and got ready to slip in. She had waited until she heard Mina go downstairs so that fewer people would notice her, and if there was a back door, she would have used it.

Cordelia had known since adolescence that her size, shape and appearance inclined people to label her. Most of the time she fought against this on principle (and, so she thought, mostly succeeded), but sometimes it came in handy. Raven used to call Cordelia her *Stealth Pixie*, and that's exactly what she'd done many times at Raven's request: sneak around looking innocent and listen to what people were saying. Sometimes with magick, sometimes without, Cordy liked to think she was a ninja eavesdropper.

Tonight, the Goddess had other ideas.

'You sit here, dear. Your feet must be killing,' said Saskia, as soon as Cordy had focused on the tableau in front of her. Saskia got up and pointed to a comfy chair. Cordy was about to thank her and say that she needed a drink first when even that option was taken away.

'Sit down and I'll get you something. I've heard you've a liking for Chardonnay,' said Oighrig Ahearn with a wild and rolling West Coast Irish accent.

When Oighrig handed over the huge glass, Cordelia knew what the Glamour was for. The Oracle of Salomon's House had long and lustrous red hair that was entirely (almost entirely) natural, but the pale complexion she sported with her Glamour was a lie. In the flesh, every inch of Oighrig's skin was covered in tiny freckles. Oh.

From a distance, the effect was to make hair and skin merge into one continuous copper covering, almost a Glamour in itself. 'It must have been a terrible long day for you,' said the Irish Mage, curling the skirt of her long dress underneath her and sitting down. 'Cheers, Cordelia. Lovely to meet you properly.'

'Cheers…'

'…You've not been in the Watch five minutes and the great lump has you parading around.' She swept a few tresses away from her face. It was something she did as automatically – and as frequently – as breathing. Before Cordelia could deny that Conrad was a *great lump*, Oighrig pressed on. 'You're making it a family thing with your ex being a Watch Captain, aren't you? Has he got the kids right now?'

Finally, a chance to get a word in, but first she had to answer the direct question. 'Yes. They're moving schools in January, so we want them to have all the Christmas fun with their friends.'

'Moving schools? Up here?'

Cordy looked down at her wine. 'Maybe.'

When her children had come to stay while Conrad was in Spain, Cordelia had taken them to look at a lovely school in Chester, not ten minutes from Middlebarrow. They looked utterly bewildered and confused. 'But Daddy's already shown us our new school in Wells,' said her daughter. 'Is he coming up here?' And then the heartbreaker. 'Is he bringing us to live together again?'

She couldn't lie. Not like that. 'No. He's staying in the Old Rectory.'

Their little faces added *abandoned* to *bewildered and confused*, until her son stood his ground. 'Do we have to come up here? Can't we stay with Dad? He said you might not be here for long, so if we stay with him in the Old Rectory, we'll all be there when you come back to Glastonbury.' He looked down at his little sister, whom he teased and protected with equal passion. 'We'll be waiting for Mum, won't we?'

Her throat was too full of tears to speak, so she nodded in agreement with her brother, and Cordelia deleted the Chester school's number from her phone. Officially it was still on the table, but…

'There aren't many of you around,' said Oighrig, breaking into her thoughts.

'Sorry?'

'Witches who've left the inner Circle of the Daughters and gone into the world.'

Instead of watching from the sidelines, Cordelia was stuck centre stage. Perhaps if she relaxed and gave Oighrig something to chew on, it would be easier to watch what happened, and that's what she did.

Food was announced shortly after that, and by the end of the meal, Cordelia was disturbed and puzzled. First was the way that Conrad and Oighrig completely avoided each other, unless absolutely forced to interact by politeness. The only other times she'd seen people behave like this was when they were having an affair. And then there was Conrad's understanding, at an unspoken level, of something painful that Dean Cora was going through.

How had they even become close, because he'd only ever spoken of her as a distant figure of politics or as a rather reserved guest at one of his parties?

At the end of the meal, Mina tapped her on the shoulder and said, 'I've volunteered us to clear up and load the dishwasher.' Part of her thought, *But Evie gets paid for that*, and another part made her get up and express loud thanks for the lovely food.

People were milling about, and she had two dishes in her hands when Dean Cora came up and said, 'Nice to meet you, Cordelia. I'm off for an early night.'

The bags under Cora's eyes said that was exactly what she needed. Cordelia hovered with the dishes for a millisecond, then smiled and carried on towards the kitchen. By the time she got back, Evie and Saskia were gone, too. And so were Conrad and Oighrig.

If they were having an affair, they'd know exactly when to sneak off for a passionate kiss. Cordelia abandoned the table and darted into the hallway. Which doors were closed? Where would they be hiding? The Study. Of course. The Deputy Constable's private den.

She went up to the door and pressed her ear against it, ready to use magick to amplify the sounds from within.

The door wasn't closed properly and opened to her pressure with a *ker-click* and a deep groan. She pressed hard, hoping to find the lovers standing apart and looking flushed.

'You alright?' said Evie, sitting in a pool of light at the desk. Of course. She was making notes for her course.

'Sorry. Yeah. I was looking for Conrad?'

Evie smiled indulgently. 'I thought you'd got used to it. A good meal is always followed by a good smoke in Conrad's book. I saw him slip out the back. While he was in Spain, the local garden centre turned up with a fire pit that he'd ordered and paid for.'

'Sorry. Thanks. I'm tired.'

She glanced into the Salon: empty. She dashed across the room and felt for magick on the locks to the garden door.

'Don't interrupt them,' said Mina from behind her.

Cordelia froze, paralysed with guilt and shame. She squeezed her eyes closed so tightly that they hurt, then opened them and turned around. Mina was carrying an empty tray and smiling with one side of her mouth, something she normally only did for Conrad.

'You get used to it,' said Mina.

'I'm sorry?'

'Conrad and his women sneaking off together.'

'I … I didn't get used to it. Not with Rick.'

Mina's laugh splashed like water running over stones, low and soft. 'Thank you for your concern, Cordelia.' She put the tray down and closed the gap between them. She put one of her hands on the window, spreading out her little fingers so that the stonking great diamond caught the light. She put the other hand around Cordy's waist in an intimate, sisterly gesture.

With night outside, all they could see where ghostly reflections of themselves in the glass. 'I am not his keeper, Cordy, but believe me, he is way too tired and Oggri is not his type. Nor is Vicky, nor Eseld.' Their eyes met in the reflections, and Mina's twinkled with something approaching magick. 'Long-term, I might have worried about you, being short, sweet and English as you are.'

It broke the moment, and they turned to face each other properly. Mina put on her courtroom face. 'Morwenna Mowbray's mother was Aisling Ahearn. Conrad is gathering intelligence. He should have told you, and he should have realised that you would notice he was up to something. Let's leave them to it.'

Mina picked up her tray, and Cordy helped her load the glasses on to it. In no time, they had the dishwasher running and the next load lined up on the draining board, ready and waiting. Mina wiped her hands on a towel, then balled it up and chucked it into the utility room where it landed perfectly on top of the table linen. 'Done!'

Cordelia did not want to talk to Mina. Not now. Not until a night's sleep had washed away some of the embarrassment. 'Nimue should be sleeping,' she said. 'I think I can risk a late-night devotion at the grove.'

'Of course. Thanks for everything today. It can't have been easy for you. I'll see you in the morning.'

Cordelia went to get her cloak from the extensive coat rack. 'When are you leaving?'

'Late enough to allow Conrad a proper night's sleep and early enough to get there in daylight. If you go out of the front drive, you won't interrupt the interrogation. Goodnight.'

The cloak was Cordy's compromise with the Goddess. She had laid aside the robes that marked her as a Daughter. She had no right to them any more. The cloak was a different matter, because it had been made for her by her mother and dedicated to the Goddess by her mother, in the days when her mother still admitted to having a daughter.

It was a measure of how desperate she'd become that Cordelia was even thinking of taking some leave to track her mother down and force her to catch up with her daughter's life and the existence of her grandchildren.

The temperature had dropped, and she wrapped the cloak more tightly, lifting the hood over her braid and going as fast as she could. She didn't need light to find her way through the gates and down the path, nor to find the grove, but when she tried to make her devotions, they stuck in her throat.

On another day, she might have thought that Oighrig was flirting with her a little tonight. She might have been flattered. Not today. Not with the hot mess she'd made of being a spy. *If only I'd had Raven to guide me. Where are you, soulmate? Where are you hiding?*

Instead of a prayer to the Goddess, she opened her heart for Raven to seek her out. Such was the power of Nimue's magick that no one else would hear. Or so she thought.

'Well met, Witch.'

It was the ball of light, the one that had sought her out at the Academy. The Spirit Orb stretched and morphed into Lucas of Innerdale, sometime Familiar of Conrad and former leader of the Pale Horsemen.

'Why are you here?' she asked.

'Because he's back, or so we thought. He spends two nights in the Lakes and then disappears. We wondered what he was up to, that's all.'

Lucas claimed that he was her friend, because the Queen of Derwent was their common enemy: hers for creating Raven and (she believed) holding Raven's Spirit captive, his for reasons he wouldn't share.

'He won't tell me.' She hesitated, but not for long. 'He's talking to a source. Talking about that Vessel who was enslaved by the demon of Derwent. Finding a weakness, I hope.'

Lucas looked disappointed. His manifestation was a good one, with shadows and depth. 'But he won't share his knowledge with his partner?'

'Don't worry. I have plans. He'll be back in the Particular before long, and if I'm not at his side, you'll let me know where he is, won't you?'

'That we will. 'Tis good to know he hasn't abandoned justice.'

Her protective nature flared up. 'He was *very* badly injured, and he knows how to play the long game.'

'He does, he does. No one knows that better than me. When I was a dog, I could feel his patience through our bond, but he's mortal, Witch. His long game may not be long enough.'

'Don't worry. I've looked into his eyes. It won't be long now.'

'Good. Until then, take care.'

'I will.'

Lucas collapsed and vanished, and Cordelia was alone. Again. She bowed and said the prayer. She forced out a drop of Lux and dropped it into the spring. It would have to do. On the way back to the Haven, she took out her phone and called Rick.

'Hello hello,' he said. 'What you been up to? You okay?'

His voice was warm, friendly and full of care for her. She sank into it with a sigh. 'I've only been hobnobbing with the next Warden,' she said, lightness coming into her voice.

'Get you. Tell me all about it.'

She did, and by the time she'd finished, she was in her room, about to get ready for bed. When the call ended, she felt a glow of warmth that lasted precisely as long as it took to peel off her jeans and turn around to tell Raven about it, but Raven wasn't there.

Part Two

Manoeuvres

6 — A Royal Family

'Make yourself comfortable,' I said to Oighrig. 'I'll try to get the fire started. Feel free to laugh if I make an arse of myself.'

'I will.' Instead of sitting down on the bench, she put the bottle of wine on the little table and came closer to watch, cradling her glass.

I placed the logs and kindling, and squatted by the fire pit. Pyromancy does not come easily for me. I drew on Lux and let it flow out of my left hand, focusing on sending *heat* to the dry wood. After a few seconds, I could feel the timber glowing, but of flames there were none.

'What on earth are you doing? Are you trying to make Artefacts?' said Oighrig.

'No. Why?'

'Because all you've done is infuse those lumps of wood with Lux. Absolutely no intent whatsoever.'

'You're not the first high ranking Mage to tell me I'm rubbish at magick. It's not news to me.'

'What are you trying to do, Conrad? I might be able to help, you know.'

I pointed to the fire pit. 'I'm trying to turn the heat of Lux into flames.'

She joined me squatting down, only she had to put her hand on my shoulder because she was none too steady on her feet. She let go with a quick, 'Sorry,' and steadied herself. 'What do you mean, *the heat of Lux*?'

'It's how I feel it. As heat, moving and flowing.'

'Aren't you the odd one? No wonder it doesn't work for you. Right. In that case, what you need to do is get the wood *excited*, if you see what I mean.'

'No. I have seen plenty of excited humans, but no excited sticks.'

She picked up a piece of kindling. 'Would you like a lesson?'

'Tempting, but not tonight, thanks. I'll put it on my to-do list and get some firelighters. You'll have to get up first and give me a hand. It's been a long day.'

'Don't move.'

She used my shoulder as a leaning post and stood up, then offered me the hand that wasn't holding the wine glass.

'Brace yourself.'

She did, and I levered myself upright. Her fingers were strong, but delicate and soft. In the shadows of her face, I could see concern. 'Should you be doing field work or whatever you call it with those injuries.'

'Probably not.' I got two firelighters, placed them in the wood and used my Zippo to ignite them. Then I lit a cigarette and poured myself a mug of hot chocolate from the flask I'd made earlier.

'I can smell that from here. The chocolate, I mean. I can smell the tab, too. Give us a couple, will you?'

I chucked her a full packet and sat down. She looked at my 7 Squadron mug and said, 'Aren't you the man of self-discipline, eh? I couldn't stop at one glass after today.'

'Yes you could, if you had to fly your fiancée, your sister and a friend in a helicopter tomorrow.'

The kindling had already taken, and the little patio at the back of the Haven was lit up. Oighrig's hair glowed even brighter in the firelight, as did her face. She was wearing a long, green woollen dress and a parka, and scooped up the skirt to sit down on the bench. She picked up on my comment about flying. 'What are you taking Sofía to Cornwall for?'

'My other sister. Rachael.'

'She's your sister! I've heard Eseld mention her a few times, but I had no idea.' She made a vague gesture with her hand. 'It's a terrible thing, I know, but I tend to tune out when people say *my mundane friend.* Why are you taking her? Is it something I should know about? And is Eseld the "Friend" you're taking, too?'

'Yes, Eseld and Rachael are taking the train to Bath, and I'll pick them up there. As to why Rachael's going…' I put on my bank manager voice. 'Do you or any of your family have assets in eight figures?'

I'd swear her fingers moved as she counted out the noughts, then double checked her workings. 'Ten million! Who are you kidding? The Ahearns of Galway may be good looking but we're not the Mowbrays or the Hawkins or the Greenings.'

'Which brings me neatly to why we're sitting out here.'

'I can't believe she's back, and I can't believe Eseld kept the secret for weeks. I couldn't do that if me life depended on it.'

The reason that Oighrig had come up to Middlebarrow with Cora was that I needed to pick her brains, and the only way she'd agree was if she knew that her cousin had re-surfaced. I had to look it up, and Morwenna Mowbray is actually Oighrig's second cousin once removed. You get the picture.

Morwenna had disappeared when she was a child after an accident that left her mother dead. Eseld had thought that Morwenna had been eaten alive, but no: she turned up at the Mowbray mansion right on the cusp of some delicate negotiations. Their father, Lord Mowbray, had known for years that Morwenna was alive but had said nothing to Eseld.

'What in the name of the Morrigan was going on?' asked Oighrig. 'All Eseld would tell me is that Morwenna had been badly hurt and that you'd saved her life. Is that true?'

'Yes.'

'How come?'

I shook my head. 'That's her story, I'm afraid. Sorry, Oighrig. I'm sure she'll want to get in touch with the Ahearns in due course, and I'll let her know you're asking after her.'

She frowned. 'Could she not tell you all this herself? I know she's been hidden away somewhere, but she must know the score.'

'I'm in an awkward position. When Morwenna first came back, she lied about almost everything. Her full brother, Kenver, dotes on her and the other Mowbrays will close ranks around her. Before I talk to her, I need a bit of background on the world of magick in Galway. I'm not saying you're unbiased, but you've nothing to gain or lose by lying to me.'

She brushed back her hair and opened the cigarettes. By the time she'd lit one, she'd come to her decision. She didn't get straight to the point, though.

'This has been eating me up since we left London. I'm not cut out to keep secrets or be a spy, you know. Because I was trying to avoid talking to you, I totally overdid it at dinner, and I think your work wife thought I was coming on to her.'

I raised my eyebrows. 'Don't let Cordy hear you call her that. She's my partner, and as you've seen, I need her magickal input.'

'True. She seemed quite sad about something.'

I slurped my chocolate. 'The Ahearns. Start at the beginning.'

She pulled out two scraps of paper folded into a small square. 'Can you read in this light?'

'Yes.'

I didn't tell her that my night vision was probably a transfer from Lloyd Flint's Gnomish magick. I unfolded the papers and found a family tree on one and the same names in a chronological list on the other. This is how she began her story.

'There's Ahearns all over Ireland, you know. There's the Ahearns of Cork, they're the rich ones. Not as rich as the Mowbrays, mind, and then there's the Ahearns of Ulster. Powerful lot, the Ahearns of Ulster, and the Ahearns of Dublin, but no one minds them. And then there's the Ahearns of Galway, the good looking ones. Us.'

If you'll forgive me, I'll summarise the rest.

The city of Galway is on the western coast of Ireland, and through it runs the river Corrib. If you follow the river upstream for only a short distance, you come to a huge lake, and I mean really huge – ten times the size of Windermere. It's called Lough Corrib, and its geography is important to what comes next.

The Fae do not live forever, despite their constantly referring to us as *mortals*. The best way of putting it is that they can live indefinitely, if the conditions are right. In the 1880s, the conditions for the Queen of Galway changed, and she died unexpectedly. No one knows how or why.

What followed was an orgy of bloodletting that saw Fae nobles attacking each other all up and down the shores of Lough Corrib and in Galway City. When the blood stopped flowing, the Princess of Aran crowned herself the new Queen of Galway, and as we know, the winner gets to write the first draft of history.

A Queen needs a court – seriously, they actually do need one, and the new Queen invited a Duke of the blood to come down from Ulster to join her. The Duke took over the estate of an Anglo-Irish lord and settled on the eastern shore of the lough, taking the title Prince of Corrib Castle. With him, he brought a coven of Witches, and one of those was the very young Aine Ahearn, from whom all the Galway Ahearns are descended.

Aine eventually became the leader of the Corrib Castle Coven and had two daughters, Deirdre and Muireann. Deirdre was Oighrig's grandmother, and Muireann was Morwenna's great-grandmother. Pay attention at the back.

The new Queen of Galway tried to secure all the territory around Lough Corrib, but it was just too big. Her sídhe was at the very southern tip, and she couldn't stop a Princess coming down from Donegal and taking over one of the many islands at the north end of the lough, and that is why Lough Corrib has two Queens: the Queen of Galway and the Queen of Inishsí. They lived in competitive harmony for nearly a century until, thirty-three years ago, the balance was upset again.

Muireann's daughter, Clíodhna, was pregnant with her second child and needed something from the mundane hospital. To keep her out of trouble, she dragged along her teenage daughter, Aisling and they stopped over at her cousin Gráinne's house, out on the coast. While they were away, the Queen of Inishsí's consort launched the Corrib Raid.

I'd have called it the Corrib Massacre if I'd been writing the history. The Prince of Corrib Castle had become the Princess by then, and she was slaughtered, along with all the other Fae and several humans, including Muireann's son and daughter-in-law. Muireann escaped.

You might imagine a chase down the lough on foot or unicorn, but this was the twentieth century. The Queen of Galway was alerted to the raid by telephone, and Muireann escaped by car. The Queen of Inishsí's consort had landed at Corrib Castle by boat, and shortly later by boat he descended on Inishlo, the island that protects the sídhe of the Queen of Galway.

Deirdre had come to look for her sister Muireann, and Deirdre was killed on Inishlo. The Queen of Galway led her own warriors into battle, and just about held off the invaders. Since then, there has been a truce, but the Queen of Galway is no longer the top dog.

In the aftermath, Clíodhna and Aisling moved to Kerry, where Éimear was born. Aisling came back to the small college of magick in Galway, and there she met Lord Mowbray. Love at first sight, apparently. Aisling moved with Mowbray to Cornwall and they had Morwenna and Kenver.

Aisling's mother and sister, Clíodhna and Éimear, moved to the west of Scotland after the wedding and Oighrig was adamant that she has heard nothing from them in years and hasn't seen them since she was a toddler. She has no idea where they live, and I'm inclined to believe her, because if she did, she'd have been pestering them mercilessly for news about Morwenna.

Oighrig spent a lot of time with her great aunt Muireann, and the closest she came to crying was when she talked about Muireann's death a few years ago at the age of one hundred and two. Even Muireann had no idea where her daughter was.

Here's the list which Oighrig gave me and the notes I added:

Name	English approximation	Who, how, what etc.
Deirdre	Dair-dreh	Oighrig's grandmother. Died at Inishlo
Gráinne	Grawnya	Oighrig's mother. Still alive.
Oighrig	Oichrigg	
Muireann	M'wirin	Deirdre's sister. Morwenna's great grandmother. Recently deceased.
Clíodhna	Klee-uhna	Aisling Mowbray's mother. Still alive????
Aisling	Ayshling	Morwenna's mother. Killed by magickal creatures at Pellacombe in Cornwall.
Morwenna		Aisling's older child. Disappeared aged nine.
Kenver		Aisling's younger child. Heir to the Mowbray empire.
Éimear	Aymer	Clíodhna's younger child. Still alive in Scotland???
Orla and Cathal	Orrrla and Cahul	Oighrig's best friend (Orla) and favourite cousin (Cathal)

'So there you go,' she said. 'Now you know all about the Ahearns of Galway and I've nearly finished this bottle of wine. What on earth do you want to know all this stuff for, and more importantly, what are you gonna do about it?'

'Morwenna disappeared for nine years,' I replied. 'And when she came back, she and her father lied about where she'd been. I can't ask Lord Mowbray, so when I talk to Morwenna, I need to know *something*. Morwenna said that her grandmother had rescued her from the police and she implied that her grandmother – Clíodhna – was now deceased.' I paused for a second. 'What are they like, the two Queens.'

Oighrig made a face. 'If I tell you something personal, does it go no further?'

'If you're telling the truth, this whole discussion is completely off the record.'

'The Queen of Galway is a hard bitch. She lords it over Galway city and has her fingers everywhere. When I was in my last year at school, we had to take tea in her sídhe. I vowed that day to leave Galway and go to the Invisible College. Do you know the Aran islands?'

'Umm. Sweaters?'

'Right. Sheep is all they're fit for. When the Queen was just a Princess, she got sent there during the Famine. For letting her people starve. That's the measure of her.'

'And the Queen of Inishsí?'

'A different creature entirely. Poet. Patron of the arts and Gaelic culture. If she'd kept a closer eye on her consort, I'm sure he wouldn't have launched the Corrib Raid.'

'Are they still together?'

'Who knows? He doesn't call himself the Prince of Corrib Castle. He calls himself Prince of the Lough now, but he lives in Corrib Castle. As you might expect, there's no love lost between him and the Ahearns.'

'If – by some chance – I find myself in Galway, whose door should I knock on? This is an impressive list you've given me.'

She laughed. 'Orla. Me best friend from school who married me favourite cousin, Cathal. She's the only one who can keep a secret, mostly because she's not an Ahearn. Should I tell her to expect you?'

'You might drop my name into the conversation the next time you speak.'

She laughed. 'Fair enough. I'll give her a warning.'

'Thank you, Oighrig. You've been a big help, and I hope the trip was worth it.'

She sat upright and stared at the fire. The light danced in her eyes for a few moments, and then she looked up, straight at me. 'Are you not scared, Conrad?'

'At this moment? No. You're not that scary, Oighrig.'

'Get away with you. I meant today. We saw the future this afternoon, and it scares the bejezus out of me. If that woman gets her way, the King's Watch will be gone. Does having Gregory Parrish as your boss not scare you? It'd scare me.'

'If I thought that was remotely possible, I'd be worried, but it's not.'

'Merlyn's Tower is not impregnable,' she observed. 'And your closest friend in Salomon's House is a busted flush. Under Lois's plan, Cora would be Vice Chancellor of an expanded Invisible College, which is great for her and all, but all the real power would shift.'

'If Cora's a busted flush, where does that leave you? I can't imagine you've had an easy time of it.'

'Being young, Irish and looking like a freak, you mean? Hasn't stopped your Mina, has it?'

That was well meant. I think. 'No matter how much wine you've had, Oighrig, you can't call Mina a freak.'

'People forget I'm a Sorcerer sometimes. I can see the swastika on her chest as clearly as I can see the scars on her face. I can see the magick in your leg, and that ring of yours is like having the Allfather standing behind your shoulder.' She paused, and the fire in her eyes grew a little brighter. 'What I can't see, what I'd love to see, is what the feck you're up to, Conrad Bloody Clarke.'

That was alarming on all sorts of levels. I opted for a version of the truth. 'Eseld. I'm doing it for her. She can't push it because she's too close, and she just wants some answers. I'd be the same in her position.'

Oighrig stood up and held her hands to the fire. 'Eseld never talks about you. She talks about Sofía, yes. Rachael even, now I know she's your sister. You, not so much, and yet you're thick as thieves with her. Strange.' She pocketed the packet of cigarettes and picked up her empty glass and the empty bottle. 'Will I see you in the morning? Saskia's taking us to the station at nine thirty.'

'Probably not, so thanks again.'

'Then I'll wish you good night and good luck.'

She left me to the fire and to my thoughts. I was indeed very concerned about Lois Reynold's plans for the world of magick, and so was the Boss. We'd discussed it over video while I was in Spain, and we'd agreed that expressing an opinion before the election would do us no good whatsoever. Now that Heidi and Selena had seen their opposition, I'm sure they would think long and hard about how to frame their own campaigns. The Warden election was now scheduled for late January, and campaigning would begin in earnest in the New Year.

I quite like Seth Holgate. He's good company and a genuinely compassionate man. What he doesn't have, though, is the capacity to lead at the highest level. I'm not sure that any of them do. Then again, I'm sure they said the same about Roly Quinn before he became one of the greatest Wardens that Salomon's House has known.

As for Oighrig and her potted history of Galway… Shall we say that it was useful? That's a good word. Useful. To what use I'm going to put it will require a lot of thought and depends entirely on Morwenna's testimony. Next stop Cornwall. Or Kernow, if you prefer.

7 — Old Wounds, New Scars

The rain that had dampened things when we left Kellysporth on the north coast of Cornwall had blown away by the time we got to the south coast. Great news for visibility, not so good for handling, because it was a lot windier down here.

'I'm going to do a loop round Pellacombe,' I announced over the intercom. 'Eseld will point out the house. Not that you can miss it. Be prepared for a bit of turbulence.'

I followed the Truro river down to its mouth, and then curved round the coast to approach Pellacombe, losing height and feeling the Smurf start to protest.

'There, there. See!' said Eseld.

'Wow,' said Rachael. 'It's… it's much more modern than I thought. How many staff have you got, Kenver?'

'Erm…'

'Leave him alone,' said Mina.

I banked to turn around again and began the descent to Lamorne Point, the Mowbrays' helipad on the opposite bank of the Fal river to their home. As I got closer, I could see the reception committee assembling on the clifftop. 'Here we go.'

The wind dropped just as I was coming in, so there was more of a bump than I'd expected, but we were down safely, and I initiated the shutdown.

It was Sunday morning, three days after my late night chat to Oighrig. On Friday, I'd flown us down to Kellysporth, home of Ethan Mowbray, and the next day I'd flown the whole family (barring Morwenna) up to the majestic ruins of Tintagel for the election of the Staff King. Mina was the officer in charge of the election and had done another excellent job. A few of the Mages even said hello and made a fuss of her.

Kenver had turned up to publicly vote for his cousin and show that there were no hard feelings, and the poll was almost unanimous in Ethan's favour. Given that magickal Cornwall is still in mourning for Lord Mowbray, there was little celebration. That would come later, so we enjoyed a calmly satisfying meal last night. Mina and Lena, Ethan's fiancée, were swapping notes on mixed weddings, and I was busy answering questions about Dual Natured wolves. Rachael? She was just in awe.

The reception committee at Lamorne Point was mostly there for Kenver, the master of Pellacombe, and was headed by Jane Kershaw, acting Steward. Lord Mowbray would have bounded out of the Smurf and started asking questions, but Kenver sat still, waiting. When the rotors had slowed, Eseld got fed up and reminded him of his duty. He led, she followed, and together they went to say hello.

I took my headset off and double-checked the status and position of the controls. It would do. I grabbed the tablet computer from the holder and opened the door. Mina and Rachael took that as their cue, too.

Jane Kershaw welcomed Mina and me back to Pellacombe, and extended the welcome to Rachael, after I'd introduced her. That completed the formalities, and allowed her daughter to get something off her chest.

Leah Kershaw is the Mowbrays' pilot, and she loves the Smurf only marginally less than she loves her unborn child. She's ex-RAF, too, and our paths had crossed in Iraq. 'How could you, sir? How could you do it?'

'What have I done now?'

'You left the Smurf in a boggy field in the Lake District! How could you do that to him?'

'Because I hadn't planned to get stabbed. I did apologise.'

Jane put her arm around her daughter. 'Easy, Leah. You don't want to go into labour out here, do you?'

'How are you?' said Mina. 'It must be very close.'

'Overdue, that's what I am. Like a bus: late and large. Are you sure he's okay?'

'Perfect.'

Jane still had her arm round Leah, and started to propel her towards the buggy that would take them down to the ferry across the Fal estuary. I told Mina and Rachael to follow them, and that left me with the Ferrymistress, her husband and their son, Michael.

'See what you've done?' said the Ferrymistress, pointing to Michael with that mixture of pride and exasperation which marks the mothers of teenage boys. Her son was now sporting the uniform of the Falmouth and Penryn Sea Cadets, a move that Michael hoped would lead to a stint in the Royal Navy. Poor lad.

He gave me the Navy salute, palm down, which I returned RAF style.

'Happy now?' said his mother. 'Right, I'll leave you to it.'

She had a job to do, piloting the ferry through the Wards, and headed off to the steps and the shortcut down to the dock. I handed the tablet computer to her husband and with it handed responsibility for the Smurf. He's the estate engineer, and a qualified helicopter technician.

'He's flying well,' I said. 'No problems or warnings, despite getting stuck in the mud.'

'Good. I'll have 'n ship-shape and ready by this afternoon.'

'Thanks.'

Michael was peering through the chopper's window. 'Where's Scout?'

I swear that dog is more popular than me. He's a menace. 'On holiday. He had a bad experience in Lakeland.'

Michael headed round the back to unload the cases. 'Just Mr Mowbray's,' I said.

'Sir?'

'Yes, I'm afraid so. The rest of us might be heading out this afternoon.' I leaned down. 'Don't say a word. Especially to Miss Clarke. Operational reasons.'

'Sir!'

They were waiting for me on the dock, the ferry ready to go. I jumped on board as athletically as I could, and joined the girls and Kenver to watch the slate and glass mansion of Pellacombe grow larger in front of us. I whispered to Mina, 'Are you going for the tour or coming to see Morwenna?'

'Tell me truthfully,' she replied. 'Do you think she will open up more if I'm there or if you're on your own with her.'

I took a risk. 'The most useful thing would be if you came along and then dragged Kenver away. I really don't want him there.'

She put her arm round my waist. 'I can do that.' She brushed hair away. 'Pellacombe is nice. Beautiful, even. I prefer Elvenham Grange, though. Or Middlebarrow. That's nice, too. And the shopping is better. Lena says we should have a wedding party there. She may have a point.'

I kissed the top of her head. 'Excellent idea. London, Clerkswell, Middlebarrow, Birkfell… All of them need a wedding. Just let me know if you want me to go to any of them.'

She gave my side a squeeze and a pinch. Luckily it was the opposite side to my stab wound. Once she'd made her point, she realised the other thing I'd said. 'Do you really want to have a party for the wolves?'

'It's that or invite them to Clerkswell. You know what they're like.'

The ferry bumped into the Pellacombe dock, and we climbed off. Eseld was already pointing out features of the house to Rachael.

'Have fun, sis,' I said. 'I've got to see a girl about a sídhe.'

Jane Kershaw had heard me. 'Miss Morwenna has asked for coffee to be served on the family terrace. I'll … Leah! Are you alright?'

'Oooo, Mum…'

The Ferrymistress leapt off the boat and joined the Kershaws.

'Shout if you need the chopper,' I said, walking quickly backwards and away from the impending birth.

We left them to it. Eseld took Rachael the long way round, up the hill to the formal entrance. Kenver, Mina and I cut through the old farmhouse and up the internal staircase to the new building. Kenver glanced into the rooms as we passed, checking for Morwenna. Pellacombe was designed to be everything the modern Staff King could need: luxurious but cozy family quarters at the northern end, then public rooms and meeting rooms for hospitality. The magick zone was well underground, dug into the hill.

We arrived at the family sitting room and saw the back of a young woman outside, leaning to put a tray on the terrace table. She was wearing the Mowbray blue polo shirt that marked her as staff, and there was no sign of Morwenna. When Kenver opened the glass doors, she looked up. 'Miss Morwenna said she'll give you ten minutes to get over the flight before she joins you, sir.'

'Where is she?' asked Kenver. Last night was the longest he's been apart from his sister since she was discharged from hospital. He's supposed to be studying with the Earthmaster, my mate Chris Kelly. Not so much at the moment.

The girl looked embarrassed. 'She said to say she'll be along and to wait for her, sir.'

Mina gave me a look and a nod. She poured three coffees and handed them around. She put her gloves back on to drink it, because the wind cut round the slate buttresses like a knife. Kenver noticed and apologised. 'Forgive me, Mina. I'll see what I can do.'

He sounded like he'd been watching Downton Abbey, and that's how he thought the lord should talk. He touched the southern buttress and closed his eyes. A few seconds later, the wind died and magick shielded us from winter. I retreated to a corner to smoke, and Mina started her charm offensive on Kenver. Poor lad didn't stand a chance.

In less than the promised ten minutes, the doors opened, and we all took a sharp breath when Morwenna stepped out.

She was wearing something more suited to a Spanish beach in June than the Cornish coast in December – a thin, stretchy shoulderless dress that started half way down her chest and finished more than half way up her thighs.

She'd done it to expose her scars: the circular puckers like craters on her leg, shoulder and arm, courtesy of an enhanced octopus. They were bad, and had barely faded since childhood, but they were nothing next to the great trench that stretched down from her jawline, across her throat and on to her right breast. A Fae had turned his hand into a claw and ripped a chain from around her neck, gouging deep into her flesh. I'd seen that wound when it was fresh. I'd seen it made. It was a few days older than my stab wound, and where mine had healed, hers was still raw. A yellow gunge coated the worst parts, and I hoped that it was one of Lena's Healing salves. To complete the revelation was a tattoo on her left shoulder, fully exposed by the low dress. It featured a Celtic triskele woven into three ravens, completed in green and black.

All that was terrible, but it wasn't the worst. That became clear when she spoke. She lifted her right hand to her face and tracked her wounds down to her thigh, as if she were showing them off. 'This is me. This is who I am.'

When she spoke, it was from the dregs of her shattered larynx, the few bits of vocal chord that the surgeon had managed to patch together. She sounded like a dying old man, not a twenty-something young woman. Mina rushed over and embraced her, and when Morwenna flinched back, she clasped her closer still, whispering something in her ear. She gave Morwenna a shake and turned to me. 'Take the poor girl away before she dies of exposure, Conrad.'

Mina neatly propelled Morwenna through the door before moving to intercept Kenver. I took my chance and followed Morwenna inside. She managed a smile at Mina's manoeuvre and waved me forward, setting off through the sitting room and into the bowels of the house.

You could tell that she was related to Oighrig, and not just from the long red hair that was held back by an Alice band, the better to expose her scars. They had the same wide eyes and the same wide mouth. They'd even chosen a similar shade of lipstick.

I followed her through a service area and up some stairs. When she turned left at the top, I knew where we were going: the junction. We passed through the magickal workshop and into the rock. A few stairs and a short passage later, we were in a cavern that glowed brightly with Lux.

Pellacombe sits on a major confluence of Ley lines, a network created by Lord Mowbray and very convenient. For him. It was also where he'd been murdered, and the only time I've been here before was to find his body. I couldn't help looking at the spot.

'It was there, wasn't it?' said Morwenna. I nearly jumped out of my skin, so clear and strong was her voice. 'Don't look so surprised, Conrad. What's the point of all this if you can't use it?' She smiled, and the pain in her eyes was almost too much to bear. 'Was it here?'

'Yes. Just there. In the gap between those pillars.'

'I thought so. Eseld wasn't too keen on specifics. This way.' In the opposite corner were three picnic chairs, the soft ones with cup holders in the arms. 'Won't be long.'

Lux can affect all other forces, and when it's moving, it can generate electromagnetic energy, which is a roundabout way of telling you that when concentrated, it can give off heat. Like here. I peeled off my coat, my jacket, and looked at my shoes. Maybe later.

A different Morwenna returned, her hair now loose and most of her scars hidden by a long-sleeved summer maxi-dress. A chiffon scarf around her neck did the rest. She saw me looking and said, 'I have a clothes rail through there. And a bed.' She fiddled with the scarf. 'And a chamber pot.' She looked up. 'I empty it myself, and I don't let myself eat in here. I go out for all my meals.'

I've heard her speak twice before. Once when she was calling herself *Medbh* and sporting an Irish brogue as broad as Oighrig's, and later when she was Lara Dent, a girl from the Lakes. This new, 100% Morwenna version of the woman in front of me could have come from anywhere south of Birmingham. Anywhere except Cornwall. She didn't roll her Rs.

'Where to start?' she said with a sigh. My eyes had adjusted to the weird light, and I realised that her mouth didn't move with her voice, like a live TV feed where the sound is fractionally delayed.

'The most important thing is how you are now,' I said. 'Is everything okay?'

'We're fine. All of us.' She rubbed her tummy when she spoke. 'Harry's little ones are coming along fine, and I'm fine so long as I stay in here. It's when I go out that the problems begin.' She looked around the chamber. 'Lena says I musn't get used to it, but it's so hard.' She rubbed her scalp and found a knot in her hair. 'You've been a Mage for less than a year, right?' I nodded. 'So, like do you get days when you're not magickal?'

'It would be closer to the truth to say that I get days when I *am* magickal. Especially now that I haven't got Scout bonded to me. I hadn't consciously used magick at all today until you brought me in here. I know it's different for born Mages.'

'Yeah, but I'm not a born Mage. That's the problem. Or I might have been. I might have been born to magick and the sea-gnomes took it away.'

Sea-gnomes? 'You mean the octopodes?'

She tried to smile and failed. 'Did you look that one up before you came?'

'It seemed only polite.'

'I felt you. When you healed me, I felt your focus. It was like being treated by a laser doctor. And now you're all kindly uncle.' She crossed her legs. 'Gnomes are all about the number eight, right? The People don't know the sea, so when they first saw an octopus, they called it a sea-gnome.'

There were two clues in that statement. First, she called the Fae *the People*, something only they do, and second, her instinct was to use the translation of a Fae word. I took her back a step. 'The sea-gnomes damaged you psychically as well as physically?'

She didn't meet my eyes. 'They sucked Lux out of me like a vacuum cleaner, and it ripped at my brain. The poison they left behind was just a side-effect. The gods only know what Aisling was doing with them.'

Aisling. Not mother.

'Whatever,' she continued. 'This is all guesswork. I have no memory of anything before the sídhe. Not a single thing. Not Father, not Kenver, not Pellacombe. Nothing. The first real memory I have is learning Irish from the Hlæfdigan. None of them spoke a word of English. They also had to teach me how to walk again. Where you saw the sea-gnome scars, yeah? None of the nerves to those sites worked.'

I sat back. The Hlæfdigan are neuter Fae, a bit like worker bees. They look female, but they're not (their ovaries don't produce eggs). They can work magick up to a point, and only within their sídhe. It wasn't them who'd cured her and re-wired her nervous system. We'd come up to the edge of the precipice much quicker than I'd thought we would.

What I wanted to know, what Eseld wanted to know, was *who turned you into a Vessel, Morwenna? Who hollowed you out like a gourd?* I licked my lips, dry from the overheated chamber, and wondered whether now was the moment to jump over the precipice or not.

8 — Memory

On my birthday last month, there had been a celebratory brunch at the Inkwell. Vicky had come, which was a treat in itself, and she'd brought Francesca Somerton, the Keeper of the Queen's Esoteric Library with her. Francesca is a good friend to the King's Watch, and she feels absurdly guilty about trying to rob my house when I was a teenager. She'd been looking for the lost books, the Codex Defanatus, and we now know that she was nearly four hundred years too late.

She'd come to my birthday because I needed a crash course on how magick can create and destroy identity, personality and memories. I needed to know exactly what a Vessel was before I met one.

After brunch and Facetime with my parents, we'd gathered round the fire – Francesca, Myfanwy, Mina and me, and it was Myfanwy who'd started. She's never had much of a social filter, and she seems to think that pregnancy gives her the right to ask anything.

'When I was a young Druid,' she'd said. 'Our Pennaeth once called you the *Merry Widow*, Keeper. How come?'

Francesca must be in her seventies, I suppose. 'I haven't heard that one in years,' she said. 'Give me another of those sherries and I'll tell you.' Glass in hand, she fixed Myfanwy with a powerful Librarian Stare and said, 'Because I married my tutor, that's why. Back in the day when it wasn't *always* wrong for a tutor to fall in love with their much younger students, and when young women could still be flattered by that sort of thing. Not that I was flattered. I didn't need to be flattered when I loved him so much.' She drank the sherry. 'He died when our daughter was six months old. I was about your age, Mina. Cheers, everyone.'

There was an awkward silence while Francesca downed half her glass of sherry. Mina had that guarded expression she used to wear almost all the time, and Myfanwy was mortified at what she'd unleashed. It was Mina who broke the silence. 'And your daughter, Francesca-ji?' It was the first time I'd heard of her having children.

'You mean *Doctor Quinn, Medicine Woman*?' Three blank faces greeted her statement. 'Good grief, don't tell me you've never heard of it?'

Mina's tiny fingers are perfectly suited to typing on a smartphone. Before anyone could object, she read out, 'An American western drama series starring Jane Seymour as a woman who practices as a doctor in a frontier town.'

'You registered her with your maiden name – Quinn,' I said.

'Correct. When she qualified as a doctor, from Boston Medical School, the series was big news. The name stuck. She's now a consultant neurosurgeon in Chicago, and no, she has no discernible Gift of magick. I sincerely hope to retire there very soon, while there's still time to indoctrinate my grandchildren. Now, what did you want to know about identity and magick, Conrad?'

'Everything?'

Over the time that followed, I learnt a lot, and like all areas of magick, you can think you know something only for it to turn round and bite you. Take Francesca's opening statement, for example:

'Identity is quantum and indivisible. Probably. Personality and memory are not.'

It's the *probably* that gets me every time. She'd expanded on her statement by looking at Mina. 'The first proof came from India, as you'd expect.'

'And why would I expect that?'

'Because of reincarnation.' She turned to me. 'Your gun is linked to your Imprint, isn't it, Conrad?' I nodded. 'That's what most people say, and that's how it's done, but it isn't really. It's linked to your *identity*, which is only part of your Imprint. Let's consider your dog.'

I told you that dog was getting to be more famous than me. Francesca went straight on to say this: 'Scout has had three completely different Identities. He was, briefly, a puppy, then he was Lucas of Innerdale, then he was a dog again. And here's the thing, Conrad. When Lucas became Scout, Lucas destroyed the Identity of the little creature he'd taken over. When he vacated the body, it should have died, but you transferred enough Lux for a new Identity to form.'

Myfanwy had chipped in at this point. 'Not everyone believes that, though.'

'No, they don't. Some believe that a body can share two Identities. Keira Faulkner believes that Helen of Troy would have shared bodies with Abi Sayer, for example Some believe that Identities are like atoms – and atoms are divisible. They believe that you can have Identity fusion and Identity fission. There has never been any proof of that, though.' She considered what she'd said. 'I'll be charitable: it's never been disproved, either. Personality and memory *and* incorporation are different. They *can* be copied. And stored.'

'Really?' I said. 'That sounds so … impossible.'

'It comes naturally to the gods, it comes quite easily to the Fae, even if they don't understand it, but you're right, for humans it's nigh-on impossible. Alcantara of Cordoba did it. His Work may well be in the Codex Defanatus.'

It was time for the blank faces again.

Francesca had turned very serious. 'I'm only telling you this because you need to know. Even then, I'm only telling you because I have to trust you not to breathe a word.'

'Were you looking at me?' said Myfanwy.

Francesca ignored her. 'Only very, very senior Mages know who Alcantara was and what he did. He was an Arabian Mage at the court of the Emir of Cordoba during Muslim rule. He used Lux to produce an exact cellular copy of a young girl. A slave, of course. As part of that, he copied her Imprint, or tried to. At the final moment, when the copy came alive, her Imprint changed because the new Farida had a different Identity to the old Farida. Is there any sherry left in that bottle?'

I was stunned. The girls were stunned.

When I'd topped up her sherry again, Francesca had moved on to Vessels, via the Fae. 'Quicksilver magick is fundamentally different to human magick. The Fae have powers with dreams and memories that humans never will, for example. The problem is that they're quite lazy and they don't like to share. They don't often write things down, and a Queen would think twice before teaching one of her Princes a good trick.'

'Like creating a Vessel.'

'Precisely. It used to be more common, when the Fae had freer rein to experiment on humans, and then the skill was lost. It looks like the secret was kept in the Codex. To a Fae, it's a very valuable process.'

'So how does it work?' asked Myfanwy.

'You scrape out almost everything that makes a person a person. Then you fill it with the stored memories and capabilities of another person. And more. You say that Morwenna as Lara Dent completely convinced Harry Eldridge?'

'I believe so. He was happy with Zina, so for him to spend the night with Morwenna, she must have made a very convincing Lara Dent.'

'I'm sure she was. I'm sure that a Construction was used as well. A complete makeover.'

It was scary stuff all right, and now you know why I was a little reluctant to confront Morwenna about it. After my lesson from Francesca, I'd been on to Eseld and insisted that she do an Identity check on Morwenna, as well as DNA test. She'd already done the DNA test, and only agreed to the Identity check when I outlined some very frightening scenarios.

Morwenna passed them all. She was the real deal.

Which reflection brought me back to the junction under Pellacombe and the awkward questions I needed to ask Morwenna. I was starting to build her trust, but it was too soon to dive in and demand that she name names.

'Have you any idea how long you were there?'

'Subjectively or objectively? Ach, it doesn't matter either way. I spent quick time and slow time. You know what that is, right?' A trace of Irish had come into her voice. Just a hint.

'Time can run faster or slower in different parts of the sídhe. I've experienced it.'

'You have to believe me when I tell you this, Conrad. You have to. From the day I woke up to the day I had my first period, I never saw daylight, and if I saw another creature but a Hlæfdige, I don't remember it.'

'What did you do?'

She spat out her answer. 'A whole load of fecking sewing. I remember that.' She paused and reflected. 'And the tales. The People's version of magickal history – and Irish history

Either she was lying or the memories had been erased. It was possible. The Hlæfdigan love to gossip, apparently. If she had spent all that time in their company – four years, probably – there would have been constant gossip about who was up, who was down, who'd stayed the night and who had been exiled, plus their favourite questions: who's slept with whom and who's been killed.

She interrupted my thoughts. 'I yearned for the full of the moon.'

'Sorry?'

'I said I never saw daylight, and that's true. They used to take me outside every full moon, from dusk till dawn. I used to wander around the wood on my own until it was time for the offering. A blood sacrifice to the Morrigan and to the Goddess. You missed these, didn't you?'

She slid up her left sleeve to show me. I *had* missed the scars inside her left arm.

'There must have been light nights. Did you get a sense of where the woods were?'

She snorted. 'Ye eejit, they were Faerie woods.'

Aah. Damn. That would have been too easy.

'I did tell Mina one truth,' she continued. 'About Donegal. When I started my periods, they shipped me out to Sliabh Liag, to the Sisters of the Grey Mountain. I'm sure if you went, they'd tell you all about me. I spent two years there, then they shipped me back. And before you ask, they weren't linked in any way to where I'd been.'

'So why there?'

'They were a refuge for the casualties of magick. I used to call them the last refuge, because Sliabh Liag is pretty much the end of the earth. Endless bogs, loughs and not a lot else. If you went for a walk, you could see the sea, and the next stop was Newfoundland. I used to think that civilisation was a lot closer that way than behind me. There was no running away from Sliabh Liag for a little girl.' She recrossed her legs. 'Are you going? That's why you're here isn't it?'

'Why did they ship you back?'

She pursed her lips. She let it drop for now, but we both knew it: I wanted to know where she'd been, and she wanted to know what I was going to do about it.

'They shipped me back because I had zero magick. Not a bit. They did teach me to read the different Gaelic scripts and they let me watch English TV once in a while. I paid them back in sewing and laundry. Are you not thirsty? I am. Eseld said you don't like sitting too long.'

'I don't.'

'Then go back there and get us a Diet Pepsi, will you? Help yourself, too.'

The junction had a border. Beyond the border was a small workshop, still rich with Lux, that Morwenna had taken over. As well as a WiFi router, I found a small, well-stocked fridge and I took two cans. While she popped the tab, I said, 'What happened when you got back?'

She slurped greedily and placed the can carefully in the holder on her chair. She sat up and folded her hands in her lap. 'It was to a sídhe on the western shore of Lough Corrib. I do not know whose sídhe it was, but not a Prince or Princess. It was someone lower than that, but on a throne in the hall was Oonagh, the Great Queen.'

'But it wasn't, I take it?'

Oonagh is the legendary Fae Queen of Ireland, only she was real. The invented part was her husband.

'She told me it was a common trope, not that I had a fecking idea what a *trope* was.' The Irish accent was stronger now, as was her determination to get a knot out of her hair. 'Sorry. 'Scuse me.' She leapt up and strode over to her hidey-hole, coming back with a large brush. 'If I don't get this thing out, I'll be reaching for the scissors.' There were a few seconds of heated struggle with her hair, until the brush went through and it cleared. As she tugged, gold glinted on the back of the hairbrush. 'There. Better.'

She put the brush in her lap, and I noticed that her fingernails were painted black, the same as the lacquer on the brush. That's not something you'd normally miss, so what other bits of magick had she been using?

She sat with her knees together and her feet apart, white trainers peeking out from under the blue dress. She'd arrived at what she thought was the heart of her tale, and took a breath. 'The Queen told me that I had no magick, and never would on my own. She said she'd fulfilled her obligations and I had two choices: I could return to my family or I could become a Vessel. I chose to become a Vessel. The rest is history.'

It was my turn to open the Diet Pepsi and drink. 'How do you feel about it now?'

'That she was a manipulative bitch who forced a child to choose between something she didn't understand and something that scared her shitless. I can remember Sliabh Liag perfectly. Rain, wind, sunburn and hard work. I thought that's what life would be like if I lived it with no magick. No one mentioned that my family owned half of Cornwall.' She considered that part. 'Then again, maybe it wouldn't have mattered. Do you know what I asked her? I said, "Will I be able to give up sewing?" And she said, "Eventually." Liar.'

'At that age, all I wanted to do was give up art and drama,' I replied. 'I can see where you're coming from. What happened next?'

'The Hlæfdige who'd fostered me came in. She took me down into the garden. You know what that is, right?'

'The deepest, most … alien part of the sídhe.'

'Alien is right. She lay me down on the grass and measured me with a piece of ribbon. She gave me Amrita to drink, and something else from a little bottle.' She was twisting the hairbrush now and glanced at it a couple of times, then finally held it up so that I could see the back. It was an exquisite spiral design in gold inlay with something I couldn't quite catch at this distance and in this light.

'This was hers,' she continued. The brush shook slightly in her hand. 'As I fell asleep, she brushed my hair. When I woke up, the brush was next to me and she was gone. Gone gone, as in dead. The ribbon was there, too, but I was an inch and a half taller.' She took out a tissue to dry her eyes.

'Let's get this over with, shall we? They took me upstairs, only upstairs was different. A completely different sídhe. The Queen was there, though, and if I had to guess, I'd say it was one of her top Prince's palaces. The whole shebang was full of the People, ready to party and all in Glamours or Constructions. I bent the knee and she gave me a chair to sit on. She said, "Morwenna, today is the day to choose your first incarnation. Would you like to be a great servant or a great performer?" Then the Queen held up two necklaces. One had a big needle with the chain through the eye, and the other had a heart on it. She held up the one with the heart and said, "This one was an athlete in bed and much in demand. Just so you know." You can guess which one I chose, can't you?'

'Was it really a choice?'

'Who knows? Maybe if the same thing had happened to Eseld, she'd have chosen the other one, if half the stories Kenver has told me about her are true. Perhaps some things are innate. I chose the needle, and after my head exploded, I was Medbh. Have I gone all Irish on you? Is it obvious?'

'Just a bit, Morwenna.'

'It comes out when I think back. They took me downstairs, and at sunset, I was delivered to my father.'

'So that was true? He said he collected you from the door of the sídhe.' It was time to push her. 'He never said which one.'

'And I don't know, okay? I was catatonic, and all I can remember is watching the moon on a big lake out of the window and stopping to pee in the bushes. It was night-time. By dawn, I was back in Donegal with the Sisters of the Grey Mountain. This time I was there to practise using Medbh's magick – I won't call it my own. There was still a lot of sewing, but at least I could use a Charm to thread the needle. And Medbh could bake, bless her heart. I really did make that barm brack I brought with me, you know. When you met me for the first time, I'd run away from Sliabh Liag. Or thought I had.'

'I'm sorry?'

'They'd tracked me down here. They'd threatened my father. When Kenver told me Daddy was dead, I thought the People had done it. That's why I ran. Thanks to you, I turned myself in.'

'Thanks to me?'

'In one day, you found his killers. Thank you for that, Conrad. Thank you very much.'

'I'm sorry I couldn't have prevented it. Why did they come looking for you?'

'I hadn't finished my service: there was another year to go. They said I could do that or go to Derwent and ride Unicorns for two years. Again, not so much of a choice, really. When the Count of Force Ghyll ripped off the horseshoe, the contract was void, and so was I.'

'What do you mean?'

'I'd lost Medbh's memories when I became Lara Dent. Most of them, anyway. Not that there was a lot to remember. When I lost Lara, I had almost nothing left in my head apart from a couple of months riding horses and Unicorns.'

For the first time since we'd sat down, she rubbed the spot where her bump was going to grow. 'I have the night I spent with Harry. I'll never forget that.' She dropped her hand. 'And a tiny, tiny amount of Gift. Just enough to do a little magick, and a little more in here.' She pointed to the third chair. 'I normally sit there. Feel in the cup holder. Go on.'

I did as she asked, and found the Artefact that governs the magick in and around Pellacombe: the badge of the Steward. I held it up and raised my eyebrows.

'Jane Kershaw can't work it, and I can't run an estate, so we divide the jobs. Perhaps I'll be full-time Steward one day.'

I dropped the badge and sat down again. 'Lara Dent. How did the Queen of Derwent come by her … properties?'

'I'm so glad you believed me when I saw you in the hospital in Preston. I was so worried that you'd go there all guns blazing. Literally. Lara submitted to having her talents scanned. I remember remembering, because I had to live through it. It was bloody painful. Worst thing I've ever felt.'

'What did Lara get out of it?'

'Freedom. She was bonded, too. Harsh, but she consented.'

The mention of consent brought me to one of the loose ends that I couldn't leave untugged. 'Did you ever see your grandmother again? I mean Clíodhna Ahearn, not Mrs Mowbray.'

She shook her head, slightly uncomfortable.

'But she rescued you, didn't she? She was the one who took you away from the police station.'

'I told you: I don't remember that. It's what Dad said had happened, so I believed it.'

'And have you been in touch with her at all.'

She shook her head. 'I have no idea where she is, and no one to ask. I'd love to see her.' She tilted her head. 'Have you any messages for me? From Matt Eldridge, or Oighrig Ahearn maybe?'

'I was going to tell you later. Matt was touched by your letter, and he'd be honoured to stand in for Harry at the Naming, but don't expect to see him before then.'

'Thanks.' She paused, then ran her hands through her hair. 'What about the Rose of Galway? That's what Eseld calls her.'

'You should talk to her. If you don't, she may spontaneously combust from curiosity.'

She dropped her hair with a smile, and then we fell silent. I had one more card to play, and I'd been saving it for the end, just in case I didn't have to play it. Morwenna had given me enough to go on. More than enough. I could take the next steps with what I had, or I could see how she responded to a gift from the gods. Or one god in particular.

On my last visit to Pellacombe, I'd left after her father's funeral, an event she'd missed, of course. When the crowds had cleared, and I'd gone to take Scout for a walk along the river, Odin had come to see me. He'd told me the truth about Raven's birth, and he'd given me something to show to Morwenna. I reached into my coat and took out the leather pouch where I'd been keeping it. 'What do you make of this?' I asked, passing her the heavy pouch.

She leaned forward to take it, and her thin wrist dropped with the weight. 'What is this? A rock?' She slipped out the polished stone and turned it over. When the glittering lines of Ogham script came into focus, she went stock still, every muscle clenched. It took a few seconds for her to jerk her head up. 'Where did you get this? Where in the name of the Morrigan did you get this?'

'I was told you could translate it.'

'Do you know how dangerous it is to have this? Where have you even kept it?'

'The one who gave it to me said that I should use it as a paperweight until you showed up again.'

Her Enhanced voice dropped away, as if she didn't want to use magick to utter the words. 'The Allfather.'

'Yes.'

Her voice returned to what sounded like normal, but wasn't. That made it a lot worse, somehow. 'He must want you dead to give you this and let you carry it around.' She put the stone back in the bag, and with a sudden, magick-fuelled violence, she threw it at a point over my shoulder, right next to my head.

I don't know how I did it, but I did. Something in the Lux merged with years of fielding cricket balls, and my left hand shot up to snatch the bag out of the air. I was supposed to duck and the stone was supposed to smash into pieces on the wall behind me. Morwenna took a sharp breath and brought her hand up to her mouth.

I stowed the rock away while I gave my heart a couple seconds to slow down and my voice the chance to even out. 'What did it say?'

'It … It's a Door stone. The People use them as shortcuts to access one of their realms. It's discharged now. If you're going to keep the bloody thing, don't let your dog lick it.'

'Does it smell of sausages or lady dogs? They're about the only things that would get Scout interested in a lump of rock.'

'Mercury. That's not gold in the letters, it's gold amalgam: gold with mercury.'

Of course it was. *Quicksilver magick*. I was grateful for the warning, but she was trying to change the subject. 'What did it say?'

'They're words of power in the People's tongue. Roughly speaking, it says *Move me from Here to There*.'

'Where's *There*?'

'Don't know. Can't say. I really can't say it. Some of those letters make sounds we can't hear, and certainly can't say. Dunno.'

The look on her face said that she didn't know for certain, but I was fairly sure that she could guess and was choosing not to.

Despite the Lux flowing around us, I could see beads of sweat pooling on her forehead as she made the effort to keep going. She dropped her head and stared at the hairbrush for a second, twirling it round. When she looked up, she was ready to move on. 'I want you to promise me something, Conrad. I want you to give me your word.'

'I don't write blank cheques, Morwenna.'

'Promise me you'll let it lie. Promise me you won't go looking for vengeance on my behalf, because I am not looking for a champion. Save your heroics for Mina. Just let me live out my life as best I can. And come to the Naming.'

'Be careful what you wish for.'

'You're not a god, Conrad. You're a man. Give me your word, for my sake and for my babies.'

'If that's what you want.'

'I do. Say it.'

'I promise not to seek vengeance for what was done to you, Morwenna.' I held up my right hand. 'As the Allfather is my witness.'

'Good. And for Mina's sake if not yours, don't go flashing that stone around near the People. They don't take kindly to their Artefacts being used as paperweights. It should be time for lunch by now. Confession makes you hungry.'

She stood up and summoned a mirror on the wall – she made the rock reflective, in other words. She brushed her hair and refreshed her lipstick. Finally, she adjusted the scarf and gave me a big smile. 'I need the bathroom, and I'll take my chamber pot. Could you be a friend, Conrad, and bring the other rubbish. I'll see you in a bit.'

Her chamber pot was actually a proper medical one, with a lid. She took it carefully away, and I went to gather the empties and a half-full black bag. The hairbrush was sitting on a bench with the rest of her makeup and toiletries, so I took a picture of the back. That design was pretty distinctive. I'm sure someone in Ireland could tell me more.

9 — A Council of War

Kenver was not a happy Mowbray when I emerged from the magickal zone. 'I knew I shouldn't have let her see you on her own,' he said.

'Why?'

'She blew out of there in tears and wouldn't talk to me. You're a bully.'

'She was carrying a bucketful of piss, Kenver, and she'd been crossing her legs for ten minutes before we wrapped up. Go and wait for her outside the bathroom.'

The girls were enjoying a drink in front of a roaring fire in the drawing room. Mina sprang up and came to take my hand. When she said, 'How did it go?' she was speaking for all of them.

'Poor girl. Woman. Yet another casualty of magick. Have I got five minutes before lunch?'

'I'll join you,' said Eseld. 'Mina, can you do the introductions when she comes in?'

Out on the terrace, we lit up, and Eseld said, 'Well?'

I looked out to the estuary for a moment. 'If she were my sister, I'd want answers. I would not be happy.'

She heard something in my tone. 'And would you want my help finding them? Because I definitely want yours.'

'The answers are in Ireland, and if I go, I can't go as a member of the King's Watch.'

'Oh.'

'I'll help on one condition.'

It's a measure of how committed Eseld is to Morwenna's future that she didn't hesitate.

'What?'

'You and Isolde. Three sessions of family therapy.'

She couldn't have been more shocked if I'd slapped her. 'You bastard!'

'Take it or leave it.'

She pivoted on her foot as if she were in a fight, turning her back on me and leaning on the balustrade. When Eseld was a little girl, her mother (Isolde) left Lord Mowbray and became a full-time member of the Daughters of the Goddess. Eseld was never happy about that, and when she became a teenager, they fell out spectacularly and haven't spoken since. Isolde did something that she thought was in her daughter's best interests; Eseld disagrees. Lord Mowbray never stopped trying to get them back together, but he was her father, and he doted on her. Completely. I think I'm the only person who's pushed it. I hoped that I hadn't pushed it too far.

What I really hoped was that she was ready to find a way back to her mother and that I could be a convenient excuse.

She spoke without turning round. 'That's a lot to take in, Conrad. I assume you want a promise rather than actual sessions.'

'Time is of the essence with Morwenna. It could take weeks for Isolde to agree, and then to find a suitable therapist. A promise is fine.'

'Yeah. Three sessions. I promise.'

'Thank you.'

She turned back and took a clearing breath. 'So. Morwenna.'

I nodded to show that I appreciated what she'd just signed up to. 'Digging into Morwenna's past won't work unless Kenver is fully on board. Look, does the Steward have full financial responsibility for the Estate?'

'No chance. There's an Estate Manager and Finance Manager for that. They do have it for the household, though. And for staffing. Where are you going with this?'

'We need to get Mina and Rachael to double-team Morwenna after lunch. I'm guessing that Jane has gone off with Leah.'

'Yeah. She's at the farmhouse while they wait for the contractions to get closer together or something.'

'Fine. Rachael would love to see the junction anyway. You set up the call, and I'll organise a diversion to keep Morwenna out of the way.'

After the cathartic conversation I'd had with Morwenna, Sunday dinner was a relaxed, friendly celebration of family. Away from the Lux, Morwenna communicated mostly by a text-to-speech app on her iPad. The basic voice was very similar to the one she'd started with in the junction. She even had a couple of phrases click-ready: just one tap to say *Shut up Eseld* and *Stop being a mother hen, Kenver*. She used them just about equally.

The one and only time she used her real voice was at the start, when Kenver proposed a toast – to me, for saving Morwenna's life. I was not expecting that. By the end of the meal, I'd come to the conclusion that Kenver needed to do two things. First, he needed to get back on the road with Chris Kelly in the New Year. Second, he needed a long spell at Pellacombe without Eseld telling him what to do.

When the coffee was brought in, Mina took Morwenna's hands and said, 'I would love to talk to you properly. And so would Rachael. She would also love to see a real place of magickal power.'

'Can I?' said Rachael. She wasn't in on the plan, but she played her part perfectly. She really did want to see the junction. She also wanted Morwenna's signature on the Mowbray Trust deeds. That helped.

The rest of us gathered in the public rooms upstairs, and Kenver looked bewildered when I drew the curtains and Eseld powered up the data projector. From Kellysporth, Ethan and Lena joined us in HD quality sound and vision.

'What is this?' said Kenver.

'A council of war,' said Eseld. 'What do you reckon, Conrad? Was she telling the truth?'

'First of all, what did she say?' interrupted Lena.

I ran through the headlines.

'See?' said Kenver. 'That's exactly what she's said to all of us.' He looked at his sister. 'I know you've been collating it, Eseld. It's all consistent. Every time.'

'Give me strength, Kenver. All that means is she had plenty of time to make up her story while she wasn't speaking to anyone.'

'While she *couldn't* speak, you mean.'

'Same bloody thing.'

'Leave her alone! She's our sister, Eseld. She's a Mowbray like you are. Why do you hate her? Why can't you just leave her alone?'

They had both stood up, and Eseld took a step closer to him. 'She's as much my sister as you're my brother. That's the point. Kerenza nearly became a Mowbray, and she lured our father to his death. Don't you want to know? Don't you want to know why she ended up like this?'

'I know exactly why she ended up like this. The Count of Force Ghyll slashed her throat open. Then to save her life, Conrad undid the Vessel Charm.'

'Did I?'

The whole family, live and virtual, stared at me. 'What did you think you were doing?' said Eseld.

I shrugged. 'What she asked me to do. She was leaking ectoplasm. I think. I stopped it.'

Eseld seized the initiative. 'You're impartial, Conrad. What do you think?'

I looked at the monitor. 'You two haven't met Sofía, have you?'

Ethan shook his head, while Lena nodded. 'No, but I know all about her, Conrad,' she said. 'She came into your life just before we did, ja? So she is like Morwenna. She has always been your sister, but only now is she here.'

I looked at Kenver and Eseld. Especially Kenver. 'It's not politically correct to say it any more, but it's true. Someone sold Morwenna down the river. Packed her off to the Morrigan knows where and let the Fae do *that* to her. I'd want answers if it had happened to Sofía. Right now, I think Morwenna is exactly what she looks like: a casualty. What about the future, though? Without answers to the past, can you really be sure about the future? What if there's another procedure that could help her recover fully?'

His eyes flicked round, from me to Eseld and then to the screen. 'It's not what she wants.' He tried to square his shoulders and look me in the eye. 'She made me promise not to go looking for vengeance. Did she make you do the same, Conrad?'

'She did. I promised not to seek vengeance for what was done to her.'

He turned to the screen. 'I'm not a Clarke, but the word of a Mowbray is still good. That settles it.'

I coughed. 'I didn't promise not to seek for answers, Kenver. I'd very much like to know what happened to her.'

'And so would I,' echoed Eseld. 'And he needs me to look out for him.'

Kenver looked confused, so Eseld spelled it out for him. 'Conrad needs a partner with more magick. He can't take a Watch Officer to Ireland, can he? I'll go with him, and I'll let him take the lead. I promise.'

Ethan spoke up. 'Face it, Kenver. Either Morwenna is lying to us or she really doesn't know what happened to her, and if you find out, you can decide whether to tell her. Your father had his reasons for not asking questions. You don't. It's your duty to look after her, yes, so let Eseld and Conrad go with your blessing.'

Kenver and Eseld were still facing off to my right and my left. He looked down and flattened a crease in the rug. 'All right.'

'Well done,' said Ethan. 'We'll leave you to it.'

Lena nodded. '*Auf Weidersehen*, Conrad. Tell Mina to call me, okay?'

The call ended, and Eseld swivelled on her heel. 'Let's get going.'

'What do you mean?' said Kenver.

'It's Christmas in less than two weeks. I've got a gig at Cherwell Roost on Saturday, and Conrad's going, too. We need to get a shift on.'

Eseld had a thick padded envelope, and I had a thinner one. We put them on the desk in front of us, and Mina brought Rachael up from the junction.

'You didn't show me this room,' said Rachael. 'It has to be your dad's study. God, you can smell the testosterone in here.' She stopped looking round and saw the desk and the single chair in front of it for her to sit on. Mina had already slipped out. 'What's going on.'

'You brought your passport didn't you? Sit down and we'll explain.'

She moved the chair before she sat on it, just to show she wasn't giving us complete control. 'Yes. You said we might hop over to France for a treat.'

'I said we might, and I meant it. What I didn't tell you was that France was Plan B. We're going to Ireland instead.'

Eseld took over. 'This is a huge ask, Raitch, but now you've seen Morwenna properly, you must have some idea of how badly she's been hurt.'

Rachael's hand moved to her throat. 'It was horrible. I can't imagine it.'

'We want to find out what happened. What really happened. And we need your help.'

'Why me? This has got magickal written all over it.'

I took over. 'We need a scout. Normally I'd ask Alain, but this one is better suited to you.'

'Is it dangerous?'

Eseld smiled reassuringly at her. 'Not if you change the habit of a lifetime and follow your brother's instructions. He really does know what he's talking about here.'

'So people keep telling me. I have seen the Elvenham sick bay, you know.' She turned so that her body was facing Eseld, then twisted her head to look at me. 'A scout? I take it we're not talking sheepdog here.'

'All you have to do is book us some accommodation. In person.'

She looked at Eseld. 'I know you two are friends. How does the rest of the family feel?'

She nodded seriously. 'This is from me, from Kenver, from Cador and especially Ethan. We'd consider it a great service to the Mowbrays.'

Rachael got the message: you scratch our back and we'll sign over all our estates to your new wealth management company. Raitch is also a good person underneath. 'How does Morwenna feel about this?'

Eseld knew she had to be honest. Up to a point. 'We don't have her blessing. We're doing this for the whole family. It's too important.'

'I see. I'm not saying *yes* just yet. What would I have to do?'

My turn. 'Fly to Shannon Airport. It's on the west coast. Hire a car and drive to the Galway Castle Hotel. Spend a night of sumptuous five star luxury, then drive around looking for self-catering accommodation that's quiet and off the beaten track. Book it for a week. Wait for us to join you, then your time's your own.'

'Why don't you do it yourselves? There is such a thing as the Internet, you know.'

'No substitute for boots on the ground,' I said. 'Especially if they're Prada boots. And we don't want the names *Clarke* or *Mowbray* anywhere out there.'

'How…?'

I slid open the envelope that Erin had handed to me at the hustings. 'Say hello to Rachael Baxter. Passport, driving licence, credit card.'

Eseld opened her envelope and took out wads and wads of Euro banknotes. 'And say hello to expenses. Keep what you don't use.'

'Fly out as Rachael Clarke, then hide your passport. Rent the car and everything else as Baxter.'

She looked from me to Eseld. She looked at the passport and the cash. 'Seriously? All that money?'

'All of us chipped in,' said Eseld. She leaned forward and whispered loudly. 'I may have asked for a bit more than was strictly necessary.'

Rachael picked up the credit card. 'Who's *Rachael Baxter*? You must have been cooking this up for a while. I won't get in trouble, will I?'

I shook my head. 'We started planning a few weeks ago. Just in case. Just don't use the card in the UK and destroy it before you leave Ireland. And remember: anything you put on *that* card comes out of *this* pile. You'll get the bill in a few weeks.'

'A couple of days? That's all?'

Eseld and I nodded solemnly.

'Then I'm in. Are we doing this after Christmas?'

'No. I'm dropping you off at Liverpool John Lennon airport in an hour or so. The flight's at 16:30.'

'What! No! I've only brought a few clothes.'

We started packing the envelopes. 'You've got all the clothes that an aspiring writer would need. That's your cover story. Gives you a perfect opportunity to ask questions. Here's your legend and some light reading.'

I passed her a copy of *How Not to Write a Novel*, along with a character sketch, both courtesy of Evie Mason. I didn't tell Rachael that she might one day feature in Evie's best seller.

'What a beautiful house,' said Eseld when we circled around the Haven. There was just enough daylight for her to appreciate it, and from the air it looked like it had been planted in the Cheshire countryside for centuries and not just a hundred and forty years. She was sitting up front with me and got the best view. We weren't landing here, but it was on the flight path to Hawarden Airport and it was too good a chance to miss.

'It's nice, isn't it?' piped up Mina over the intercom. 'The Deputy's Suite upstairs is sumptuous, if dated. Conrad doesn't know this yet, but his wedding present to me is going to be a new bedroom and en-suite at Elvenham. One of his presents to me.'

An hour later, we were back at the Haven, this time on four wheels not four rotors. Saskia turned out to welcome such an honoured (i.e. rich) guest, and when she'd taken Eseld to her room, Mina and I ended up at the car. It was the first time since we'd got up this morning that we'd been alone.

'Do you really want a new bedroom?' I asked.

'Of course I bloody well do. The set-up at Elvenham is barely fit for the last century, never mind this one.' She frowned. 'But it's not my top priority. Unless Myfanwy and Ben buy a new place and get permission to live there, we need to do something for her. Her twins will be nearly two when her Seclusion is finished.'

'They will, and you're right. We owe it to her. Let's hope I arrest a seriously rich Mage in the near future and they're wearing enough bling for a total refurbishment.'

'We can wish. When are you going to tell Eseld what's really going on? She is going to be furious with you'

'I don't mind her venting a bit. After supper. I've turfed Evie out of the study for the night.'

'You're forgetting something.'

'What?'

'It was the semi-final of Strictly Come Dancing last night. We'll be glued to the TV.'

'Even better. I've had two texts from Hannah since this morning. She wants me to call.'

'I don't think she does,' said Mina, taking my hand. As usual, she rubbed it between hers to get some warmth. 'I think she wants you to get me to call. I shall Facetime her later and tell her all about the election in Cornwall. And I shall tell her all about my new job.'

While we were in Ireland, Mina was going to be visited by a senior official from the Edinburgh division of the Cloister Court. Word of her skills and impartiality was spreading.

'Come on, then. If you're going to Facetime, you'll need to do something about your helicopter hair.'

I ran into the house before she could take retaliatory action.

'When did you get this done?' asked Eseld when we adjourned to the study. 'It's a bit in-your-face.'

She was admiring (or criticising) my new coat of arms, one copy of which now hung over the study fireplace. It looks like this:

And if you're seeing it in monochrome, the grey bits are bright red. All of them.

'Does it mean something?' she asked. 'And why did you get it? Oh, hang on, those triangly bits are rotor blades, aren't they?'

'They are. The book is for magick, and the Plough is for my old Squadron in the RAF. You can guess who the Pole Star represents.'

'Mina. Or the Allfather, I suppose.'

'Heraldry is always ambiguous,' I said diplomatically. 'The red is because I was in combat, and the reason I got it is that it's the only thing allowed on that wall. It was a bit bare without it. Can you light the fire for me?'

While she did, I made myself comfy. She stood, leaning on the mantelpiece and looked down at me. For the first time since we'd met up on Friday, she looked troubled. 'Go on, then,' she said. 'What's changed since you were in Spain? You've gone all quiet on the details of this trip, and that's not like you.'

'Indulge me for a minute. Lloyd re-set the locks on that cabinet for me. Have a go at trying to crack it, will you.'

She moved over to the fire-resistant secure cabinet and examined the magick. 'Nope. All good. An acetylene torch would be quicker than trying to break these locks.'

'Here. It's the green one.'

I chucked her my bunch of keys, and she found the stamp that opened the locks. 'What am I looking for?'

'See that pile of boring looking files on the right? Half way down, there's a folded piece of paper tucked in.'

She rummaged inside and found it, then locked up the cabinet and sat down by the fire. She offered me the keys and the paper. I took the keys and said, 'Read it. You need to know.'

It took her less than a second to ask, 'What's the *Codex Defanatus*?'

'A book. I'll explain more in a minute.'

It took her a couple of minutes, and a big drink, to reach the end of Tom's report. She sat back and shook her head. 'You are a piece of work, Conrad Clarke. You set me up, you bastard. You got me to agree to family therapy when you were always going to go after the Fae because of this.' She waved the paper around. 'This Codex Defanatus stuff is serious shit and goes way beyond our little problem with Morwenna. If the rest of the family knew I was getting in to this, they'd have serious second thoughts. I should back out now, then I wouldn't have to sit in a comfy chair trying not to strangle my mother.'

I gave her a moment. 'If I hadn't made you promise to go to therapy, and I'd still shown you that, would you back out?'

She snorted. 'You're still a conniving bastard though. Here.' She passed the paper to me, and I fed it to the flames before topping up our glasses.

'How did all this come to light?' she asked.

'I met my eleven times great grandfather this summer. Thomas Clarke. This is his story, not mine. Or not until the end anyway.'

I gave her the edited version – that Thomas had come into possession of a book of very old magick, and that a gathering of powers had sealed it until the day I was born. At some point in the intervening years, it had been stolen from its custodian. Stolen by one of the Fae.

She pointed to the fire. 'And you believe that those Mages went to Galway to buy parts of the Codex.'

'I do.'

'Bloody hell, Conrad. That's a shitstorm and half. No wonder you've been up to your arse in Dragons and blood.'

'What that report doesn't say is that it's likely to get worse before it gets better. This is my one chance to cut it off at the source.'

She considered that. 'Why you?'

'My family tipped over the first domino, and if being a Clarke means anything, it means that I have a duty to stop it.'

She nodded slowly. 'And because the trail leads over the water, you can't involve the Watch. No wonder you're keen to "help" find out what happened to Morwenna. And I see what you did with that promise to Kenver – you won't be seeking vengeance for her. You're doing it for yourself.'

'Myself, the Clarke family and others. Including yours, as it happens. This isn't quite the Rubicon, Eseld, but we're getting very close. If we go to Ireland together, I'll be looking to prove that one of the Galway Queens had the Codex, that she opened it, that she sold some of it off, and that she kept some of it for herself. That she used some of that magick on your sister.'

'And then what?'

'Let's go outside for a moment.'

We took our glasses and stood on the back steps. The distant lights of Chester allowed us to pick out the grove that surrounded Nimue's spring. 'I want three things, Eseld. First, I want to know who sold Morwenna down the river and why. Second, I want it to stop. Now. And third, I want to know what else is out there. What to look for.'

'You don't want much, do you?'

'Vicky has a wonderful Geordie saying. *Shy bairns get nowt.*'

'Terrible accent, that. And if you don't get what you want?'

'Then we come to the Rubicon. Whether you cross it with me is up to you.'

'And how do we get there?'

I stubbed out my cigarette. 'Come back inside and I'll tell you. The first thing is that we're not going to fly.'

10 — Over the Water

Monday morning brought a real surprise: a cup of tea in bed. From Mina. She carried it across the room, and I sat up straight. 'I didn't hear you get up, love.' She brought it to my side of the bed, and I put my arm round the soft silk of her dressing gown to give her a kiss. I ran my hand up her back, under her hair and stroked the nape of her neck. 'Mmmm.'

She pulled gently back. 'I couldn't sleep, and for once you were dead to the world. I think the last week has been catching up with you.'

'You're right. I feel a lot better this morning. Are you coming back to bed?'

'No. Lloyd has messaged. He'll be here in an hour, and I need a shower. Oh, and Lloyd wasn't the only one who messaged. Leah Kershaw had a healthy boy. They're going to call him Arthur, after Lord Mowbray.' As compensation for not coming back to bed, she leaned back in for another kiss. 'Drink your tea before it goes cold.'

It wasn't just Lloyd who turned up after breakfast. I saw a familiar face get out of the white van, and limped over to shake his hand. 'Albie. How are you?'

Albie is a sort of adopted nephew of Lloyd, and his right hand man in Clan Salz. The last time I'd seen him was when they loaded him into an ambulance.

'Much better, thanks. Settling in nicely to the new place.'

'Good. If you wait in the kitchen, someone will look after you. C'mon, Lloyd.'

We collected Eseld and went to the study. Lloyd had a number of things with him, most obviously a long sword in a plain black polycarbonate scabbard. He put that aside for later and emptied the contents of a plastic wallet.

'As requested, one unmarked van with automatic gearbox. It's registered to one of my companies and you're both listed as drivers. Keys, logbook and insurance. I have to ask: why aren't you using your own car with a Glamour on the plates? Or just drive through as it is?'

'Letter of the law, Lloyd,' I replied. 'If we take my car, the further south we go, the more likely it is to trigger an alert on their systems. If I use a Glamour, and I get found out, or if I use a fake passport or anything like that, it's a real risk. If I keep to the letter of the law, they can't get me on a technicality.'

'Fair enough. Is that why you wanted me to book and pay for the ferry?'

'Correct.'

'But you've only put Eseld down. Are you gonna smuggle yourself in?'

I shook my head. 'We'll add me to the manifest at Cairnryan. It won't even go on the system until we're already half way to Galway.'

He nodded slowly. 'I've said it before, and I'll say it again. I'm sure you're part-Gnome Conrad. Here's the printout of the ferry booking. We'll do the cash part first. Who's settling up?'

'Me,' said Eseld. 'And the fact that I'm paying suggests he's more than part-Gnome. I'm also paying the alchemical gold fee. This "mission" is costing us a fortune.'

'Absolutely,' I agreed. 'And you know what, Lloyd, I even forced them to underwrite the cost of my funeral.'

He handed two envelopes to Eseld and said, 'Quite right, too. Okay. The sword. I don't know why you don't use Great Fang. It's got a cold-forged tip.'

'And it's got the badge of Nimue on it. I am not taking that to Ireland. Let's have a look.'

While Eseld counted out banknotes, Lloyd picked up the sword, not touching the exposed hilt. 'All the magick is dormant. It'll bond to you when you draw it for the first time, and talking of bonding, this is totally experimental. Ceramics do not play nicely with metal *and* magick. There you go.'

I gripped the scabbard in my right hand and grasped the hilt in my left. I closed my eyes and felt for the magick in the sword. Woah. In the name of Mother Earth, what's going on? To my limited magickal senses, the sword seemed to have a beating heart – a low, slow pulse. I waited to see if it would settle down, and I realised that I'd got the image wrong. It wasn't a beating heart, it was the rhythmic thump of a trip hammer sounding deep underground. I started to draw the blade.

The pounding got louder, and the sword was reluctant to leave the sheath. I pulled harder, and now I could hear a heartbeat: mine. And the sword got stuck. I remembered back to when I'd bonded with the First Mine of Clan Flint. Gnomes love synchronicity. It was just a question of adjusting my heart to the rhythm of the sword.

No it wasn't. Only Indian yoga masters can do that. I had to reach into the sword and adjust the hammer to suit me. Down, deeper. Hammer, hammer, hammer…

With a crash, the sword came out and I had to stop my left arm jerking it too close to Eseld.

'You don't half make a meal of these things, Conrad,' she said.

'He gets there in the end,' said Lloyd. 'How does it feel?'

'Bloody hell, Lloyd. This is something else.' I transferred the blade to my right hand. It was like no sword I've ever seen before, and for a good reason.

Given our potential enemies, I'd asked Lloyd to make me a blade of cold-forged iron. The old legend about the Fae and iron is mostly nonsense and comes from the days before we knew about haemoglobin containing iron. Having said that, because Fae biology *is* different, especially when using their Quicksilver magick, they are vulnerable to iron that's had Gnome magick worked into it while cold. It's not easy to do, and that's why it's rare to find a whole weapon made of the stuff.

Lloyd had made a long, thin rod of cold-forged iron with a wickedly sharp tip. It was magickally very powerful, but physically brittle. To compensate, he'd created two ceramic blades and bonded them to the core, and to make the whole thing even lighter, he'd put holes in the ceramic. 'It's the future of weapons,' he'd told me. The only traditional feature was the steel hilt holding it all together and acting as a focus for the magick.

'Just how experimental is this?' I asked, testing the balance and being very impressed.

'Not really. I wouldn't do that to you, Conrad, it's just that it's the first of its kind. If you use it, I want a full report. I've given you a discount.'

Eseld opened the second envelope. 'Bloody hell, Lloyd. This is *after* discount. I'll tell you what, Conrad, I'm keeping that thing after we've finished.'

'Of course. You're paying for it. What the hell will you do with it?'

'I don't know. I'll make the transfer before we set off, is that okay, Lloyd?'

'No probs. Right, I'll go and grab a cuppa.'

He left, and I sheathed the sword.

Eseld stared at it for a second. 'Well? Got everything?'

I scooped the documents back into the wallet and put them at the left of the desk, next to the sword. I opened the secure cabinet and got out the other items I thought I'd need: the Door stone from the Allfather and a very masculine looking case with *TAG Heuer* stamped on it.

'You've always said you hated bling watches,' said Eseld. 'What's that for?'

'It's the most accurate totally mechanical watch I could find. No electronics at all. And it was a birthday present from Mina. As to why, I may need Rachael for something other than being a scout. There's just one more thing. Would you mind getting Mina to come in and leaving us to it?'

'Of course. I'll grab a coffee and go pay the Gnome. Are we off soon?'

'We are.'

Mina found me making a pile of other things. Things I wouldn't be taking. Things like Great Fang, the Hammer and my RAF ID card. I was most definitely *not* going to Ireland as a serving officer of the British armed forces.

I locked them in the cabinet and handed the keys to Mina. 'There's one more thing I need, love.'

She put it in a box and handed it over. 'If you're sure. It feels like exactly the wrong time to be giving it up.'

'It's only a symbol,' I replied, and that was the cue for a goodbye kiss, one that we were both enjoying when the door burst open and Cordelia stormed in.

Cordelia knew why she'd been told to enjoy a long weekend with the kids the moment she saw who was lounging against the outside wall of the Haven, smoking, looking at her phone and playing with her long hair. There was a coffee mug on the floor next to her.

Long hair? Since when did Eseld Mowbray have long hair?

Cordelia had been forced to drive right down the side of the house because a plain white van was parked in her normal spot, and an unfamiliar Range Rover was hogging the visitors' space. Because she was so far down, she'd glanced at the sheltered smoker's corner first to see if Conrad were out there, only instead of Conrad, she saw her nemesis. One of them.

As she got closer, she realised that the hair must be extensions. What did Eseld think she looked like, with Hollywood hair on top of those big shoulders and thick thighs? She looked exactly like what she was: a rich, spoilt tramp.

Cordelia had known of Eseld even before the Daughters of the Goddess had invited Cordelia to join Ash Coven at Glastonbury – after all, Eseld's mother was their Guardian. It was only when Raven chose Cordelia to be her Page that Cordelia started to hear the whispered (or not so whispered) stories about Raven and *the Mowbray girl.*

Raven got her a bat Familiar was one. *Seduced her in the heart of the Grove* was another. She never did get the full truth, but before she'd let Raven remove the last of her clothes, on the first night they lay together, Cordelia had said, 'You and Eseld. Did you?'

And Raven had replied, 'No. I was barely a woman and she was still a child. She ran back to her father before we were old enough to be lovers. Why are you so beautiful, Cordelia? Why has the Goddess sent you to me?'

And all that was before Cordelia knew just how badly Eseld had treated her own mother. Was still treating her. The scene in the hall at Pellacombe during the summer, when Eseld had treated her mother like shit, was one of the most embarrassing moments of Cordy's life.

If all that wasn't enough, she'd seen Eseld and Conrad come back from their *morning ride* at Pellacombe. She'd seen Conrad treating Eseld like she was more than a friend. And even in her new, lonely life, she'd heard the stories from Rick: *Eseld Mowbray is doing a show with Conrad's sisters.* Even worse: *Eseld is Sofia Clarke's tutor at Salomon's House.*

'What are you doing here?' she demanded.

Eseld looked up and flicked ash off her cigarette. 'Oh, hi Cordelia! I didn't recognise you at first without the robes. How are you?'

She looked as if butter wouldn't melt, and it made Cordy even angrier. 'Have you been here all weekend?'

Eseld gave a slight frown. 'No. We were in Kernow for the election. Flew back last night. Conrad told you, didn't he?'

Damn. She'd let her anger get the better of her. Of course she knew that. She was tired. Tired from the drive up so early, and from all the tears she'd cried last night after she'd signed the consent forms for the kids to join Wells School. She'd cried so much that she couldn't go to bed, and rather than see them again in the morning, she'd crept into their rooms at five o'clock to kiss them goodbye in their sleep and slip out of the Old Rectory while Rick was still snoring. And she'd come back to this. To her.

And then the other reason for Conrad's journey had come back to her. 'He's been talking to Morwenna,' she said, more to herself than Eseld.

Eseld crushed out her cigarette and put her phone away. 'Yeah,' she said, her eyes on alert now.

Cordelia snapped back into the moment. 'So if you're here, you must be going in search of whoever made your sister a Vessel. Where are we headed?' Another thought struck her. 'You were going to go without me, weren't you? I have a right to be there, Eseld, and I'm not going to let you stop me.'

'Hey, Cordelia, calm down.'

'I was hers and she was mine. Not yours, *mine.* We were partners. She was nothing to you, really. *Nothing.* She was just a teenage crush you abandoned.'

Eseld had gone red. She took a step back before she spoke again. 'Are you on about Raven? This has got nothing to do with her.'

'Whoever made the Vessel made Raven. I will find her.' Cordy bit her lip before she gave herself away by saying *again.* She said it in her head, though. *Again. I will find her again.*

Eseld looked at the back door, desperate to escape. She was clearly embarrassed now that she'd seen Cordelia's love for Raven. Did Eseld love anyone or anything except herself and her own pleasure? Had she even loved her father, despite the crocodile tears at the joint funeral pyre?

Eseld took another step away from her, and was going to say something, but the back door opened first, and out stepped Lloyd Flint.

He smiled when he saw Cordelia, and was going to come over to say hello until he saw the two women's faces and body-language. Instead, he said, 'Is everything alright out here?'

'Cordelia's just got back,' said Eseld to Lloyd. She glanced briefly at Cordelia. 'Is Conrad in the study, Lloyd?'

'Arr, he is. You might wanna knock first.'

Cordelia forced herself to be polite. After all, the Gnome had been nothing but pleasant to her at the hustings. 'Are you staying, Lloyd?'

'No, we're done. I'll catch you later, yeah?'

She flashed him a smile and she headed into the house, through the cloakroom and into the kitchen. Evie was doing something at the chopping board, and Cordy used a quick Silence to pass by unnoticed; Evie Mason had so little magick that the Morrigan could walk through undetected. She took the short side-passage that bypassed the hall and arrived at the study door. Conrad was up to something, and she had to know what. She burst into the room to confront him.

She should have known better. The last time she'd tried to catch Conrad up to no good (with Oighrig), she'd found Evie Mason. This time she found Conrad locked into a passionate embrace with Mina. Or they were, until he twirled his fiancée round and put his hand on a sword that was lying on the desk.

'Ohmygod! I'm so sorry,' said Cordy.

'That's quite all right,' said Mina. 'At least we weren't in the bedroom.' She paused to make sure the point had got home, then smiled. 'Conrad was going to have a word with you anyway. I'll see you later, Cordy.'

Cordelia felt confused *and* embarrassed. 'I really am sorry. I thought you were about to go off, Conrad. Are you not going, Mina?'

Mina shook her head. 'Not on this one. There is nothing that I can bring to this party.' She patted Conrad's hand, then slipped round the desk and out of the door, closing it softly behind her.

Conrad sat down behind the desk and pointed to the chair in front of it. Cordelia couldn't help notice the pile of stuff on the desk, including the wallet with a set of vehicle keys in it. Conrad had told her since day one that he would rather she spoke up than kept quiet. In the back of her head she could hear her mother's voice saying *But preferably not when he's in mid snog.*

She sat down and said, 'Where are you going?'

'The Emerald Isle. With Eseld. To finish my convalescence.'

She pointed to the sword. 'And that's for the good of your health is it?' When he did nothing but raise his eyebrows, she sighed. He wasn't going to make this easy, was he? 'You've been to Cornwall. You've talked to Morwenna. You've found out that she was made a Vessel in Ireland. You're going to find out who did it and you're going off the books. We'll take that as read, shall we?'

No response from Conrad. She had to raise the stakes. 'So. I have an interest in this. Whoever made Morwenna a Vessel almost certainly created Raven.' She had to tread carefully now. 'I swore that I'd punish whoever did that, just as I'm sure Eseld has sworn to punish whoever interfered with Morwenna. Now tell me I'm wrong.'

She saw his eyelids lower a fraction, and pushed on, moving past the confession. 'You could be in serious trouble with this. You need all the help you can get. I can put in for a few days leave, too. Eseld is a powerful Mage, yes, but she doesn't have much experience of field work, does she?' She could see that he'd taken that on board, so she decided to go all-in. She leaned forwards and put her hands on the desk. 'If nothing else, I could be your chaperone.' That was it. She'd given it everything, including a joke as bad as one of his.

He frowned and pulled at his lip. It was his most obvious tell, and he didn't bother to hide it. Unlike Tom Morton rubbing his shoulder. That was a different order of obsession altogether.

'It's why you joined the Watch, isn't it?' he finally said.

Damn. She wanted the conversation to be about him, or failing that, about Raven. She did not want it to be about her. Unfortunately, he took her hesitation as an admission.

'I'm glad you've spelled it out for me. We have been wondering.' His eyes glanced to the door. 'Mina said that you were looking for something specific, and she was right. As usual.'

'Not really,' she said quickly. 'I joined the Watch to learn from the best hunters, including you. I never intended it to be part of my service. It was for later.'

He stood up and went to the open cupboard. While he looked for something, he said in a matter-of-fact voice, 'And if you came to Ireland, there's a good chance you might not have a career to come back to. I can afford to get demoted. You can't. Ah. Here we are.'

He turned round and brandished a printout. From this distance, she could just about make out a map of Europe with splodges on it. 'There's another very good reason why you shouldn't go,' he said. 'Would you agree that the Fae are actually quite lazy?'

Where had that come from. 'In some ways, yes,' she said. 'Why?'

'Because I took a sample of Raven's DNA and sent it off for analysis.'

She recoiled. 'What! How could you do that?'

'It was post-mortem, Cordy. I wouldn't have done it if she were alive.' He pulled himself up. 'Well, not without a good reason.'

'That doesn't make it any better. You know that won't tell you anything, right? The magick shrouding her Imprint disappeared with her.'

He gave a slight frown at her choice of words, then shrugged it off. 'I know, but that's not the point. The point is that Raven's starting point was human, and that had to come from somewhere. Would a Fae Queen send to England for her raw material?'

'I … what? No.' She could see where he was coming from and thought it through. 'No. She'd send a minion for the nearest suitable host and donor.'

'Quite. According to the DNA lab, Raven was 80% British, 10% Scandinavian and only 5% Irish. The other 5% is generalised North West Europe. There are people like that in Ireland, but they're all immigrants or the children of immigrants.'

'Can I see?'

He hesitated, then handed it over. 'Of course. If anyone has a right to this, it's you.'

She stared at the paper. It was more sophisticated than a generalised report, and included a lot of technical information that meant absolutely nothing to her. Conrad was standing expectantly, so she had to hand it back.

'Thank you,' she said, and as she said it, she realised just how thankful she was. A trip to Ireland with Eseld Mowbray was not what she wanted. 'Don't worry, Conrad. I'll mind the shop while you're gone.'

He put the report away. 'Thanks. All of this wasn't the main reason I wanted to see you. I need a favour.'

'How can I help? Do you want me to keep the Boss off your back?'

'I'm leaving my phone with Mina. That should do the trick.'

A little shiver ran down her back. This was clearly bigger and more risky than she thought. 'Then what?'

'I know that you're not Eseld's biggest fan, but how did you get on with her mother?'

That was a question she could answer honestly. 'I had a lot of respect for her. I still do.'

'Then can you, or someone you trust in the Daughters, get in touch with her? Tell her I'd like a word when we get back. And if you know of any therapists with experience in magick…'

'No! How come?'

He shook his head and glanced at his watch. 'I'd better get a move on. We've a ferry to catch.'

Part Three

Queen Gambit

11 — Accommodation

The highlight of the journey to Galway was undoubtedly our first sight of land, not that we'd exactly been far out at sea. The ferry from Cairnryan isn't a long trip, and we'd barely recovered from the endless drive along the Solway Firth before it was time to take our coffee on to the deck and admire the scenery. On the way out, we discussed the fact that this might be the last chance we had to enjoy the view: there was a cold front on the way, bringing lots of rain. Only to be expected, I suppose.

The Stena ferry goes all the way along Belfast Lough, right into the city, where the sun was setting and the lights were coming on. The giant yellow cranes of Harland & Wolff were both majestic and threatening. I tried to work out if they were an omen, and suggested as much to Eseld.

'Conrad, sometimes a crane is just a crane. Shut up and give me a fag.'

After that, I can report that Irish motorways are pretty similar to English ones. Apart from the distances being in kilometres, of course. What's that all about? It was a very ratty Eseld and a very stiff Conrad who arrived on the west coast several hours later. 'I hope my sister's done her job,' I said as Eseld drove us out of Galway City.

'Of course she has,' said Eseld. And she was right.

Once you've left the university city of Galway, you first go through the family fun outpost of Salthill, complete with amusements, then all of a sudden you're in the countryside, and you might as well be on the dark side of the moon at this time of year. No streetlights, no traffic and only the occasional rooftop Santa Claus to remind you that you're still on earth. Or perhaps Santa Claus lives on the dark side of the moon. I told you I was tired.

'Right turn in half a mile,' I said. 'Should be signposted to … nowhere. I cannot see that this road goes anywhere.'

'Sure it goes where we want it to, so it's the road to everywhere.'

I left a pause. 'If you try that Irish accent out here we may be lynched. Slow down.'

We entered a tiny village and I was right: the road was totally unsignposted. I guess you have to live here to know where you're going. 'Another mile.'

Our final destination *was* advertised: Clover Cottage, 200 yds. I expected something on the road, but Rachael had indeed done her job. We had to turn through a narrow gate and go down a track through a field before we found a utilitarian box that had all the architectural merit of an RAF base, apart from the colour. It was pastel green. Either that or the lights on the van were broken. As I leaned on the roof to unkink my aching back and leg, I turned a full circle, and I couldn't see a single lit window from any other building. Perfect.

Rachael had already given Eseld a hug, and I told her how well she'd done when she did the same to me.

'Sod the spy stuff,' said Eseld. 'She's been cooking. Smell that.'

Rachael gave me a happy, simple smile and handed me a glass of red wine. 'Welcome to Ireland. Now take your boots off and sit down. Sorry there's no roaring peat fire. There's no fire of any description, I'm afraid.'

Raitch had cooked Irish beef slow braised in Guinness, served with sourdough bread. While that disappeared into the black hole of my stomach, she explained how the cottage had come to be here.

'The owner's a lovely bloke. He said that everyone who owned land where there had once been a dwelling was allowed to put up a house without permission.' She topped up our glasses. 'I read an article about that once. The Celtic Tiger boom. Anyway, it was his father who did it. The guy's older brother got the farm, and he got this place. He's a software engineer in Dublin, so he rents it out. I've got it on a week's trial with the possibility of a winter lease so that I can commune with my muse and compose the great novel of multicultural Ireland that's just crying out to be written.'

'And he bought that, did he?' said Eseld.

'I don't think he gets out much. You won't be disturbed here.' She leaned her elbows on the table and swirled her glass. There was already one empty bottle by the sink. 'That hotel you put me in last night was amazing. I've booked in again for two more nights from tomorrow. I'm having the all day Spa Journey on Thursday. Don't worry, no one from the hotel knows about this place.'

Eseld and I looked at each other. If I ordered her to fly home tomorrow, there would be an almighty row, and although she'd go eventually, I'd pay the price for months. Eseld didn't have that problem. As such. She thought about it for a second, then shrugged. I was inclined to agree.

'Sounds good, Raitch. What are your plans for tomorrow?' I asked.

Rachael didn't answer me straight away. 'What are the chances of you making it to Lady Hawkins' Christmas bash on Saturday? Both of you?'

This was a sore point with all sorts of people. My little sister, Sofía, is trying to break into the magickal entertainment business with her Fire Games show, and Rachael is her glamorous assistant. Eseld also has a role to play.

'You don't need me,' said Eseld. 'Celeste can be Hostess for the magick. Are you sure that Sofía is ready? I know she wasn't happy that you disappeared over here instead of rehearsing with her.'

I hadn't said anything because I have a lifetime's experience of Rachael's stratagems, and the main thrust always comes second.

Rachael sat back from the table. 'I think we should cancel. It would be really good if you told Sofía and Lady H.'

See? I told you.

Eseld was not happy. She started mopping up the gravy with her bread and thought about it. Unfortunately, Rachael was right in this instance. I hate it when that happens. Eseld chewed for a moment, then checked the calendar on her phone. 'When's Sofía getting back from Spain?'

'New Year's Eve,' I said. 'The Clarkes are going to the races on New Year's Day.'

'Hmm. Term doesn't start at Salomon's House until Monday the 11th. I'll nip outside to call Lady H while Conrad does the washing up.'

Rachael smirked. Luckily Eseld didn't see her. She also came to help me, giving me the perfect opportunity to ask a favour that only she could accommodate. I piled up the dishes and took some papers out of my adjutant's case. 'Can you solve these equations?' I asked.

Rachael may be a wizard when it comes to investing other people's money, and I swear that there's magick involved in some of her decisions, but the foundation for her financial sorcery is firmly rooted in her double first from Oxford. In maths.

'Equations? Are you winding me up? Let's see.'

I handed them over and started to fill the sink with suds. It took a few minutes for the significance of what she was reading to penetrate the fug of wine, then she swore. 'What on earth do you need these for? Or should that be *what in space*?'

'I can't say. If I told you my life might depend on it, would that help?'

'Seriously?'

'Completely. And don't tell Eseld. This one's for the Clarke family only.'

She looked at the papers again. 'Yes. No. I don't know. What values do you want them solved for, and why is there a red ring round *g(h)*?'

The outside door banged open. 'I should know tomorrow night,' I whispered. Rachael nodded and shoved the papers in her handbag.

'How did you get on?' I asked Eseld.

'Team Gitana is back in action on Saturday 9th of January. I think Celeste was quite relieved, actually, given what happened last time. I don't know about you two, but I'm knackered. And I don't know how you can drink that much coffee and sleep at night, Conrad.'

'It's a gift. See you in the morning. Did you get anything for breakfast, Raitch?'

'Yep. It's the one thing I know you can cook, dear brother.'

That was harsh. Harsh but fair. 'See you in the morning,' I said. 'I'll lock up.'

I went outside to call Mina, who was already in bed. It wasn't a long call, but I felt a lot better after hearing her voice. I flicked the light on in the little lobby so that I could check the door properly. On the wall was a deep picture frame with a green spot in the middle and text underneath. I went over to look and the green spot turned out to be a tiny plant, pressed behind the glass.

The heading said *A Galway Five Leaf Clover.* This is the text underneath:

The original building on this site was called Clover Cottage because it was in a meadow where the plant grew thickly. The cottage fell to ruin over a hundred years ago, and when it was rebuilt, this five leafed clover was found growing next to the doorstep. It is estimated that only one in 20,000 clover plants has five leaves and they are said to bring great luck. We hope that some of the luck rubs off on you and that you enjoy your stay.

I touched the glass over the plant and thought of Mina. Right now, I'd take whatever luck I could get.

Wednesday morning brought rain, three full stomachs and a message from Orla, the best friend of Oighrig Ahearn. She wanted to meet us at the Spiddal Craft Village, a few miles along the coast from Clover Cottage. The only one who was unfazed by the weather was Rachael. 'It's dry in the shops,' she noted.

Is it possible to drive along the edge of Galway Bay without *Fairytale of New York* running through your head? It wasn't for me. I'm sure it's beautiful out there, though whether the NYPD Choir would sing about it on a day like this is another matter.

We parked at the Craft Village at the same time as a coach with Ulster Tours blazoned on the side disgorged its unhappy campers. Rain was already running off my new waterproof hat like a leaky gutter, and I pointed to the tourists. 'Why?' I said.

'Search me,' replied Eseld. 'Pre-Christmas shopping trip? Cheap rates at the hotels? Maybe they were on their way to Knock Shrine and got lost.'

'I don't think you can get *that* lost and still not know where you are, especially as it's half way between here and Belfast. You've forgotten your extensions.'

'What?'

'When you pulled your hood up, you forgot your hair extensions. They're outside the hood.'

'Shit. Damn the bloody things. It's your sisters' fault. Both of them, but especially Rachael. Can we go somewhere dry to wait?'

'We won't get in the café, that's for certain. Which places are even open?'

We walked into a central plaza surrounded by squat craft outlets and workshops. I think they'd used the same architect as Clover Cottage, squat boxes hunkered down against the wind. The bright orange they'd chosen for some of the exteriors probably looked good in the summer.

'That one's got a light on,' said Eseld, pointing to *Andrea Rossi – Art Studio.* 'Do you think she's Italian? If she is, wouldn't she rather be painting sunlight on the Arno or something? I know I would. And try not to drip on the paintings, Conrad.'

The little shop was a haven of warmth, and we both stood inside the door for a moment, enjoying the heat and letting some of the water run off us. The room was crammed with fixtures and boxes of framed and unframed paintings. To the left was a raised counter, behind which a dark haired woman was attacking a small canvas.

I sent Orla a quick message to say where we were and shook the last drops off my coat. Now that it was safe to browse, we passed through a brightly coloured realm that banished the rain outside. We glimpsed strange worlds of nostalgia, surrealism, yearning, and often raw emotion.

Orla responded that she was in the queue at the café and asked what we wanted. 'You put our order in,' I said to Eseld. 'I'm just going to buy something.'

As well as the feature pieces, Ms Rossi also had a good amount of small block canvases aimed squarely at people like me: those who had wandered in and felt guilty for not buying something. I chose one with a pint of Guinness that said *The Glass is Half Full* and took it to the till.

I've been in a fair few art galleries over the years, and what impressed me most about this one (apart from her talent) was that every single scrap, from painted rocks to giant canvases, was from her distinctive hand. I passed some Euros over the counter and said, 'You must spend a long time building up your stock for the main season. It's impressive.'

She wrapped the canvas block quickly and gave me a smile. 'Sure, the winters in Galway are awwwwful long.'

Definitely Irish.

I followed Eseld back into the rain, my purchase safely in my poacher's pocket. I had absolutely no reason to be suspicious out here, but old habits die hard. I scanned the few people outside and checked to see if anyone was watching from one of the workshops. Nothing.

I caught up with Eseld and we repeated our rain dance inside the café door. It was easy to spot Orla in the queue: she was the only one who looked under thirty. I expected her to have red hair, but she's not an Ahearn, of course, being a friend of Oighrig's and not a cousin. Her hair was actually a light brown and she was dressed for a trip to the gym. In fact, if she'd been in a queue of young mothers and not seniors, you might not notice her at all.

She reached the serving station, and we joined her. 'Orla?'

She smiled an open, welcoming smile. 'I am. Pleased to meet you guys. I see you brought the weather with youse, because it never normally rains in Galway.' The server coughed politely. 'Sorry, that'll be two cappuccinos and a tea.' We looked round the room. There was barely a single seat left. 'We'd better get them to go, thanks.'

Eseld and I stood back until the order was complete. Orla handed out the drinks and said, 'Let's go to my car, unless you've hired yourselves a limousine or something.'

'We haven't. Thank you.'

Orla had a decent sized 4x4, and Eseld didn't argue when I called for the back seat so that I could stretch out. It only took me a minute to move the coats, boots and assorted junk out of the way. I was tempted to make a joke about women, handbags and the back of cars and then I remembered that there were two female Mages sitting in the front.

'Have you got a nice place to stay?' said Orla.

'A B&B in Salthill,' I responded. 'The full Irish breakfast was a feast, especially the white pudding. That was why we didn't want cakes.'

'Don't talk about breakfast, you'll make me hungry,' said Orla. She took the lid off her tea and blew on the liquid. 'Oighrig said I should answer all your questions and say nothing to anyone about youse being here. Now if that's not a red rag to a bull, I don't know what is.' She looked at Eseld. 'Your Da was Lord Mowbray, right? Does that make you Lady Eseld or something? I'm just asking because when you're all gone, I can say as I had a Lady in the car.'

Eseld pointed at me. 'He would say that I'm no lady, with or without a capital letter. If it's titles you're after, try him. He's got more of them than a library catalogue, but he's 100% Lord Guardian of the North.'

Orla looked at me and found me wanting. 'Nah. You're not selling it, Eseld. I love your accent by the way. I thought *Poldark* was great.'

That stumped Eseld completely, and she opted to drink her cappuccino rather than reply with more than an *Mmm.* I stepped in. 'You heard about Morwenna turning up last summer?' I asked.

'Too right I did. Has she reappeared?'

'In a way. We'd like to track down something she may have lost when she was here.'

Orla's eyes narrowed. 'Here? In Galway?'

'Somewhere around the shores of Lough Corrib, yes.'

'It's a big lough.'

'We'll stick to the two Queens,' said Eseld. 'Both of us want to be home for Christmas, so we might as well go to the top.'

'How very English of you,' said Orla. Her tone was dry, so dry that I couldn't work out how serious she was being. 'What do you want to know.'

'Not much,' I said casually. 'Where they live, what they're like, how to get in touch with them. That sort of thing.'

'Oh I like that, Lord Guardian. Are you serious?'

'He was born serious,' said Eseld. 'Unfortunately, I agree with him today.'

There followed two minutes of negotiation in the front seat while Orla sent Eseld a map with two pushpins in it, one at the north of the lough and one at the south giving the exact locations of the two Queens.

Having done that, Orla put her phone down and glanced from Eseld to me, then back to Eseld. 'I can't stop you turning up on their doorsteps, but I really wouldn't. If you want an audience with the Queen of the northern lough, I'd go to Corrib Castle first, and for the Queen of Galway, try the Menlough retreat. If they'll let you in.'

'Thanks,' I said. 'You live here, Orla. What are they like?'

'What are any Fae Queens like? Full of themselves and dangerous is what they're like. Let me open a window, it's getting steamy in here.'

She dropped the rear offside window and my feet started to get wet; Orla didn't seem to notice and carried on. 'The Queen of Inishsí is what you might call a social animal. She loves to throw a party and she puts a lot of money into the mundane arts community. She takes a very live-and-let-live attitude to most things, so long as you pay your tribute. The Queen of Galway is another creature entirely. Have you heard about why she got sent to the Aran Islands?'

'We have.'

'Well, she's up to her old tricks and no mistake. Because she lost so much territory after the Corrib Raid, she's been turning the screws on Mages all over the south of the county. It doesn't pay to get on the wrong side of her.'

'And people put up with this?' said Eseld.

Orla paused before answering. 'If by *people* you mean the likes of me, then yes, we do. The Queen of Galway also sponsors our little college of magick. If you're from the area, it's much easier to get a post there. Like I did.'

The way she looked at Eseld when she said the last part made it clear that she'd heard all about Eseld's appointment at Salomon's House, or at least she'd heard Oighrig's version of it. Pretending to change the subject, I said, 'Oighrig didn't even say whether Cathal was a Mage.'

'In a tiny way. He's a farmer, which is why I didn't ask you to come to the house. It's miles up a dirty lane. The only good thing about this time of year is that he doesn't have to get up so early for the morning milking.'

Eseld looked as if she were about to say something, so I got in quickly. 'Thanks for your help, Orla. And for the coffee – it's good. I'd better not tell Tom's girlfriend about it or she'll be over trying to buy the place. You remember Lucy, don't you Eseld?'

'Of course,' said Eseld, slightly bemused at the random shift in the conversation.

'We'll try the Menlough Retreat first,' I said. 'We'll stop off at the B&B on the way in case you want to do something with your hair. One problem I don't have.'

Eseld's hand snapped straight to the visor, and she slid back the cover on the vanity mirror. 'Shit. I'm gonna have to get these re-done or taken out before Christmas, aren't I? And I need to change out of these jeans. They're soaked.'

I'd started to move the detritus of the rear seats back to where I'd found it. 'Don't bother with that,' said Orla. 'Youse have got my number if you need it.'

'We have. Thanks again.'

'Yeah. Cheers, Orla. We'll keep you posted,' said Eseld, pulling up her hood and remembering to tuck her hair away.

I clamped my hat on my head, and we left the car. Our van was only a few metres away, and I chucked Eseld the keys. 'Head back to the city.'

She caught the keys and unlocked the doors. 'And while I drive, I presume you're going to tell me what the fuck's going on, are you?'

I got in the passenger side and looked over at Orla's car, giving her a wave. She smiled and waved back through the rain. When our doors were closed, I opened my rucksack. 'I need to multitask. Head off while I get my stuff lined up.'

I waited until Eseld was focused on exiting the car park before I pulled the units out and switched them on. We drove for a mile until I was satisfied. Eseld was far from satisfied.

'Right,' I said. 'I was just checking our van for listening devices or trackers. We're clear.'

'Isn't that a bit paranoid?'

'Not at all. It's what I've just done to Orla.'

'You came prepared,' she said angrily. 'Why didn't you tell me? And don't you dare say that you're telling me now.'

'I was giving you plausible deniability. Not that Orla's likely to report us. Let's get the audio on.'

Orla seemed a fairly cool customer, given that she doesn't have to lie for a living. I didn't think she'd have got straight on the phone, and I was right: all we could hear was background noise. I looked for a landmark and checked it against the map on the tracking screen. Orla was about half a mile behind us. 'Slow down a bit. Then when we get to Salthill, turn left at the roundabout.'

'Salthill? That godawful haven for grockels? Why on earth did you say we were staying there?'

You can take the girl out of Cornwall… In case you didn't know, a *grockel* is their word for tourists. 'First place I could think of with hotels. There's a straight bit coming up. Tell me what you can see in the mirror.'

'I can see … a blue Transit van.'

It is notoriously difficult to detect a Glamour on a vehicle behind you while you're driving. 'That's her.'

'Why is she following us?'

'To see where we're staying, I imagine. I doubt she'll linger once she's seen us go inside.'

Eseld's hands were gripping the steering wheel. She loves to roleplay and provoke people, and if I'd told her to have at Orla, she'd have done it with abandon. This was different. This was the girl underneath the powerful and confident woman.

'What did you think of Orla?' I asked.

'That she's kissed the Blarney Stone, or whatever the magickal equivalent is. She wasn't telling us everything, and her husband is not a dairy farmer. They get up at the same time every day of the year.'

'Well spotted. And there wasn't a trace of farming in all the assorted rubbish on the back seats.' I was going to ask her what else she'd picked up, until I remembered that she was not my work partner and told her anyway. 'Would you even dream of not meeting us somewhere proper, Eseld? Taking us where there was absolutely no magick was pretty brazen.'

She thought for a moment. 'Yeah.' After that insight, she lapsed into silence, increasing her speed without realising it.

We arrived at Salthill and turned left, heading away from the esplanade and up the High Street. I scoured the buildings for something suitable ahead. 'There. There's a B&B with a café. Pull over on the other side. She won't get too close until we're inside.'

She stopped, and we legged it over the road and into the café. I looked over my shoulder and saw a blue Transit flash past. I didn't get a sense of magick, but I wouldn't, would I? Eseld would have done, but she was too busy looking at the menu. 'Get sandwiches and tea to go,' I whispered. 'I need to get back to the van.'

I got inside just as the microphone picked up Orla making a call. Thankfully, she was doing it hands-free so I could hear Oighrig saying *Hello?* I pressed *Record* and prayed that I wouldn't need a rush job translating an illegally obtained recording from what I've learnt to call Gaeilge – the Irish word for their language.

'They've gone,' said Orla in English, and I breathed a sigh of relief.

'How did it go?'

'I have no fecking idea how it went because those two are up to something.'

'Of course they're up to something. They're not over there for the good of their health, are they?. Was the whole "How do I find the Fae Queens?" not a big enough clue for you?'

'Knock it off, Oighrig. You haven't just had Lady Muck and her gamekeeper dripping all over your seats and stinking the place out. It's no wonder the British lost the empire if that's what their ruling class is like.'

'Why? What did they say?'

Orla huffed out a sigh. 'Sorry. I was just venting. They were politeness itself really. Now, are you sure that the big fella didn't have any help with that Dragon he's supposed to have killed, because he's little more magick than

Cathal, and that'll be why all he could snag for himself was a *drawck cael-yawk*. No wonder he left her behind. Now your cousin Eseld is another matter. She's powerful enough all right, but him…?'

'She's not my cousin. About Conrad? Who knows? Half the stories people tell about him *can't* be true. Hang on, you didn't see any kids hanging around, did you?'

'Kids? What do you mean?'

'Teenagers. He's got his own wolf pack, you know.'

At that point, Orla did switch to Gaeilge. Her remark was short, and almost certainly obscene. When she'd got that off her chest, she continued in English. 'No, there were no fecking teenagers, no dogs, no wolves, no Gnomes and no giant fecking moles. Just him and his bond-partner trying not to look at each other. You cannot be telling me they're just going to walk up to Inishsí and knock on the door.'

'Ach, who knows. They didn't ask about the family did they?'

'Not really. Conrad asked about Cathal in a very English, polite-conversation kinda way, but that's it. I span him the old farmer yarn. Dunno whether he bought it.'

'What are they doing now?'

'Back at their digs in Salthill. They said they were going to Menlough Retreat. No idea whether they were telling the truth.'

There was a pause, and I thought one of the connections was broken until Oighrig came back on the line.

'Do you think they have a suspect? Do you think they know which one did it?'

'They don't have a fecking clue. If they did, would you want to join in?'

Another pause. 'No, Orla, that's all in the past. Fear would be barking at their heels, though.'

'This is getting serious, Oighrig. Some of us have to live here you know. If they do something stupid, I don't want to get caught up in it. And there's your Ma and Sionainn to think of, too. If Conrad and Eseld upset one of the Queens and they come looking…?'

'They won't.'

'And if something happens to one of 'em, will they have friends looking for revenge?'

'Look, Orla, I've seen enough of both of them to know that Conrad isn't stupid and he won't do anything stupid either. I think he'll skulk around for another day or so and then drag Eseld back to England.'

'I hope so.'

'Thanks. If they call you, don't answer it. Let them leave a message and let me know what it is. I really do owe you one, Orla.'

'You can pay me back when you come home for Christmas.'

The next pause sounded awkward even with five devices separating me and Oighrig. 'I'll do me best. Catch you later and love to Cathal, yeah?'

'Right. Bye.'

I peered through the rain at the café. There was no queue in there this time, but it looked like Eseld had been trapped by the patron. I decided to rescue her and scratch one of the many itches that the telephone conversation had generated: the one about *fear barking at their heels.*

Eseld's eyes had gone slightly glassy, and she jumped when I got to the counter. 'Oh, Conrad, Martha here was telling me about the new developments out Aughrim way. I let slip that we were looking to buy a holiday home.'

'Well, we need as much local knowledge as we can get,' I said. 'Talking of which … Martha, I've just had a strange conversation with an estate agent. Either they're trying to sell us a haunted house, or *Fear* is a name.'

Martha gave a low chuckle. 'It's a proper name all right. F-I-A-D-H. *Fiadh.*'

Martha was guarding the food and drinks as a way of keeping Eseld captive, so I used my long arms to reach over. 'Thank you so much. Are those ready? How much do we owe you?'

Eseld already had her purse out, and handed over the money with a generous tip; on the way out, we promised to come back for the special breakfast.

'What was that all about?' said Eseld as we climbed back in to the van. I stashed the food, passed over her drink and lit two cigarettes. 'Head off, turn right ahead and head back the way we came. I'll play you the tape.'

By the time it had finished, we were nearly back at Spiddal, and Orla's car had come to a stop half way between the Craft village and Boliska Lough, and straight inland.

'What are you going to do?' said Eseld, eyes fixed firmly on the road.

'I'm sorry you had to hear that. It's not always good to know what people really think of you.'

'I've heard worse. Dad used to call them *The Koi*. Big fish in little ponds, and not just Ireland. So, what are you going to do?'

'We. I'm going to suggest that *we* pay them a visit. Have a proper chat. Because without more intel, we've got nothing, and I really will go back to England. Oighrig is right: until we can narrow it down, we don't know which of the Queens is our target. And clearly they have no idea either.'

'They've got a suspect, though,' she replied. 'They think it's Galway.'

'Or they want to think that. Turn right ahead.'

She ignored me, and actually returned to the Craft Village. 'I need a pee before we go any further.'

'Good. We can swap over. I need you to scan for Wards.'

'Glad I'm good for something,' she muttered. I chose to ignore that one.

Back in the van, we were past the straggle of houses and into the countryside before she spoke. 'Are you going to be armed?'

'The last time I called on an Irishman without my Ancile, he shot me.'

'Is this the Rubicon?'

'No. This is just a normal day at work for me.'

12 — Cousins

We turned off the narrow country road and I slowed right down.

'Nothing yet,' said Eseld. I drove another couple of hundred metres further. 'Stop. There's something. On the right. A concealed drive.'

'What level of concealment? Wards?'

'Undergraduate stuff. I can pick that apart without getting out of the van. Good job, too, that rain's got worse again. Close your eyes.' It took her less than a minute. 'Open them.'

I turned into the lane, and the slope increased, as did the density of trees. We'd soon be at the river. The lane ended at a T-junction, joining another lane that ran up and down the river. Orla's car was somewhere to the right. Out of habit, I looked left and quickly put my foot on the brake. Coming down the lane was a man in a long waterproof coat, carrying a staff and accompanied by an enthusiastic Irish setter. Boy, I would not want to be drying that dog's coat when they got home.

Eseld had turned to see what I was looking at. 'Do you think that's him?'

'Bound to be. There was a dog chewing ring in the rear footwell of Orla's car. Let's say hello.'

I grabbed my new sword and slung it over my shoulder before getting out. Now that Lloyd has got to know my magick better, the bond he'd created allowed me to activate the Ancile without touching the hilt first. Handy.

I limped round the car, and Eseld joined me. The man had stopped and told his hound to sit. The dog looked very reluctant to do that.

'Good morning,' I said. 'We're looking for Cathal Ahearn.'

He'd been looking at Eseld, as usual. Well, she is the proper Mage, isn't she? He turned to me. 'Who wants to know?'

Whenever people say that, it's as good as saying *You've found him.*

'I'm Conrad Clarke, and this is Eseld Mowbray, half-sister to your cousin, Morwenna. We've been talking to your wife, and we left something in her car.'

He frowned. Deeply. 'You tracked her down at the gym?'

''Fraid not. We met by appointment at the craft village.'

He was not a happy bunny, and we were the only ones he could direct his anger at. He thought about it for a second and reached into his pocket. I tensed for half a second until he withdrew nothing more threatening than his phone. Orla answered almost straight away, and this time I had no clue what he was saying because he went straight to Irish. He listened. He gave what sounded like an order. He listened again, and then he disconnected.

'She's coming up. I'll not have you at my home. Either of you.'

If Eseld was thinking about telling him that it was Orla's home, too, she kept it quiet. Probably because Orla was even less likely to invite us in for a dish of tea. As they don't actually say in Ireland. Talking of tea...

'Of course, Cathal,' I said. 'Excuse me a second.' I opened the van door and slung my sword inside. I retrieved our cups of tea and passed Eseld hers, along with a smoke.

I turned my attention back to Cathal. 'Orla told us you were a dairy farmer for some reason. Were you out in this weather for business or pleasure?'

He looked down the lane, from where his wife would appear, and he pursed his lips. I'm sure the words *You had no right* would be spoken when they were alone later.

'I'm a *Walker of the Ways*, as we call it. Junior Geomancer is what I'd be at Salomon's House. I find that if I don't put in a few miles every day, I get very itchy.'

According to Britain's Earthmaster, I'm a bit more advanced than a *Junior* Geomancer. Cathal was like me a few months ago – he could find and trace Ley lines, and probably pronounce them sound or damaged. From his age, that would be about his limit. On the other hand, he'd never be short of well-paid work.

His left eye twitched, and he blinked slowly. Some inner struggle had come to the surface. He turned to Eseld. 'Is Morwenna alive? Do you know where she is?'

Eseld nodded. 'She's alive. Alive but hurt. Badly hurt. She was made a Vessel, Cathal. Here in the West.'

An oath in Gaeilge. 'I want to ask if you're sure, but you wouldn't be here if you weren't, and you wouldn't lie about that. I'll ask anyway: are you sure?'

'About being a Vessel? Absolutely. About who did it?' She turned to me. 'Conrad? You questioned her, not me.'

'I wouldn't stake my life on it, Cathal, but I'd stake almost everything else, yes. That's why we're keeping a very low profile. Morwenna said it was one of the Queens.'

'You do right to lie low, then,' he said. 'I take it that you got to Orla through Oighrig? No need to answer, it's obvious. Which one of ye?'

We glanced at each other, and I spoke. 'Eseld works with her, but it was me who saw her last week.'

'You work at the College, eh? Bit of a come-down for a Mowbray, I'd have thought.'

Cathal and Eseld looked at the road behind me, which meant that they'd heard something. The dog stood up, too. Before I could turn round, I heard it as well, the growl of Orla's diesel engine going too fast for the gear she was in. I turned round just as she slammed her brakes on, blocking the drive to their home. She jumped out and strode towards us, a "hers" version of Cathal's long coat now covering her gym gear.

She threw the bug and the tracker at my feet from a distance. 'Yours, I think.'

I bent down and picked them up, shaking the water off them and checking for damage. Both were still live. I shoved them in my pocket and smiled at her. 'Thank you, Orla.'

Her cheeks were red, and she pulled her coat tightly around her; the rain was already sticking her hair to her head. She turned to her husband. 'I'm so sorry, Cathal. I should have known they wouldn't deal fairly with us. We can't trust them.'

The dog whined at her mistress, and for a fraction of a second, Cathal's eyes met mine. He nudged the setter's neck. 'Go on, say hello to mammy.' The dog shot across the wet ground, splashing in puddles and diving at Orla's feet. Orla let go of her coat to brace herself, and the dog jumped up, thinking it was an invitation.

While his dog was plastering mud, water and slobber over his wife's pastel outfit, Cathal spoke up. 'Talking of trust, did you have a good time at the gym, Orla? And when were you gonna tell me about Morwenna, eh? She's my cousin. My choice whether to see these two or not.'

Orla fended off the dog and pulled her coat closed again. 'And Oighrig is also your cousin. She doesn't want you dragged in to this, and neither do I.' When he said nothing, she started to blink back tears, as well as rain. 'I was wrong, okay? I should have told you. Sorry.'

'Here, girl. Come on,' said Cathal, summoning back his dog. When she was at his side, he looked at us. 'What do you want? Whatever it is, you'll have it standing here or not at all.'

'Fiadh. Who is she and where can we find her?'

'Ca…' Orla started to speak, then thought better of it.

Cathal removed his hat and wiped water off his face. Underneath the headgear, he had the Ahearn ginger, but shaved close to his head. He put the hat back. 'She's Dara and Sorcha's girl. Find Moycullen and leave the town on the road north. Half a mile you'll see a turning to Loch an Rois – Ross Lake – and the Market Tavern. That's her place. It's common ground, so don't take that sword of yours in there. You'll be safe without it. Tell her I'll see her at the weekend and that we're both looking forward to it.'

Eseld surprised me by saying, 'Is that a coded message?'

It surprised Cathal, too. 'You what? Heavens, no. It's a pre-Solstice dinner I'm talking about.'

'Will Fiadh be there?'

'She's nowhere else to be,' he said, somewhat cryptically.

'Then thank you, Cathal. One last thing, if you don't mind. What's a *drawck cael-yawk*?'

'No!' said Orla.

Cathal glanced at her. 'A Droch Cailleach is a poor excuse for a Witch, Mr Clarke. If that's what Orla called Ms Mowbray, what did she call you?'

'Nothing, and it wasn't Eseld. We'll be on our way as soon as we can turn round.' I looked at Orla. 'And I won't tell Mina what you called her. You can thank me later.'

I touched my hat to them both and went back to the car. Cathal and his dog retreated, then Orla got into her car and reversed back from the junction. Another minute and we were on our way.

'We are not going straight there,' said Eseld with a degree of finality that brooked no opposition.

'Why?'

'Because we are going to Clover Cottage and I am going to do my hair and change my clothes before I dissolve into the mist.'

'One condition.'

'What?'

'If this place really is a tavern, I should point out that I've been in Ireland nearly a whole day and the only Guinness I've had was in last night's dinner.'

'No chance. Either we toss for it or we both stay sober.'

It was a tavern. A big one by Irish standards, and in the middle of nowhere. Given the weather and the isolation, I didn't expect to see a dozen cars in the large car park, nor the stable with three horses in it and an ostler sheltering from the rain.

Ostler. Now there's a word you don't get to use very often. 'Ten Euros to park your horse,' I said. 'At least that's what I think the sign means. I'll drop you by the door so you can run in.'

Eseld slipped off her seat belt. 'Thanks. I still think you cheated. Sofía must have shown you how to make that coin come up heads twice in a row.'

I pulled up by the door. 'She couldn't teach me that if she tried. Lloyd does a nice line in double-headed fifty pence pieces, though.'

She couldn't decide whether I was being serious, so settled for a, 'Sod off, Conrad,' before she exited. I parked the van and joined her inside.

The Market Tavern had not one but two roaring fires, both very popular. As soon as I walked in, the smell hit me: earth and sawdust, and it was good to know that my Nimue-given sense of magickal hadn't worn off. At least some of the patrons in here were Fae, and it was hard to tell which because they were *all* staring at Eseld. This was very bad news. I had one chance to salvage the situation.

I waved at the room. '*Guten tag!* Hallo.' I pointed to an empty table from where you could see the fire. 'It is okay to sit here, yes?'

A smooth voice from behind a pillar, deep and masculine, spoke up. '*Willkommen in Irland, Herr...?*'

'*Georg und Fraulein Kathe Bäcker auf Mainz.*'

It was a desperate throw, and if the nosy punter asked a follow-up, it wouldn't be long before we were in serious trouble. Not now, but soon. Not here, on common ground, but somewhere dark and out of the way.

There was movement from the bar. A young lad, no more than eighteen, hurried towards us. 'I'm so sorry sir, but the kitchen's closed now. If you're wanting a drink, please, make yourselves comfortable. All are welcome in the market, not that there's an actual market today.'

'Thank you,' I said slowly, keeping up the German accent and pulling a chair back for Eseld.

'*Danke*,' she responded, not to me but to the lad.

I stuck to German and asked Eseld if she wanted coffee, hoping she'd at least guess.

'Ja, bitte.'

'One pint of Guinness and one coffee, please.'

'Coming right up.'

It had worked. For now. The rest of the punters had gone back to their conversations or their solitary drinking, but we were under no illusions: at least one of them would be using magickally acute hearing to listen to every word we said.

Eseld was now wearing a long skirt in a subdued tartan which meant that her phone was no longer in her back pocket. It was in her hand. With actorly aplomb, she pretended that she'd received a message. She unlocked the screen and opened the app, pretending to read. She said, '*Auf Klaus*,' and passed it to me.

I peered at the empty screen, then nodded my head and passed it back, saying, '*nach Weihnachten*.' *After Christmas*. This gave her an excuse to tap a message quickly and show it to me.

What the fuck are we going to do now??????

Direct and to the point. And then it struck me. This was a place of magick. I raised a Silence and turned my lips away from the crowd before touching Eseld's arm.

'As soon as the Guinness arrives, I'll send word to Fiadh. Hopefully she won't want to talk in public.'

'I'll play with my phone. Hang on, you didn't introduce me as your wife, did you?'

'Sister.' She gave me the look. 'What?'

I glanced at the bar and saw that the Guinness was getting its second pour. In a moment, the lad was coming over, and I handed him a business card wrapped in a twenty Euro note. 'Thank you. Is Frau Ahearn in the building?'

'Erm, danke you, I mean, thanks, sir. I'll just see.'

On the back of the card, I'd written *Cathal sent me. Could we have a word?*

The lad didn't head to a back room, he headed round to a nook at the side of the second fire in the far corner. I was just savouring my Guinness when a woman stood up and stared at us. She said something to her unseen companion and started to work her way over.

If this was Fiadh Ahearn, you wouldn't guess she was Oighrig's cousin. Her father was Dara Ahearn, Muireann's son who'd died in the Corrib Raid. Fiadh must take after her mother, Sorcha, who'd died alongside her husband. Fiadh had dark, almost black hair and lines around her eyes that went with her likely age. She was wearing a black woollen dress, black tights and black boots, the professional woman's winter uniform. Her expression was welcoming in a way that hid whatever it was she was really thinking.

'I'm sorry, sir, I didn't know you were here. You're a bit early, or I'd have been waiting on youse. I'm Fiadh Ahearn. Pleased to meet you.'

'Georg Bäcker,' I said, shaking her hand. 'My sister, Kathe.'

'Hi,' said Eseld as they shook.

'Come with me.'

We followed her out of the bar, through a darkened dining room and into a comfortable office, the sort that said she did more than run an oversized pub. There was a tiny fire in here, and she added another couple of sods of turf (dried peat). This room must have been in the oldest core of the tavern, so old was the stonework. She had a desk at one end, with a laptop, and an antique display cabinet with all sorts of weird items in it. The lighting was dim at that end of the room or the spirit of my father would have driven me to examine it.

I'd sent one of my *George Baxter* cards over to her in the bar, and she held it up. 'How the hell do you know my cousin? And which is real, *George* or *Georg*?'

'Neither. I'll let Eseld explain.'

As soon as I said Eseld's name, Fiadh's eyebrows shot up. 'This is going to be good. Have a seat, and I'll be back in a second. Are you alright with coffee?'

'I'm driving.'

We sat down on one of two small couches, and Fiadh slipped out of the door. She was only gone a second and returned with a glass of wine. There was no welcome, no lifting of glasses or offers of food. She just sat down opposite us and said, 'Go on.'

Eseld told Morwenna's story while Fiadh's eyes burned into her, not dropping once. Eseld finished by saying that she was there on behalf of all the Mowbrays, including Ethan.

Fiadh frowned and looked at me. 'Are you not Ethan? I heard he had a German fiancée.'

'Tyrolean, not German,' I replied. 'I thought you'd have guessed. I'm Conrad Clarke.'

Her next question shocked me. 'Did the Wanderer send you?'

'The Allfather? No. He's not my patron.'

'Wearing that ring, you could have fooled me.'

'You could say he's invested some capital in my future. That's all.'

Eseld pressed on. 'Why did Oighrig want to keep you from us?'

'Because she loves me, that's why, and she wants to keep me out of trouble, and when it comes to the Queens, I'm nothing but trouble. Trouble Incarnate.' She paused and wetted her lips. 'I'll help youse any way I can, but you're in a terrible bind. If you pick the wrong one…' She lifted her eyebrows. She didn't need to fill in the rest.

Eseld looked at me. Her shoulders had hunched up under her velvet jacket. The close encounter in the bar had brought it home to her just how exposed we were out here. We needed allies, and we weren't doing well so far. 'Excuse me,' I said. 'My leg's playing up. I'll just lean against the fireplace for a minute.' As I stood up, with my back to Fiadh, I pointed at Eseld, then dragged my finger to our hostess: *Your call*, was what I hoped she got from the gesture.

Eseld finished her coffee and put it on the floor. She flicked her eyes to me, then back to Fiadh. 'Conrad doesn't do subtle when it comes to magick. Everything here seems so … amplified. I'm sure the whole place knew when he put a Silence on in the bar, and I can feel something radiating out from the back buildings. I've not been somewhere like this before.'

Fiadh settled back and crossed her legs. 'Do you not have common ground over the water?'

Eseld shook her head. 'Not really. We have Dwarves and Gnomes instead. They handle most of the magickal commerce.'

'Aye, and haven't they made an almighty balls-up of it? Weren't you connected to that, Conrad?'

'You could say that.' I was anxious that Eseld took the lead, so I pushed it back to her by saying, 'What did you mean by *amplified*?'

Fiadh answered. 'We have a Truth Stone. No one knows whether the market is here because of the stone or vice versa. Folk come from all over to strike bargains and have a natter.'

'It's powerful. It must take a lot of maintenance,' said Eseld. She waved her hand, searching for the right term. 'Isn't there a re-folding combinant in those?'

Fiadh shrugged. 'Sure there is, but it's not as though I've anything else to do.'

Eseld frowned. 'I'm sorry?'

Blank look from Fiadh. 'Cathal sent you, so he must have told you.'

'He told us where you were, and only because we asked. Your name came up in another conversation.' She remembered something else. 'Oh, and he asked us to tell you he's looking forward to tomorrow night. I think he wanted to be sure you'd remembered.'

'How could I forget? And he didn't tell you why I'm here?' Fiadh was getting worked up a little. She sat up and uncrossed her legs. 'He didn't tell you about the price on my head?'

Eseld's eyes bulged. 'Erm, no…'

Fiadh roared with a dirty Irish laugh. 'I don't know who's the biggest eejit: youse two, him or me. I haven't gone beyond the Market's boundaries for fifteen fecking years. Fifteen years.' She shook back her hair and finished her glass of wine. 'As you no doubt know, I have no parents, and no one to pay for me at the college. Grainne and Michael had to save every penny for Oighrig 'cos they didn't know if she'd get a scholarship.'

Eseld and I glanced at each other. We both knew that Oighrig had studied at Salomon's House in London, so…

It was as if Fiadh had understood our glance. 'Oighrig went over the water because of me and what I did.' She rubbed her hairline and looked at the ceiling. 'I had to sign a bond with the Queen of Galway for three years service. When it came due, she wanted me to serve in the sídhe. I said *Hell No*, she said *Hell Yes* and sent a Count of the Grove to pick me up. I killed him, stole his horse and fled. The dogs caught up with me at Ross Lake, and the Queen herself wasn't far behind. I just made it here, so you can see that I don't get out much.'

'And the Fae have long memories,' said Eseld, finishing off my thought for me. 'You've done well, though.'

Fiadh snorted. 'There's two empty glasses here. Your man'll have another pint, so can't I tempt you?'

Eseld put on a theatrically pained expression. 'He has many bad habits, most of which are catching. Abstinence before driving and flying is one of them. Immunity to caffeine is another.'

'Right you are.' She sprang up and went to the door. She opened it a fraction and shouted, 'Donal! One Guinness, one merlot, one coffee. Soon as you like.' She stayed at the door and turned back to us. 'I've *done well* as you say because the tavern was a near ruin and the old dear who ran it didn't give a rat's arse about the place outside market days. I've also done well because the Queen of Inishsí lent me a stack of money to do it up, just to put Galway's nose out of joint. I've paid her back, but Galway won't set a blood price, and I can't force her.'

'I … I'm sorry,' said Eseld. 'I didn't mean… It must have been very, very hard for you.'

'The first couple of years were terrible. You know what, Eseld, every day I give thanks to the Morrigan for her creating Internet shopping.'

Eseld stood up to pass our empty glasses to the barman, then stood next to Fiadh. 'Conrad's fiancée claims that Ganesh invented Internet shopping and bought shares in Amazon. From what I've heard, it's not the Morrigan's style. Or am I wrong?'

Fiadh took the tray of new drinks and closed the door with a bump of her hips. 'Hey, I'm not gonna argue, but I'll tell you this: I sacrificed to the Morrigan and the next thing you know, Net-a-Porter start delivering in Ireland. Cause and effect, obviously. Now how can I help?'

Eseld had done a good job, but she'd reached the limit of what she could fish for. 'Conrad has a few questions. I hope.'

I lifted my glass. 'How is it pronounced, exactly?'

'*Sláinte*,' said Fiadh.

We joined in and drank each other's health. The women looked at me, and I said, 'Fiadh. Tell me everything you can about the Corrib Raid, starting with how you escaped.'

13 — You Pays your Money

'My Grandma saved me. She had a choice, a choice no mother should have to make: stay and try to save her son or run and save her granddaughter. She ran, and she barely made it. I've felt her guilt every day since I was old enough to understand, and it didn't stop when she passed. And before you ask, no, I didn't get to go to the funeral, and Oighrig wouldn't let the hearse come up here. I've a bone to pick with her about that. What else do you want to know?'

I'd moved back from the fireplace to sit next to Eseld. Fiadh was sitting with her back ramrod straight, holding her glass of merlot like a chalice. 'How the Queen of Inishsí did it.'

She nodded slowly. 'That's the question I've been asking myself all these years. It's one of the reasons I fell out with the Queen of Galway: she won't let it be mentioned in her presence, and I wanted answers. As far as I can tell from fifteen years of eavesdropping in the bar, there was a traitor. He or she somehow gave them access to Corrib Castle during the night. Most of the Princess's guards were dead before the enemy landed on the shore. That's the bit they don't talk about.'

I opened my case and took out the bag containing the Door stone. I slipped out the rock and showed it to Fiadh. She leaned forward to examine it, but didn't touch it. She gave a low whistle and looked up. 'That's your proof of treachery, alright. The Prince used that to enter Corrib Castle sídhe, and it could only have been set from inside.' She sat back. 'I'll not ask how you came by it, but I'd love to know.'

It could almost have been Mina speaking: two contradictory statements jammed together to form a new sort of truth. I shook my head. 'Sorry, Fiadh. Maybe later.'

'Still doesn't answer the question, though: we've always known that Inishsí carried out the Corrib Raid. Doesn't tell us who made Morwenna a Vessel.'

'It doesn't. Two more questions and I'll have my answer. First, and I'm sorry to ask, but what happened to the mortals who didn't escape?'

She closed her eyes, and her lips moved in a silent invocation before she spoke again. 'They were lined up on the dock and beheaded. The bodies were left to the birds until the peace was signed, then the new Prince of the Lough sent the families the price to recover them. Bastard.'

It is amongst the Fae's least admirable traits: if they kill a human, they charge you to get the body back. I nodded sympathetically, then asked my final question. 'Can you name all the mortals who died?'

'I can.'

And she did, and one of them clinched it for me.

'What can you tell me about Medbh?'

On my left, Eseld drew in a sharp breath.

'Not a lot. She was a member of the Coven of Corrib and her parents had no magick. They also had a great respect for the Church and cast her out. Why? I know that Morwenna called herself Medbh, but it's a very common name.'

I took out my notebook and flicked back to the time that Morwenna had given the first account of where she'd been. I held my thumb under the statement and showed it to Fiadh.

She read it out, 'I was in the sídhe of the Princess of Corrib herself. So?'

'We didn't suspect at the time that Morwenna was a Vessel. I think that one of the original Medbh's memories spoke for her, out of panic. There hasn't been a Princess of Corrib since the Raid. Only someone who'd actually been there would have said that. Nerves added a moment of truth to the lie.'

Fiadh sat back, blinking sudden tears away. 'I don't know what to say. Is that enough?'

'It is for me. I have other evidence that I can't share with you, mainly that one of them came into a lot of old magick the year before you were born. Enough to mount the Raid with confidence.' I turned to Eseld. 'And you?'

'Yes.'

I turned back to Fiadh. 'Thank you. You've unlocked the puzzle. We know who our target is now: the Queen of Inishsí.'

'And what are you going to do about it? Knock on the door and ask for a polite word?'

'I'm going to see the Queen of Galway, of course. My enemy's enemy is my friend and all that. The only problem is that I don't want Inishsí finding out.'

'To Hell with it. You're a sign, you are, a sign that I need to bite the bullet and get out of here.'

'Fiadh!' said Eseld. 'You can't do that.'

'Can't I? I haven't told you the most embarrassing part of my captivity. When Inishsí lent me the money, you know what Galway did? She pronounced a death sentence on any man who fathered a child with me.' She gave a bitter smile. 'I've not been short of male company over the years, but it's cramped my style a fair bit. It's time for me to face her down.' She looked around the room, her eyes lingering on the cabinet in the shadows. 'Would it be too much to hope that youse two know horses?'

'We do,' I said.

'No, Fiadh,' said Eseld. 'This isn't your fight.'

'Morwenna is as much an Ahearn as she is a Mowbray, and my quarrel with Galway is *very* personal. You've no choice in the matter.'

Before Eseld could protest any further, Fiadh shot up and went to the door. She held the latch and looked at us. 'Get back in role, Georg and Kathe. Stand up and look German!'

She opened the door and used her best landlady's voice to shout across the tavern. 'Oy! Ballycraig! Get your useless arse in here now, before I chuck you out.'

We scrambled to our feet and stood together in front of the fire. Fiadh stepped back from the door to stand by her desk and waited. A few seconds later, a Fae noble appeared in the doorway. He looked half-cut, and looked like he spent a lot of time in the bar, judging from his waistline. He still radiated power, though. 'What's up, Fiadh?' he said. I doubt this was the first time he'd been called to the headmistress's study for a telling off.

She pointed the finger at him. 'I know you and your little pal Oughterard are only hanging on to see if you can find out what my German friends are doing here, well I'm about to tell you. Shut the door and listen.'

I'd felt magick in the door earlier. Presumably an anti-eavesdropping Work. Ballycraig closed the door and glanced at us. I'd folded my arms and Eseld had put her hands on her hips. Not exactly *German*, I know, but in Ballycraig's state he'd probably go home and swear that I was in lederhosen. He looked back to Fiadh and said, 'What's the craic, Fi?'

'Go back to your mistress and tell her that I've had enough. Tomorrow, I'm going to the city.'

Ballycraig looked very alarmed. Presumably he was Queen Galway's official spy here, and he probably thought his nice little job was about to come to an end. 'What for, Fi? What's up?'

She spat out the words. 'I'm going to get me fecking Christmas shopping in, you great gobshite. It doesn't matter why I'm going to the city, the fact is I'm going, and these two are coming with me.'

The Fae was sweating now. 'Oh?'

'Oh is right. They're both in the Riders of the Rhine, and their job is to keep the riff-raff away from me. If the Queen wants a civilised discussion, she's more than welcome to come along. Tell her we ride out at dawn.'

Ballycraig had had enough. 'Of course, Fiadh. I'll go now. Thank you very much, Fiadh.' The last was delivered as he backed through the door, closing it behind him.

'Riders of the Rhine?' I said, raising my eyebrows.

'It was the first thing I could think of. They won't be able to prove me wrong because they don't exist, do they? Right. Now that's over I need another drink because I'm suddenly very scared. How about youse?'

'I think I need a smoke. Is there somewhere dry?'

'There's a little smokers' bothy out the back. I'll show you.'

'And could you get a map while you're at it.'

Safe in the sanctuary of the old cattle pen, Eseld and I looked at each other. 'Are we mad?' she asked.

'Probably. I didn't expect it to work out this way. Not that I'm complaining.'

She looked at the rain (still falling) and sighed. 'Do you think Fiadh has a drink problem?'

'No. I clocked her little nook earlier, and there was a big mug of tea in her spot. On the other hand, I'm not denying that drink played a part in her little showdown there.'

'Do you have to see the Queen of Galway?'

'Yes. I'll tell you why.'

When I'd shown her and explained, she wasn't exactly happy, but she did understand. Before we went back in, I called Olivia Bentley at FERC. 'Part one is on, Liv. Head to Earlsbury.'

She groaned. 'Do I have to? It doesn't seem such a good idea any more.'

'If you want to pay for Christmas, I don't think you have a choice. If I haven't been in touch with Lloyd by ten o'clock tomorrow, hold your position and wait for advice.'

'Why?'

'Because I'll probably be dead. See you soon.'

Eseld was in deep enough to see the funny side. 'Great pep-talk, Conrad. Let's go back. What time *is* dawn tomorrow?'

'About half past eight.'

Back in Fiadh's office, she'd put on the lights over her desk and spread out a map. 'Do you want to stay here tonight or shall I help you get away without being followed?'

'I am not going riding in this,' said Eseld. 'And I've a few Artefacts back at the cottage.'

'Fine. What now?'

I stared at the map. Fiadh had marked the boundaries of the common ground – much bigger than I thought. We were south of Ross Lake, and the ground was in our favour. The lake drained into Lough Corrib via a series of small meres (or whatever that is in Irish), which meant the route to Galway took us downhill from the tavern. Perfect.

I traced a route with my finger. 'We'll go this way. You know her, Fiadh. How close to the tavern will she be waiting?'

She looked at the map. 'That farm, there. That's one of hers. She bought it specially, just to keep a better eye on me. She'll have a Sprite keeping watch on the tavern, and when she gets word, she'll come out to meet us.'

'Who will she bring?'

'Just her household. This is personal.' Some of what we were contemplating had sunk in while Eseld and I were out of the room. 'I've heard the stories, Conrad, but would you really take on a Queen in single combat?'

'No. I don't even want to take on her household. I just want two minutes of her time.'

'You don't want much, do you? Right, I'll show you the horses then get you on your way. It's going to be busy in here tonight. Should I say anything or should I hide myself away updating my last will and testament?'

'I think you should wait an hour, then appear and tell all who'll listen that you've had a change of heart. Pretending to get snivelling drunk would help, too. An audience is the last thing we need.'

'Fair enough.'

'One last thing: what are your magickal strengths?'

'Sorcery, you'd call it.'

'Good. Let's see these horses, then.'

There was a second lot of stables round the back. We'd glimpsed some of the market buildings when we went for a smoke, and in the last of the daylight they looked more like an abandoned barracks than a thriving business. Fiadh took us into the stables. 'This is the only thing likely to get me in trouble. I don't actually own any of these beasts.'

Only three were suitable for our purposes, all of them old and steady mounts who wouldn't mind a few scares and plodding through mud. Decisions made, we stood around for a second. Fiadh pulled down the sleeves of her dress over her hands and shivered at the wind. 'I don't know which of us is the madder: you, me or him, Eseld.'

Eseld gave me a vote of confidence. 'Oh, him. We'd not be in this boat if it wasn't for his family.'

'*Your* family, Conrad? How come?'

This was not a conversation I wanted to have with Fiadh. 'There's a question we haven't asked yet: how come Cliodhna was at the clinic on the day of the Raid? She didn't let in the attackers, but I don't think her absence was a coincidence, do you Eseld?'

'That's for another day, I think,' said Fiadh. 'I'll go and lock the tavern doors so no one follows you.'

14 — Ill Met by Daylight

We didn't sleep much last night. Not only did I want to talk through what might happen with Eseld, I also wanted to stop her self-medicating with the ample supply of wine that Rachael had left for us. Talking of Rachael, she sent me a message saying that she'd had a lovely day in Galway and that she'd bought my Christmas present. I dread to think.

I banged on Eseld's door at six o'clock. 'I've got you a cup of tea. Can I come in?'

'Umrgnhgha.'

I took that as a yes. I placed the tea by her head and dropped a package on the bed. 'One winter combat set, size twelve, women for the use of.'

'Unh?'

'They're warm, mostly waterproof and very hard wearing. And without badges, they're just clothes. See you in a bit.'

The Market Tavern's ostler was standing by the locked gate when we arrived. A black pickup had parked further down the lane, and a pair of beady eyes was watching us from it. 'That's one of Queen Inishsí's people,' he said when I lowered my window. 'Now you're here, I'll go and saddle up. Fiadh's in the kitchen.'

There was coffee and bacon sandwiches on the go when we found the back door. 'Don't youse two look the part, eh?' said our host. 'Very *Riders of the Rhine*. I must have been inspired.'

'How are you feeling?' said Eseld.

Fiadh placed her hands on the stainless steel counter. 'Scared shitless. How about you?'

'Sick. If this all goes brilliantly, we have to do it all again later.'

I do not normally hug my team. I put my arm round Eseld's severely belted waist and squeezed. 'There's such a thing as too much honesty, you know. Now eat something.'

She'd put her arm round me, and didn't let me go. 'Is that an order?'

'If it means you'll eat, then yes.' I pulled gently away and propped myself up. 'How was last night? I see there's a watcher in place.'

'Last night was humiliating. I learnt a few home truths, I'll tell you. Made me determined to go through with it, though. I'll be settling a few scores when this is over.' She dished up two plates of food and poured coffee. 'Now you've been spotted, Queen Inishsí will have someone watching discreetly.' She shrugged. 'Only to be expected, I suppose. At least it's stopped raining.'

'True,' said Eseld.

It wasn't true, but Eseld is from Cornwall, Galway's wet British cousin. For them, medium drizzle counts as a drought.

Fiadh drank her coffee. 'Tell me about Morwenna.'

It was a good way of focusing Eseld's mind. Twenty minutes later, with levels of protein, nicotine and caffeine nicely elevated, we led our mounts out of the stables and across a field. At the other edge was a gate, then a boggy field sloped down into the valley. I took a long, hard look at the terrain, verifying it against the map in my head: woods (avoid), a big pasture by the river (also avoid), a smidgin of smoke rising from the farmhouse (good), and several smaller pastures that could easily be a quagmire given the rain we'd had (take your pick).

'When we leave the common ground, pick up the pace and head to the left of the farm, okay?'

'Right, Chief.'

We mounted up and made our way across the field. 'There he is, on the wall to the left of the tree,' I said.

'Who? What?' said Eseld.

'A Sprite.'

'How the feck do you know? I thought you had no Sight at this distance.'

'I eat my carrots. Little fucker's laughing his arse off.'

'I see him now,' said Eseld.

'Aye, and I think he's got a message or he'd be gone. Ignore him. They hate that.'

We plodded on. The ostler had been out earlier and opened the gate to save us dismounting. We certainly weren't going to risk jumping on this ground unless it was life or death.

'Hey! Hey you! Stop!'

When we didn't, the Sprite launched itself off the wall and flew ahead of us, landing in Fiadh's path. Even in the rain, its wings glistened beautifully, picking up the greens of the field around it. A Sprite is effectively the larval stage of a Fae, and they look like toddlers.

Naked, sexless toddlers with too many teeth, an evil light in their eyes and wings. Yes, they have inspired both nightmares and horror movies. Fiadh would have carried on, but her horse wouldn't go near it without a lot of persuasion. Wise creatures, horses.

'Shift your shitty arse out of me way,' said Fi.

They have deep voices, too, just to add to the whole demon-child vibe. 'The Noble Queen says that if you come alone, on foot, she will consider being merciful.'

'Does she now? Well, tell your mistress that I'm going shopping, and if she wants a word, she should drop into the tavern tonight. I'm sure we can work something out. Now can a goblin like you remember a message that long?'

The Sprite worked its oversized jaws for a moment and spat out his response. 'You will suffer.'

'Not as much as you will if you don't shift out of my way.'

Sprites are not normally allowed out of the sídhe. For one thing, they're vulnerable to magick, and for another they can be very impulsive. This one repaid the Queen's trust by spitting on the ground and flying away, keeping low to the ground and running after a hundred metres or so.

'Ready?' said Fiadh.

I pulled my goggles up from round my neck and seated my hat firmly on my head. 'As I'll ever be.'

Eseld nodded, and Fi said, 'Let's go.' At little more than a trot, we headed down the slope. Half way to the next wall, I saw the creature reach the farmhouse. A section of the upcoming wall was down, and Fiadh headed for it. On the other side, a track appeared, running next to a small wood.

'Fiadh, check the trees,' I shouted. That point was exactly where I'd set an ambush, and the only thing stopping me from changing our route was the knowledge that Fae Queens don't wait in the rain for mortals.

We got nearer. 'Clear. No magick in there.'

Over the wall and on to the path. We picked up speed with a firmer footing under the horses' hooves. I also lost sight of the farmhouse now that we were lower down the slope. There were two more small fields between us and the river, and I changed my plan because the gate ahead was tied shut with baler twine.

'We need to gallop,' I shouted. 'Jump the gate and make sure they don't get us in the next field. Come on!'

I dug my heels in and urged my horse forwards. He responded, and his movement gave the other two mounts the impetus to follow. Onwards, faster. 'You can do it, boy … Up!'

He launched himself at the gate, and years of experience carried him over. I risked a glance behind, and saw Eseld sail over second, her hair trailing behind her now that her hat had blown off. I expected nothing less, and it was Fiadh who bottled it. She may have ridden round the common ground, but she was woefully out of practice in the wider world.

Shit, shit, shit.

I slowed and Eseld caught up. 'Can you make the next one?' I shouted. 'She can catch up.'

'Beat you over! Come on, girl!'

Bravado. Sheer bravado. So long as it got her over the wall, I didn't care, and I pushed my horse to follow. He did it again, a second behind his stable-mate, and as we rose up, I saw Eseld's horse plunge into a dark figure, pitching her off its back and into the field. Fuck. They'd moved faster than I'd thought.

My horse landed safely, and I scanned around. There were three or four shapes dodging in and out of visibility. Not the whole party, then. Just sentries. That didn't help Eseld, though. Time to make a stand. I pulled hard on the reins and dismounted.

Her horse had surprised a Fae and basically smacked straight into it, with both of them collapsing in a heap. Eseld had been lucky: this field was very, very wet, and her landing had been more of a slide than a fall. It had still winded her, though, and another of the Fae was heading for her with a drawn sword.

I couldn't reach her in time. I reached for my SIG, then changed my mind. If the Fae had an Ancile, I'd achieve nothing. As the Fae approached, he headed straight for a great pool of water. *Odin give me strength,* I prayed, as I swivelled, raised my left arm, and chopped it forwards, energising the air and sending every ounce of Lux I could summon into a blast. With an Ancile, it would do nothing. Without an Ancile, it wouldn't even trip him up, but I wasn't aiming at the Knight: I was aiming at the water.

It fountained up, into his face, and he tried to stop, flinching away and skidding. His feet went from under him and he landed on his back. Eseld struggled upright, and she was going to attack him until I shouted, 'No! Back to the wall.'

I drew my sword and headed to join her, via the Fae who'd been hit by Eseld's horse, a Squire judging from his size and androgynous face. In the niceties of things, they'd started this. The threat from the Sprite, and the Knight's drawn weapon meant that there was no peace here. I tested Lloyd's new sword by running the fallen Squire through the back. It worked a treat.

Until it got stuck. Damn those bloody cutouts in the blade.

'Conrad! Behind you.'

We were stuck, exposed. The Knight was making for Eseld, and I had a Squire bearing down on me.

KABOOM!

A noise like a small bomb bounced round the field from my left. The two-legged creatures (including me) all dived to the ground. The horses were totally spooked, and ran away from the noise, right at the Fae Knight.

The Squire who'd been coming after me had no clue what was going on, and that gave me the moment I needed to retrieve the sword. I would be having words with Lloyd about that.

The Squire brought up his weapon, I beat it down and thrust into his abdomen. The scream was almost as loud as the fake explosion. I turned, and had just enough time to force the Knight attacking Eseld to draw back from her. If he hadn't disengaged, I'd have had his exposed back as a nice target.

He saw the two bleeding Squires, and he could smell the cold-forged iron in my sword. It's the blood that makes it stink, apparently. 'Do you want to taste it?' I said. And then I switched to the Mother Tongue, the dialect of proto-High Germanic that Gnomes speak. I gave him a mouthful and stepped forwards. He called out in his own language, and they fell back in good order towards the farmyard, one of them trying to help the Squire I'd spitted.

I joined Eseld. 'You okay? No damage?'

She dipped her hand in a pool and wiped some of the mud off her face. 'I'm good.'

'That sound effect was spot on. I didn't know I had it in your locker.'

She shrugged with her face, too taut for the rest of her to move. 'Old party trick with a bit of *oomph*.'

'Help me over, you feckers!'

Fiadh had arrived at the wall on foot, out of breath and struggling to get over. The wall was barely rib-height for me, but Fi hasn't been out much lately. We heaved her over, and she surveyed the damage. 'Where are they? Oh, here they come. I can see magick building in the farmyard.'

'Right. You know what to do.'

We set to our allotted tasks and got ready to receive fire. When Eseld had finished, she retreated to the wall, and I took up guard, with Fi's hand on my shoulder. I've met a Queen once before, and she had ridden out in splendour with her court, and dressed to impress. That was not going to happen today.

We were up a slope, backs to the wall, and the farmyard was in the right hand corner downhill. On my own, I'd have known something was coming, but with Fi's Sight to assist me, I could see a dozen riders canter into the meadow and spread out, with three more behind them. The one right at the back wore red, a bright red waterproof, not that she needed it. Her black hair streamed out behind her, unbothered by the rain, because why get rained on when you're a Queen? Umbrella Charms are so easy when you're that powerful.

'Any without Anciles?' I asked.

'The four on the right. Your right.'

Now that they'd seen us, and seen that we were in a field where there was little room to manoeuvre such a number of riders, their leader shouted new orders. In the couple of seconds while they reined in and shuffled around, I crouched down and swapped my sword for the SIG inside my jacket. I've upgraded it a little recently, adding a laser sight to the rail. 'A Silence would be good.'

One of the Squires got his mount under control, and I had a second to draw to my sights and estimate the distance. As soon as I saw the green dot on his head, I fired. Without the noise of the gunshot, the Fae didn't know what was happening at first, and that gave me the chance to get another one. The Silence also meant that I didn't hear Eseld's warning.

A great weight smacked me in the back, flattening me into the water. Fingers scrabbled at my face, trying to rip my goggles off and get at my eyes. Tiny fingers. The Sprite. I reached behind, or tried to. I missed, and the creature's right hand ripped off my goggles. And then an even bigger weight landed on me, and with a gurgle, and then a *snap*, Eseld broke its neck.

'They're coming!' screamed Fiadh.

We were on our knees, and the riders with Anciles, all eight of them were heading towards us. I grabbed my sword, left the SIG where it was, and reached out to Fi for a hand up. Eseld had other things to worry about.

With twenty metres to go, the onrushing Knights hit the two Wards that Eseld had laid out for them. A few seconds of calm consideration and they'd have been able to unpick them, a few seconds that they didn't have because the Wards were aimed at the horses, not the riders.

Instead of a line to overwhelm us, the beasts swerved to follow the course of an invisible funnel, stronger in their minds than steel rails. Four of them smashed into each other at the opening of a bottleneck, two more pulled up short, and the two that made it through were spooked so badly that their riders couldn't control their mounts and their blades at the same time. Not only that, the spout of the funnel took them to my left, and with Fi's help I could just see the edge of the Ward. I stood behind it, knowing that the horse would pass close enough for me to…

Slash at empty air, because the rider threw himself to the ground to avoid my blade. The second one wasn't so lucky. His mount reared to avoid the fallen Fae, and I stepped forward to cut open his side.

'Out of my way ye eejits!'

It was their leader, and the only other Fae on the field to have taken female form. I knew she was the leader from her attitude, but I'd guessed before from the bright red leggings and white jacket, the Queen's colours. A bit like mine. If you fancy being a target.

The others backed or milled away and she had a choice: try to dismantle the Ward or come through the funnel and risk her mount panicking. She did neither in the end. She dismounted and came at me on foot. Good. 'Now, Fi!'

Behind me, Fiadh and Eseld joined hands and projected their voices so that they could be heard on the other side of the field, through the rain and over the sound of running water from the swelling river.

'A truce! A truce and parley!'

I squared up to the approaching Countess and engaged the magick in the sword fully. She had a long, fine blade, opting for length to counteract her lack of natural reach. The tip shimmered in the air, a Work of some sort held ready to discharge as soon as she got a thrust on target.

'Truce.'

The Queen's words whispered through the air so quietly you could almost miss them, and the Countess considered a bit of selective deafness. For a second. Just enough to make the point – to me. Then she put up her weapon and stood aside. Her Queen's horse splashed through the waterlogged ground and stopped ten metres away.

'Why should I parley with you, Fiadh Ahearn?'

I only found out that's what she'd said when Fi translated for me. I bowed a little and said, 'Not with her, your grace, with me.'

'And who might you be, stranger at my door?'

'Some call me the Dragonslayer.'

Now that I could see her face, I wondered at this Queen. She made no pretence of extreme youth, and a hundred people would guess her age from a photograph at around thirty-five. Her high cheekbones were a little too wide to be classical and her jaw a bit too square. Strong, though. It was hard to really know, because her eyes were hidden by riding goggles that were magickally darkened.

'A Queen always has something to learn,' she said. The ethereal voice she'd projected was gone, replaced by something thicker, a country voice used to winters on the farm. It still had a beautiful lilt, and she tilted her head when she'd spoken. She was intrigued. Good.

I bowed. 'Thank you. Shall we talk here under silence, or would you ride?'

She snorted, a bit like a bull. 'I would rather get out of this bog. Chase down your mounts and I'll see you in the farmhouse parlour.' She wheeled round and trotted off towards the farmyard.

I wiped my blade on the grass and sheathed it under the scrutiny of the Countess. As soon as it was on my back, she turned and went to supervise the collection of horses, the wounded and the dead. Except the Sprite. She left that to rot in the field.

I joined Eseld and Fiadh for a group hug. 'Thank you. Thank you both,' said Fi. 'You don't know how much that meant to me.'

Eseld was shaking with adrenaline and near-shock.

'You did brilliantly,' I said. 'You saved my life. All of our lives.'

Tears had started to run through the mud on her face. 'I couldn't let a Hawkins beat me. I saw Saffron break someone's neck at King Mark's Barrow. I know this was only a Sprite, but they don't need to know that, do they? Do they?'

I put my arms on her shoulders. 'A couple of deep breaths, Eseld.'

She nodded and blinked her eyes, then she looked at Fiadh. 'Do I look a total mess?'

'Sure, you look like a fecking hero to me, kid, and that's all that matters.'

15 — Parley

It is a very, very rare thing for a mortal to have a private conversation with a Fae Queen. Once we knew that Galway was not our target, I could have spent a month going through the levels of bureaucracy, and probably the odd duel, and still only had five minutes in a public audience.

Once we'd corralled the horses, one of the Fae who'd been right at the back made an appearance. It was a he, and he was no warrior. Some sort of chamberlain, probably. He offered my partners refreshment in the kitchen, and showed me through to the parlour for the parley. Sorry, couldn't resist that.

'For the love of the Morrigan, could you open a window. You stink, Dragonslayer, you really do, and I don't know which is the most obnoxious: the bog, the tobacco, the blood, or the whiff of Gnome you have around you.'

'And you smell of earth and rotting leaves, your grace. I'll open the window.'

A hastily lit fire was sputtering to life in the grate, and she'd taken the good chair in front of it, leaving a hard-backed thing for me, to which she pointed. 'That's not a snub, by the way, it's because you've mud all over you.' She wasn't wrong, and I sat with a nod of thanks.

The chamberlain appeared and fussed around with side tables and a tray. Even a Queen takes off her boots when she's a guest, and although she owns the soul of this house, it is not her home. Underneath the black breeches, she sported a pair of pink fluffy socks. She saw me looking and wiggled her toes, and that wasn't the most surprising about her indoor appearance. That was the black framed glasses. Whatever else they did for her, they made her eyes violet, and that was incredibly creepy.

When the chamberlain had gone, she drank some tea and looked at me. 'So, we have the Deputy Constable of England running around a bog in Galway dressed like a toy soldier. A man whose word is backed by the Allfather, no less, and he's consorting with a pub landlady. We've not figured out who your girlfriend is yet.'

'My fiancée is in Cheshire, and my friend in the kitchen is no doubt texting her even as we speak. Oh, and I'm an Airman, not a soldier. You'd be wise not to forget that, your grace.'

'Would I now?' The violet eyes bored into me. 'It was a close run thing out there, Mister Airman. It was only the fact that you'd risk death for a parley that swayed my hand. That and wanting to teach my bodyguards a lesson about risk assessment, the eejits. You have my attention for two cups of tea. Don't waste it.'

I drank some of the tea myself, because my mouth was suddenly very, very dry. 'It's simple, your grace. I want to bring down the Queen of Inishsí. You want the same. With your help, I can do it.'

Her hand jerked a fraction, enough to spill a drop of tea on to her high-necked silk blouse. She put down the cup. 'Tell me why.'

I pointed to the kitchen. 'My friend is Eseld Mowbray. Your rival made her sister into a Vessel without her true consent. She'll do it again, and worse, to other mortals. And I have my own reasons.'

'Morwenna Ahearn, eh? The Mowbrays would take in a Vessel and claim her as their own? Strange family.'

'She's no longer a Vessel. Apparently that was my doing.'

'She's still an Ahearn. Still a traitor's spawn.'

'Your grace?'

'Cliodhna sold herself and her child into bondage to escape the Raid. When I found out, I sent them packing. Or they were rescued by Inis, depending on your point of view. Aisling's premature death meant that the bond passed to Morwenna.'

'I saw it voided. She is one hundred per cent Mowbray now.'

'Voided how?'

This seemed important to her, for her own reasons, and I took a moment to explain what the Count of Force Ghyll had done, and how I'd laboured in my cack-handed way to fix it. I left out the bit about Harry Eldridge's twins. At the end, I moved on to the main event. 'I have found out what I can about the Fair Queen's people beyond Inishsí. What more can you tell me?'

'That the greatest of her offspring is well away from her over the water, and that the Prince of Lough Corrib is a preening peacock who's not fit to clean the jacks in Corrib Castle, let alone sit in my Princess's chair. The rest are useful idiots. Useful to her that is.'

She wasn't going to give me any more without knowing exactly what I was up to, so she made her position very clear. 'You do realise that you've almost no chance of succeeding, don't you? That doesn't bother me in the least, as I'm sure you know. What bothers me is any comeback. I cannot allow the Fair Queen to see my hand in this.'

I got that. I didn't need the Queen of Galway's army at my side. Or only one of them. I could also see her naked greed and desire for vengeance. This Queen has seen better days, and she's embattled here. Further discussion with Fiadh last night had let me plot the locations of the sídhe surrounding her heartland, and that was just the ones on the west coast. She had many, many more years to enjoy as Queen of Galway, but unless something changed, those days were numbered, and she knew it. When you can live indefinitely, any finite number of days is too short.

'I understand, your grace. I also believe that you are too wise not to take this chance. If I'm right, the Fair Queen won't be able to resist.' I let that sink in for a second. 'I hesitate to compare myself to a fruit, but I'm going to turn up on her doorstep like a ripe plum, to be eaten today or left to rot.'

'What do you want?'

'Four little things only. First, and this is non-negotiable, I want you to set a blood price for your late Count, the one that Fiadh killed. A price that's discounted for every year she's spent in captivity.'

'Go on.'

You'll notice that she hadn't said yes. She hadn't said no, either, so I continued. 'Second, I need an escort, up front and open, to the door of Inishsí. I'll simply tell her that I spoke to you first, and you passed me on. This is on me, not you.'

'I can live with that.'

'The third is your Favour, secretly. For afterwards. If I prevail.'

'I wouldn't double-cross the man who took down Inishsí. That's not my style, Dragonslayer. You shouldn't believe everything the Gnomes say about the People. My Favour, openly given after the event, is worth far more to you. And that's non-negotiable from me: I'm showing trust, so should you. What's number four, because you've not asked for much so far.'

I ramped up the politeness to somewhere beyond parody. 'Your grace is as wise as her years. The fourth boon is indeed the greatest.'

'Knock it off, I'm not here to flirt with you.'

Only a Queen would confuse flattery with flirtation.

'I need you to explain something to my sister. The mundane one, if you're interested.'

'Explain what?'

This was tricky. It does not do to patronise the Fae. 'In her terms, she wants some solutions to Einstein's Field Equations as they apply to gravitational time dilation within a sídhe. In your terms, I don't know the words.'

The violet eyes blinked behind the lenses, and the firelight was trapped in them. What she said threw me right off balance. 'D'you know Hledjolf the Dwarf?'

'I do.'

'It's said in London that what drove him mad was the realisation that he couldn't automate Lux. He wanted a machine to move his Hall out of this realm and on to a higher one. They say he scrambled his own brain trying to do it. Something to do with not being able to pull yourself up by your own bootstraps. I'm not a Dwarf, so I wouldn't know.'

She clearly thought that would make sense to me. I tried to show that it hadn't, and that it was my understanding that had fallen short, not her explanation. She wasn't interested, though.

'I agree, Mister Clarke. I will post the blood-price on the Solstice, and I'll waive Fiadh's bond even though you didn't ask for that. See? I told you not to believe everything the Gnomes say about us. We can be generous.'

'Thank you.' I deliberately hadn't mentioned the bond because I didn't think she'd agree. 'I'd like to say that Fiadh will be grateful, but I doubt it. I certainly am.'

She poured her second cup of tea. 'The escort isn't a problem. When and where?'

I checked my watch. 'Noon at the Market Tavern.'

'Fine. The Favour I've covered, so that just leaves your sister.' She broke off and looked at the door, then shouted in that weird language of theirs, when bits of sound drop out because the frequency is too high for humans.

The chamberlain came in and bowed. 'Your needs, Noble Queen?'

'My needs are his needs,' she said, indicating me. 'Give him your number, and contact my Privy Keeper. Tell her to give all help to the Dragonslayer's sister.'

The chamberlain's eyebrows rose a fraction. About a millimetre. Quite a shock, then. 'Of course. Anything else?'

She shook her head in a self-deprecating way. 'Today is a very strange day. Tell all the People that Fiadh Ahearn is free to go wherever she wishes, and tell Countess Portarra that she and her Squire are to meet the Dragonslayer at the Market Tavern at noon and escort him wherever he wishes. I will return to the city in half an hour; right now, I need to do some thinking.'

'Very good, your grace.'

He withdrew, and I stood up. I bowed and offered my thanks.

'May fortune smile on you, Mister Clarke. What do you think your chances are?'

'About the same as finding a five leafed clover.'

'I can see why the Allfather chose you. Until we meet again.'

'Your grace.'

I found a cleaner and dryer Eseld on the phone when I was shown into the kitchen. Fiadh was talking to the Countess of Portarra – assuming that she was the one I'd faced off with earlier, and they broke off when the saw me.

'She won't believe I haven't a clue what you're up to,' said Fiadh. 'Can you put her right, for goodness sake.'

There was a brightness to her voice, covering the emotion she clearly felt. I hadn't planned that she'd hear about her freedom from a flunkey, but that doesn't matter: she had put her life on the line for me this morning, and it's nice to see good deeds rewarded for a change.

I stretched out a hand, and Portarra reluctantly took it. 'She's telling the truth,' I said. 'Fi has no idea what I'm up to.'

Eseld had finished her call and gestured to the phone. 'Lloyd is on his way. No problems. Whatever that means.' She paused, giving me a dark look. When I'd asked her to call, I hadn't mentioned that Lloyd was already in Ireland. She carried on, 'And Mina says she has made an offering of thanks.' She smiled. 'She also said that the Napier crowd have arrived, and that only now can she concentrate.'

The Countess of Portarra coughed politely. As politely as she could. 'So what *is* going on? What should I prepare for?'

'This afternoon, you are going to escort Eseld and me to the gates of Inishsí, and then you're going to wait outside with her while I go in.

'What?' said Fiadh. 'If you're going, then I'm going.'

'And if you're going inside, then I am, too,' added Eseld.

I shook my head. 'I need you outside, Es,' I said. 'I'll explain why you can't help me inside when we reach the Rubicon, and I want you waiting for me when I come out. I really will need help then. And if I don't come out…'

She nodded. 'You need me to tell Mina.'

'I do. Hopefully it won't come to that. And you're welcome, too, Fiadh, but I don't want to keep you from your Christmas shopping.'

'The Devil take that,' she said. 'There's none of them worth more than what I can get from Amazon. I'm with you, Conrad.'

16 — A Gathering

There was a reception committee waiting for us at the Market Tavern. A committee of Ahearns, and none of them looked happy. I scanned the crowd, putting names to likely faces, and their expressions ranged from furious (100% Orla) to worried (probably Grainne).

Eseld and I hung back from politeness. From the back of her horse, Fiadh said, 'What's up with youse lot? You look like you've gone to a funeral and found it's cancelled 'cos the corpse got up and walked. Away with youse. I'm free, thanks to this pair of psychos.'

I've been called a lot worse, and smiled my greeting. Eseld just looked confused.

'What have you done, Fi?' said Grainne. 'This can't be good.'

'Yes it fecking well can.'

The professional hostess who'd first greeted us yesterday was now a distant memory, and there were issues here that didn't concern the English party. I hoped. 'Do you need us, Fi?' I whispered. 'We need to get ready.'

'What? Right! No, I don't. Thank you so much, Conrad, and you Es. Just leave the horses here.'

'See you in an hour or so.'

We dismounted, and an older man who had to be Cathal's father stepped smartly over the ground to take the reins. His eyes were full of questions as they studied us, but the questions didn't make it to his lips. When I thanked him, he gave a quick nod and turned back to his family.

We headed for the van, and reaction started to kick in. My leg ached, I was wet through and very, very cold.

'I don't know about you, but I need a bath,' said Eseld. 'How long have we got?'

'It's not so much the time as the size of the hot water tank. At least there's an electric shower.'

She bumped her shoulder into my arm. 'You can have the bath after me, you lucky devil you.'

'I've warned you about that accent. Your Irish is even worse than my Geordie.'

Cleaned, much warmer and a lot drier, we returned to the tavern at eleven thirty. The gate was still firmly locked, and there was now a whole bunch of (mostly) men milling around, and I got some very dark looks when I got out of the van.

One of the smaller men stepped forwards. 'Excuse me, sir, but would it be you who knows what's going on in there? We can't get sense out of the boy other than that the tavern is closed. It's never been closed in my lifetime.'

'Here he comes,' said an older voice from the back.

The ostler had been keeping watch from the shelter of the stable, and ran across the car park. Only when I went closer to the gate did I realise why they hadn't hopped over the wall: some very strong, very obvious Wards.

The ostler got to the gate, and the older voice shouted out, 'Is she open yet? Will she not take pity on us?'

'I'm to let in these two and no one else,' said the boy, pointing to me.

Smell of earth and rotting leaves. I whipped round and saw a man getting out of a pickup, his eyes fixed on me. I banged on the roof of the van and motioned for Eseld to drive through the gate. I slipped in behind her, and the way was barred again. The Fae noble came up to the gate, and the deprived drinkers gave him a wide berth.

This lot were The Regulars, Entangled men with not much else to do on a wet afternoon in December. There's a similar crowd to be found in the Inkwell most days, and for just a second, I felt homesick. I love Middlebarrow Haven, and wherever Mina is will always be my true home, but just for a moment I wanted to be away from this wet place and its dangers.

'What's up, Conrad?'

'Sorry, Es, I must be getting old.'

'You are. Is that…?'

'Oughterard, or his boss. Inishsí's agent at the Market Tavern, yes. Let's get inside.'

As we went in through the back door, the sound of voices told me that the assembled Ahearns were being shown out of the front. Fiadh appeared, still in her riding gear, and I said, 'Everything okay?'

'For now. I've told them a great pack of lies that should keep them happy for a while. Has Oighrig been in touch with you?'

'Probably. She hasn't got this number, though.'

She laughed. 'Wise man. Have I got ten minutes to get changed? Good. Chef!'

She jogged out of the back room with a spring in her step, and a lugubrious man in whites appeared. With a picnic hamper. 'Boss says I've to show you this and ask if there's more you'd like, miss.'

'Me?'

'Yes. Boss says if you're in for a long wait, you might get hungry.'

He placed the hamper on the table and lifted the lid. Eseld examined it and said, 'Wow. This is great. You must have been busy.'

'No lunchtime service, miss. I've flasks of tea, too, and I'll bring two mugs of coffee while you wait.'

We took the coffee outside, and I finally got a message from Rachael.

You don't change, do you? Well, you've nearly ruined my spa day with this, but if YOU think it's important, then I suppose it must be. And who was the freak on the other end of the phone? I think this is what you want:

*For each n, where n is a transition value, t`=√(n*1.618)*

Tell Eseld that if she fancies joining me tomorrow, she's more than welcome. You owe me a leg massage and a hot stones session.

Take care,

R. X.

I showed Eseld the message. 'How do I measure a transition value?'

'You don't. Only the Fae can do that easily. And the likes of Tamsin Kelly. For you, not so much.'

'Damn. I hadn't planned for that. This could all be off unless I can get some help.'

The sense of anti-climax and frustration was almost more than I could bear, and when the ostler showed in Countess Portarra, I did something very stupid.

She'd swapped the white coat and red leggings for a red leather biker's jacket with white stripes up the sleeve and across the shoulder. She was shorter than Eseld by a good few inches, but much broader. A bit like a boxer, really, but boxing would be too tame for her.

After saying hello, I almost blurted out my question. 'How do I measure the transition levels inside a sídhe? Can you tell me?'

An evil smile twisted up her mouth. 'I can help you do that. There's a price, though.'

Of course there was a price. There always is. 'Can I afford it?'

'I don't know. Depends on how much you value your life. If you survive in there, and I don't think that's very likely at all, then I call you out. You and me, sword to sword. Let's finish what you started this morning.'

'We could argue about who started it, but life's too short. Deal.'

She looked down at my proffered hand. 'We don't shake on a contest.'

Eseld's face was a mask, lips pinched in and brows lowered, the whole thing frozen. She didn't look at me when she said, 'I'll go and put a rocket under Fiadh. If she's got in the shower, we're going without her.'

Portarra had removed a ring from her right hand and offered it to me. I took the ring and nearly dropped it, so strong and alien was the magick. 'What in Odin's name does this do?'

'We're not all the same, you know.'

'Sorry?'

'You have your gift, Eseld has hers. The Noble Queen is a born plane shifter. It's said that she came out of the egg and flipped two levels before her wings were dry.' She looked at me. 'That's a story, by the way, but it tells a truth. I can't do that, so I need a little help. It really is your lucky day, Dragonslayer.'

'Is it safe for me to wear? Does it have any hidden properties?'

She considered for a moment. 'It may drive you mad. Oh, and you'll lose your ability to see through Glamours. If you have any.'

'I'll risk it.'

'Then put it on and tell me what you see.'

I looked at the ring, and bugger me if it didn't start pulsing like a beating heart. The Countess of Portarra might be built like a boxer, but she still has small hands compared to mine. That ring would barely make it past the first joint on my little finger. I stared at it and had another mad idea. It was a day for them.

With closed eyes, I slipped on the ring, and a kaleidoscope pattern exploded into my vision. I waited a few seconds to see if it calmed down, and it slowly turned to violet blobs that faded in and out of focus. It was the same violet as Queen Galway's eyes. Relevant? Who knows. I risked a peek.

'You have rainbow hair, Countess.'

'Good. It works, then. I can't hold this for long, so try to work out which bands are the biggest.'

I heard Eseld and Fiadh come in, talking about me. It took a great effort of will to keep focused on the layers in the Fae's hair, and even more to separate them. 'Call them out,' she said.

'Red is about middling. Orange is slightly smaller and yellow the thinnest. Green is huge, blue is the same as red, and … there are three more. Why can I see three more?'

'Because I'm busting a gut to show you, that's why. Focus on the last one.'

'It's the same size as red, a bit bigger than indigo but smaller than violet, if that's violet.'

'Focus! Get them in your head!'

I stared until the shifting colours made my eyes ache, then there were only seven again. No… there were eight. The bonus violet had gone, and it was replaced by a ruddy brown colour, as best as I can describe it, and then they were all gone.

I told Portarra what I'd seen, and she shook her head. 'Must be an illusion. There's nothing below red. The rest is easy: your Royal Violet is one, got that?'

'Royal Violet. One. Yes.'

'This is the hard part. When you see any other colour, or combination, ignore how big it is and focus on the colours. What would red and yellow be?'

'About one and a quarter, I suppose.'

'That's your transition value, then. Just add them up.'

In my own head, I added this: Add up several fractional colours and multiply by one point six one eight. Then take the square root. This little adventure could well turn out to be death by algebra.

'Did it work?' asked Eseld stiffly.

'You're a stupid fool,' added Fiadh, 'but we knew that already. How are you gonna keep the thing on your pinkie?'

'Glad you asked. When we go out, could you ask Oughterard if I could borrow his nice leather glove. Just the left one. I spotted them earlier.'

'Oh, I'm sure that will be no problem for him. Eejit. How am I supposed to do that?'

'Tell him that I'm on the way to Inishsí to deliver a message from Morwenna Ahearn, but make him give you the glove first. Let's go.'

Because I had to hold my left hand up in the air to keep the ring on, the chef was summoned to help carry things, and then move things because of who we found waiting outside.

It was the older Ahearn, and Fi introduced him as Donal before she went off to play with the Fae Count.

'I've left you my car,' he said. 'You won't all fit in that van of yours. No rush to get it back. The Road to Donegal can be murder.'

Donegal? What on earth had Fi told them. 'You're very kind.'

Donal is a single, retired man. His BMW X5 was filthy on the outside and clean on the inside. Eseld sorted the gear, and Fi returned with the glove.

'You've a warm welcome waiting for you on the Lough,' she said. 'Warm as in the same welcome you get in Hell. I'm not gonna ask if you know what you're doing, because you're clearly beyond that. Here you go.'

The glove was a little tight, but it did the job. It's a measure of how keen we were to put off the journey that there was a discussion about whether I could start a Michael Jackson tribute act on account of the single glove, but was it the correct hand? When the Countess of Portarra offered to Google the answer, I ordered everyone into the vehicles.

Eseld was driving Donal's car, because Fiadh hasn't driven more than fifty yards in fifteen years. When we passed through the gate, she asked Es to pause, then lowered the window. 'Right you useless lot, the tavern is now open, and I've got news for youse: it will be closed at Christmas. Put that in your pipes and smoke it.'

The journey to Inishsí took less than half an hour, and during it, something very strange happened: it stopped raining. Properly stopped, as in blue sky visible.

'Shit,' said Fiadh when I pointed it out. 'That means it'll be cold tonight.'

'That's why I told you to wear thermals and pack blankets. You did wear thermals, didn't you?'

She looked a bit sheepish. 'I was gonna wear a miniskirt until Little Miss Practical here found me half-dressed and put me right.'

'I am going to cry,' said Eseld. 'I have spent my whole life trying *not* to be practical, and now I am reduced to this.' She took her eyes off the road for a second to glare at Fiadh. 'And you are too old for a miniskirt.'

'I am not so too, and besides, I am going to re-set my social life to when I arrived at the tavern, so from tomorrow I am twenty-two and on the pull.'

'That'll give you something to do while you wait,' I said. 'You can help her create her Tinder profile. Look, sunlight on the Lough.'

The countryside around Lough Corrib is quite flat, with no dramatic plunges to give you a view. When we finally got near the water, the many islands dotting the lake glowed such a vibrant green that I was tempted to take off Portarra's ring and see if that was their true colour.

'We'll soon be there,' said Fiadh, suddenly sober.

This would be the point where I described the majestic island of Inishsí to you, but I can't, because I couldn't see a bloody thing: Glamours. What I could see was a large gravel semi-circle leading to a gate that had a tiny slipway on the other side. 'This is tough,' said Eseld. 'I could learn a thing or two about these effing Wards. Nnngrhs.'

The BMW wobbled alarmingly, then swerved on to the gravel. And I blacked out.

'You should have thought of that,' said an Irish voice.

'It's what he wanted,' said another, deeper one.

'He did not want to pass out.' That voice was English, or something. Aah. It was Eseld.

'I am still here, you know.'

A hand on my neck and face, warm and gentle. Definitely Eseld. I smiled and opened my eyes. Oops. It was the Countess of Portarra.

'He's fine,' she pronounced. 'Sit still, Dragonslayer. Take deep breaths.'

I'd expected to be prone, but I was still held in place by the seatbelt. Someone had lowered the back enough for me to rest, and that's what I did. The others carried on their argument.

'What now?' said Eseld. 'I know him, and he won't go in there unless he has that ring, and if he can't wear it near the sídhe…'

'There's another way,' said Portarra.

I raised the back of the seat and unclipped the belt. 'What happened, and what's the other way?'

'I think the protective Glamour fought with the presented Construction — two different views of the island. Your Sight couldn't cope. As soon as I took the ring off, no problem. As for the other way … your friends won't like it, but it should work, and if I can't get you to see transitions in there, our contest is off.'

'That's not my primary concern. Let's do it before I have second thoughts.'

When Portarra took out a hunting knife, Eseld jumped forwards. 'No!'

'Easy,' said the Fae. 'It's for me.' With that, she slashed her forearm. 'Open wide.'

I went to drink the blood, but she held me back with her other hand and popped the ring in my mouth first, then pressed her bleeding arm to my lips.

Eurch. I can now report that Fae blood tastes disgusting. Like I imagine the run-off from a compost heap might taste. She placed her right hand behind my head, and the magick made a circuit. Royal Violet and rusty brown shapes swirled in my vision, chasing each other until the violet washed the other away.

Portarra removed her hand and arm. 'Swallow the blood, then spit out the ring into my palm. Don't touch it.'

I did as she asked, and when I glanced up, I could see the island in all its glory. Wow. I turned away for now; there would be plenty of time for sightseeing in a moment.

'It's a bit late to ask, but what about mercury poisoning?'

Portarra nodded. 'We don't trick people like that. When I removed the ring, I checked your Aura. You've a base of Earth-spawn in you. Your body will reject my blood over the next few hours and purge it. No lasting effects. As promised.'

'Earth-spawn? Gnomes?'

'As you say. Let's check your Sight.'

She did the thing with her hair again, and I could see it fine. I made her do it for a little longer, because the more I studied those colours, the more chance I had of solving that equation. And there was definitely that rusty brown underneath it. Never mind. I walked round the cars to centre myself again, and I had a shock when I glanced in Portarra's vehicle.

I'd forgotten that her Squire was supposed to be with her, and I'd seen no sign of him at the Market Tavern. Something in the light off the windscreen told me that he'd been there all along and that my attention had been drawn away. By magick.

'Isn't he a bit young for this?' I asked the Fae Countess.

'He's on probation until the Solstice. So far he's learnt to make a decent cup of tea, but that's about it.'

I lit what might be my last cigarette and called Eseld over to me. For a moment, we stood looking at Inishsí, bathed in winter sunshine. From the gate in front of us, a road flew straight over a causeway to the island proper, where low cottages looked trapped between the lake waters and the hill behind it.

Instead of a dome or mound, the home-hill was an uneven, undulating carpet of green, and it wasn't easy to work out where the highest point was. 'Put up your best Silence,' I said.

Eseld did, and hooked her arm through mine. 'I've added a couple of Wards, too. Is this the Rubicon? I had to Google it, you know: Julius Caesar's career isn't on the curriculum at Salomon's House.'

'Well, it should be. If you're willing, I've a plan. Agree to it and you'll have no way out.'

'Go on, don't keep me in suspense.' I outlined the plan, and she gave my arm a squeeze. 'I was never going to say no, Conrad. Let's do it.'

I placed a call to Lloyd. 'We're on. At midnight.'

'Right you are,' he replied. 'At least it's finally stopped bloody raining. What a miserable place this is.'

'See you on the other side, Lloyd.' I disconnected and went back to the car. 'Time to go.'

Eseld, Fiadh and Portarra gathered round and watched with growing mystification as I placed my coat, jacket and sweater in the back of the BMW, along with my phone and, finally, all my magickal Artefacts.

'Eseld?'

She picked up the case with my new watch in it, and swapped it for my old one. This was something I couldn't do on my own, because Lloyd had adapted the fastening. Eseld looked up, and I had a weird flashback to something that had never happened to me – a lady fastening on her knight's armour before he went into battle.

'I wish Mina could be here to give you a kiss,' said Eseld, blushing slightly and giving my hand a squeeze.

'To hell with that,' said Fiadh. She almost pushed Eseld aside, and before I could react, she put her arms round my neck and dragged me down for a full-on lip lock. She only held it for half a second, then pushed away. 'That was to say thanks. Whatever happens today, I've got my freedom back. If I die tonight, I'll die a free woman, thanks to you.'

This was getting too much. 'You should thank Eseld as well, but wait until I've gone. It'll give you something to do while I'm away.'

Fi's laugh was interrupted by a shout. 'Incoming,' said Portarra, looking along the lake road.

'I know that car,' said Fiadh. 'It's the ear-hor.'

'The what?' I asked.

'The Iarrthóir. The Seeker.' When I still didn't get it, she rolled her eyes. 'The FAE – the United Inquisition.'

'Time to go.'

I grabbed the three other things I was taking with me: my new sword, a jewellery box and a packet of curried worms. I slung the sword over my back and shivered. Cold? Definitely. Fear? Absolutely.

I was walking towards the gate when a small hatchback burst through the Wards. After that, the driver had to slam on the brakes and take evasive action. I passed through the gate and set foot on the bridge. Behind me, I heard a woman's voice shouting, 'Come back here! You don't know what you're doing!'

Unfortunately, I knew *exactly* what I was doing.

17 — The Isle of Inishsí

The Scottish party were still closeted in the Deputy's Study with Mina when Cordelia's phone rang, and she nearly ignored it.

She'd had a call earlier, nothing to do with this one, which tipped her off that a coven of Witches in north Shropshire was planning a Summoning outside their Grove on the Solstice. It was the fourth call like this she'd had this week: it seemed that a lot of things had crawled out of the woodwork now that Piers Wetherill had retired. Cordy suspected that a lot more went on like this in Lancashire and the Palatinate, but people weren't used to having the Watch in residence. Yet.

She'd talked over the first call with Vicky, and Vicky had persuaded Saffron Hawkins to attend. When the second came in, Cordy made a rendezvous with Saffron and they dealt with it together. It had been galling to play second fiddle to a kid barely out of Salomon's House, but when push came to shove, Saffron had been brisk, no-nonsense and efficient.

Cordy had taken the third job herself (a lot less briskly), but the fourth one, this morning, would have meant driving nearly to Herefordshire in the pouring rain. She'd put it off and planned to deal with it tomorrow, on the way down to Wells and a weekend playing Happy Families with Rick and her children. As a guest. No wonder she nearly ignored her phone until she saw that it was the Boss calling.

'Where's Mina? She's not answering her phone.'

'The committee from Napier House are here today. They had an early lunch, and…'

'Go in there, drag her out and put her on the phone. Use reasonable force if you have to.'

Cordy nearly dropped her phone. *Use reasonable force!* Yes, Hannah was the Peculier Constable, but she was also Mina's Matron of Honour.

'Why can't I hear you moving?' said Hannah. 'Put me on speaker.'

Cordy shot up from the kitchen table and knocked over the stool she'd been sitting on. It clattered across the flags, and she stumbled. At least the Boss would know she was on it. She slapped her feet along the passage for added effect and knocked loudly on the study door.

'What is it? I'm busy.' Mina's voice was muffled through the thick oak, and Cordy didn't want to shout back, so she tested the handle (unlocked), then pushed the door open, holding her phone flat on her hand.

Mina was at one end of the big desk, with the two women and the man from Edinburgh around it. Papers were spread all over, and folders had been stacked on the empty Deputy's chair.

'Sorry to bother you, Mina, but it's the Constable. For you.'

Mina frowned, opened her mouth, then changed her mind and closed it. She pushed her chair back from the table and stood up. 'Excuse me. I'd better take this.'

Cordy stepped out of the room a couple of paces and waited for Mina to take the phone off her, but Mina didn't do that. She came out and closed the door behind her, then started walking backwards towards the kitchen.

'What is it, Hannah-ji?'

'You have to stop him. I've had the United Inquisition on the phone, and he's about to start a war. I had no idea he was in this deep.'

Mina didn't look surprised. Morning, noon and night since Conrad and Eseld had left for Ireland there had been messages and hushed conversations. Mina knew exactly what Conrad was up to. Or did she?

'What do you mean by a *war*?'

'The Chief Seeker of Ireland tells me that the Queen of Galway is gathering her people and getting ready to ride out. She tells me that it's a total mess, and that Conrad's been seen with Galway's personal Guard, driving north to Inishsí. This is madness. Certain death and madness. You have to stop him.'

As the details of the Boss's message piled up, Mina's eyes widened. 'I know nothing of this war, Hannah-ji.'

'Well, what *do* you know?'

'I last spoke to him at twelve-thirty. He said he was off to see the Queen of Inishsí and turning his phone off. To avoid distractions. As far as I know, the only people with him were Eseld, this Fiadh Ahearn woman, and an escort. He would have mentioned an army, I think.'

If Cordy's phone had water in it, steam would be coming off now, so angry was the Boss. 'Stop pissing me about, Mina. This has gone too far. What is he up to? Tell me. Now.'

Despite this being a voice call, Mina was gesticulating and moving her head as if Hannah were in the room.

'All I know is that he's going to see the Queen. Honestly, Hannah, he has never kept so much from me. He needed a horse transporter, and Lloyd Flint is in Ireland with it. I have been so worried, because he keeps making jokes about your solution for the Dragon problem.'

There was a pause. 'You don't mean that old contingency plan?'

This was news to Cordelia. Conrad had never mentioned it to her. Yet another in-joke that she was outside.

'Yes,' said Mina. 'The nuclear strike.'

Cordy couldn't help herself, and she blurted out, 'Where would he get a bomb?'

Mina looked strangely at her, and Cordy felt the Boss was doing the same down in Merlyn's Tower, and it was Hannah who answered.

'This is Conrad we're talking about.'

'Precisely,' added Mina. 'The only thing that makes me think otherwise is that he would never put Lloyd and Olivia at risk like that.'

Hannah took an audible breath. 'Please, Mina, if you have any way of getting in touch, do it. I'm asking you, not ordering you. Please.'

Mina already had her phone out. She placed a call and tapped the Speaker button. 'Eseld?'

'Hang on,' came the Cornish whisper. 'Let me move away … Hi.'

'Eseld, I have Hannah-ji on another line. She says that the Queen of Galway is gathering her People for battle.'

'Double shit. Really?'

'According to the Chief Seeker.'

'Yeah, well we've got the Galway Seeker here now, screaming blue murder, but I've no idea what she's saying, and the others are too busy to translate. If you can hear me, Hannah, I had no idea. Conrad had no idea. This is nothing to do with him.'

Hannah could hear, and she spoke even louder. 'This has everything to do with him, Eseld. You must stop him. Please.'

'I'm sorry. He's gone. Truly. I swear it. We need to hold the line here. I'd better go.'

Mina lowered her phone. 'When I came out of hospital the first time, Hannah-ji, I would have said that this is in the hands of the gods. Now I know better, and I hope that they keep their hands well away from this.'

'That won't stop me praying,' said Hannah. 'When I've tried stopping an international incident. Let me know the second you hear anything, and that *is* an order.'

'Of course.'

Cordy's phone went dark. 'What do we do now, Mina?'

'I shall finish my meeting as quickly as possible, then I suggest we go for a long walk before it gets dark.'

'Why?'

'Because I don't want to start drinking until it's over. Apart from tea. I am going to need a *lot* of tea.'

Away from the shore, the wind cut through my shirt, and I wanted to get over that bridge and on to the island just to warm up. My eyes watered, and I blinked. Oh. That's good. That's very good.

The steel and concrete bridge, with its low railings and room for a truck, had been replaced by a ribbon of glass that stretched fifty metres away to a small tower, framed against the green hill, through which you had to pass. Or swim.

Water lapped gently under the unsupported glass deck, and the more you looked at it, the less you could see what was holding you up. Glamours within Constructions within Glamours. What was real: the steel girders? The glass fancy? The guard tower?

It's one thing to *know* that to the Fae this is all a game, a display of magickal one-upmanship; it's quite another to walk through it. No wonder every story, tale and legend has the same core: *don't go into the sídhe.* I was beginning to wonder if I'd bitten off more than I could chew here, not that there was any going back now. I shivered, and my internal thermostat overcame my reluctance. With a deep breath, I strode towards the gatehouse and the figure who'd appeared there.

I idly wondered what Countess Portarra wears when she's on formal duty – probably the leather jacket. Things looked a bit less casual here. The Fae noble waiting for me sported a handsome coat in vivid golden yellow and an immaculate pair of white trousers that would pass inspection in the Household Cavalry. A big lock of blond hair threatened to fall over his eyes, and I regret to say that his eyes matched his jacket: a most vivid, unnatural yellow. Just to make sure I knew why he was there, his right hand rested on the hilt of his sword.

'Greetings wayfarer,' he called out when I was still ten metres away. 'Who crosses the waters to Inishsí?'

'Conrad Clarke, Lord Protector of the Elvenham Pack, known by some as the Dragonslayer. I seek an audience with the Fair Queen of this land.'

'And I am Lord Cartoor, Guard to the Fair Queen. Welcome in peace and cross the threshold. You could say that She has been expecting you.'

He gave a small bow, then a massive grin. 'Would you be wanting a hand, there?'

'If it's not too much trouble.'

He held out his hand, and when it crossed an invisible line, it flashed gold sparkles. I closed the distance between us at a smart walk and grasped his hand. When I crossed that line myself, I got a flash of yellow across my vision as I left the natural world. He didn't notice as I glanced at my watch. For every minute that passed in this place, one minute twelve seconds would pass outside. That was epic: the Queen had raised *the whole island.* Way to go, your grace.

When I looked up, I could see why.

The green hill was gone, or rather it had been edited and intercut with a palace. Not just any palace, you understand, but a proper Irish royal palace of piled turf, wood and the occasional stone support, the whole thing ornamented with banners, outdoor tapestries and bright pigment on the timbers. I've seen a bigger version of this – in books. I think.

'Not seen above ground since the days of Saint Patrick,' said Cartoor. 'A junior version of the Great Queen's home, if you're wondering.'

I looked at him when he spoke, and his eyes had reverted to a pleasant but still unnatural bluey-green. 'I *was* wondering, actually. Very few of my friends are interested in magickal architecture.'

Cartoor seemed a jolly chap. For a Fae warrior. He clapped me on the back and said, 'In that case we should get on fine, 'cos I've no interest in architecture either. Shall we?'

The Queen's Guard wasn't just good looking – he was as tall as me, broad in the shoulder and looked a lot younger. Then again, I'm finding that most of the people/creatures I meet these days look a lot younger than me, the Queen of Galway notwithstanding. A theory tickled the back of my neck, then blew away on the wind.

The path to the door wound up a slope, through terraced beds of mostly bare earth. Cartoor saw me looking and said, 'We're too close to the natural world, here. The winter gardens are within the Fair Queen's palace. Are you not cold without a coat, Lord Dragonslayer?'

'I'm not a Lord over here, just a concerned citizen, and I hope that the Queen's radiance will keep me warm.'

He chuckled. 'That it will.'

'Tell me something, if you can. Who decides on the honorific? I know why the *Great Queen* is Great, but…?'

'Now that's a question that no mortal has ever asked me before. Congratulations … What do I call you, if you're not a Lord?'

'Conrad will do.'

I wondered if he'd just used the classic Fae misdirection, but no, he actually answered my question. 'The honorific comes from the mouth of the first noble to bend the knee to the new Queen. Shall I let you into a secret? I think the Fair Queen might have planned it that way, but I'm fairly sure that the Noble Queen of Galway didn't.'

'Oh?'

'As I've heard the tale, her rival submitted on the battlefield and begged for mercy on his knees, declaring her the Noble Queen. She accepted his submission, then cut his head off. She's like that.'

That theory was tickling my neck again. I scratched it, but to no avail, and I had to put it aside because we were at the gates, big wooden ones painted in stripes of yellow and white, clearly the Fair Queen's colours.

'Give me your hand, Conrad. We're going up again.'

Up we went, and through we went, bypassing the doors and arriving in a high passage with wooden walls. It was high because the Queen would no doubt leave her palace already mounted.

This time I felt the transition as a lurch inside me, accompanied by a flash of purple. I'd memorised the solutions to Rachael's equations for all the colours – what? You didn't think I was going to work them out on the fly, did you? What I did have to do was add them together: we were now on one to one minute thirty. I also had to check my watch, and this time Cartoor noticed.

'Do you have somewhere else to be, Conrad?' he asked with a smile.

'Sorry. OCD behaviour.'

'Eh?'

I am not OCD, nor am I trying to make a joke out of a psychological disorder. Just so you know. 'Compulsive time-checking. I used to fly helicopters in war zones, and you had to log *everything*. Sorry.'

'Never mind, just try not to do it in front of the Queen.' He turned and raised his voice. '?'

And I've no idea what he said, because he said it in Gaeilge. I could guess, because a Squire who'd barely shed his wings came running down the passage. Cartoor gave an order, and the Squire shot off.

'I've asked him to tell the Chamberlain that I would present a visitor, and I should warn you that only Gaeilge is spoken in the sídhe. I'll translate for you.'

I forced my shoulders to relax now that I was out of the cold, and I fell into step with Cartoor as we walked down the passage. The area immediately inside the doors had been lit by two flaming torches; beyond that, golden globes hanging from the roof shed a warm light that cast no shadows. About thirty metres along, we reached an open room, more of a junction really, with lower passages to left and right. If you took one of those ways, you'd move from granite slabs to packed earth. The royal way led ahead, through a proper stone arch. On the keystone was a symbol: the radiant sun on a white background.

'Here we wait. Sorry there's no chairs.'

I was starting to believe my own propaganda, because I checked my watch. Cartoor smiled a sympathetic smile. 'Might I ask a question?' I suggested.

'Course you can. Not saying I'll answer, mind.'

'I know that High Unicorns aren't native to Ireland, but I wondered if the Fair Queen – or any Queen – had brought any over. After all, Irish horses pretty much have racing sewn up in England.'

'Do they?'

Just when you think you're talking to a human, they remind you that you aren't. Lord Cartoor clearly had no idea about mundane racing. He knew about Unicorns, though. 'Not that I've heard. The Fair Queen has Her own steeds. If you've an interest in mounts, you might get to see them. Or you might be unlucky and get to see them anyway if She puts you to the hunt.'

And then they double down and let you know what they really think.

Cartoor reflected for a moment. 'Not that the Fair Queen makes a habit of putting mortals to the hunt. In fact, I can't recall her doing it during my lifetime.'

It was my turn to clap him on the shoulder. 'I can see why you're her guard and not her press secretary, Cartoor.'

I think that went over his head, because all he did was smile and stand further away from me. 'Tell me about the Dragon,' he said. It made a change from asking about my dog. It took the Fair Queen another twenty minutes at least to send word, and when she did, Cartoor was clearly impressed on my behalf: the Chamberlain herself appeared.

I knew from her bearing that she was important, and Cartoor supplied her identity when he translated. 'Her Chamberlain says that Fair Queen of Inishsí would be honoured if you could grace Her hall.' And if you're wondering what the Chamberlain of a Fae Queen wears, I only have a sample of one to judge from. Somehow I could not see her counterpart at Galway wearing a white trouser suit with a gold waistcoat.

'It is me that is honoured,' I said loudly.

The Chamberlain barely waited for the official translation before she beckoned us through the arch. The flaming torches were back now, and not a trace of soot on the roof above them. The doorway ahead of us was shrouded in shadows, despite the bright flames. That way you got maximum impact when you stepped over the threshold.

You also got a flash of orange. I'd checked my watch as we went down the passage, so I didn't need to do it in the hall. All I had to do was remember that we were now on 1:1.70.

18 — The Queen's Hall

The hall of the Fair Queen of Inishsí was a space I'll never forget, and I so wished that Mina was with me to see it. Not only because my heart ached to be near her, but because she would have sold her soul (or at least mortgaged it) to have her wedding here.

It was round, for one thing, so no one would ever be too far from the dancefloor in the middle. The walls rose straight for about fifteen feet, then domed towards a lantern from which a soft light illuminated the room. It was high enough to give a real sense of space, but not so high as to feel like an arena. From the top of the walls hung a huge selection of banners, and every other one was the gold sun on a white field. I didn't get to see any other others properly, except for the big standard that hung next-but-one to her throne: the gold triskele on green of the Great Queen. Bear in mind that no two humans can agree on whether there is still a Great Queen, and if there is, whether it's the same Great Queen as in the legends.

As well as the banners, the wall was decorated with tapestries depicting Fae life and the doings of Queens. I didn't have time to linger over these, either, nor to count the openings and passages, so I crossed the floor with my eyes down.

I was looking at flags to occupy my eyes and to avoid the butterflies hatching in my innards as the Chamberlain led us across the granite floor to the throne. Closer to it, and I scanned the Court, ranged on either side and around the dais. Two more guards, dressed identically to Cartoor, flanked the dais, and I don't think there was a Fae there who didn't have a gold *something* in their dress or in a badge. I guessed at forty or so, and most of them were female.

The nobles were nearest to the dais, of course, and to the Queen's left, one of them stood on the lowest tier. That meant he was a Prince, and there was a Princess at the Queen's right hand. I didn't get to spend any time looking at the top noble because it was time to face the Fair Queen.

In a wet French field, I once saw Helen of Troy herself emerge from a rock. If Helen is your bar, where did that leave the Queen? I don't know, because I'm not so shallow as to go around giving magickal creatures a score out of ten for beauty. All I can say is that it depends on whether you prefer blondes.

Shimmering white silk, gold embroidery, golden slippers and cascades of honey-gold hair all built up to a face that made me fall in love immediately. There and then. On the spot. Sculptured cheekbones and sad eyes, flawless skin and ruby lips, a long neck and elegantly pointed ears. Who wouldn't fall in love with that? It was clear in a glance that the Fair Queen was wise, beautiful and full of all the gifts of Mother Nature.

I came as near to the throne as I dared, and bowed low. The Chamberlain announced me exactly as I'd introduced myself on the bridge (she did that bit in English), and the Queen said something to her. The Chamberlain bowed and sat in the only chair at ground level, and the Queen turned her attention to me.

When I heard her soft voice wrap itself around the words of welcome, even though I didn't understand them, all I wanted was for her to sing to me in her beautiful mezzo-soprano.

'The Queen welcomes you in peace and asks what brings you to Her home.'

Lord Cartoor's voice was a poor substitute, but I had my welcome.

'Please tell her grace that I am honoured beyond words.'

He did, and she responded via his translation. 'The Fair Queen says that as you are from a foreign shore, you may speak directly, so I won't be translating your words.' He'd stuck pretty close to me, and touched my arm to whisper under a Fae Silence (they're like mine, but much better). 'Now would be a good time to offer your gift.'

Gift? Who said anything about a gift? Shit, what do I do now? I was starting to sweat, heavily, and reached for my handkerchief. On top of the folded Irish linen was a gift from the gods, or from one in particular. *Always take curried worms when you go underground.* It was literally the only thing I had that I could give to the woman I now loved with all my heart.

Okay, I'll admit that I'm exaggerating. I *did* love the Queen, in an aching, you-are-beautiful kind of way, and that love was a bit like my bad leg: it was part of me, but it made it hard to get around, and it hurt like hell for no benefit.

I pulled out the packet of spicy invertebrates and offered them to Lord Cartoor. I also got to address the Queen directly. 'I have nothing that would compare to your riches, Fair Queen. This token is something that once saved my life, and I offer it to show that this is all my life is worth in your presence.'

Was that a bit OTT? I crossed my fingers as Cartoor went up to the dais and knelt in front of her. She peered down and asked him to pass them up. When she saw what I'd given her, she chuckled a deep-throated chuckle.

Cartoor returned and translated. 'The Queen finds your gift to be … witty. That's right, *witty*. And She would like to know what you think of Her realm.'

It took a full twenty minutes to get to the point, during which I complimented her home, her looks, her wisdom, her contribution to the arts, the valour of her men and her exquisite skill in Glamours and Constructions.

The Court listened attentively throughout the exchange, the ones she could see anyway. Her throne (of gold) was not against the back wall: it stood out about six feet, and behind it was an archway. On either side of the arch were padded benches, and on the benches were her Hlæfdigan, her ladies, or some of them. There must have been a one-way audio barrier, because they came and went and chattered to each other without me hearing a thing. My declarations of praise also allowed me to look at the Princess.

A Fae Princess can look like she wants, and this one had chosen to look as little like her Queen as possible and still be beautiful. She had dark hair, round eyes and a voluptuous figure that suited the belted green gown. She also frowned occasionally; the Queen does not allow frown lines to sully her countenance.

When I'd finished extolling the virtues of her realm, the Queen looked at me properly, taking in the man that I am, and it gave me a great thrill to see that she was not disappointed. She held my gaze and asked me a question.

Instead of translating, Lord Cartoor jerked my eyes away from the Queen by saying, 'You're bleeding, Conrad.'

'Sorry?'

'There, on your shirt. Blood.'

He was right. Over my left breast was a small patch of bright red. Cartoor leaned down to have a closer look, and then he recoiled with a disgusted expression on his face. 'What have you done? You stink of that bitch Portarra.' He grasped his sword and only stopped from drawing it when I raised my arms in the air.

'Forgive me, your grace. It was only a small dose, to help me cross the bridge. She said I had too much of the Gnome about me.' I turned theatrically and glared at the entrance. 'She also said that it would purge naturally, and I imagined a sudden urge to use your bathroom.'

She spoke, and Cartoor translated with a frown. 'The Fair Queen does not believe you. Approach Her, and keep your hands where I can see them.' I'm fairly sure he added the last part, and he followed close behind me with his hand never leaving his sword.

The Queen spoke to the Prince at the foot of her dais, and he came to examine me. Whatever he said to her finished with a shrug, and he stepped back. Round about this time, another patch of red appeared on my right breast, and the Queen must have caught the scent, because she sat up a little straighter. Finally, she gave her answer.

Cartoor stepped back, giving me a bit of space, and said, 'The Fair Queen was going to ask you for the truth about that Dragon, and how you managed to become a Pack Protector, but She does not want you bleeding on Her floor. She is ready to hear why you came.'

I took that as a sign to lower my arms, and no one shot me. Always a bonus. 'I brought the gift of worms to show how little I value my life here. I have also brought another item that your grace might be interested in trading.'

'The Fair Queen was not expecting that,' came the translation.

I reached slowly into my other pocket and drew out the jewellery box. It looked like a standard, rather cheap item. It wasn't. It was a very expensive, custom-made barrier-box. I'd felt it get warm the second I crossed to Inishsí, and it was now getting almost too hot to handle. 'Might I humbly suggest to your grace that this item is for her eyes only?'

I didn't expect her to take the bait straight away. For the Queen to take me away from the Court like this would be extremely unusual. After all, I'd only managed to secure the private audience with Galway by violent confrontation in an out of the way field, and it was now clear that the Queen of Galway's stock is much reduced. Much lower and she'd have been giving me her number and suggesting drinks at the Market Tavern. Only joking, your grace.

The box in my hand got hotter still, and I realised that the collective magickal attention of the entire Court was causing the enmeshed Work to fight back. I fished out my handkerchief and placed the box on top.

The Queen rearranged her dress and smiled at me, a radiant smile that made today a good day, whatever else happened.

'The Queen is intrigued,' said Cartoor. 'She would like to see what you have to offer. Please give it to the Chamberlain.'

'Alas, the box is a riddle. Everyone wants what's inside it, but only your grace knows what it really means. Anyone can use it, but it can only ever belong to you.'

By directly addressing the Queen, I'd just committed several faux pas. A couple of the lower ranked courtiers gasped, but only because they hadn't twigged what I'd said. The brighter ones frowned, looked amazed or took a step back, presumably to avoid getting splashed by blood if things got nasty. Human blood can be difficult to remove from Fae fabrics.

The Court froze for a second, all waiting on the Queen's response. She'd got the message alright, and it was just a question of whether she was going to deal with me or destroy me and take the box anyway.

Her tongue ran over her ruby lips and she shifted on her throne. She looked at Cartoor, and I didn't see murder in her eyes. She gave him an order, and he took his hand off his sword to whistle at one of the tapestries. It moved and it disappeared, revealing a narrow gap in the wall. Neat. Perhaps *all* the tapestries were illusions – it would make it easier to redecorate. From the gap came a slim female figure in green, a bow strapped to her back. She jogged over, bowed to the throne and looked at Cartoor.

I could tell that things were getting serious because he switched from the Irish vernacular to Fae, asking several questions in rapid succession. She replied, and he dismissed her. With another bow, she ran back to her hiding place, and once again all eyes were on the throne.

The Queen thought for a moment, then things suddenly got a lot more serious: she addressed me in English. 'Why is the Countess Portarra at my gates, Dragonslayer?'

'She is standing vigil with my old friend and my new one. You might say that they're all waiting for something different.'

This was the tipping point. She knew that to strike at me out of hand would have consequences, and those consequences could be very bad for her image. They might even be inconvenient, and the Fae do not like to be inconvenienced.

'Your bleeding has got worse,' she said. 'Perhaps some refreshment and some music in my privy chamber would help you recover.' She stood up, and the Hlæfdigan jumped to it, some running down the tunnel behind the throne, and others picking up the bits and pieces of sewing, reading and embroidery. The oldest of the crew reached underneath the throne and dragged out a Sprite. Had the bloody thing been hiding there all this time? Oh, judging from its expression, it had been asleep.

The Queen smiled on her court, and as one they bowed their heads. I didn't, because I wanted to feel the beam of that smile as often as I could. She said something to them that could have been *You're dismissed until dinner*. Or it could have been an instruction to ready the torture chamber because it wasn't translated. Finally, she spoke to the Princess and to Cartoor.

'Astra, you will play for us. Guard, bring the Dragonslayer to my privy chamber.'

She turned, and the Sprite hopped on to the back of the throne, then down behind her. When the little creature had picked up her dress at the back, she processed out of the hall, down the passage.

The two bodyguards by the dais moved to a tapestry on the throne's right, and this one I'd had a chance to study. It showed the Fair Queen seated below an even bigger throne than the one she owned herself. Most of the throne was off the top of the picture, and it was obviously empty. Her grace was busy plucking at a small harp, and her audience was the creatures of the forest.

It was a good representation, and on its own a nice adornment. What made it special was the magick, because the Fair Queen didn't just play and sing, she also shone like the sun, casting shadows and lighting up the faces of the deer, wild cattle and sheep. Even the rabbits were in awe. I scanned the tapestry's ground, looking for something, and then I remembered that there are no moles in Ireland.

The bodyguards carefully lifted the tapestry and fastened it around a hook. This one was real, then. They disappeared down the tunnel and they were followed by the Chamberlain and the Princess. The rest of the Court had started to break up, some leaving immediately and others forming groups and deploying Silences to hide their conversations. I didn't have to look to know that a lot of glances were being cast in my direction.

The only one who didn't avoid us was the Prince. He came over and nodded his head. I was expecting an awkward conversation, but he carried on by and out of the main entrance.

'That's the Prince of An Mám,' said Cartoor. 'Her Grace's voice in the mundane world. He's off to keep an eye on your friends over the bridge.'

'Not the only one, presumably.'

'Quite. It's a shame we didn't know you were coming: the Court is rather sparse today, what with preparations for the solstice and all the Christmas festivities.'

I smiled and checked my clothes for further purging of Portarra's blood. Not yet. I also checked my watch, and although things were ticking along nicely, there was still a way to go in the outside world.

'Her Grace is ready for you,' announced the Chamberlain. 'This way please.'

'I hope you're ready for this,' said Cartoor. 'It's going to be a real treat for us.' There was no guile in his voice: whatever we were going to face in the Privy Chamber, he clearly thought it was going to be a good time.

The jewellery box had cooled down enough to put in my pocket, so I stowed it and followed the Chamberlain out of the hall and into the unknown. Lord Cartoor followed close behind me.

19 — The Queen's Chamber

The Privy Chamber of the Fair Queen wasn't far from the great hall, and we didn't need to leave the tunnels to get to it. When we got there, the chamber was private only in the sense that you had to be invited to get in. Private, yes, intimate, no. At least it had seats: my leg was starting to hurt from all that standing.

The lady herself was missing, and when we arrived the room was a hive of activity. Tables were being moved by Squires in their yellow coats, a pair of Sprites were trying to drape a protective cloth over a chair which sat next to a comfier version of the throne. Opposite them was a small stage, and on the stage the Princess Astra was tuning a harp.

I looked around, and all of the tapestries in here were real, judging by the way they moved gently when someone walked past. They also rippled with magick, and whatever scenes of glory or celebration they held were in suspense, darkened and shadowy.

The Chamberlain entered, followed by two women, one young and one old, and both human by the look of it. They carried food and drink and placed it on a table at the side of the room, job done the older woman disappeared. The Squires and the Sprites stood back, looking at the Chamberlain for approval.

'Closer,' she said, pointing at one of the chairs. It was moved, and she dismissed them.

The throne, the chair with the dust-sheet and one other were placed to watch the stage. Three other chairs and a table had been placed at the back, behind where I was going to be sitting, and yes, it did make me feel uncomfortable.

'An Bhanríon!' said one of the bodyguards. I'd picked that word up: *The Queen*. The soldiers took places by the wall, and Cartoor and I bowed as her grace wafted into the room. She took her place on the throne and crossed her legs.

'Please, be seated.'

I'd seen shadows follow her: three Hlæfdigan. They sat next to the wall, and I took my place on the covered chair.

'Would you do me the honour of sharing food and drink?' she asked.

Who knows? Maybe my luck is in today. 'The honour is mine, Fair Queen.'

The human woman served us the mostly symbolic food: exquisite salted fish canapés and mead from the hives of Inishsí.

She raised her glass in a toast. 'To new friends.' I was more than happy to drink to that.

I've said it before, but it's worth repeating. The Queen was very interested in the box in my pocket. She could easily drug my wine, take the box and feed my corpse to the fishes of Lough Corrib if she wanted. That she didn't was down to two things.

First, the watchers on the shore represented four powerful interests: the Queen of Galway, the Mages of Galway, the magickal law of the Fiosrúchán Aontaithe na hÉireann, and my friends in England. The Fair Queen could afford to upset one of those, but not all four of them.

The second reason is the law of magickal hospitality. To harm me after feeding me in front of her Guard, a Princess and her Chamberlain would damage her image and put a stain on her reputation that no amount of washing would remove. A bit like the bloodstains growing slowly on my shirt.

The smokeless flaming torches were the only source of light, and they warmed the Queen's skin, giving it a soft glow. 'Astra will play for us a while, and after that I have a special treat for you. Do you recognise her instrument?'

I gave the harp my full attention (I'd been more focused on the player up to now), and I couldn't help a twitch in my face. I'd last seen that harp in the Tangi château in Brittany, on the night we dragged Adaryn ap Owain away to face justice. Adaryn had opted for suicide by cop instead of a cell, and I hadn't given her harp a second thought since. Why would I?

'I do, your grace. It's travelled a long way to be here.'

'It's a fine instrument. Listen.' I never did get to hear Adaryn pluck those strings, and I'll never know if she was as good as Princess Astra or better. If she was better, she'd have been bloody good.

Princess Astra made no concession to me in her choice of music. She played for nearly twenty minutes, and I didn't recognise a single tune, other than that there were jigs and, for a finale, a haunting Irish lament that used the magick in the harp to brush the breeze over me and take me down to an unknown lakeside where water lapped gently at the sides of a boat.

I stood up to applaud, and earned a nod from the Princess in return, as did Cartoor, who'd been applauding even more enthusiastically than me. When I sat back down, the Queen leaned her head towards me and lifted back her golden hair. 'I'm glad you came, Dragonslayer. Any excuse to hear my Astra perform. Now for that treat I promised you – one of my students is going to sing.'

Of course the Queen of Inishsí has students of her own. She's a great patron of the arts and strives for beauty throughout her realm. Or so her PR tells you. The Queen of Galway probably thinks that PR stands for Proportional Representation.

While we waited for Astra to re-tune and for the student to appear, the theory that had first tickled my neck on the bridge came into view. Much of what we perceive in the Fae world is an illusion, that's obvious, and doesn't tell you much more than "Dwarves are strange". It was the extreme contrast at either ends of the lough that were getting to me. The Fair Queen presents herself as generous, as a patron and as being vulnerable to all that is beautiful in nature. Galway not so much.

The Noble Queen's affect is *you don't mess with me.* When you're under threat, you make threats, and if you want to know what triggered this moment of reflection, it was the pink fluffy socks. Underneath, neither Queen is what they seem.

'Here she is,' said the Queen. From a doorway to the right, a young (human) woman appeared. She was lifting her long dress off the floor, and I couldn't see her face, only the mane of red hair. She joined Astra on the stage and turned to face us. There was something familiar about her, and I'd nearly worked it out when the Queen told me. 'This is Medbh. I think you've met.'

This was a massive middle finger in my direction, delivered with mead and a smile: *I know who you are and why you've come. Suck it up, mortal.*

The girl on the stage was a Vessel. The gods only know how she'd got to this point, but right now, all she looked was nervous. Astra played, Medbh sang, and I fell in love with the Queen of Inishsí all over again.

Morwenna hadn't picked up any singing skills from the original Medbh, so this girl had been made a Vessel purely so she could access magick and add it to her natural talent for music, and her singing made the world a better place, a bit like the way the church used to procure castrati for their beautiful voices.

'Thank you, Medbh,' said the Queen. 'We're going to have to work on your relaxation techniques, because when you lost yourself in the music, you took me to a special place.'

The girl who'd been made Medbh blushed and bowed and hurried off the stage as quickly as her legs could carry her. When she'd gone, the Queen stirred herself and stood up. Cartoor and I followed suit as quickly as we could.

'I think that the Dragonslayer and I have business now,' she said to Cartoor. 'He's truly welcome in my home, so you can leave us. All of you can.'

Cartoor bowed. 'Thank you for letting me hear the music, Fair Queen.'

He left through the door to the great hall, the Hlæfdigan the other way, and the Queen pointed to the bodyguards, saying a couple of words in Fae. 'They are in their own world, now. It's just you and me. Have a seat and show my what you've got in your pocket. I'm dying to know.'

Yes, the Fair Queen was now flirting with me. I sighed inwardly, allowing myself a moment's pleasure, then took out the box before I sat down. I placed it on the table away from the Queen and turned to shield it with my body. I had other business to deal with first.

'In a moment, Fair Queen. I would first talk about Morwenna, if it pleases you.'

She drew back a little, withdrawing her light from me. 'I'm not sure that it does.' She considered for a second, then decided to get it over with. 'Have you spoken directly to the Noble Queen?'

'I have. She was less gracious than you, but she did give me a moment of her time.'

'Of course. Then you will know about Clíodhna.'

'That she and her daughter received your favour, yes.'

It doesn't do to state the truth on these occasions: *You bought her off and bound her to you.*

'Then you can rest assured that my interest in Morwenna Ahearn ended when that great oaf ripped Lara Dent out of her. You were there, were you not? Why did he do it?'

'I think it was because Lara Dent was all too human, your grace. The Count of Force Ghyll dealt with it the only way he knew how, as I dealt with him.'

She lifted her left hand, not quite pointing at me, but letting me know I was being measured. 'I think you named the wrong culprit there. I think you meant to say that *Morwenna Mowbray* was being all-too-human. Before you ask, I did not send her to Pellacombe – she fled there because she hadn't come to terms with her fate. I had no hand in the death of her father, and now she is released. I wish her well, and that's the end of it.'

Did I believe her? That's the question. You cannot bind the Fae to the truth in the same way that you can other creatures, and don't ask me why – it's something to do with their Essence, which is to say that no one knows. Or if they do, they're not telling.

She had given me her answer freely, and probably the only bit that really mattered were her final words. *That's the end of it.* You can't bind them to the truth, but they do stand by their word. I am interested in Morwenna for all sorts of reasons, but I wasn't really there for the Mowbrays, I was there for the Clarkes. I retrieved the jewellery box and placed it on my knee.

'Is that what I think it is?' she asked. 'Does it have my Name on it?'

'It does, your grace. One second – this catch is stiff.'

Not all magickal creatures have secret names: Lloyd Flint is Lloyd Flint is Lloyd Flint, for example, but the Fae most certainly have a secret name, one that both has power in its weaving and gives power to those who know it. The greatest of Fae magick has their name woven into it, if you know where to look, and I had a prime example of that in the jewel box.

In 1618 (or 1619, he was vague on that), my ancestor Thomas Clarke did a deal to get rid of the Codex Defanatus. It was sealed by the Morrigan in the Grounds of Elvenham Grange and carried away by the Dwarf, Niði. The seal was so strong that only a unique set of events could unlock it, and until that day it was an asset that no one could exploit. But if they could…

Eighty years later, in 1689, a visitor called at Niði's Hall and swapped the Codex for a rare and priceless Artefact: the Rockseed, the Philosopher's Stone of Dwarven magick. Naturally, given that the visitor was Fae, the Rockseed was a fake. A good one, yes, but worthless magickally, except for the diamond at its heart, and at the heart of the diamond was the name of its maker. I was sitting next to her now.

The box finally unlocked, and I prised it open.

In the low light, the diamond didn't just sparkle, it sang, a beautiful note of sweetness echoed round the room as it found its namesake. My ancestor did the deal, and it was my birth that unlocked the book. Ever since then, the Fair Queen has been selling old and dangerous magick to the highest bidder, and using some of it herself; the Vessels are evidence of that.

'Why is my little trinket in a ring?' she asked. 'A tiny ring.'

'My fiancée has small fingers, your grace.'

Her laughter tinkled, higher in pitch than her normal voice. 'You made *that* into an engagement ring? You were either brave or foolish.'

'Or both. She's worth it, though.'

'I'm sure she is. You can put it away now.'

I closed the box and put it on the table. When I looked at the Queen, she was fingering her necklace and staring at me. My arms ran cold, and something gave my heart a gentle squeeze. 'Speak to me truly,' she said.

A mundane human would know that something was wrong, and I knew that I was now being subject to the Fae equivalent of a lie detector. She wouldn't have done it with witnesses present, but we were on our own now. I thought about using what I'd read to fight it, then relaxed and let it sit.

'What would your grace know?'

'Did the creature send you?'

'Niði, you mean? No. He doesn't know where I am.'

She thought about that. 'But does he know whose name that is?'

'He does not.'

She smiled, reassured, and sat back a little. 'How did you come by it? I knew that you trafficked with him, but this? Did you steal it?'

'I did not. He gave it to me. He wanted to trick me, and when the casing dissolved, I was left with this. It's taken me a while to find you. I'm glad I did, despite the dangers.'

'And I'm glad, too. Your visit has been the most unexpected pleasure. Tell me, what do you want?'

'I want to broker an exchange. A fair deal.'

'You sound like you already have terms.'

'I do. I will give you the ring with no word to anyone, especially not Niði. In exchange, you give me all the remaining sections of the Codex, and a list of all those you've already sold. With buyers, obviously.'

She didn't laugh or get angry. She gave me a sad smile and said, 'A high price. What would you do with such riches?'

'Hand over the Codex to the Esoteric Library and pay a visit to those on the list. I am sure that it will prevent many more deaths.'

'Who else knows the true nature of your mission?'

'A few. They are all bound so closely to me that they will keep the secret forever.'

The grip of the lie detector faded, and she was left with a problem. Like any great leader, she also knew that every problem is an opportunity in disguise. 'Will you negotiate, Dragonslayer?'

'Call me Conrad, please, now that we're alone, and yes, I've come to negotiate, not to issue ultimata.'

'Good. There are too many waiting for us here, too many hanging around the doors. Shall we go somewhere truly, truly private?'

'I … I hadn't hoped for such an honour.' She stood and clapped her hands. The acoustics of the room changed, and the Chamberlain appeared. The Queen spoke to her in English and said, 'Tell my ladies to prepare the bower. I will be entertaining our guest privately.'

'Your Grace.'

She offered me her arm. 'Your leg is giving you great pain, Conrad. Let me support you.'

I took her arm, and for the first time, I got to look down on her. She looked up and her face radiated pleasure. She squeezed my arm and said, 'Let's go.'

20 — *The Queen's Bower*

She led me into the gardens. The hall was in the main part of the hill, and only if you scaled it did you see the dip at the top, the hidden, sheltered place where roses bloomed in winter and a wall of sunflowers, taller than me, cast a gentle light over the garden.

Yes, that's right, the sunflowers glowed with the light of the sun. Well, it was night, now, wasn't it? To get to the gardens, the Queen had helped me up and over another threshold that flared orange. Through the door, I pretended to stumble so that I could get a glimpse of my watch. From having too much time, it was now running out. I had to strike my bargain soon or die trying.

'Very few mortals get to see this place,' she said. 'Which is a great shame, really. In the summer, my coven celebrate the solstice, and I try to have as many concerts as I can out here.'

'I had no idea such beauty existed,' I said, and when I said it, I looked at her. She got what I meant.

'Even fewer mortals get to see what lies below,' she whispered.

The steps at the back of the gardens wound down, turning back into the hill, and going down a long way. 'I have a more direct route,' she said. 'This one is better for you, because you got to see the gardens, and this Way is easier. We can do it in steps.'

In yellow steps, to be precise. Several of them. By the time we got to the arch at the bottom of the stairs, the clock was definitely ticking.

The passage on the other side of the arch led through the hill, and joined the bottom of the stairs that were her normal route to and from her bower. Lord Cartoor was waiting for us in the antechamber, and he had a frown on his face.

'What is it?' snapped the Queen.

He answered in Fae, one hand on his belt, the other on his sword, and both eyes fixed on me. Oh dear.

The Queen was not happy, in fact I'd go so far as to say that she was disappointed. With me. She unfastened her arm and gripped my shirt with her delicate fingers. 'Tell me true, Conrad, does the Noble Queen have an army in the field? What is she doing? Tell me!'

I was devastated that she was angry with me. I'd do anything to get back on her good side. 'Your grace, I know nothing of this! I know of no army, no plans or anything of what the Noble Queen is doing. Nothing. I give you my word as a Clarke. She knows I'm here, but she knows nothing of the ring or my plans.'

The Fair Queen had been gripping the material where blood had made a growing patch, and I'd noticed that the colours of transition had been getting harder to see. Much longer and I wouldn't have a clue. She released my shirt and her magick released my heart. When she went to move her hair off her shoulder, she gave a tiny sniff, then she did something no Fae has any need to do: she coughed. And when she coughed, she licked her own hand.

'That's good enough for me, Cartoor. Return to your post and keep watch. I need to finish my business with the Dragonslayer, and I've no doubt that Galway is just flexing those mighty muscles of hers. Thank you.'

Cartoor bowed and stepped backwards. The Queen took my hand in hers and led me on a final, green transition into her bower.

Mortals have returned from a Queen's bower. It would be bad for business if they didn't, although most have little memory of what happened to them. What they all agree on is that here, Mother Nature is at her most concentrated.

The sunflowers were back, warming as well as lighting, and the grass in her bower was as green as any field of clover. Her ladies were waiting for her by a little sloping grove of trees, and they placed golden cushions for us to sit on. 'Fetch mead and my jewels,' said the Queen.

'Your grace, not for me, thank you. I find it a little sweet, if I'm telling the truth.'

'Lace it with Amrita for him. Just a drop. We'll need something to seal the deal, won't we, Conrad?'

'As your grace wishes.'

We sat, and she told me of some of the flowers. One of them in particular made the hairs on the back of my neck stand up. 'This is the Morrigan's flower.'

'But that looks like a yew tree.'

'It is. It is said that when Cú Chulainn died she was there in the form of a raven. She flew away and wept, and when the raven's tears fell on the oldest yew tree in Ireland, it bloomed. This is a cutting from that tree. You know of Cú Chulainn, Conrad?'

'I do. He made the mistake of not listening to good advice from women.'

She laughed, and placed her soft hand on my scarred arm. 'You took the words from me. Cú Chulainn was the Hound of Ulster. I shall call you the Hound of Gloucester.' She lifted it away when the Hlæfdigan returned, leaving a tingle behind it. Two goblets of gold were placed on the ground in front of us, and a plain cabinet of Irish oak was offered to the Queen.

She knew instinctively what she wanted, and opened three drawers, palming the contents. 'Give me some cloth from your gown,' she ordered the youngest of the ladies. Teeth were bared and a square of yellow silk was placed on the ground between us.

On to the silk, she placed a huge diamond, two rubies and two emeralds. 'I think this is a fair exchange,' she said. 'What do you think, Hound of Gloucester?'

'I think that none of these are the fairest jewel.' I paused, then continued with a sigh. 'My family name and the fate of innocents are at stake, your grace. I must decline.'

She took my hand, massaging the palm and trailing her fingertips up my arm. 'Cú Chulainn was brave. I think that you are braver, Hound of Gloucester. I think that you would have no fear if you walked with me to the pool. I think that you could take those gems and let the rest of the world take care of itself. I think you would seize the chance to drink, to explore and to leave something. You are no boy, Conrad. You are a man. Brood from your seed could be a new Great Queen. I think that's the real reason you're here.'

I looked down at the gems. 'Your grace can see right through me. I … I had no idea you could be *so* beautiful. If you are willing to let the chips fall where they may, then so am I. These gems and a night with you in exchange for the ring. I name my price.'

'I think we can manage more than one night, Hound of Gloucester. I accept your price. Do you not find it warm here? I do. Let us go and cool down.'

She used her strength to help me up, then gathered the gems into the square of silk and held them in her right hand. With her left, she led me away, downhill and towards an arch of trees. Although the arch was shallow, whatever was on the other side was blacked out with no light escaping it. She called for her ladies, then said to me. 'Let them help you, as they help me.'

Three of them used magick and long arms to lift off the Queen's golden gown and shoes, leaving her in a loose silk shift that reached to her knees; it was so white that it almost hurt my eyes. While I was looking at what had been revealed, the Hlæfdigan had my shirt, boots and trousers off in no time. The only thing I removed myself was the sword that I'd been carrying; when it came to the watch, they struggled, but couldn't work the clasp, so they left it be.

The Queen stared at me, and pointed to two places where more blood was leaking slowly from my skin. 'It will soon wash away,' she said.

I held out the box with the ring. 'As we agreed,' I said.

'Now?'

'If it please your grace. Then I can forget all about it, and what it represents.'

'So be it.'

I swapped the box for the twist of silk, and laid my prize next to my sword and my clothes. 'It is done,' I said. 'Let the chips fall where they may.'

She took my hand and led me through the arch, with a burst of violet, edging into Royal Violet, because we were now in the deepest heart of the sídhe, the pool. It was exactly where Morwenna had awoken, right here next to the water.

The youngest Hlæfdige had followed with the cups, and by the water we drank to our agreement. I checked my watch while the Queen gave an order, and if I was right, I'd made it with about half an hour to spare.

When we were alone, the Queen took off her shift and revealed herself completely, every smooth plane and curve, every inch of flawless skin. 'Your turn,' she said, and I joined her in total nakedness. Apart from the watch. Right now, time was my only friend. She sat me down on the bank by the pool and began to sing, and I had no choice but join in her dance.

In the end, it was the Countess Portarra who saved me, because on my own, I couldn't have lasted. The Fair Queen wanted two things from me: yes, she wanted my seed, but that only takes a moment. It was getting me to drink more Amrita that she really desired, an extra dose that would make me forget everything but her beauty and bind me to her with an invisible thread, and she was well on the way to getting it until she started to lick my chest.

Tasting the blood of her rival's brood was far more intoxicating than anything I could give her. We hadn't moved much further than that when I felt it: something in the ground called to a part of me I didn't fully realise existed, and when I twisted to look away, I saw that the wall of green was getting rusty spots.

'Did the earth move for you, too?' I asked.

'We've barely started,' she said, scarcely noticing my words.

'There!' I said. 'You must have felt that.'

She climbed off me and looked around. 'What's going on?'

The third time I felt it, the ground didn't just move, it shook. Violently.

'What have you done?' hissed the Queen.

I made myself comfortable on the bank. 'Nothing. If you'd taken the exchange I offered, I'd have walked out and made a phone call. I'd have called him off.'

When running in a familiar course, the Fae are quick. Quick as quicksilver. When trying to take on something new, they slow down. 'But I felt it! You told the truth. How can this be?'

'When you asked me, Niði was sealed in a box on a boat on the lough. He had no idea where he was or who you were. When I didn't call, my blood-brother broke the seals and told him the truth.'

It still hadn't penetrated. 'You can't have brought him here. It's impossible!'

'I'm sorry, your grace. Truly sorry.'

It was my sympathy that broke the dam inside her, and she realised that yes, she was under attack in her sídhe from an angry Dwarf. She showed some of her true nature then, and I'd like to say that it was black and evil, twisted and a thing of the night. It wasn't: it was more beautiful still.

Great shimmering wings of gold appeared at her back, and her eyes shone the same colour. Her arms moved and the magick-sodden bower came alive with colours. She was trying to shift us even further away from the natural world, up on to higher realms and away from Niði's vengeance. Much further and we'd end up having breakfast with the Morrigan.

Golden sweat ran down her face, mixing with golden tears. Her mouth was open in struggle, and all her Fae teeth were bared in determination. The bower flared again, but yellow this time. Then it didn't flare at all, and it was suddenly quiet. She collapsed to her knees and looked at me. 'Why, Conrad? Why?'

'I said I was sorry, and I am. Sorry for you and the beauty you've created, but mostly sorry that others have paid the price for your greed.'

Her wings faded away, and she stood up, hooking the soaking hair away from her face. The moment of silence was shattered with a growl, and Niði the Dwarf appeared, carrying a great axe and wearing a huge diamond on a chain round his neck. His eyes glowed red with fire, and parts of his leather harness were smoking. Even his beard looked singed.

The Queen of Inishsí lifted her arms and tried to work magick. There was a flicker in her fingers, but it made no difference. Niði stepped forwards and swung his axe. He chopped her in two at the waist, and the explosion blew me backwards into the pool.

21 — The Chips Fall

The shock of the water nearly killed me. Humans are not meant to bathe in that pool. Be washed gently in its water, yes; immersed and take a mouthful, no.

My mind filled with gold, a great golden sky with a black sun that was going to burn out my eyes, until the sun reached down a hand and pulled me out of the water. As I lay gasping and hallucinating on the bank, I heard Niði say, 'Is that what I think it is?'

I heard a splash, and then some thumps. By the time my eyes cleared, Niði had climbed back out of the pool and he had a dozen eggs lined up in front of him.

'Thank you,' I said. 'Thank you for that.'

'The pleasure is mine. I have waited a long time for this moment,' he replied without looking up from the eggs. 'And thank you for finding the cockroach who robbed me.' He looked up and looked around at the devastation, and he was greatly pleased with himself, and satisfied with what he had done.

There was one question that I've been wanting to ask but scared of. Now that she was dead, it didn't matter so much, and I wasn't fit to stand up yet. 'When you gave me the diamond, did you always mean for me to find her?'

'It was bait. I knew you and the Watch would be tempted, and you did what it would have taken years for me to accomplish. You were happy enough to follow her.'

I couldn't deny it. When I'd told Niði that I'd found the Queen who'd robbed him, I thought I was being clever asking him to break into the sídhe. No. He'd been expecting it. He'd even been working on how to plane-shift while he waited centuries for chance to get revenge. He was right, though, I'd gone into this with my eyes open. I tested my extremities and magickal Sight: all in working order. Time to survive.

'Shouldn't we be going?' I asked. 'We're rather high up here.'

'We are. She fought hard, and we're nearly in Ásgarðr. If she'd managed a couple more jumps, I'd have been lost, and now that she's gone, we'll sink most of the way. I never thought I'd get to taste these.'

And with that, he took a Fae egg and bit into it. The look of happiness on his face nearly turned my stomach when the smell hit me. I looked at this muddy, singed and grotesque creature stuffing his face with the Queen's brood, and then I looked around at the peace of the bower, at the intricate Works woven into the sunflowers and the golden cups lying on their sides, their sweet nectar drained away. Of the Queen herself, there was no obvious trace. She, and all her beauty were gone forever, and I had had a hand in it.

Niði finished a second egg and belched loudly. 'They're rich,' he said, hovering his hand over the selection. They glowed still, for a moment, and different colours shone from them. It was time to pull myself together or sit by the pool until the sedge withered and no birds sang.

'We did a deal,' I said.

'And I've fulfilled my part. Don't worry, I'll push you out of the bower when the time comes.'

'And then? There are going to be a lot of angry Fae out there.'

He glanced up. 'You didn't think this through, did you? This flea pit nest of cockroaches is collapsing. The earth around us is reclaiming the space, and we're going to be on top. Time is passing so quickly out there that it will be dawn by then. You know what will happen to me.'

Oh shit. Oh shit, oh shit, oh shit. If the sun's rays strike Niði, he will turn to stone. I was suddenly in very deep trouble.

He continued, oblivious of my worry. 'I was going to give you the axe, but you've taken too much of the Fae into you. Don't touch it or you'll die. Aaah. We're close, now. I can feel my selves again. This is good.'

The diamond around his neck glowed even brighter, and I had to look away. Back at his Hall in Dudley, there was another Niði, and when not locked in the back of a horse transporter, they share consciousness in ways that the single-minded will never understand. That's what they call us when they're being really abusive: single-minded. And right now, the other Niði was discovering what Fae eggs taste like.

I was furious, and I couldn't think in here. Not caring what happened, I knocked the next egg out of his hand. 'Get me out of here. Now.' I pointed to the diamond. 'Listen, if you don't help me, it will be known.'

Somehow, the different parts of Niði thought it over, and the one in front of me got up reluctantly and walked towards the arch leading back to the rest of the bower. I grabbed the Queen's shift and put it on to cover my nakedness.

Niði had promised to push me out of the bower, and he kept his promise with a shove in the back that was so hard that I flew into the air…

…And landed face down on the sweet grass.

Women's screams. A cry in Gaeilge. A shudder from the ground as Mother Earth and Mother Nature struggled to reconcile several different structures that occupied the same space. Smell of leaves, the Fae were close. Time to move.

One of the Hlæfdigan was approaching me, the younger one who'd donated part of her dress earlier. Her face was a mask of terror and shock, and every single one of the Queen's children, no matter where in the world they were, now knew that she was suddenly, violently dead.

Like all her sisters, this one wore a long gown that could have come straight from a pre-Raphaelite painting, if she'd been the only subject. Only a really third-rate artist would have had *all* his female figures in golden yellow.

'How…?'

Either she couldn't find the words in English, or she couldn't find them in any language. I got to my knees, then to my feet, and looked around. The greater bower was already dimmer, the source of Lux for the sunflowers was rapidly running out and the structures that held it together were disintegrating. The Hlæfdigan in here were running in pairs, or forming groups, then splitting up and running again.

'Why are you still here?' I asked, looking closer to home. Aah. There they are. I moved to my pile of clothes and she stepped back when she saw me reach for the sword. 'I'm not going to hurt you. You should leave.'

'We … we cannot. The portal…'

The Queen must have dragged the greater bower up along with the inner grove. No wonder she was in no fit state to fight when the Dwarf arrived, so I had a moment. I also had an idea.

'Shout loudly and call them here,' I said. 'Tell them I will help you escape.'

While she shouted, I moved the sword out of sight and jammed my feet in my boots. The Hlæfdigan hurried over and gathered around. At a safe distance. 'Who speaks the best English?' I asked.

It was the youngest, or youngest looking, who fell on her knees. 'Mercy, great lord. Have mercy on us.'

'Listen and translate. Quickly. Once we leave, you will be fought over. You will be dragged and grabbed and killed one by one.' I paused, and she stammered out the words. In Fae. 'I offer my protection. Come with me, be my eyes and ears, and I will protect you with my life. This I promise.'

As soon as the second part had been relayed, an argument broke out. The oldest drew a dagger and pointed at me. The message was clear: *there are eight of us against one human. Let's get vengeance now.*

The translator and the one who'd first approached me broke ranks and dashed to my side, skidding to their knees and lowering their heads. 'Quickly,' I said to them. 'Tie my laces, then we're off. Hurry!'

It took them half a second, then they got to it. At that moment, the dagger-wielding Hlæfdige looked at where my sword was and charged me, knowing I couldn't reach it in time.

The Lux in the bower was fading, but it was still a Queen's sídhe. I drew on it and, in my clumsy way, created a blast that staggered her back. One of the others launched herself at the creature and started struggling for the knife. She won, and plunged it straight into their elder's chest. One by one, the other four dropped to their knees.

'It is done, great lord.'

'What are your names?' I asked the translator.

'Rose. This is Fern. We are all the flowers in the Queen's garden. We … what is happening, Great Lord? How did you kill the Great Queen?'

'Get up, Rose and Fern. Let's get moving.' I grabbed my sword and the twisted square of silk containing the jewels. I shoved it in Fern's hand and said, 'Put that somewhere no one can see, and grab a cutting from that flowering yew tree. Rose? Translate everything I say.'

I strode forwards towards the portal, pausing between sentences. 'Follow me and keep together. I did not kill your Queen. Rose called her *Great Queen.* She was not the Great Queen. She did great harm to a Dwarf.' At that point they stopped to have an argument. Clearly the idea of an actual *Dwarf* in the sídhe was too much.

'If you stay behind, you will die. This bower is going to be pushed outside very soon. I doubt that anything will survive.' That got their attention. I reached the Portal and realised that I had absolutely no idea what to do next, because the arch in the bower wall led to nothing but blackness. 'Who knows most of these things?' I demanded.

Rose shoved one of her sisters in the back and propelled her towards me. 'She does, but she has no English. She has said that she has no power to make the bridge.'

'What's her name?'

'Clover, great lord.' There was an unspoken *Why do you care?* In her voice.

'Clover? That's a lucky name.' I held out my hand. 'Come here.' She came reluctantly, and stopped between me and the Portal. 'Rose, get the others to join hands. When I lift my hand out of the ground, grab it hard, and for Odin's sake hold on for your lives.'

I reached for Clover's hand and pointed to the Portal. She looked like she'd rather grab an iron from the fire with no glove than touch me. Rose shouted something, and Clover reluctantly slipped her silk-soft fingers into mine.

I plunged my other hand into the grass and dug down with my Sight. No matter how Fae this magick was, underneath it all was Lux, and when Lux flows through Mother Earth, I can feel it.

A tingle. A warm waft over my fingers. Close, but no cigar. I tried to stand. Ouch. Then a tug on my other hand as Clover figured out what I needed, and with her strength, I got to my feet. I moved further right and plunged my hand back down.

Better. Now we're talking. A rich vein of Lux was flowing *in* from the Portal, and I've done this often enough now to have some control as I channelled it back to Clover.

Except she screamed. Too much. I dialled it down, and she staggered; this time it was my strength holding her up. She focused on the Portal, and I felt the draw of Lux. The blackness of the arch started to sparkle with stars. I nearly lost my grip when she started to sweat badly, and then the darkness glowed, and when it was shimmering, Clover spoke.

'Now,' said Rose.

I lifted my arm, Rose grabbed my hand, and Clover led us through the darkness and into the light.

22 — *The Queen is Dead*

Half of the torches had gone out in the antechamber, and Lord Cartoor was mostly in shadow. I saw his sword, though, and it glowed brightly as he lifted it to attack me.

I let go of the two hands I was holding and tried to step back and draw my own weapon. I barged into Rose, and it was too late anyway, because Cartoor was too close. He would have sliced me open if Clover hadn't stepped in front of me and dropped to her knees.

It stopped him long enough for me to shuffle sideways and hold up my hands. 'The Queen is dead, Cartoor, and her ladies are under my protection. Do you want vengeance or do you want to be the one who names the new Queen?'

That stopped him alright. He shouted at the Hlæfdigan and gestured behind him. Led by Clover, they backed away and gathered behind me instead.

'Hand them over, Dragonslayer, and I'll let you escape with your worthless human carcase intact. I'm sure someone else will catch up with you.'

'Your Queen didn't listen to me, Cartoor, and she's dead. Don't make the same mistake. This bunch are under my protection. Join me and you'll be in pole position to offer them *your* protection if they choose to take it. Or we can waste time in combat. Your choice.'

Rose said something in Fae that made Cartoor screw up his face.

'A *Dwarf*? In the sídhe? Impossible.'

I held up my hand, displaying Odin's ring. 'She speaks truly.'

I also noticed that Clover hadn't been sweating into my hand – she'd been bleeding. I looked at her, and realised there was almost nothing remaining beyond her wrist except bloody bone and sinew. Fern was trying to do something to help.

'I don't understand,' said Cartoor. He clearly didn't. I think that Portarra would have grasped the situation in the blink of an eye, and that was another mistake the Fair Queen made. You shouldn't choose your chief Guard for his looks.

'We're leaving by the back stairs to the upper gardens. You'd better go in front. You know the way. I'll take the rear.'

He understood that much, and sprang into action; Rose ordered the others to follow him, and I waited until their backs were turned before wiping my hand on my leg. It seemed disrespectful to wipe the blood of her brood on the Fair Queen's shift. Job done, I drew my sword and turned for one last look at the archway. On either side were two disgusting pools of goo, and soaking in them were the uniforms of the Queen's bodyguards. They were so closely bound to her that they must have expired the moment she did.

A sorry figure was waiting for us at the top. Still in the primrose yellow evening dress that clashed horribly with her red hair was the 'new' Medbh. She was cowering behind a raised bed of dying sunflowers, and didn't have a clue what to do.

Cartoor ignored her and turned to me. 'What do we do now? Is it safe here?'

How the fuck should I know that?

'Rose, ask Clover what's going to happen to the garden when the merging is complete.'

While the question and answer were rendered, I beckoned Medbh over. 'Are there any other mortals inside?'

'Sure I don't know. I was practising when the place started to shake. Is it true? Is she dead?'

I nodded to Medbh, and Rose started to translate Clover's opinion on the unravelling of the sídhe. 'We should go higher. Closer to the eastern edge.'

I led the party towards the wilder area of the Queen's gardens, up a slope and beyond the warmth of the sunflowers. Something was happening to the sky here. When the Fair Queen had brought me through, I hadn't been able to see what was above me, though I was fairly sure that we hadn't been "underground". On a different plane, yes, but not below the rocks of the natural world. After all, the sunflowers were there to harvest Lux, and for that they needed daylight as much as their mundane cousins.

At the edge of the gardens, daylight was struggling to break through a fog of some description, and the cloudless skies of the Fae realm were about to be replaced by something naturally Irish.

The small Fae realm at the bottom of my garden in Clerkswell has been without its Count for centuries, but it's still there: a young Knight could move in and be at home in no time. It doesn't work like that for the sídhe of a Queen.

The Fair Queen's bower was at the bottom of a time dilation well and physically underground. At the same time it was on the summit of a high hill of magick, twisting space and creating its own little pocket of time, making an equation that only balanced by the injection of huge amounts of Lux on one side.

The creation of those opposite elements was instinctive to the Queen, like making a hive is instinctive to bees, and I presume that's where they get it from. In the making of her bower, she'd tied herself so strongly to it that without her, the Lux no longer flowed. We were about to see the values of that equation reach stability.

At the far end of the gardens, where the great hall, privy chamber and other constructions were located, earth started to move. The underground spaces had been made well, and as they reappeared at natural level, they were pushing the earth aside like water. Soil and rock rippled out in a wave and smashed through the beds and borders, drowning the Queen's planting.

The sound hit us, a roaring cry of pain from the earth that I heard with my ears and felt with my feet. Then, with a flash of light, Mother Earth shuddered and became still, and from behind me, sunlight fell on Inishsí. I turned to see where we were, and there was the water of the Lough, spread out in front of me at the bottom of a steep slope. Before I could get my bearings properly, a scream made me turn.

A flash of yellow and red. I brought my arm up and deflected Medbh's sword, but she still crashed into me. We both dropped our weapons as we tried to keep our footing, and we both failed.

I was rolling and falling, down the slope. I threw my arms and legs out to slow me down only for my bad leg to hit a rock. It stopped me, but at the cost of blinding pain. More pain as Medbh hit me, too, rolling me on to my back.

I couldn't stop her getting on top of me and pinning my shoulders down because I couldn't breathe. Her hands reached for my neck and squeezed. I bucked up my shoulders, and she panicked when I drew half a breath. Her fingers were too small and too weak to do the job quickly. She reached for her belt, and I was able to get my right hand down, enough to lever her off me. Too late. She had a dagger out.

Just before she could strike, a crack of thunder filled the air and her eyes bulged wide. She coughed up blood and collapsed in front of me; in the back of her yellow gown was a gaping hole, and standing up the slope was Lord Cartoor.

'Put yourself away, man. No one wants to see that first thing in the morning. Well, I don't, that's for sure.'

I pulled the Queen's shift down to cover my nakedness, and he kicked something down the slope. My sword. It came to rest on Medbh, and Cartoor followed it; the rest of our little gang coming down slowly. They weren't dressed for rock scrambling, and neither was I. It was bloody cold out here. At the very least I had to figure out if I was fit to stand and get off this soaking grass.

Cartoor arrived at Medbh's body and grabbed her head. He tugged hard, and as well as rolling her over, he also pulled off a great red wig. 'That's the trouble with humans. You can't fecking trust them most of the time. Astra always said this one was away with the fairies.' His mouth split in the Fae smile as he brought out his extra teeth. 'I'm allowed to say that.'

Underneath the red wig was greying brown hair, and underneath the makeup and magick was a woman well into her forties. Cartoor saw me looking. 'Sent over from America, would you believe. Here.' He held out his hand, and I had my way of getting up. 'I'll give you this, too, before you die of cold.'

He opened his coat by force, ripping the buttons and letting them fly around. I took it gratefully and put it on. 'Thank you. Your intervention was unexpected.'

'On the way up, I asked Fern all about the bower, and she told me you'd offered them all protection *before* you knew you needed them to get out. Killing this trinket was nothing compared to that.'

Sword now firmly in hand, I turned and looked around. I'd fallen and rolled on to a natural ledge, two thirds of the way down the hill, and I could feel the bruises starting to form already. Clover spoke and pointed to the slope to my right. 'It is coming,' said Rose.

'It is, and so are a lot else,' said Cartoor.

Small figures were running along the strand at the water's edge, heading our way, and getting bigger. Others were following our route down the slope, but it was the Lough that held my gaze. A small flotilla of boats was approaching, and somewhere on each vessel was a red and white flag. Oh dear. I opened my mouth to speak, then grabbed at Fern to keep myself upright because the earth was shuddering again.

There was no tidal wave of soil this time. Instead, a fountain of water gushed out of the ground like a geyser powered by light, blinding me and making me look away. I heard a deep groan, and as the spots cleared from my vision, I saw this Niði for the last time, reaching towards the dawn and then freezing. Freezing solid. Solid, steaming, red-hot rock.

Cartoor clapped me on the back. 'I should never have doubted you, Dragonslayer. A Dwarf! I'll be old before I see that again. You're still on the hook for bringing him in, mind.' He was about to go on, then he fell silent as from the steam around Niði, a huge figure emerged. 'Gracious Lady, have mercy,' he said, and fell flat on the ground.

'Well met, Dragonslayer,' said the Morrigan.

And I thought the day was going quite well.

Part Four

Legacy

23 — Long Live the Queen

She is the god of war and death. She has a necklace of ruby skulls around her throat. Her knife is longer than my sword. She towers over mortals and immortals alike. She is the Morrigan. I bowed low.

She was also the guarantor of the Codex Defanatus, and she came to Clerkswell when Thomas Clarke told his story. I was scared then. No, I was terrified. This was ten times worse.

She bent down from her enormous height and picked something off the statue of Niði. With a flick of her wrist, she threw it at me, and I caught it, then dropped it because it burnt my hand. At my feet was the diamond that the Dwarf had used to enter the Fair Queen's bower.

'Take that foul thing away back where it came from,' said the goddess. 'I don't trust any of these lot with such an evil object. And don't worry, Dragonslayer, I'm not here for you. Whenever a Queen falls on this isle, I am there. Whenever the People lose a mother, I am there to bury her. When the sun sets on Inishsí, it will be sealed for as long as its Queen lived. Five hundred and forty years in this case, if you're counting. After that, I wonder who'll come looking inside it for treasure, because there's plenty in there. And ghosts. Them, too.'

The other figures we'd seen were getting closer, and one by one they arrived at the edge of an invisible circle and fell flat on the ground.

'Why am I the only one standing?' I asked. It was the only thing I could think of.

The Morrigan had already started looking around on the ground, oblivious. 'What? Oh, it's that ring of yours. Aah. Here we are.'

She bent down and picked up something tiny from the grass. She held it in her cupped hands and blew on it gently. After a few seconds, she opened her hands and a big insect flew drunkenly into the morning sunshine. It *looked* like a bumble bee. It flew like a bumble bee, and like a bumble bee it was soon out of sight.

'If you've a wise bone in your body, you'll tell no one you saw that,' she said. She paused and looked around for a second, and I recovered something of my equilibrium.

'Great lady, have you got what you wanted?' I asked.

As soon as the words were out of my mouth, I regretted them, because it meant that she turned her full attention on me. When she said nothing, I decided that I was so deep in this hole, I might as well keep digging. Shame I'd given away the curried worms.

'I can't help wondering how the Allfather came by the Doorstone to Corrib Castle. It meant nothing in the end, because it wasn't a smoking gun, but it convinced me that I was on the right track. Somehow I don't think that the Wanderer was here when the Corrib Raid happened.'

'Get in where a draught wouldn't, that one,' she replied. 'Are you saying that I would conspire with a Power in Britain to bring down one of the People? That would be dangerous talk, Dragonslayer.'

That's exactly what I thought she *had* done, and she could see that from the look in my face.

'You would have come here sooner or later, would you not?'

I looked down, and she knew her words were true. 'Don't question our ways, mortal. That's a piece of friendly advice. I'll also point out that I didn't make you come here. That was your choice.' She paused again. 'I don't normally do this, but I'm going to ask *you* a question. How did you get him here without me or the Fair Queen having a sniff of him?' She gestured to the stone Dwarf and raised her eyebrows.

'In a horse transporter, great lady. Specially adapted by a Son of the Earth. And then a boat.'

She nodded thoughtfully. 'I'm off underground now. I'll see you at your wedding, if not before. Go well.'

I bowed again, and by the time I'd straightened up, she was gone, and everyone else was waking up. Or disembarking in the case of the Queen of Galway's party.

The already assembled crowd were all members of the late Fair Queen's household, from Princess Astra down to a couple of Sprites who had managed to survive, and still running to catch up were four familiar figures and one extra, last seen on the other side of the bridge. I couldn't keep a huge grin off my face as Eseld, Fiadh and Portarra struggled over the rocks, and behind them came Portarra's Squire and another woman, presumably the Iarrthóir, the Seeker of the United Inquisition.

As soon as they realised I was there, Eseld and Fiadh took out their phones. Eseld put hers to her ear, and I hoped that she was calling Mina. Fiadh held hers up and stopped to take a picture of me wearing nothing but a yellow coat, a white shift and a pair of boots. And carrying a sword. It was at that point I leaned my head back and started to laugh.

'Prepare to die, mortal.'

'Knock it off, An Mám,' said Cartoor. 'This is not the time or place.'

The Prince who'd been there in the great hall was squaring up to me. He had a shock of grey hair over a face that Vicky would call *chiselled*. Unlike the household, who'd all worn yellow coats, he was in a very smart suit, with only a yellow silk square poking out of the pocket to show his allegiance. The coat was already half way off when I saw the blade on the floor. Oh.

'He saved the Hlæfdigan, ye eejit,' said Cartoor. 'Out of nothing but pity for them as far as I can gather. If you've any sense, you'll back off.'

'And they are going to be mine,' said An Mám, 'as soon as I've paid him back for his treachery. Now back off, Cartoor, like the good boy you are.'

Cartoor turned to me. 'Shall I get rid of him?'

I'd been willing to die in the sídhe. Willing to give my life for this adventure. Nothing had changed now that the Queen was gone. I offered my hand to Lord Cartoor. 'In peace, my lord. Clover, Rose, Fern and their sisters: I entrust them to you with thanks.'

'Are you sure?' When he saw my face, he shook my hand. 'In peace and with thanks,' He pulled me closer and whispered under a silence. 'Don't take my coat off, Lord of Death.'

That was not a title I wanted to adopt. Thankfully, no one else had heard it. Cartoor stepped back towards his charges, and I turned to face the Prince.

'No, Conrad,' said Eseld. 'Let us finish him off. It's over. I've only just told Mina that you're alive. Don't make me ring her back.'

Eseld, Fiadh and the Seeker actually looked worse than I felt. The time dilation meant that they'd been up all through a long night. It was still a low blow to bring Mina in like that. I shook my head and went *En Garde.*

Things went well at first, even though An Mám hadn't been through what I'd been through. He was very wary of the cold-forged steel in my point, and I had him for reach. Then he cut towards me, and I didn't see it coming at all, and had to jump back. Then he did it again, and his blade slashed my right arm.

Or it would have done if Cartoor's coat hadn't turned it aside. The Prince swore and changed his stance to aim at the exposed parts of me. I was dimly aware of a shout to my right, and ignored it until I saw Clover and Rose run into my field of view.

'Lick your fingers,' said Rose. 'You need the blood.' What? If you say so…

There was a big patch of red on my wrist that I'd missed. All I had to do now was put him off. I swapped hands and used my Sight to access some of the magick in the blade, but it was hard with no Artefacts to help me, and I am not ambidextrous, so I couldn't risk engaging him. It took him less than two seconds to work that out.

I used the reserves of Lux in my titanium tibia to activate one of the Works in the blade, and it flared with light, blazing enough to rival the morning sun. I advanced a step and turned to offer my side. The Prince fell back while he tried to work out what I was doing.

Before he could see that the light was just that – a big lightstick for convenience, I was scuttling back over flat ground and licking my wrist. When An Mám came at me again, the sword was in my right hand, a foul taste was in my mouth and I could see that he was plane shifting his blade when he attacked.

I feinted and let him strike at my chest. This time, I knocked his blade right down, and the point caught in the grass. He had to let go or get skewered. A few more steps, and he was on his back and the tip of my sword was at his throat.

'Tell me who bought the segments of the Codex,' I said. 'Tell me and I'll spare you. You might become Queen yet.'

'I don't know what you mean.' He didn't look afraid. Yet.

'You were the Fair Queen's bridge to the mundane world. You would have organised the auction or whatever it was. You know who came here. Rybakov. Adaryn. Debs Sayer.' I could see from his eyes that he recognised the names. 'Tell me who else.'

'Never. You will soon be dead.'

'I gave the Queen a chance to deal. She refused. I'm giving you one last chance to deal for your life. Tell me.'

He flicked his wrist, and Lux flared. He tried to kick my bad leg from under me, but before he could flex his muscles, cold-forged iron had ripped him open. When he started to scream, and his flesh started to dissolve, I finished him off.

'That's one less to worry about, I suppose.' Enter the Noble Queen.

I stepped back and put up my sword. Eseld and Fiadh chose that moment to sprint across the open ground to my side. Eseld came in for a big hug, and through tears, she whispered, 'Mina loves you. That had to be the first thing I said. She made me promise.' I squeezed her in return, and had to slowly detach her before she'd let go.

'It may be of no use to ye at all, but I'm standing by ye,' said Fiadh, doing exactly that.

This was nice, but not my priority. 'Lloyd and Olivia?' I said.

Eseld was crying too much to reply, but she did nod, and it was Fi who spoke for her. 'Back on dry land and half way to Dublin. They're going to rest up for a few hours and take the late ferry. Oh, and you are in so much shit, Conrad, that I have to salute you. Fair play to ye.'

I think that was meant to be an Irish compliment.

As soon as I'd kissed Eseld, I'd been scanning around over her head. The Queen of Galway had come ashore with her warhorse, a great black stallion that might as well have had glowing eyes. A truly fearsome beast. To add to the effect, she was wearing a black leather riding coat, long, with inserted skirting spread out behind her. The pleats of the insert were red and white. Nice touch.

She was surrounded by her People, all armed and all ready for combat. The Countess Portarra had gone to her side and was whispering up to her Queen. To her left was the Seeker of Galway, a very scared looking woman in her late thirties who was still trying to get her breath back after running here. She was not built for running.

Opposite the Noble Queen was the bulk of the Inishsí survivors, separated by a small distance from Lord Cartoor and the Hlæfdigan; we were to the Queen's right, and between us and her was a lump of rock. Niði.

The Queen spoke to Cartoor, and he replied, pointing at the rock, the Hlæfdigan and finally at me. She turned her head, and behind her riding goggles, I could see violet light. 'Is that true? You guaranteed their lives?'

'Yes.'

She roared with laughter. 'That's priceless. Absolutely priceless. Right, Cartoor, or should I call you *Lord Queenmaker*? Who are you gonna bend the knee to?'

Cartoor looked at his brothers and sisters, then out to the Lough. He licked his lips before replying. 'We are bound for Corrib Castle, if it please your grace.'

'Suits me. I'll even lend youse a boat. The Prince there is already gathering what People he can.'

Cartoor looked confused, poor bloke. I decided to help him out. 'I think you'll find that the Noble Queen has been assembling *her* People for twenty-four hours, with a view to an assault on the castle. I'm sure she'd be quite happy for you to be there.'

'There's no flies on this one,' observed the Queen to Cartoor. To me, she said, 'Stop spoiling me fun. You can go off people, you know.'

Was it just the scent of blood in her nostrils, or did she actually look younger? Her hair was certainly glossier than yesterday.

Cartoor's face didn't give much away, possibly because there wasn't a lot going on behind it. 'If not to the Prince of the Lough, we will go to the Princess over the water,' he declared.

'Nope,' said the Queen. 'It will be a terrible distraction, and I'll have to take on the Dragonslayer to do it, but if you try that, I'll cut you down here and kill everything on Inishsí that's not wearing red and white.' She let that sink in a second. 'I don't know why you're messing around, Cartoor. There's a perfectly good Princess of the blood over there. You of all People should know that.'

Every eye turned to a rather bedraggled and bewildered Princess Astra. The name gave it away: Fae only get a proper, public name if they have they have their own household – Cartoor, Portarra, Force Ghyll and so on. If they live in another's sídhe, they are given what amounts to a nickname, *Astra* in this case. She was biologically a Princess, yes, but that's about it.

Cartoor looked at her with real affection. 'Are they…?' I whispered to Fiadh.

'Sure are. There are even songs about it, I'm told.'

Astra spoke in Fae, first to what I now knew to be her great love, and then to the Noble Queen. After taking the grin off her face and replacing it with something more solemn, the Queen inclined her head in approval.

Slowly, hesitantly, Cartoor led the Hlæfdigan across to Princess Astra. He bent the knee and lowered his head. He spoke three times, in Fae, Gaeilge and English. 'Will you accept me, Star Queen?'

She spoke three times as well. 'I am your Queen, and you are my Guard and Consort.' When she'd finished, she held out her hand. He kissed it and stood up.

Astra was now a Queen Proclaimed. She wouldn't be the real thing until she had undergone a final transformation and started to dig her own royal sídhe. She looked around, and some of the other Fae started to approach her. Some held their ground, and a few used magick to slip away. One even took out her phone. The Hlæfdigan were already on their knees.

'Enough!' said the Queen of Galway. 'You can finish when you've heard my word. Astra, Star Queen you are, and you are welcome to plant your sídhe anywhere north of here. If you or any of your People move south, I will root you out. Hear my word.'

'I hear you,' said Astra, trying to find some regal dignity.

'Right,' said Galway. 'Go well, Star Queen, and you, Lord Dragonslayer. Youse lot can party on. I've got a castle to besiege.'

She turned her horse and trotted towards the boats.

'Let's get out of here as quickly as possible,' I said.

'Hear hear,' echoed Eseld.

Fern broke away from the rest of her sisters and came over, followed by Cartoor. She took a square of yellow cloth from a concealed pocket and offered it to me. I took it and went to embrace her, but she ran, back to her new Queen. Cartoor was less reluctant, and took me in a big Irish hug.

'It's a terrible shame, but the Lord of Death can never be welcome in our hall. Should we meet elsewhere, I hope I can really test your mettle and see who can drink the other under the table.'

'That's a contest I'm definitely up for. Go well.'

'And you, oh and I wouldn't rely on that coat again if I were you. A lot of the Charms were in the buttons.'

There was one more goodbye for me. I patted the stone Dwarf on the head. 'See you soon, old chap,' and then we started to make our way round the hill and towards the bridge.

We hadn't got far before the Seeker barred our way. 'In the name of the United Inquisition, stop there,' she said.

I wasn't going to disobey her, was I? On the other hand…

'Eseld? Light me a cigarette, would you? I think I've earned it.'

The Seeker of Galway was large and fair and approaching forty. She too had been up all night, and there were black bags under her eyes, eyes that held a mixture of fear and fury.

'By what Right are you here and have you acted?' she demanded.

I waited for Eseld to pass me a smoke before I answered. 'By right of free passage and self-defence. No other.'

'By Order of the Chief Seeker, your Free Passage is withdrawn, and you are to leave this island immediately.'

I breathed out the smoke slowly. Good. They weren't going to arrest me.

Before I could speak, Fiadh piped up. 'Shove it where the sun don't shine, will ye. I'm taking Conrad and Eseld back to the Tavern for a bath, a sleep and a party tonight. I'm sure he'll leave tomorrow when he's ready. If your Chief Seeker wants to bring a warrant on to common ground, he's welcome to try. He's got my lawyer's number.'

The Seeker braced herself to come back, but Fiadh wasn't finished. I'm guessing that these two have history, probably something to do with smuggling, trading in stolen goods and tax evasion. 'If ye don't shift your arse out of me way *right now*, I swear by the Morrigan that I'll throw you in the Lough.'

The Seeker held her ground, but only for a moment. 'You have until sunset tomorrow, Conrad Clarke. Is that clear?'

'Much appreciated,' I said. And I meant it. I put my arm on Fiadh's wrist and held her back for a second. Once the Seeker had made her point, she turned left and skirted round us, heading for the gathering of the Queen Proclaimed. Maybe she was going to give her a ticket or tell her how to apply for a royal licence.

We continued our way, and I had to get some of it off my chest: how close a call it had all been, and how come I'd ended up custodian of the Hlæfdigan and not spitted on the end of Cartoor's sword.

'That reminds me,' said Fiadh. 'When it all kicked off, and we knew that the Queen was dead, Portarra gave me a message. She said, "Ask the Lord of Death if we can make it a game of chess instead of a duel by weapons." I think it was her way of backing out.'

'About that title. Can we make sure it stays in Ireland?'

'I should bloody well hope so,' said Eseld.

We stopped on the shore, and a great shock was waiting for me: the bridge was neither concrete and steel nor glass: it was actually made of wood. Amazing. It already had cracks in it. We hurried over and reached the refuge of Cathal's BMW. Eseld popped the tailgate and opened a bag full of clothes. 'Look away now,' I said.

'No,' said Eseld. 'Not yet. I want to check some of those bruises, and you've been trying to limp on both legs.'

And there was me trying to laugh it off. She was right though.

I needed a couple of plasters, but no more, and I was glad to get some warm, clean clothes on. That bath at the Market Tavern sounded very attractive right now.

I balled up the late Queen's shift, and Fi asked what I was going to do with it.

'Give it to Mina. She'll probably put it in one of her wedding outfits.'

Fiadh was nonplussed. 'Why in the name of heaven would she do that? She seemed such a sweet little thing when we Facetimed before.'

Eseld laughed. 'Mina will do it to show that she won, and because it's the finest silk that money can't buy. Hey, Conrad, did you get an exchange? Was that in the packet?'

I fastened my coat and got out my phone. I also took the packet of cloth and unwrapped it. I took the two emeralds and palmed them into my pocket, then showed off the rubies and the diamond. 'They should make a nice replacement ring, with enough left over to make some matching earrings, I think.'

Fi's eyes were like saucers. 'I have never seen the like. And what's that bit of twig?'

I wrapped the piece of yew in the cloth. 'Must have got trapped when we fled down the hill. Is there any coffee left?'

'Not here. There's a fresh pot waiting at the tavern. So's breakfast. If you sit in the back, I'll put a Silence around us so that you can call Mina in private.'

'Before you do,' said Eseld, 'you should know that I've ordered a pilot to pick up the Smurf tomorrow morning and fly over here. He'll drop you at Middlebarrow by lunchtime.'

I insisted on another smoke before we set off, and Eseld and I discussed who should know what had happened and in what order they should be called. And how much of the truth to tell them. My first call was to Augusta Faulkner, telling her to deliver that Opinion I'd paid for. Out of my own money, no less.

When I got through to Mina, she spent a good third of my journey back to the tavern crying down the phone. Most of what we said was what you'd expect us to say, except for the news she saved until nearly the end of the trip. It seems that the contract chopper pilot is not the only one on the move.

'Hannah-ji is on the train,' said Mina. 'She is staying with a cousin of Moshe Kaplan in Manchester tonight and for Shabbos. At sunset tomorrow, she is coming to the Haven.'

'Did she say anything?'

'No. I messaged her constantly, giving her all the news, and she did not respond until I told her that you were alive. After that, she messaged her thanks to Hashem for your deliverance. I didn't tell her it was Ganesh's doing, really.'

As you can tell, the smile was back in her voice by then, and I'd swear that I heard a champagne cork go off in the background. Me? I was ready for that coffee. And bacon sandwiches. Most definitely.

24 — *Farewell to Galway*

Barney's uniform still fitted him, which was no surprise: he'd only been a trainee detective for ten days. The same could not be said for Liz, who'd had to beg and borrow some of the kit. Not that you could call what police officers wore on the street *uniform* in any meaningful sense of looking smart. By the time you've got the stab vest, the equipment harness and the bright yellow coat on, you've moved beyond uniform into another category that Barney didn't have a name for.

Liz returned from the depths of the station with a scowl on her face. 'The useless git won't give me a Taser. Says my bloody training certificate is out of date. I'd like to see him last ten minutes of Black Eye Friday without one.'

The market towns of northern England are mostly quaint havens with tearooms and boutique fashion shops. During the day. At night, the preferred hobby of the local young men (or some of them) is alcohol and random violence. Barney had carted more than his fair share to A&E or the cells over the years, especially on the last working Friday before Christmas: Black Eye Friday. It was why a proportion of the detective team had been ordered back in to uniform for an evening shift. At least they'd get overtime.

Liz made the final adjustments to her equipment and checked the pockets of her coat for Haribo: all present and correct.

'Briefing in a minute,' said Barney.

'Not for us. I know where we're going.' She gave him her happy smile, which was not to be confused with her evil smile. That one she saved for drug dealers. 'For tonight only, Barney, I am very glad you are here. Oh, how did the course go?'

Barney had been down in Manchester for a day and a half at a training course and seminar entitled *Anatomy of an OCG: How Organised Crime has adapted to the 21st Century*.

'Scary, Sarge.' Seeing her in uniform had made him forget the first names rule of the detective division, and he wondered whether he could share Erin's news. Why not. 'Something big happened today, according to Erin.'

'Oh?'

'Yeah. Special Constable Clarke's been up to his tricks again.'

There was almost panic in Liz's voice. 'Here?'

'No, Sarge. In Ireland. Should be a safe distance.'

'That's a relief.' Now that her brain had switched to its magick track, she remembered something. 'It was Full Moon on Wednesday. How did the Pack get on?'

'It went very well, actually. Erm, I know it's a bit short notice, but is there any chance of a day off on Tuesday? Erin wants me to celebrate Yuletide at Birk Fell on Monday night.'

'No need for a day off, Barney. We'll do that drugs exercise at Charlotte Mason together on Monday, then you can take me to see for myself.'

Something lurched in his stomach. This was not right. His worlds should not be colliding in this way. 'I'll have to check with Erin, and she'll have to check with Conrad.'

'Don't worry about him. Special Constable Clarke won't say no. I wonder if DCI Morton will be there? Right. Enough gossip. Let's go and get sworn at, attacked and puked on.'

'You make police work sound so attractive, Sarge.'

'Why do you think I couldn't wait to get out of uniform?'

'I've brought you a cup of tea.'

Mina???? No, of course not. It was Es or Fiadh putting on a funny voice. I opened my eyes. Oh. Rachael.

'What are you doing here?'

'Charming. Move your legs so I can sit down.'

I started to move, and flinched with pain as today's war wounds made themselves known.

'Are you okay?'

I gritted my teeth and rolled to give her some room. 'I'm not in hospital. Always a bonus at this point. And thanks for the tea. I need this.' She'd brought it in an Irish sized mug, and she'd made it just how I liked it. Boy, that was good. 'Now tell me how the fuck you found us.'

'When Mina called to tell me you were okay – and thanks for putting me top of the list, by the way – I simply said, "How are the others?" and she was so out of it on adrenalin and lack of sleep that she said, "Lloyd and Olivia are safe and resting up." I had no idea they were involved. After that, I rang Lloyd and browbeat him into telling me where you were. You'll be pleased to know he didn't let on until he knew you were safe here.'

Of course that's what she'd done. I felt almost proud of her. Almost. 'Why did you come?'

She grinned. 'I wanted to make sure that you and Eseld were in separate beds, of course.'

'Don't tell Es that. She doesn't have your sense of humour.'

'Nah. Just joking.' She looked at the window, where night had already fallen. I looked at my watch, only it wasn't there: removing it had been the last thing Eseld did before we went to enjoy a hot bath – separately. 'She let slip a while ago that she's been seeing someone. Or trying to. She was drunk, obviously, so it was hard to figure out what she meant. And that someone wasn't you.' She patted my leg, making sure it was the good one. For once, it hurt worse. 'Apparently you turned her down, not once but twice. Impressed.'

More tea went down. 'How long have you been here?'

'A few hours. She's a feisty one, that Fiadh, isn't she? Uncle Donal is running the pub in her absence, and after ten minutes acquaintance, she put me in charge of the war room.'

'Am I still asleep? What's going on? And if I'm not asleep, why didn't you wake me?'

'That made no sense whatsoever, Conrad. Never mind, I'll tell you anyway. You know who Ballycraig and Oughterard are, I presume?'

'I do. The two Queens' agents here. Bit of a Laurel and Hardy tribute act, from what I can gather. Is Oughterard even here?'

'He is. When he heard what had happened from Fi, he declared for the Star Queen apparently. Before I arrived. Since then, he and his pal have been working the phones and moving chess pieces over a big map of the Lough in Fi's office. I was told to help out, and they were told to keep me in the loop in case we needed to make a sharp exit. We don't, by the way, and I stink of peat smoke.'

'What *is* happening?'

'Ouhterard rang several friends of his at Corrib Castle, and they spread the word about the Star Queen, who sounds like a total lame duck if you ask me. Anyway, when this Prince bloke heard, he got himself proclaimed Queen, which sounds totally wrong, but who am I to argue. A lot of the "People" joined in. And a lot snuck away from the castle or never went there.'

I flopped back on the bed. 'The Queen in battle. Of course. No wonder Galway was so chipper this morning.'

'Yah. When Ballycraig explained it, I felt very, very ill.' Her face had gone from slightly merry to stone cold sober. She gathered the quilt in her hands and squeezed it. 'Does it have to be this way, Conrad? Do all of them *have* to die?'

When a Fae army takes to the field, if their Queen, even a Queen Proclaimed, is at the back, they never retreat. They fight until there is a truce or until the last one dies defending their Queen.

'You haven't met the Noble Queen. This is revenge for the Corrib Raid. The ones who stayed knew what would happen if they lost. What they probably didn't consider was that Galway would throw *everything* at them, including herself.'

'I get that, but does it have to be like this? Total slaughter?'

'Would you stop one ant colony attacking another? It's the same biological imperative, but with swords and magick. Maybe the ants don't have a party afterwards.'

She hung her head and straightened the quilt. 'But they seem so … *human*, and don't tell me humans have done worse, I know we have. It's just the way that every single Fae thinks it's normal. Natural. Who they are.'

I sat up again. 'You know what, Raitch, I heard a story last night. Or yesterday. I have got serious sídhe-lag, if that's a thing. Fiadh told me that the Fae have a legend that Saint Patrick visited them. They invited him in, fed him and for a diversion, they let him preach to them. When he'd finished, the Great Queen took him down to her inner bower and showed him the truth. They say he ran screaming into the night.'

She did something very unusual at that point. She took my hand and held it close, squeezing my fingers. 'I haven't told you the worst. When they weren't on the phone, they kept asking about you.'

I didn't say anything at that point because I trust her completely. She knows exactly which stories are and are not for public consumption, but that wasn't the point. Not here.

She squeezed my hand again. 'They called you the Lord of Death. As if that were a good thing. An honour. I'm just checking to see if you're still alive, and you are, so I'll settle for that. Maybe one day I'll understand why you did it.' She dropped my hand. 'I'll give you some space. It's going to be an epic party.'

It was an epic party, especially at midnight, when the whole room fell into a deathly hush as the Queen of Galway strode in, still in her leather riding coat. At her side walked the Countess Portarra, who had a bandage around her head and her arm pinned into a sling.

The Noble Queen stopped in the centre of the room, where the crowds had parted, and looked around, her black framed glasses back in place and her violet eyes gleaming. A good number of the punters were down on one knee already, and the rest bowed. Including me, of course, and it was me she was looking at.

'I hear you've a liking for peated whiskey, Lord of Death.'

Really? Even her?

'Yes, but not the title you're so keen to bestow. I have killed no Queen.'

'Hear my word everyone. Fiadh Ahearn, come here.'

Fiadh approached, stepping out of the circle and bowing. Her face was grave, and you had to look to the trembling in her left hand to see the fear in her. 'Well met, Noble Queen.'

As the hostess of a common ground hostelry, it was within her right to say that. Just.

The Queen returned the bow with a nod. 'Well met indeed. You owe me a bond and a blood price, Fiadh Ahearn. I pronounce it as one bottle of Connemara malt and four glasses.'

By Fae standards, that was unusually generous, and Fiadh showed an appropriate degree of gratitude. Fiadh's like me: there's a time and place for attitude, and this was neither. Behind the bar, Uncle Donal nearly slapped the young lad until he ran off to fetch a full bottle, then Donal himself brought the goods on a tray. While this was going on, I could hear a murmur in the shadows, but no one in the circle around us had spoken a word. Rachael and Eseld were by the fire, and slipped round the edge of the crowd to join me.

'Pour four measures,' said the Queen.

With a quick wrist, Donal filled the glasses and handed them to the Queen, to Fiadh, to Portarra, and finally to me.

The Queen lifted her glass and raised her voice. 'After I'd cleansed Corrib Castle of every last ounce of Inis's spawn, I was reminded by Portarra here that I was in such a rush earlier that I'd forgotten to grant a Favour. Well, that won't do, will it? And I have other news as well, but first, to Fiadh. The price is paid. Let there be peace between us.'

I took my cue from Portarra and stayed my hand as the Queen and Fiadh drank to each other. From the look on Fiadh's face, smokey malt is not her first choice for drinking neat. The Queen seemed to like it.

'And now for the rest,' said the Queen. 'For her service and her bravery today, the Countess Portarra is named Countess of Corrib Castle, and Prince to come. Here's to her.'

It was noticeable that not everyone joined in that toast. If the Queen had any sense, she'd ignore that.

'And finally, the Favour.' She reached into her coat and pulled out a piece of silk, red and white shimmering in the tavern's light. 'Let it be known that Conrad Clarke of Elvenham Grange is Favoured of me, free to walk through all of my lands, and let him be named Dragonslayer, for that is what he is. To the Dragonslayer!'

That got a slightly less popular response than Portarra's elevation, but only in terms of numbers. Those who did join in were a lot more enthusiastic. Remember, that this was a human crowd, and freeing Fiadh from her bonds was by far the most popular thing I've done here, a fact I decided to reinforce. After I'd received my favour, of course.

I walked up to the Queen and bowed. I don't kneel for anyone but Nimue. I did, however, kiss her hand, and received the small banner in exchange. It looked like this:

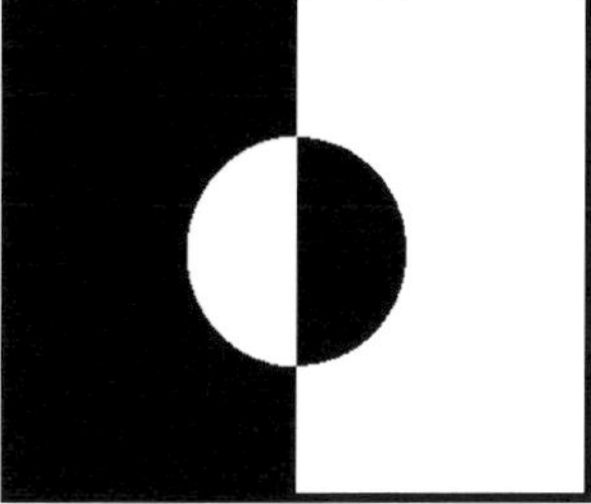

Red and white, in case you're not reading this in colour, and the black border is just for contrast; the original has no such thing.

When I stepped back, I retrieved my glass from Rachael and seized the moment. 'Another toast, to one who deserves all our thanks. To Fiadh, Queen of the Market.'

That went down well. Very well. Even the Queen of Galway joined in, and she amazed me by staying for a couple of drinks, though she spent the time talking to Ballycraig and Oughterard rather than the mortals.

Portarra – sorry, *Countess Corrib* – came over and we clinked glasses. We've scheduled a game of chess for when we next meet. 'Then again, I don't think the Seekers will be letting you back into Ireland in a hurry,' she observed. She's probably right, and I'd need to practise Fae chess: it's exactly the same as regular chess, but you have to capture the Queen, not the King. The King is pretty dispensable in Fae Chess.

I asked her about the siege, and she shrugged. 'It had no glory in it. No one will be singing songs about it.' She paused and swirled the last of her whiskey. 'Unlike you.'

Rachael had been hovering, and said, 'Will they inflate his ego?'

'Depends on how you look at it. I've heard a whisper that Astra is working on the lament for her Queen. I've also heard that she's going to call it *The Fair Queen and the Hound of Gloucester*. You can make what you like of that. Cheers.'

I've turned a lot of blind eyes recently, and relied on a lot being turned in my direction. When I saw Rachael slipping the Countess a business card, I let it go, but made a mental note. If she really wanted to work with the Fae, I needed a couple of people to give her the heads up first.

A lot of people bought me a drink, asked for stories and clapped me on the back. A lot of people also gave me a wide berth, including Orla and Cathal. I don't think I'm on their Christmas card list.

There was even a small crowd the following morning when the Smurf arrived to take us away. Ballycraig was there, as was Uncle Donal. Parked down the road, I recognised the Seeker's car, but she didn't come to wave goodbye. I tossed the keys of the van we'd brought over to Fiadh. 'Yours. Make Eseld a good offer for it.'

'Make me any offer you like,' said Es. 'Sod the bloody van.'

After a protracted Irish farewell, I told the pilot to follow the western edge of Lough Corrib before turning east.

'Can you see anything?' I said to Eseld when we flew over Inishsí.

'No. Gone completely.'

I could see it. The bridge was already reduced to a few piles sticking out of the water, and the cottages looked abandoned. The banners were all gone from the entrance, and only fading yellow and white paint remained of the Fair Queen's empire. And songs. They would endure.

25 — Homecoming

Lloyd was the first, and most welcome visitor, when I returned to Middlebarrow Haven. He'd been paid well for his work and for the risks he'd taken, and had found it an interesting if uncomfortable adventure, partly because horse transporters are uncomfortable, and partly because of Olivia. She was not on good form. He took away the Fair Queen's jewels with a commission for his relative in the Jewellery Quarter, and there was one final gift for him: Niði's diamond.

'Are you sure?' he said dubiously. 'The Dwarf'll pay loads for to get this back.'

'I know he will, and it's a useful bargaining counter for you. It's a good job we're blood brothers, Lloyd, because keeping track of favours owed and received would keep Mina up all night.'

I tossed him the diamond, and he bounced it in his palm. The magick inside it is so powerful that it's inert to humans, and even Gnomes. He stared at the diamond, tossed it in the air and caught it with his new prosthetic hand. 'You've risked your life for me, and me for you. That's what's counts, mate, not the other stuff. Take care, alright?'

'You too.'

The last visitor arrived at six o'clock. Seth Holgate brought her, saying that he had nothing else to do now that he wasn't campaigning for Warden, and he had the good sense to drop her off with the barest moment of conversation through the driver's window ('You're always welcome at the Society.').

Hannah waited until his car had reversed and disappeared before she gave Mina a big hug, then me. We didn't say anything, and she wouldn't let me go until she'd stopped crying.

'Let's get this over with. I'll use your loo and we'll get Cordelia.'

'She's here. Inside.'

'We're doing this at Nimue's spring.'

'In that case, I shall need to get changed, Hannah-ji,' said Mina. 'I am not dressed for standing around in a bog. I don't think Cordy is, either. Shall we say fifteen minutes in the kitchen?'

Hannah nodded, and I picked up her bags. The conversation on the way in was rather stilted, to say the least.

Not needing to get changed, I sat waiting at the kitchen table. Hannah was back first, and looked at Great Fang. 'Why have you brought that? Oh. How did you manage to move your Badge?' Comprehension dawned. 'You summoned her! She did it!'

Now was not a time for lying. 'I did it myself. After a close encounter with the First Daughter.'

A dark, very dark, look passed over Hannah's face, and she shook her head. If she'd been going to say anything, she swallowed it when Cordy and Mina came in. 'Let's go.'

I led the way, collecting three lightsticks from the supply that Saskia had created recently. Saves lugging LED lanterns everywhere.

Nimue's spring was bubbling nicely, sparkling in the illumination from the planted lightsticks. Lux calls to Lux, they say. In the still night, our breath was freezing in the air, and we turned to Hannah. This was her show. To start with, any way.

'Mundane business first,' she said. 'The oversight committee has considered what happened in Ireland, Conrad, including Augusta Faulkner's legal opinion. However, they put more weight on the strongly worded complaint from the … I'm not going to attempt the original. From the Combined Authority of Ireland.'

She took a deep breath before continuing. 'You're not allowed to read the minutes, but if you do, you'll see that I objected strongly to the Irish trying to subcontract the washing of their dirty laundry to us. If they had a problem with what you did, they should have arrested you. The rest of the committee disagreed, and with only my vote against, they have dismissed you from your post in the King's Watch, effective on delivery of this letter. As you know, it's a post at Her Majesty's pleasure, so that's that. For what it's worth, I proposed a one month suspension without pay and a written warning.'

She offered me the letter, and I accepted it.

'Was it worth it?' she asked.

'Later, ma'am. Let's get the rest over first.'

'You can drop the *ma'am* now, Conrad.'

'You're still a senior officer. Your committee doesn't have the power to remove my commission in the RAF. Or institute a court martial come to that.'

She flinched back and blinked. 'Really? You're going to go down that route?'

'I will accept medical retirement and a transfer to the Reserves. If offered.'

She shook her head. 'I'm past caring, I really am. You can do the Summoning.'

I didn't complain about that. I am the Priest of this Altar. At least for now. I unsheathed Great Fang and focused on the image of Caledfwlch. It didn't take her long to appear.

'A treat,' she said. 'Both my living swordsmen at once. Who will make the offering today?'

She'd said the last bit with a smile and a gaze firmly directed at me. I sighed and rolled up my sleeve. If this wasn't about to stop, I'd think seriously about getting a cannula fitted. At least she wasn't too hungry this time: it's only been a week since the last donation.

With my blood giving her shape, she turned to Hannah. 'How fares the realm?'

'Troubled, my lady, and especially troubled today. I must ask you to take back the Deputy's Badge. If it pleases you.'

'Why?'

That was a stumper. For Hannah.

'He is dismissed from his post,' she said bluntly.

'For what reason? I have heard nothing of him. In fact, I was going to ask him where he had been.'

'For actions in Ireland.'

Nimue flowed and re-flowed, a sign of agitation. 'In Ireland? How many men did he lose?'

'None, my lady, it was that he acted without authority.' Hannah looked at me, and I shrugged.

I tried to focus on Nimue's non-eyes. 'I found out who had tricked the Dwarf, Niði, and the Queen of Galway preferred to settle the matter by combat. She was slain. I had no part of that contest, though I did help the Dwarf cross the Irish Sea.'

The Nymph laughed. Peals of laughter echoed around the grove, and the lightsticks flickered in a wash of Lux. 'You should be celebrating him, not casting him out,' she said to Hannah. 'You may dismiss him from your posts if you wish. He is Lord Guardian of the North and Bearer of Caledfwlch at my pleasure, not yours, and it still pleases me for him to be so. There is much work for him to do yet.'

A silence descended. Shock, mystification and laughter flicked through the air as we looked at each other. I had not been expecting that. Nor had Hannah.

Three times she tried to find words, and three times she stopped. On the fourth time, she shrugged helplessly and said, 'You are wise beyond our years, my lady. If you sever the bond to the Haven, we will depart in peace and gratitude.'

Nimue laughed again. 'The Haven is the home of the Guardian. It is not yours to dispose of, nor are the farms which supply it. Or perhaps you had forgotten that, given that you never lived there.'

Hannah looked at the path leading back to the Haven and wetted her lips. She looked very keen to get out of here as quickly as possible. 'Forgive me, my lady, and thank you.'

We all bowed, and by the time we'd stood up, she was gone.

Hannah turned on her heel and stormed out of the grove, leaving us to remove the lightsticks and follow her. 'What does that mean?' whispered Mina.

'No idea, love.'

'Ow! Shit! Fucking brambles.'

'I'll catch her up.'

Hannah had wandered off the path in the darkness, and I had to pull a dead strand of thorny bramble off her coat.

'I should kill you now and die in the Undercroft,' she said. 'The only thing stopping me is the thought that we'd both be stuck there as Ghosts, and that you'd spend eternity making my death as miserable as you make my life.'

Mina had caught up and spoke before I could. 'I hope that's not the only thing stopping you, Hannah-ji. You cannot be Maid of Honour if you are dead. I would happily marry Conrad's Ghost, though.'

In the much-reduced light, Hannah's eyes glowed as they darted around. 'Perhaps I'm dead already and this is my Hell. Or at the very least a nightmare. What the fuck are we going to do now?'

I felt Mina's hand on my arm, warning me off. 'We are going to go inside, I am going to get changed for the fourth time today, and then we are going to get drunk and talk about it. Come on.'

Mina brushed past me and took Hannah's arm. The Boss (ex-Boss?) flinched, then relented, and they walked off together towards the lights of Middlebarrow Haven.

I beckoned Cordelia to come closer and took the lightsticks. They were as tall as her, and she'd nearly fallen twice. 'I'm sorry, Cordy. I have absolutely no idea what this means for you. You know I wrote a statement saying that you had nothing to do with it?'

'Fat lot of good that will do. Guilt by association is a very powerful force in politics, Conrad, and in a lot of eyes, you're very guilty. Not mine, obviously. I thought you did a brilliant job, but who cares what I think?'

'Me. You know that.'

'I do. And other than not being at your side, I don't regret what you did one bit. I've got quite used to being here. And working with you.'

'Ditto. Let's see what happens, shall we?'

The first thing that happened took place before we'd finished taking our coats and boots off, when Hannah asked for my guns, 'Before we get too drunk for me to put them in a safe place.'

'Sorry, ma'am. They're under the authority of Commander Ross. He might still have a use for me. You can put it in the pot with my medical retirement.'

She shook her head. 'I'm not going to argue.'

Mina took that as her cue to lead Hannah away on the pretext of showing her something upstairs. When they came down, we carried on as if nothing had happened at the Spring and that everything was normal. We all knew that it wasn't, but tonight was one of those nights where everyone agrees that tomorrow is another day.

I was last to go to bed, mostly because I couldn't face getting up off the sofa and abandoning the embers of the fire for the cold of the bedroom. A shadow came into the room, and Mina was back from escorting Hannah upstairs.

'How is she?'

'Anaesthetised. She will know tomorrow how much she hurts.'

'I know how she feels.'

Mina turned off the lamps, and I was about to lever myself off the couch, but she came and sat next to me. Where was this going?

She took my hand and said, 'I thought I was stronger than this, Conrad. I thought I could cope, but I can't. When I told you not to hold back from … relations with other creatures if it saved lives, I also told you not to tell me. The whole world of magick will soon know that you engineered the death of a Fae Queen by distracting her in bed long enough for a Dwarf to break in. I find that I cannot put a face on this if I don't know what happened. What it was like.'

I could tell that she'd thought this over and over, and that her words had been rehearsed. It didn't make them any less genuine or her need to know any less pressing.

'She was Beauty. Beauty personified. Everyone who met her fell in love with her beauty. It's who she was.'

'Everyone? Including you?'

'Everyone. Especially me.' She flinched back and blinked her eyes quickly, but she didn't let go of my hand. 'The Queen of Galway must have met her, and she probably fell in love with her beauty, too. But there's a big difference between loving an attribute and loving a person, especially when you're already in love with the most beautiful person on earth.'

'Don't. Don't flatter me like that, not when you went to bed with her. And don't pretend you didn't enjoy it.'

'I wasn't going to. You know I've always said that it's possible for one action to have many motives, well that's what happened. I had to let go, Mina. I had to let the part of me that wanted to embrace her run ahead full steam, otherwise the part of me that wanted to kill her would have stood no chance. It's hard to accept, I know, but it's the only truth I have.'

She was silent for a moment. 'You wanted her to die? Even when you were inside her?'

'We didn't get that far. If you want the details, I'll tell you.' I gave her a fraction of a second to decline, and when she didn't, I rushed ahead. 'I was drugged, don't forget. She wanted to give me the Rapture and help me forget all about the Codex. I'd have begged for more Amrita eventually, and her price would have been my amnesia. It didn't get to that point, because she found that licking Portarra's blood off my chest was the biggest aphrodisiac she'd had in years.'

'And now I regret asking you. How did you feel when she died?'

'Even when Niði sprayed her blood all over me, I still loved her beauty.'

'Still? Still today?'

'Yes. She created something I've never seen before or will again, probably. Her palace, her court, her People and above all herself were beauty incarnate. She had to die, but I can still mourn its passing and love what it was.'

'It? Not her?'

'Never her. She had a black heart, and why love a dead Queen when you have a live Rani? I will always love you, for who you are and who we are together. That's all that really matters.'

She snuggled up to me and squeezed me, and we kissed.

When she moved away, she said, 'I wish you hadn't had to do it, Conrad, but I could have stopped you, and I chose not to. I shall wear my new engagement ring with pride, just tell Lloyd's friend to hurry up with it.'

She stood up, and helped me clamber out of the squashy old sofa. We linked arms and headed upstairs. 'Eseld has sent me pictures from the Market Tavern. Unless it doesn't come over on camera, I wouldn't say that the other one, the Noble Queen, is the personification of Beauty.'

'She's not. Not in the same way. The way her eyes look at you, and that weird violet colour behind the glasses. She's the Queen of mystery, perhaps. I don't know, and I'm not in a rush to find out.'

On Sunday morning Cordelia and Evie were first in the kitchen. 'Where's Conrad?' said Evie. 'It feels weird not having him here, bright eyed and bushy tailed and asking what we want for breakfast.'

It did feel weird. Cordy hadn't realised how much she had already got used to the routine of collective living here, and with a sharp stab in the chest, she realised it was how she'd lived for years at Glastonbury – everyone pitching in and rubbing along in a common cause. Only Conrad was no substitute for Raven. She touched the raven-shaped badge of office around her neck and forced away the tears.

She pasted on a smile and said, 'I think we can allow him a lie-in on today of all days. Can you remember what was supposed to be in a kosher brunch?'

Evie scratched her armpit. 'Dunno. Let's have a look in the fridge, shall we?'

The others emerged with matching hangovers, and Hannah only paused to grab a large mug of coffee before saying that she had to catch the Vicar of

London Stone before Sunday service and tell her what had happened on Saturday night. It did not go down well.

Hannah returned from making the call, threw her phone on the kitchen table and said to Conrad, 'There's going to be a committee to look into it. Hah! In the meantime, she suggested that I ask you to resign as Guardian of the North. I told her to ask you herself. Can you give me a bone to throw them? Anything?'

Cordy went still and waited to see what would happen. Hannah had been – was still – upset, but the bond between her and Conrad didn't seem broken.

Conrad pulled his lip and said, 'Tell them I'm taking annual leave until the fourth of January. That should allow everyone to have a joyful Yuletide followed by a merry Christmas and a happy New Year.'

Hannah grunted. 'More coffee. I need more coffee, and I need it now.'

Cordy re-entered the conversation with a quiet cough. 'I don't want to add to your troubles, ma'am, but…'

'But you're going to add to them anyway, aren't you, Cordelia? I don't know. I'd tell you I don't care, but what would that leave me with? Ach, carry on as you are. You're not a kid like the other Officers, and you've done a good job – with Vicky's help. Mind you, you'll have to be nice to the Guardian or you'll be homeless. I cannot believe the taxpayer is going to fork out for this house *and staff* for you to sit in it and thumb your nose at us, Conrad.'

'I agree,' he said. 'I think you should restore the eight hundred acres of prime Cheshire farmland to me, and then I'll be self-sufficient.'

'Where's my coffee?' said Hannah.

After brunch, Mina volunteered to take Hannah to the mainline station at Warrington. Conrad suggested a walk to clear their heads, and Cordy agreed. She was desperate to know what was in his head.

'We drank so much last night, I can't remember whether we agreed or not,' she said when they were clear of the Haven.

'There was nearly a fight over the result of the Strictly final,' he replied. 'I remember that much. What else did we need to agree on?'

'Whether the Queen Gambit had been worth it. In the end.'

It had been Conrad's suggestion to call it that. Cordy thought it was a bit cheesy, but it neatly avoided words like "Slaughter on the Lough" and "Massacre at the sídhe."

'Who says the Queen Gambit was the end? It's the end of the Codex Defanatus, that's for sure, and it was worth it for that. I think so, anyway.'

'If it had been sold already, then you've not achieved much.'

'But it hasn't all been sold. The Fair Queen only had it for my lifetime, which was nothing to her. If I hadn't tracked her down, she'd be selling bits of that book off to the highest bidder for generations to come.'

'I suppose.' She walked a few more steps. 'No, I don't suppose, I know you're right. At Solstice tomorrow, I shall pray to the Goddess that I never have to make that choice. It sounds like you couldn't have done it without Eseld.'

He looked at her sharply. 'There's no *suppose* about it. I couldn't, and not just because she's Morwenna's big sister.'

Cordelia blushed. Even after last night's raking over the coals, she didn't know exactly what shape or size was the hole in his life that Eseld fitted, and of course that made her think of the Raven-sized hole in her life. She drew a deep breath: Eseld had broken Raven's heart, but if Eseld was someone that Raven could love, then she couldn't be *all* bad. She reached into her pocket and pulled out a piece of paper. 'Here.'

Conrad took the paper and gave her a quizzical look.

'It's the contact details for a Mage-aware family therapist. She's in Salisbury, because the ones in the West Country are a bit too close to the history…'

'…It's a small world,' supplied Conrad. 'Thank you.' He held the paper for a second before putting it away, and she cringed at the thought that he might ask her whether she and Rick had gone for therapy. They hadn't. Instead, he heaped coals on her head by being nice to her again. 'Are you sure you don't mind being up here for Solstice? And on your own?'

'In an ideal world, would I like to be celebrating with my children? Yes. At least I've still got a home here, and Saskia's invited a few people round who aren't doing the full Yuletide. What have you got planned at Birk Fell?'

'The pack have been busy. Erin says I won't recognise the place, and I've only been gone two weeks. We're having the usual: slow roasted venison. For festival feasts, it has to be something they've caught themselves. At least they're allowed to buy in the bread and beer. I get to see Scout, too.'

'Are you going to take him to Clerkswell for Christmas?'

'You've got me there, Cordy. I'm in a real quandary, because he's become very attached to Maria and her daughter. Then again, now that I'm my own master, I might re-think.'

He paused and took his phone out of his pocket. He had it set to a really loud vibrate, and it had already gone off umpteen times. This time he scrolled through the list of messages and missed calls before grunting to himself. 'It's not going to be a quiet night in, that's for certain. Half the world wants to know what I've been up to and is it true?'

He looked up at the house. 'Light's on. Mina's back. We can divide the list between us.'

He lengthened his stride, as he always did when he was about to see Mina again. He realised that Cordy had been left behind, and turned to apologise. She waved him on and said, 'I'll catch you later.'

She turned and made her way to Nimue's spring while there was still light left. Evie had told her that Karina used to worship here as if it were an altar of the Goddess. Wrong. Nimue was not the Goddess, though Cordy was sure that they aligned on most things. As the year drew to an end, and the sun's life was at its lowest, it had been very hard to feel the presence of the Goddess anywhere, and without that, what did she have left? Nothing. No children, no home and above all, no Raven.

Did the Goddess mean for her to be alone in the world? Was that her will? Was her obsession with finding Raven just that, an obsession?

The clouds coming in from the west obliterated what was left of the dusk, and Cordy could make out nothing apart from the trees around the spring. She opened herself and felt out into the world. No, she wasn't alone, because the hole next to her was still a hole. And where there is a hole, there is something to fit it. Raven was out there somewhere, and Raven would fill the hole.

She stood up and thought back to Friday night. Mina had rambled a bit, but one of the things she said came back to her: Ganesh is the god of doorways. Cordy needed to see Conrad's sudden dismissal from his post as a door opening, not one slamming closed. She hastened her steps back to the house, because by now the tea would be ready, and now that her spirit had been warmed, the rest of her needed it, too.

26 — *Visitors*

Erin was right. I almost didn't recognise Birk Fell when we arrived on Monday afternoon.

It wasn't just the new wooden shed making a third side to the yard (a joint effort with the Skelwith Gnomes), or the mini-amphitheatre with a fire pit big enough to burn half a tree (ditto), it was the general air of homeliness that comes from a whole bunch of young, energetic people caring about the place they live and wanting to make it better for themselves and their children.

The first one to greet us was Scout, of course, followed by Maria's daughter, and then Maria herself, who had now fallen in line with the Pack dress code. She still curtsied, though.

'We were very worried about you, sir. When the Guardian said that you'd gone *off the grid*, we thought that meant you were dead, until she explained it. Please don't do that again.'

'I'll try not to.'

'We can't wait to hear all about it,' she replied, with way too much anticipation. 'I shall fetch Alex.'

'And I can't wait to have words with Erin about oversharing,' I muttered.

'They care about you,' said Mina. 'And they will always be worried about their future, given their past. It's only natural.'

'True.'

Alex appeared, and gave us the guided tour. Well, he gave Scout and me the guided tour, because Mina went into the cottage to check that our bed for tonight didn't smell of wet canine and to discuss with Erin the plan for making the Pack pay its way. And also to discuss Erin's list of items that she said were, 'Totally essential and totally capital investment.'

Mina was waiting for me when we got back, and she had that *She's done it again* look on her face. 'What?' I said.

'We have two more guests on their way. Barney we knew about, but he's bringing his sergeant as well. Erin claims that she invited herself.'

'The Daughter of the Earth?'

'The same. Down boy! This dog has got worse not better since he's been living with the pack.'

I took Mina's hand and led her towards the amphitheatre. 'Sergeant Swindlehurst has heard that you throw epic parties, so naturally she wants to come. And it's not as as if we have anything to hide, is it?'

Her nose twitched down. 'Apart from an illegal development, lots of unregistered children, oh, and the fact that they change into wolves every month? No, we have nothing to hide. I take it that Dawn and Erin have renewed all of the Occulting and the Wards? I feel rather exposed here.'

'The occulting, yes. Erin was able to more or less copy what the Ripleys had done and use the Artefacts they'd put in place. Unfortunately, they took the Ward stones when they cleared out the cottage. She's working on it. Then again, who's going to attack a pack of Mannwolves?'

'That sounds like famous last words, Conrad.'

'I know, but who? The Derwent Queen isn't going to be deterred by a few Ward stones, and who else would want them gone?'

There was a fire burning at one end of the fire pit, big enough to accommodate the iron rod on piles of bricks that was the spit, and on the spit was a big red deer buck. The smell of roasting venison had my mouth watering already, but food was a fair way off yet. I was about to take a seat for five minutes, when there was a shout from the gate, and a big Toyota pulled in.

We switched direction and went to join the kids who had crowded round the strange vehicle. The adults were expecting visitors, so they just got on with what they were doing: to them, human business was something they rarely bothered with. After all, they had Erin and me to worry about that sort of thing for them.

A rather nervous looking Barney Smith got out first, scanning the yard for Erin, then breaking into a smile of half relief and half extra worry when he saw me. I knew that he'd been here before, but only when the compound was unoccupied. In seconds, he had an audience of rather grubby children, and one very excited dog. The dog he could cope with.

'Hello Scout. Who's a good boy, eh?'

'Arff!'

The children knew from Scout's reaction that Barney was a friend, so they looked at him with curiosity, and being well brought-up cubs, they didn't talk to strange humans. I think that unnerved him most.

The driver's door opened, and the large frame of DS Swindlehurst emerged, her police officer eyes scanning everywhere.

'Conrad, Mina, this is Liz.'

There were handshakes and a, 'Pleased to meet you,' from Liz, followed two seconds later by, 'I had no idea it would be like this, sir. None. I've heard about this sort of thing, but…'

'It's rather rough round the edges, I'm afraid, but they're getting there. With help from your father's family.'

'He told me. When I asked. And when he'd checked with the client first.' She looked rather put out about that, and what daughter wouldn't be? Especially a Daughter of the Earth who's also a detective sergeant. That was her problem, though. I was more interested in how long Erin had known she was coming.

Scout had come to investigate, and was showing a particular interest in Liz's coat pocket. 'Gerroff, mutt, they're mine,' she said, removing his head with a firm grip that no doubt also worked on drunks. 'I thought that seeing the First Mine was a special treat. This is just, so *different.* Thanks for having me.'

Her eyes had switched to a point over my shoulder, and I turned to see Erin quick-walking up from the cottage. Mina dragged me subtly out of the way so that Erin could size up her boyfriend's boss and Liz could get the measure of her DC's Witchy girlfriend.

It all went rather well, even if Barney looked disappointed not to have been greeted more romantically than, 'Did you bring more gin?'

Erin turned her attention to the children. 'This is my special friend. He's called Barney, and he's a policeman. This is his boss, Liz. They're both friends of the pack.'

Liz seemed unsure about that part, especially when one of the boys piped up with, 'Why aren't they wearing guns and armour?'

'This way,' said Erin. 'It's nearly time for the log.'

Liz fell into step with me. 'Never mind armour, which hat are you wearing today, Conrad? I hear on the grapevine that you're no longer with the King's Watch.'

'Even you?' I said.

'I think every Mage, Son and Daughter and Fairy in England knows by now. It was over a day ago, so plenty of time for the bush telegraph to buzz.'

'Yes. I spent nearly all day yesterday on the phone. Mina had to help out.'

'So what's the official line, if you don't mind me asking?'

'That I am still convalescing and that my position will be discussed in due course, and it's a line I support. My friends and extended family deserve a quiet Christmas.'

'Just wait until you have kids. There's no such thing as a quiet Christmas.'

'Liz, any Christmas where I'm not attacked is a quiet one in my book.'

She lowered her voice. 'I've got bags of sweets in the boot. Are the cubs allowed them?'

'They're children most of the time, not cubs. Hand them over to the adults publicly and everyone will be happy.'

'Where are they? The adults, I mean.'

'There's the queen. Cara.'

'Where?'

'There. By the Pack Hall with the bucket and sponge, trying to spruce up the kids.'

Liz stopped walking to stare. 'She's a child.'

'She's expecting her second child, as it happens.'

Cara saw me and waved. She dumped the sponge in the bucket, put her hands to her mouth and howled. Yes, they do do that in human form. It's partly because the sound carries with magick, and partly to get the kids used to the limited communication they have as wolves. I've already learnt *Gather Round* and *Danger*. At the sound of their queen, everyone stopped what they were doing and came towards the amphitheatre.

'That was the spookiest thing I've seen or heard since Midsummer,' said Liz.

The humans were seated in positions of honour opposite the raised bank of terraced seating, with the fire pit between us. We also got chairs. We'd barely made ourselves comfortable when a different sort of howl came from the woods to the east.

'What the fuck was that?' said Liz in a hoarse whisper.

'They can hear you,' said Erin. 'Wait and see.'

The woods echoed again, accompanied by human shouts, and it wasn't long before all eyes were on the path to the yard, almost invisible in the dusk. It was even spookier when a large wolf padded in at the head of a small procession. All the adult males, and the adult females without children, were pulling on ropes, dragging a tree trunk behind them.

They built up a head of steam and the trunk bounced down the path. The pack guiding the tree into the fire pit, then hauling back on the ropes and stopping. The wolf howled a final time, and yes, the hairs on my arms did rise up in horror. I hope never to hear that sound as the hunted rather than the hunter.

The wolf, Alex, was supposed to Exchange at this point, according to my briefing, but he trotted to the end of the fire pit where the buck was sizzling on the spit. He carried on out of the amphitheatre, away from the smells and into the trees, then he turned right and disappeared out of sight, loping up the hill.

'That's not part of the plan, is it?' said Liz. I was already on my feet, reaching for Great Fang when the howl of *Danger!* ripped through the twilight. The pack started ripping off their clothes, and I turned to Erin.

'Where are the keys to the boat?'

'In the ignition. It's Occluded.'

'Get down there and get ready to scarper.'

The first wolves had Exchanged and were heading away from the fire in different directions.

'I can't leave them!' said Erin. 'I'm supposed…'

I cut her off. 'I'm their Protector, not you. You look after the humans, I'll look after the wolves.'

I threw the sword over my shoulder and jogged into the yard, which would have been pitch black if it weren't for my still improving night vision. I stopped dead when I saw why Alex was howling. We had visitors. Fae visitors. I could smell the rotten leaves from here.

27 — The Year's End

They'd come at us from downwind, so Alex hadn't smelled them coming, but horses make a lot of noise, and four of them were at the top of the compound, as were a dozen Fae on foot, some with bows, some with knives.

The pack were spread out, in twos and threes, none of them standing still as they circled the intruders. The horses were bucking a little, but not as much as I'd expected, then the lead rider applied the spurs and came forwards.

I came out from the shelter of the new shed and was going to make a stand until I heard more howling from behind me, then *barking*. Scout. Then a howl of pain, then a woman's scream. I was torn between running down to the boat and dealing with what was in front of me.

'Pack! To your Guardian! Help her!' I shouted.

The silver shapes flooded down the yard and around me, except one. Maria was abused more than any of the wolves here, and she has a ring of pure white fur around her neck. You do not want to see the un-Glamoured version of her human form.

She held back, watching the Fae approach me and giving them two things to think about, not that the leader was bothered. As the horse got closer, I could see that the rider was female, her face hidden inside a cloak. She held the reins in her right hand and carried a spear in her left.

I moved to put myself to her right and stood to block the way. She reined in her horse at a distance from me, and the other riders stopped behind her. The footsoldiers spread out, moving to encircle me, all of them keeping half an eye on Maria.

Before I could speak, I heard a shout, then Mina's voice. 'Conrad! We're okay. I'm coming.'

I kept my eyes roaming, checking for sudden aggressive movements. Light footsteps, ragged breathing. Mina. 'They intercepted us by Harry's clearing. They were going to handcuff us, but Liz fought back. She's been cut. The pack are keeping them at a distance. Erin is doing first aid.' She swallowed hard and tried to catch her breath.

'Get ready to shout for the pack,' I said as quietly as I could. 'And watch the ones behind me.' I lifted my head and spoke up. 'Who trespasses on Pack land?'

The lead rider flipped her spear so that the point faced down, then jammed it into the ground with a crack of steel on stone and a flash of light that had me blinking. I reached for my sword, but Mina didn't shout, so I relaxed and realised that the spear was now a lightstick. Three or four others did the same, and the yard was a blaze of light. I could now see that their leader's cloak was in a deep blue with a yellow trim. She lowered the hood and shook out her waves of blonde hair. The more I looked at her, the more familiar she seemed. Something about her nose, perhaps? No. When she lifted her left hand to move her hair, I knew her. We've met before.

When she spoke, it was with an accent from the north, half way between Belfast and the Highlands.

'Lord of Death, I am come for you. In the name of my Queen, I am come for reckoning.'

'I say again: who trespasses on Pack land?'

There was a fractional pause before she answered. 'I am Princess Lussa, proclaimed the Fair Queen and heir to the Queen of Inishsí. I will return to the Lough and reclaim her lands. I come in her name, with my sword arm, Countess Kintra.'

I closed my eyes for just a second. Had it all been worth it? In less than a year, I've come to know magick, learned of my family's less than glorious record, and tried to put some of it right. In doing so, I've brought four innocent humans and a whole pack of innocent wolves into a desperate situation. I opened my eyes, and saw movement as Maria changed her position again. The white fur glinted as she moved. Yes, it had been worth it.

'You should have called, your grace,' I said. 'I could have messaged you Niðï's address in Earlsbury. It's him you want, not me.'

'You are the Lord of Death, and from you there must be a reckoning, and from all your creatures if they defend you. Or if you allow them to defend you. You have my word: surrender, and they will live.'

'You're not going to surrender, are you?' said Mina in a tone that was both loud and scarily conversational.

'No.'

'Good. Maria! Fetch the surprise. Bring it here.' What on earth? Mina stepped to my side and bowed to the Princess.

Mina straightened up. 'If your grace would wait a moment, I think that what my fiancé is about to say will make more sense.'

'I hope it makes sense to me, love. What are you doing?'

The Princess was not impressed. 'Close in. Take them alive.'

The three other horsemen/women, all still concealed, moved away from their leader, and the Fae on foot took two steps towards us, looking at each other as they did so.

I was about to call for the pack when Maria dodged between the soldiers and ran to Mina, on two feet, not four, and carrying a package wrapped in brown paper. She handed over the package and moved to stand behind me, back to back.

Mina was already ripping paper. 'Your Yuletide gift,' she said, thrusting a large piece of fabric at me. 'It's the Galway flag. For the Pack Hall.'

Oh. Right. I am indeed engaged to a genius. I took it and shook it out so that the Princess could see it. Her retinue had already stopped advancing.

'Hear me! Your proclaimed Queen has no reckoning with me. I am not your Lord of Death. I was named Dragonslayer by the Noble Queen of Galway, and granted of her favour. When I left Inishsí, I parted in peace with the Star Queen. If your Queen would seek a reckoning, let it be with the Dwarf, but I think your Queen is too scared. Would you follow a coward's orders? You won't kill us all, and word of this will reach the Lough. The Star Queen and the Noble Queen will both be waiting.'

That stopped them alright. One of the cavalry lowered her hood and a flicker of magick told me that she was speaking under a Silence, and she wasn't talking to Princess Lussa, she was talking to the other two riders. I'm guessing she was Countess Kintra.

I had to seize the initiative. I bowed for the first time, and said, 'You are Princess at Lussa. Be Queen there and depart in peace. Or issue a personal challenge.'

Countess Kintra nudged her horse forwards. Princess Lussa was about to issue more orders, but her right-hand woman spoke first. 'A Queen is not afraid of a mortal. Issue a personal challenge and be done.'

Another rider lowered their hood. A man. 'I will bear your sword, Fair Queen.'

Fae politics makes no sense if you think like a human. A mortal. To understand their code and their traditions, you have to imagine that your eternal youth is dependent on Amrita, and Amrita is only produced by Hlæfdigan. The Princess of Lussa would have a couple, perhaps three, enough for her to become a true Queen and dig out a royal sídhe on the Isle of Mull. But she wants more. She wants Lough Corrib, and she sees taking out me as her first step on the road to Ireland.

Not all of the late Queen's People in Galway rallied to Princess Astra. A good number will have been waiting to see what Lussa did, and coming to Ireland as the avenger of the Fair Queen would be a big boost. On the other hand, Lussa's people clearly didn't fancy their chances if the Queen of Galway was likely to step in. After all, they'd rather be at the extreme fringes of Astra's Court than have their rotting corpses chucked into the Lough.

As soon as I'd revealed my Favour from the Noble Queen, I'd as good as guaranteed the safety of everyone else, so why had I pushed for the challenge? Mina deserved to know, so I spoke up.

'I remember our meeting, Princess. I remember you ripping out the heart of my prisoner and eating it. You had the law on your side, but I will let it be known to Ivan's heirs unless you tell me who else you did business with. My family let the Codex into the world. I will do my best to undo that harm.'

'She looks and sounds nothing like her,' murmured Mina. 'Are you sure?'

I didn't get to answer the question, because Lussa had reached the tipping point. She unfastened her cloak and dropped it behind her. 'Come,' she ordered one of the footsoldiers. When he'd taken the reins, she swung herself down and took her sword from the saddle sheath.

'Mortal, I challenge you. If you lose, you will bear the name Lord of Death.'

'I hear you, Lussa. Maria, fetch the others and tell the pack to stand ready. We will do nothing until I see that they are safe.'

The male rider dismounted and went to stand next to his lady. I turned to Mina, handed over the Galway flag and said, 'It's the ring. There aren't two like that in circulation, and that's how I knew her.'

Grey shapes slipped into the yard. The Fae raised their weapons instinctively and tracked the wolves as some of them passed through and out the other side.

'Ow! Fuck! Careful, Barney.'

'Sorry, Liz.'

With Alex in wolf form taking the lead, Erin, Barney and Liz appeared. Barney had his shoulder under Liz's right arm, and her right trouser leg had been cut off. Someone's scarf was tied round her thigh, holding a folded cloth in place.

'It missed the artery,' said Erin. 'She needs the hospital, though.' With an impressive shot of venom, she pointed at one of the Fae bringing up the rear. 'That one. He did it. I've marked his card.'

'Where's Maria?'

'Gone to the Skelwith amphitheatre to check on the Elders and the children.'

What in Odin's name was she on about? Skelwith amphitheatre? If Erin was trying to give me a message, she seriously needed to work on her allusions.

She waggled her eyebrows then rolled her eyes, giving up. She looked at the Fae nearest the Pack Hall and said, 'You. Fetch a chair, or let me pass to fetch one.'

Countess Kintra gave a command in Fae, and the warrior ran to get a chair for Liz. There was no putting it off any longer, and I faced Lussa.

'I accept your challenge on condition that you name those you sold the Codex to. If you lose.'

'I am in a hurry, so yes. I'd tell you to make peace with the Allfather, but I am going to eat your Essence.'

The time for talking was over. I took off my coat and handed it to Mina. She grabbed me and gave me a big kiss. I rolled my shoulders and gripped the haft of Great Fang.

Lussa drew her blade and tossed the scabbard to her second. Her sword was a classic of Fae workmanship: long and slender, with the finest edge and the sharpest point. She was tall for a female, but still half a foot shorter than me, and her blade was in proportion. Having a longer reach was my only advantage in combat, and that's before we started on the magick.

In a challenge, general use of Works is frowned on, so no blasts of air, no Pyromancy and no use of poisoned bites. Small comfort. I drew my sword and faced her.

Thrust. Parry. Block. Block. Retreat. Shit.

If she hadn't spent a hundred years practising, I might have stood a chance. In ten seconds, she was all over me, and I was barely keeping her at bay, and she hadn't started to use the magick in her sword yet.

I was running out of options here. A single slip and she'd get the first cut. There wasn't even any point in taking out the lights, because her night vision was as good as mine. I was getting desperate. All I had to do was get a decent slice with the cold-forged tip of Great Fang, and I'd be on top. One slice.

I missed, and her riposte flashed by my neck, putting me off balance.

'Now!'

The Princess was ready to cut my sword arm, but something stopped her. Her eyes blazed with light and pain, and she turned round. Four arrows stood out of her back.

'Again.'

Four more hit home, this time in her chest. She staggered back, sank to her knees, then fell forwards, her sword hitting the ground with a tinny *clang*. When the echo stopped, there was no noise in the compound but the gentle wind and my heavy breathing.

I looked up and saw the Countess Kintra with her sword in her hand and half a dozen archers clustered around her. The Queen's second gripped the scabbard in his hand and stared at his dead mistress as if he couldn't believe what he saw. Sod that, *I* couldn't believe what I saw, because next to Countess Kintra was Maria, and she was holding up a phone like the Statue of Liberty holding her torch, the face flat and close to Kintra's thigh.

'Why?' I said.

Kintra shrugged. 'She had her chance. I will follow no Queen who cannot dispatch a mortal in ten seconds. Her fate was sealed when you parried her third thrust, and then this one appeared. You can put that down now, she-wolf.' Maria lowered her arm and stepped away from Kintra's horse. She moved closer to the fourth rider, the only one who hadn't shown their face. 'Stay,' ordered Kintra. Maria stayed.

Kintra rested her sword on the pommel of her saddle. 'I saw your Badge, Lord Guardian, and I heard what you said. I give you my word, with my blood if you will, that the last of the People who knew of the Morrigan's book is now dead. Had she lived, the King's Watch would have been after us, and I know that because of her Chief.' She indicated the scene behind me, where Liz was combining a grimace with a grin of triumph.

'That Maria is good,' said Liz. 'When she came to see my wound, she put on a Silence that fooled the Fairies, and leaned in. I told her to take my phone and call the Chief.'

Kintra finished off. 'The Chief of Clan Skelwith is not happy. He heard the challenge and the Dragonslayer's response. He told me that he was mobilising all the Clan to cut off our retreat.' She shrugged. 'It seems you have more friends than we do, Lord Guardian.'

I took the scabbard for Great Fang and sheathed my sword. 'Let there be peace between us, Countess.'

'In peace, thank you.' She put away her sword and ordered the others to do the same. She gave an order in Fae, and Lussa's second argued back, then reluctantly took the dead Princess's ring and blade. He offered them to Kintra, and she took both.

'What will you do now, Countess?' I asked. 'Or should that be *Princess* Kintra. Perhaps even Queen.'

She pointed a finger at me. 'Do not try to sow discord. We will return to Mull and conduct our business within the sídhe, as it should be done, not here amongst mortals and wolves.'

'Go in peace, my lady.'

She hesitated. 'In peace, thank you, Lord Guardian. Let us hope that if the sun returns, it shines more brightly on both of us. This has been a dark year.'

'And for me. May the sun shine more brightly on your People than it has.'

She nodded and took the reins. One of the Fae leapt on the back of the spare horse, and they all moved off. Grey shapes shadowed them through the gate and into the night.

28 — And a New Beginning

Neither of us wanted to let go. I had my arms wrapped around Mina and my face buried in her hair. My eyes were closed, and I was desperately trying to forget the world around me while she sobbed into my chest. It was only when I couldn't control the shivering that she backed away and wiped the tears from her eyes.

'Put your coat on before you freeze to death.'

I struggled into my coat, and she dabbed her face with a tissue. We had an audience of three: Maria (now clothed), her daughter and Scout, but Scout was being cradled in Maria's arms.

'How is he?' I asked.

'He has a broken leg. We know what to do. I will take care of him.'

I went over and kissed Maria on the lips (it's a wolf thing). 'Thank you. Without you, I would be dead. Many of the Pack, too.'

'Every day of freedom from the Evil One is worth risking my life for.'

I smiled. That just about summed things up. I looked down at Scout, and his eyes were barely open. 'Lowri has drugged him.'

'Good. Where are the others?'

'By the fire, waiting for you, my lord.'

Oh. Right. I took Mina's hand and we walked down the yard. We passed a wet patch where someone had hosed away what was left of Princess Lussa. Were my legs shaking? Yes. This was not a hero's entrance, because I was a mad fool, not a hero. Any victory tonight had been a collective one. I took my seat and reached into my coat pocket. 'Why are you still here?' I said to Liz. 'And thanks, by the way.'

'You're welcome. Dad and the Chief are coming to collect me, but they'll be a while. I didn't want to miss the fire, so I told them that no one could drive. Besides, I'm gonna need Dad's help to calm my husband down.'

The only one still in wolf form was Alex, back where he'd been when he first sensed danger, right by the tree trunk. He waited until everyone had settled down, then stood up and turned to the west, where the sun had long since set.

He howled three times at the sunset, three times at where it would rise tomorrow, then three times to the north, and then he lay down. Cara stood up and shouted at the night. 'Who will make a fire? Who will help us return the light?'

Maria had handed off Scout to another pack member, and she stood up. 'I will make the fire, with a token of our victory tonight.'

From the ground, she took the lightstick/spear that the Fae had left behind. She raised it over her head, then plunged it into the log turning all its

Lux into heat instead of light. Flames licked along the dry wood, and broke out all over the trunk. She held the spear in place for a few seconds, then stepped back. 'We have light until the sun returns.'

Alex howled for one last time, then Exchanged his form. Cara walked up to him with a big tankard, carrying it carefully with both hands. He took it from her and he turned to me. 'Would you drink, Lord Protector?'

I knew my lines. 'I would drink deeply, but the pack must drink first.'

Alex took the tankard to the youngest adult, a boy who looked about twelve, and he took a big sip. In silence, the tankard circulated through the whole pack, refreshed a few times, until it was back with me. I took it and drank as much as I could without choking. Hawkshead Bitter, delivered by the Gnomes, if you're wondering. When I'd finished, I stood up. 'Let everyone drink!'

And that is about as complicated as Mannwolf ceremonies get. They have a slightly longer one on Walpurgisnacht, and one at Midsummer and Samhain, but to them, the monthly full moon is the one that matters.

Amidst the general celebration, Mina turned to me and whispered, 'Put a Silence on us. Their hearing is way too good.'

I did as she asked. 'What's up, love?'

'You nearly died again. That's what's up, and I had to watch it, and there was nothing I could do about it. I cannot live with that. Do you believe that there is nothing more to come from your search for that book?'

'I believe it. I can't see any other avenue to pursue.'

'Then promise that you will never again choose single combat.'

I thought about it. Mina would expect me to think about it, and I couldn't think of any circumstance where I would be the sole target of an invasion. 'I promise.'

'Good. Now let's enjoy ourselves.'

Which we did for half an hour. When Liz's father arrived, the pack did the heavy lifting of getting her up the yard to his car, for which I was very grateful. You can drink a lot of Hawkshead Bitter in half an hour after a near-death experience. I was introduced to her father, but he didn't linger: Liz really did need to get to hospital. His only notable comment was, 'The Chief will be here shortly.'

When he arrived, the chief of Clan Skelwith came alone, except for his driver, a Daughter of the Earth who remained nameless and didn't get out of the Mercedes. Saul Brathay is one of the younger clan chiefs in England, and has only been Top Gnome for fifty years or so. He was wrapped up well, but I didn't fancy the chances of his shoes if we went far.

'Welcome to Birk Fell, sir,' I began.

'Namaste.'

He shook my hand, then Mina's. He had a fairer complexion than most Gnomes, certainly fairer than Lloyd's.

'I'm sorry to have dragged you away from your Yuletide party. Would you care to join us and meet the pack?'

He grunted. 'I was glad to get away. Yuletide isn't what it was at the Clan. Yes, I would like to meet the pack, but not tonight. If I start enjoying myself, I'll be in trouble. Is there somewhere we can talk in private?'

'There's a fire in the cottage. This way.'

Being a Gnome, he couldn't resist a detour to examine the Pack Hall. He ran his fingers down the boards for a second, examining the joints, then stared around. 'You'll have plans for this?'

'I always have plans. Except for tonight. I had no plan for single combat with a Fae Princess. Thank you for your intercession. It made a crucial difference.'

We moved to the cottage and made ourselves comfortable. Saul surprised me with his first question. 'What's this book you were talking about to Lussa? It strikes me that you were willing to give your life for it.'

Mina looked at me. 'Are you going to tell him? Because if you are, I am going to make tea.'

I gave Saul the edited highlights, missing out the involvement of Tom Morton and other secrets of the Watch. Mina returned with the tea as I was summing up my trip to Galway.

He sipped his tea, pronounced it good, and stared at the fire. 'Do you think the Allfather planned this when he Enhanced you?'

'That's a question I've asked him a few times,' I replied. 'Now that it's over, I think I finally understand what he was up to. If he'll forgive the Biblical metaphor, I think he was casting his bread upon the waters. He had no idea whether I'd be interested, or survive, or even find out what was going on.'

'So now you've got a title and Nimue's Badge, but no authority in mundane or magickal law until the London elite stop running round like headless chickens and make their mind up. That about the size of it?'

'Close enough.'

'George speaks very highly of you, Conrad – if I can call you that? Thanks. I prefer Saul, too. Yes, George speaks very highly of you, as does Matt Eldridge.'

'And I'm grateful for your support behind the scenes. Saul.'

Where was he going with this, I wonder? Mina wondered, too, but only I can tell her puzzled face from her polite one.

'We can't go on like this,' said Saul. 'Philippa Grayling is too old and set in her ways to run the Assessors.' For a Gnome to call someone *set in their ways* is pretty extreme, but there you go. He made eye contact with me and continued, 'I'm taking over as President of the Grand Union on the first of January. If I propose to appoint you as Guardian of the Lakes, over Philippa's head, will you accept? I want to do it, but I won't if you're not on board.'

Mina and I looked at each other. I raised my eyebrows, and she found my hand with her fingers. She gave it a squeeze and turned back to Saul.

'I'm definitely interested, but I won't make a decision tonight. In fact, not until after I've had a few days rest in Clerkswell. What would Philippa say, do you think?'

'I think she'd fight it until the Grand Union agreed with me, then she'd retire in disgust. Especially if I threatened her with an enquiry into the Sprint Stables business.'

'And what would be my brief? As a Watch Captain, I pretty much trashed the reputation of the Assessors.'

'You did, and it was justified. The first priority is to make the Assessor team fit for purpose in whatever way you think works best. Long-term, I want the Watch to have oversight. If they take you back, great, if not, you could hand it over to your replacement as Deputy with the satisfaction of a job well done.'

I drank some tea and thought it over. 'I'm not saying yes by any means. Have a think over the holidays and put a package together: salary, support and accommodation. Unofficially, of course.'

'Of course. And I'm not going to say anything until you're fully on board with the idea.' He paused, to make sure I got the point. 'Until you've given me your word.'

'Of course. And I'd like to sound out the Queen of Derwent first. I don't expect her to approve, but I've taken on enough Fae Queens to last a lifetime.'

He gave a wry smile. 'Understood. She'll keep our secret well enough. You won't be surprised to learn that I've already spoken to the Greenings, and they're content with the idea. At least their leader is.'

'Good.' We nodded to each other in agreement, and I risked a gentle dig. 'I should point out that I'm already Lord Guardian of this area, so that's not a job you can offer me.'

He smiled. 'Nice touch. I suggested *Guardian* because you need something that's one up from Chief Assessor.'

'I'll get back to you on that one. Put some thoughts together and we can talk after Christmas.'

We parted with handshakes and wishes for the sun to shine on each other.

'Where've you been?' said Erin, a little unsteadily, when we returned to the amphitheatre. Actually, getting Clan Skelwith to sponsor it might not be a bad idea.

Children were dancing around the fire, or curled up on the grass, asleep. The adults were passing around platters of venison, and I couldn't wait to tuck in.

We lasted as long as we could, and I think that Barney could have lasted a lot longer. When Erin started to nod off, I stood up and made a couple of toasts and told the pack that they were the finest assembly of wolves that England had ever seen, that they were led by the greatest ever king and queen, and that they were blessed to have a Chantress like Maria and an Elder of such wisdom as Lowri. And after a fair amount of kissing, it was time for the humans to depart.

We arrived at the cottage after a somewhat meandering progress up the yard, and Mina gave a little squeal of fright when Maria stepped out of the shadows to waylay us.

She dropped to her knees and lowered her head. 'Forgive me, Lord Protector. Forgive me, Guardian. There is something I must tell you.'

Erin grabbed her and hauled her up. 'What's going on, Maria? We've talked about going behind Cara's back, haven't we? I thought you'd got the message.'

Maria looked wretched, and the Glamour she'd put on for the party was nowhere in sight. 'But for this, I have to. All the Brookford wolves swore an oath never to reveal where they came from. We did not. It's the only thing that really divides us. If I went through Cara, it would make things worse.'

'Oh,' said Erin. This was not her problem, it was mine.

'Tell me, Maria. I want to know.'

'The fourth rider tonight. The one who never showed herself. She was the Mistress, I'd recognise her smell anywhere.'

I reached through the fog of memory. Maria had been barely weaned when she was taken from her mother and sold to the Ripleys. The only thing she could remember was that the pack where she'd been born was run by a human, not a Fae, and they called that human the Mistress. Another wolf had been a little older when he left, and he had said that the Mistress was neither cruel nor loving, and that she ran the pack with a mixture of care and brutal efficiency.

'What was she doing here, I wonder? I take it you didn't recognise any of the Fae, Maria.'

'No. None of us did.'

'Then thank you for telling me. Is there *anything* you or the others can remember?'

'She glowed. I remember that. Griffon thinks that was a Glamour, because she had red hair. I don't know.'

'Thank you. You did the right thing, Maria.'

We stripped off our coats, and I suggested that some hot chocolate might be a good idea before we went to bed. 'There's something I need to say,' I added.

We gathered in the kitchen and Erin started on at me about an upgrade while we waited for the kettle to boil. I agreed with everything she said, and promised nothing.

We adjourned to the fire and I told Erin what I – we – had decided. 'Mina thinks I'm taking advantage of you, Erin, and she's right. I know you love the pack, but you can't do this and be Pihla's tutor. You need a live-in Pack Witch, Assistant Guardian, whatever.'

Erin let out a rush of air with an oomph. 'I'd like to argue, but I can't. Barney's been saying the same thing. Shall I start asking around?'

'No need. I'd like to offer it to an old … sparring partner of yours. Karina. You heard about what she's been up to, I assume.'

'Karina! Oh my god, Conrad, are you serious? Of course you're serious. Well, she'll fit in round here: just one more mad bitch to join the pack. Is that your *best and final offer* as the robbing estate agents say?'

'I will interview her,' said Mina.

'Right. Karina. Hey-ho.'

I lifted my mug. 'May the sun shine on you both.'

'And on you two,' Erin replied. 'Especially on your wedding. *Weddings*, plural. You know you'll have to have one here, don't you? And one of the pack will have to attend the *actual* wedding in Clerkswell. At least one. It's in the rules.'

Mina nodded as if Erin had been speaking with authority instead of spouting total nonsense as a wind-up. 'Of course. It shall be Maria and Cara, if she can travel, and Maria's daughter will be a flower girl. I have some material to use in her dress. A piece of silk. She will be beauty itself.'

Conrad will be back in the Tenth Book of the King's Watch, Four Roads Cross, due out from Paw Press in Autumn 2021.

And before then, we will get to see how Karina copes when she takes over the Birkfell Pack in

Arrow in the Dark

A King's Watch Story

By Lucy Campbell

The Seventh King's Watch eBook novella will be available from Paw Press on Amazon in the Summer of 2021.

Coming Soon from Paw Press

Four Roads Cross

The Tenth Book of the King's Watch

By

Mark Hayden

The last time Conrad was unemployed, he got a visit from the Allfather. Look where that got him.

And now the Gnomes of Lakeland want him to be the new Commissioner.

A simple job: sort out the Assessors and put the Union on a stable footing. They're even willing to pay for an assistant to help him with the difficult magick stuff. What could possibly go wrong?

He soon finds out that everyone has their own agenda here, that no one wants him to succeed, and that someone is determined that Conrad will do their dirty work for them.

It all starts with a race down Great Langdale and it ends with an appointment at Lakeland's oldest boundary marker, the Four Roads Cross.

Available Autumn 2021 from Paw Press.

And why not join Conrad's elite group of supporters:

The Merlyn's Tower Irregulars

Visit the Paw Press website and sign up for the Irregulars to receive news of new books, or why not join the Facebook Group? Search FB for *Merlyn's Tower Irregulars.*

Author's Note

Thank you for reading Conrad's latest adventure – and it is very much *Conrad's* adventure this time, something he had to do for himself and (so he says) for the honour of the Clarkes. I'll let you decide about that.

This book was written during the UK's second full lockdown in winter/spring 2021, and it remains the case that Anne and I have been very lucky during this pandemic. So far. One of the first visits we're hoping to make outside Britain is to follow in Conrad's footsteps from Cairnryan to Belfast and see our new great nephew. Ethan Thomas Simpson was born in mid-May, and this book is dedicated to him. I hope the welcome we get is slightly more peaceful than Conrad's.

Extra thanks are due this time to Lucy Campbell and David Gillespie. Lucy has written the King's Watch novella *Marshlight*, and was good enough to read this book ahead of publication.

David Gillespie has contributed in a unique way, by being my Irish correspondent. He helped with the Irish language phrases (okay, he totally supplied the Irish language phrases), and did me the honour of reading the manuscript to check for Irish clichés.

Shakespeare said that A good wine deserves a good bush. In other words, a good book deserves a good cover. I'll never be able to prove it, but I strongly believe that The King's Watch would not have been the same without the beautiful covers designed by the Awesome Rachel Lawston.

An additional note of thanks is due to Ian Forsdyke MBE for casting his eye over the final draft. Any remaining typos/errors are all mine.

If you've followed Conrad through nine books and many novellas, you'll know that sometimes he visits places that are clear for all to see, and sometimes the locations are shrouded by Occulting. This book has a cunning departure: it features a real life person. Should you find yourself on the Wild Atlantic Way in Ireland, I urge you to visit the Spiddal Craft village and buy something from Andrea Rossi. Tell her that Conrad sent you.

Finally, this book could not have been written without love, support, encouragement and sacrifices from my wife, Anne. It just goes to show how much she loves me that she let me write the first Conrad book even though she hates fantasy novels. She says she now likes them.

Thanks,
Mark Hayden.

Printed in Great Britain
by Amazon